HENDRIK HOITINGA

THE ITEM

novum pro

This book is also
available as
e-book.

www.novum-publishing.co.uk

© 2023 novum publishing

ISBN 978-3-99131-869-9
Editing: René Nel
Cover photos:
Elena Schweitzer, Andreykuzmin,
Tennesseewitney I Dreamstime.com
Cover design, layout & typesetting:
novum publishing

www.novum-publishing.co.uk

Climate neutral
Print product
ClimatePartner.com/16547-2201-1002

BOOK I

TWO TRAILS

DEDICATION &
ACKNOWLEDGMENTS

In memory of Klaas
(19-8-1954 – 5-8-2015)

Adventures on rooftops and alleys, playing in the street
Summertime journeys on trains and the girls we would meet
Canoeing on rivers and lakes we did too
And our friendship just grew and grew.
Across the seas we sailed, new challenges ahead
Brick laying, painting and carpentry in a shed
Motorcycles you tinkered with, a Matchless comes to mind,
bringing to some a frown
For with an engine so loud and distinctive, it could be heard
right across town.
In time, as we grew and different paths we followed, no worries, no bother
For the bond we forged, was truly like no other
You were the best friend.

Thanks to;

Gilly, my loving wife for over 42 years.
Daughter Suzy, for her valuable input,
assistance, guidance and research.
Margaret Alison for her encouragement
and prayerful support

Author's favourite passage of Scripture;

'Trust in the Lord with all your heart,
and lean not on your own understanding.
In all your ways acknowledge Him,
and He shall direct your paths'.
Proverbs 3: 5-6

And finally a big thank you to NOVUM Publishing.

PROLOGUE;

PARIS, FRANCE

MONDAY 19ᵀᴴ JANUARY 2015

When he saw it he recognised it immediately, and when he did, he also knew straight-away, that something just wasn't right.

He stopped walking, tried to focus, tried to recollect what it was that had made him stop.

Some moments passed and once again he realised that his mind had wandered. Pictures and scenes, flashing around in his mind, faces, people, events, all jumbled together.

Why couldn't he just focus? Why couldn't he just breathe and make sense of it all?

Lost in thought, lost and unsure, feeling emotional, yet suppressing those feelings. Through the mists of his mind, he sensed someone approaching.

Letting out a deep sigh, he briefly closed his eyes, then opened them once more and stared at the painting that was hung on the wall before him. One of many that were lined along the wall.

But this one had drawn his attention.

A voice, a man's voice, spoke to him, in French.

'Sorry, my French is not great,' he said in English, turning to face a smartly dressed gentleman wearing a shiny gold name badge that said he was the director of the Paris Fine Arts Auction House, Emmanuel Sauvonne.

'Is Monsieur interested in the Gauguin?'

He looked again at the painting, his mind seemingly, at least for the moment, showing signs of clarity, 'It caught my eye, but for the wrong reason. There is something about it' he answered.

Again turning to face the director, he said, 'But I can't put my finger on it. A feeling, a hunch if you like, but it seems ... wrong. Does it have good provenance?'

Less than two minutes later he stood in the director's office. The director, who had picked up the phone and was speaking in rapid French, had opened a filing cabinet.

He stood and waited. His mind losing focus once more and drifting away.

Sonja had died.

Acknowledge it. Accept it.

Her words came to him, slicing through the mist in his mind, pushing aside all else that was around him, the opening of the office door, the presence of someone else, the quick conversation, ...

... her words so soft, and yet so clear.

His mind suddenly bringing the scene to the forefront taking him back, back to earlier in the day ...

She was holding his hand; her face was a picture of confidence. Her eyes were bright, and despite the tears in his eyes, he saw her so very clearly.

'Go and find someone to love,' she had said, her eyes totally engaging his, 'You have so much more to give, and thank you so very much, for all the love you have given me ...'

'Go and find someone to love ...' Well, he thought, back in the present time, it certainly wasn't going to be the woman who had entered the office and now stood before him, looking up into his face and berating him in strongly accented English. Her fiery French temper had brought a red blush to both her cheekbones.

She had asked him what expertise he had in judging the painting, but before he could even begin to formulate some sort of response through the confusion in his mind, she had gone on to say that she had studied at Atelier 115,School of Arts, had been the curator of a well-known Parisian Art Gallery for five years, the first woman and the youngest to ever hold that post, before joining the Paris Fine Arts Auction House in 2009.

Finally, taking a breath, still looking at him intently, she asked again, 'and why do you think the Gauguin is not genuine? What expertise do you have?'

Finding his voice, he held her gaze, 'I just walked in. The painting, well, just caught my attention, I'm sure I've seen it before, but I just have a sense that it's not right. I merely question its provenance, but if you are satisfied, well, all is good. Sorry to have taken up your time.' His voice, surprisingly calm and firm, 'Good day to you.' Nodding to them both, he turned and left the room.

Strangely, his mind was suddenly clear and sharp.

He headed back to the room which housed the paintings that were to be auctioned later in the day, made a note of the Gauguin's lot number, checked the brochure he had picked up for the auction time and left the building.

Ten minutes later he sat in a sidewalk cafe, a black coffee within reach and looked up at the grey sky which threatened to produce some rain sooner rather than later.

He thought back, though with more clarity now, more in control of his senses and his emotions.

He had left the hospital in tears. It was only just starting to get light. She had called him to come in. He had called a taxi, had showered and dressed and was by her hospital bedside twenty-five minutes later.

This moment had been expected.

But how do you prepare for it.

His wife had, after speaking to him so softly, so sweetly and with such confidence, simple closed her eyes and slipped away.

He needed air, he needed to walk, to take it all in. He needed to breathe.

After walking in somewhat of a daze, he realised he had entered the grand Rotterdam central railway station.

He studied the electronic departure board, made up his mind, purchased a return ticket, and boarded the high-speed train to Paris eighteen minutes later.

Sipping his coffee and beginning to accept the events of the day, he checked the time and headed back to the auction house which, earlier, he had stumbled upon just walking through the streets of the French capital.

He registered for the auction and wondered why it had been that the Gauguin painting had brought that reaction in him.

He nodded to the director, who watched him and who, after he had sat down, had checked his registration form.

THE PRESENT;

FOUR YEARS LATER
BAARN, THE NETHERLANDS

11AM TUESDAY 5ᵀᴴ MARCH 2019

She pressed the doorbell. Almost immediately the door opened.

'Miss Price I take it?' please, come in. said the man, stepping aside.
   'Thank you.'

The woman entered, waited while he closed the door, then followed him along the hallway, the clicking of her heels on the wooden floor echoing all around.

He entered a large room, the front lounge. It was nicely furnished, a couple of couches, two armchairs that looked invitingly comfortable to sit in, several casual tables, two standard lamps and, against one wall, a large, solid oak, bookcase.

There were several paintings adorning the walls and, above the chimney, a large flat-screen television. The room was fully carpeted, and the man strode through to the dining area and kitchen beyond.

She followed, glancing all around, taking in her surroundings. The carpet ended, another wooden floor began, and her heels, briefly muffled on the carpet, once again clicked audibly.

He walked around a large dining table, gesturing for her to come around as well. She did and watched as he proceeded to unfold a cloth that lay on the table, revealing what lay tucked beneath.

The man stood back. The woman placed her handbag on the table, her eyes fixed on the item. She admired it for a moment, then, opening her bag, she took out a pair of white cotton gloves. These she put on, then looked at the man, who nodded.

Carefully she took the item, lifted it from the table, looked at it closely, from all angles, then placed it back on the table. She reached for the camera that was slung across her left shoulder then took several pictures, front and back, before focusing her attention on the piece of paper that lay next to it.

It was an old document, a very old document. It was faded, a little torn, had a couple of stains upon it and several creases.

She looked at both sides, then also took photos of it.

She turned to the man, 'Thank you.'

The woman took the gloves off, flung the camera back across her shoulder, then, putting the gloves away, said, 'That's fine.'

'So, you'll be in touch then?' the man asked, putting the cloth back over the items.

'I'll get the paperwork sorted. Your suggestion of two million seems valid. We will add it to your existing policy, I will send it by registered mail tomorrow, with the amended premium costs, sign the relevant pages, and send it back in the prepaid envelope. Then you'll have peace of mind.'

'Excellent' he replied and set off to escort the woman back to the front door.

'Here's my card,' she said, handing it to him as he opened the door, 'any queries, just give me a call.' She smiled at him. He nodded as she walked past him and down the three steps to street level where she turned left towards her car, parked only yards away.

THREE HOURS LATER

He pressed the doorbell and waited. It was an overcast day and it was cold. He heard footsteps and the door opened.

'Mr Price is it?' the woman asked,' Please, come in'
'Thank you'

The man entered, waited whilst she closed the door, then followed her along the hallway.

The heels of her shoes clicking on the hardwood floor and resounding through the passageway.

She entered the lounge. He followed as she led him across a deep pile carpet towards the dining room and kitchen area beyond. He took in the furnishings as he followed, particularly drawn to a couple of fine paintings on the wall.

Her footsteps hushed until she once more clicked and clacked on a wooden floor and walked around a large dining table.

He joined her as she bent forward to reveal what lay beneath the cloth on the table.

'Wow' he said, peering at the object, then looking around and up at her asked, 'may I?'

She nodded and he, just using his forefinger and thumb, carefully lifted the item and studied it from all angles.

Then, after just as carefully replacing the item, he took hold of the old document. This too he studied closely before laying it back down on the table. The man then reached into his jacket pocket, took out a small digital camera and, again being very careful handling both the item and the document, took several pictures.

Standing back, he turned to the woman and said, 'Okay, yes, we will put it into the catalogue at a suggested price of between two and two point two million euros, with a fixed reserve of two. If that is still okay with you then I'll go ahead and prepare it, in readiness for our next auction, which is seven weeks tomorrow. Now, remind me, I was told that this was an inheritance, in a box of items you recently decided to go through and found?'

'Eh, yes, my husband's uncle,' she replied, offering no further information.

Then, covering the object again with the cloth, she led the way back to the front door, saying, 'and that price is fine. Thank you for coming so promptly.'

'No problem' he answered, smiling at her as she opened the front door.

Handing her his card, said, 'Any queries, or any other information you might find regarding this item, please call me. The more history we can attach to this piece, the more it may raise at auction.'

'Yes, of course, thank you' she said as he walked past her, down the three steps to street level and turned right to head for his car.

The woman closed the door, walked back towards the kitchen.

Her husband, having heard the front door close, came down the stairs and followed her.

They both stopped by the kitchen table, looking down at the item and document that lay on the cloth.

His phone rang, he answered.

THE PAST;

PERIOD 1

FEBRUARY 1578

It was just after midday on a bright but cold day. The two horses, still breathing heavily, were unhitched from the wagon and taken to a nearby stable block for watering and a rubbing down. Meanwhile inside the stone and wooden building that lay adjacent to the long and wide wooden pier, a woman was showing two men her documents.

Viana Vanetti was a striking young woman, twenty-four years of age.

She had very long dark hair and very vivid blue eyes, was around five foot ten inches in height, and stood much taller than both of the men she was talking to. Whether they were impressed with her documents, her stature, or her calm and self-assured manner wasn't clear, but they bowed and hustled and scurried away to accommodate her.

She arched her back a little, rolled her shoulders to ease her body as she felt a stiffness setting in after her journey. She brushed the dust from her long skirt and walked over to a rectangular window.

Of the eight panes of glass, set in two rows of four, several were cracked, and most needed a good clean, but she peered out to view the twin-masted schooner that was tied right outside, noticing the many men busy with the loading of the vessel.

She glanced behind her where she had placed her own luggage, two large and one small leather and cloth bags, on the dusty wooden floor.

Standing by the window, she took a pouch from somewhere within her clothing, a black, soft leather pouch with a cord tie.

Viana opened it and slid out the item it contained. This she placed on the wooden windowsill, looking at it intently whilst managing, with the pouch in her hand, to re-arrange her wind-blown hair somewhat.

It was a thing of beauty; she adored it.

Retrieving the item, she kissed it lightly, then returned it into the pouch and tucked it away.

She looked at her surroundings.

It was late in the month of February.

She was in Port Civitavecchia.

About fifty miles or so from Rome.

Viana had set off before dawn had even begun to break. A maid helped her dress and get ready; a manservant had brought the wagon and horses around to the front door and had put her luggage inside.

Then two young men who would drive her to the port arrived on the scene.

She had embraced her mother, then turned and climbed into the wagon. A basic carriage, one seat high up front for the drivers with two seats behind, facing each other.

Viana did not look back as they set off. Little did she know that she would never see her mother again.

Now, all alone in the old port building, she reflected on the events of the past month and wondered what might lie ahead as she was about to set off on her journey.

Giulio Clovio had died.

A very fine and renowned artist that specialised in painting miniatures.

As a little girl she, Viana, had often watched him at work, being one of very few who were ever allowed into his studio area.

Many other artists had also been there, coming and going over the years as they stayed with the Farnese household, where her mother was in charge of all the servants and a confidante of the Cardinal himself.

There had been one, among those visiting artists, one, who was a good friend of Giulio. One who had stayed for some considerable time. One who had a special relationship with her mother, resulting in her being in this world today.

When she was in her teens, her mother had told her about him.

Often, when she had spent some time watching Giulio at work, watching some of the other artists that still called regularly, she wondered about her father. Trying to imagine him at work at one of the easels, but, obeying her mother's wishes, had never asked Giulio or any of the other visiting artists about him.

All she knew was what her mother had told her, which, sadly, was very little.

Viana had been schooled by the best and took to learning very well.

At the age of sixteen she could speak Italian and French fluently, as well as Latin and knew a fair amount about poetry, art and philosophy.

The Cardinal also enjoyed her being around as she was an excellent hostess to the many visitors who came calling.

Giulio had died.

He had written a will and among the items listed were six pieces attributed to the artist and friend who had been in that relationship with her mother. When the will was read, these items were to be given to Viana. This brought a little smile from the Cardinal and made her mother blush.

Over the past few weeks she had looked at and thought about these pieces of art, which had been brought to her. She had never seen them before. Giulio must have stored them some place. One item in particular had drawn her attention.

It was this item that brought her to the decision to find him. To find the man who had so beautifully painted it, to the man who, according to her mother, was her father, a fact surely supported by Giulio himself as he had purposefully desired for this item and the other five to be given to her in his will.

She spoke to her mother about her idea. Seeing the determination in her daughters eyes, and knowing that if Viana was set on doing something, there was no stopping her, she agreed with her wishes.

She did, however, strongly advise her daughter to be careful in revealing who she was, as, firstly, this might cause upset within his family and secondly, he actually did not know Viana existed.

The following day they had together spoken to the Cardinal who had initially not been too pleased at the idea of a young woman travelling such distances, a journey that could be fraught with danger.

After realising his concerns were not going to put her off, he recommended someone should travel with her.

Viana had been resolute. This was her quest, her intentions, she would do so alone.

The Cardinal had looked at her mother. They had then shrugged, both knowing there was no stopping this young lady. He told her he would prepare a number of documents that would provide her with passage and accommodation, told her he would miss her greatly, then gave her a huge hug.

The two men came back into the old building. After some more bowing and scurrying, one of them handed back her documents, then they picked up her luggage and gestured for her to follow them.

They exited the building, stepped onto the wide wooden pier, the air brisk, and for a moment, it seemed all the work stopped, like a moment frozen in time, as the men working the dock and the cargo watched the young woman walking along the pier, then up a narrow wooden ramp onto the ship.

It wasn't until she was gone from view that work continued as they hustled and bustled the last of the cargo aboard.

The captain of the ship, a rotund man in his fifties whose jacket could no longer be done up, greeted her cordially. She smiled at him, sensing he was a little uncomfortable with the situation, then followed the now three men to her cabin. It was small, but tidy. She wondered who had been tossed out to make room for her as her luggage was placed on the floor. She thanked the men, then, turning to the captain, asked what time they would sail.

Within two hours, was his reply and he turned and left her to it.

Just under two hours later Viana stood on the deck as the schooner sailed out of the harbour into the Tyrrhenian Sea, making sure she kept out of the way of the men who were attending to the sails.

A light breeze filled the four sails and Port Civitavecchia was soon in the distance as they headed for Genoa.

It was only early afternoon but already beginning to get dark.

The sea had a gentle swell, and as the wind caressed her face, Viana felt both calm and excited.

Calm because she felt comfortable and relaxed, and, as she had never been on the sea before, she enjoyed the experience.

Excited, because she wondered what might lie ahead.

The Farnese household was well known and respected. The documents she had with her carried a lot of weight. Genoa, an independent state at this time, had been chosen as Viana's first stop as they had strong connections, including with the Grimaldi household, who held much power there.

Late in the afternoon of the following day, having had good weather and a favourable wind, they sailed into port.

Several hours later Viana sat on a low stool in front of her dressing table. Brush in hand, her eyes staring in the mirror at her own reflection.

Behind her, a few steps away, a young girl quietly stood, waiting.

She had been taken from the ship to a house not far away from the port.

A man, second cousin of the Cardinal, and his wife had greeted her warmly. The woman had taken her upstairs where she was given a room and a maidservant was summoned to help her bathe and change. She was informed of the time for dinner and just to ask if there was anything she required.

21

Viana was tired. The maid, a young girl really, was helpful, obviously pleased to be meeting someone new, and was totally in awe of the visitor, though a little nervous.

She chatted practically the whole time about everything and nothing, all the while either brushing clothes, tidying them into drawers or seeing to any other of her new mistress' needs.

Despite the chatter, Viana enjoyed her company and came down to dinner feeling quite refreshed.

Dinner had been quiet at first. Numerous candles lit the dark wood-panelled room. A fire was burning in the hearth.

A square dining table stood on a bare wooden floor, there were two sideboards in the room, and above the wood panels several paintings adorned the walls.

The food smelled good when it came.

There were just the three of them. After a little while, Viana opened up the conversation, which had been virtually non-existent till then.

She spoke about her plans, related how things were in Rome, expressed her gratitude to them for hosting her and listened as the lady of the house told of how things were in Genoa.

Finally, the man, rather shy and retiring, spoke. Obviously, he had been listening to Viana's plans and gave her some bad news.

She listened thoughtfully as he spoke.

Now she sat at her dressing table, deep in thought.

The young maid sensed the mood of her new mistress and remained quiet, waiting for instructions.

The room was warm. Whilst she'd been at dinner someone had lit the fire and had drawn the curtains. The maid had lit three candles that stood upon a chest of drawers and a further candle on a small table by the bed. Outside it was now raining.

Viana suddenly noticed her maid in the mirror. Holding up her brush she caught her eye and said 'please.'

The young girl immediately responded, took the silver and pearl handled brush that matched the hand mirror that lay on the table and began to brush the long dark hair, still not speaking.

She brushed softly and carefully.

Smiling into the mirror, Viana said, 'You can brush a little harder, I won't break.'

'Yes Miss, 'the girl answered, smiling back.

Viana returned to her thoughts about what her host had said at dinner. She had hoped to obtain passage from Genoa to either Antwerp or Amsterdam, however, he informed her that the Spanish were at war with the low countries, in what would become the eighty-year war. It had started some ten years ago, and there were over seven thousand casualties so far. The war had recently intensified, with a siege on Antwerp that had resulted in the destruction of at least eight hundred houses.

To travel by sea into that region would be too dangerous at this time and an overland journey would be equally fraught with danger.

He told her he now had a responsibility for her and could not allow her to travel under these circumstances.

Briefly she had wondered if the Cardinal had been instrumental in this decision, but then realised, looking him in the eye, that he was genuinely concerned for her well-being.

The lady of the house spoke up at that point, saying that she would be more than welcome to stay as long as she liked. An offer that was generous and genuine.

Viana sighed.
'That will be all for now, thank you.'
The maid handed back the brush, folded the bedclothes back ready, then, saying goodnight, left the room.
February ended and rolled into March, then into April.

A letter came from another of the Cardinal's widespread cousins with an offer to come and stay with them in Monaco.

An offer she accepted.

She thanked her hosts and gave her tearful maid a hug goodbye when the day came to leave.

Viana once more stood on the deck of a ship. This was a similar schooner, and she stood on the starboard side watching as they approached and sailed into Port Hercule, Monaco.

In her hand she held the leather pouch, having moments earlier taken it out to admire again.

She gripped the pouch tightly and wondered if she would ever meet the artist who created it. The man who had loved her mother. The man, who had no idea of her existence.

A step closer, she told herself, and watched as the vessel docked, and then prepared herself to disembark.

She was greeted warmly by the Cardinal's cousin and his young and curious daughters, ten-year old twins.

Little did she imagine that her journey would end here.

THE PRESENT;

BAARN

10AM SUNDAY 10TH MARCH

Wouter and Mies Wagenaar sat on the same side of the dining table. A police detective from the Amersfoort Branch, sat opposite them.

The couple were both in their late fifties. He was a now retired company director of a small shoe factory, of which he was still the owner.

She was a retired legal secretary.

'So, you didn't notice anything last night?' the detective asked, going over his notes again.

The call had come into the Baarn Division a little after eight this morning.

Being Sunday, there weren't many personnel around, so the case was put through to the larger Amersfoort Division once it had been established that no-one had been hurt.

'No,' Mr Wagenaar replied, 'we had been out, to see a show in Utrecht. When we came home we did notice that the alarm system didn't beep when we entered, I figured that I must not have set it in the first place.

We went up to bed, but, as we said, this morning, we came down for breakfast and noticed the back door', looking at the door on the other side of the kitchen, 'the handle was down, was out of place.'

'So, then you realised someone had broken in?' the detective said, writing down a few more notes.

'Yes, I suddenly noticed that it was gone. It was right here, on this table.'

'And why was it just here, on the table?' the policeman asked.

Again, it was Mr Wagenaar who spoke. His wife was very quiet and pale.
'We kept it wrapped up in a cloth as we had just added it to our insurance last Tuesday. Our insurance agent came over to view it, as it was such an expensive item, in order for it to be added to our policy.'

After a brief pause and glancing at his wife then back at the detective, he continued, 'We also had an auction valuer come, because we wanted to sell it.
As I have said, we have only recently discovered it amongst some bits and pieces that were in a box of items we inherited.
We found out it's possible worth, didn't want such a valuable item in the house. The cards I gave you,' he said, referring to the business cards on the table beside the detective's notepad, 'are from the two people who visited here last Tuesday.'

The detective briefly looked at the cards, then once again looking at Mr Wagenaar, asked, 'And how many others knew of this item that you describe as an oil painting on ivory, a miniature?'
Glancing down at his notes, he went on, 'What about family, children, anyone?'

It was Mrs Wagenaar croaked, 'We have two children,' she cleared her throat then continued, 'our son, Erik, well, eh, when he was younger he got into some trouble with the police, but, about ten years ago, he moved out. Went, we believe, to Mexico, we don't know, we have not heard from him since,' she paused. 'Our daughter, Elsa, she is a lecturer at the university of Leiden, but she is away in Greece at the moment, for a couple of months, doing research for her lectures.'

'So, neither are around,' the detective confirmed, 'and your daughter, does she know of this item?'

'No' Mr Wagenaar replied, 'when we found it, we did some research ourselves, found out its value and decided it was best to sell it.'

The detective, a man in his late thirties, looked at them both, down at his notes, and said, 'So, these two,' picking up the business cards, 'you said they both viewed the item, and took pictures. You don't have any yourself?'

'No' answered Wouter.

'Very well, 'the detective said, standing up. 'I have checked the door. It was definitely tampered with, but I will send someone to check for prints and so on, so, in the meantime, please don't touch it or the alarm box. I'll write this up and send you the paperwork. You'll need that for your insurance claim.'

'Yes, of course. Well, thank you, detective,' Wouter said, also standing up. 'Let me show you out.'

Mrs Wagenaar remained seated. Still rather pale, the detective noted as he nodded a goodbye.

ROTTERDAM, THE NETHERLANDS
THE FOLLOWING DAY

'Are you related to Samantha Price?' The question puzzled him. He was pouring out two cups of coffee. The Dutch, as fifth ranked coffee drinkers in the world after the Scandinavian countries, would be unlikely to refuse an offer of the beverage.

The detective, a man who stood as tall as Samuel but was at least ten years younger, had said yes to the offer of a coffee, as expected, after introducing himself and given a reason for his visit.

Though puzzled by the question, he brought the drinks out of the kitchen, placing them on the low table.

'No. Well certainly not a close relation. Why do you ask?' He went back into the kitchen area to fetch the sugar, then sat down opposite the detective.

'It's a name that popped up,' the detective, the same man who had interviewed the Wagenaars the previous day, said, 'Not important. So, as I mentioned, there was a break in, on Saturday evening at some point. Now, you were at the house, last Tuesday, right?'

Sam helped himself to one teaspoon of sugar and stirred his coffee. Pushing the sugar across the table, he answered, 'That's right. They had contacted the company I work for. Wanted to place an item in our fine arts auction.'

The detective shovelled a couple of spoons of sugar into his mug, stirred it for a bit and asked, 'This auction house is in Paris, I gather?'

'Aha. We specialise in fine arts, paintings, sculptures, pottery, china, glass, also antique books and maps.

I was contacted to visit the Wagenaars, see the item, check it out, photograph it for the catalogue.

I then send the info to Paris. They send correspondence to the owners to sign, company policy, transit insurance cover and an exclusivity form, so that they will not sell it through another auction house or dealer.

Closer to the auction I would arrange for collection of the item or items.'

'So, you have photos of this item?' the detective asked, taking a sip from his mug.

Sam got up, crossed to the other side of the room and pulled out a sheet of paper from a small writing desk, walked back and handed it to the detective.

'This is the format for the catalogue, the description, history, photos and so on.

This is what I have prepared so far with the information I have. Should I or the team in Paris come up with further relevant details, these will be added. The catalogue is due for printing in three weeks' time, then it's another three and a half weeks before the auction.

Head office have a copy of this, so, please, have that. I have the details on my laptop and can easily print another.'

'I take it, then,' Sam continued, sitting down again and reaching for his coffee, 'that this item is among things that were stolen. I mean, you did say there had been a break in?'

'Yes,' the man answered, studying the photographs on the sheet of paper he had been given. He took another sip, looked up at Sam and asked, 'Are you an expert then, on this sort of stuff? Is this item really that valuable?'

'I have a wide knowledge of art, but I'm not an expert. I'm an assessor. I cover an area from Brussels all the way up to the Scandinavian countries, even been to Estonia and Latvia. I'm given an address, then check out what the people have for auction, check its provenance where possible, get a feel for the articles as well as the people selling them.

I take pictures, then draft a catalogue page. I will do some research myself on the pieces of art, as will the team in Paris. The better or more information we can have on the art, the better price we can achieve at auction.

Also, provenance is very important. We cannot offer an item as a genuine, say Vermeer or Rembrandt, Gauguin or whatever, if we don't have conclusive proof.'

'Mm, and this item?'

'Not sure, Sam answered, 'the bill of sale that was with it looks the real thing, but the item itself is not signed and it's on ivory, which is hard to date just by looking at it, or by feel, but it could be, yes.'

'And if it is, it would be that valuable?'

'Absolutely, if we can track it back, find out more about its history, then yes, it would be worth two and half million, maybe more.'

'Would it be hard to sell on the black market?' was the next question.

'This is a rare piece. A piece of art deemed lost. You say the house was burgled. The Wagenaars have some lovely pieces in their home, from what I saw when I was there, I noticed nice vases and some good paintings.

This item, wouldn't seem at all special, unless you knew what it was, so, as a piece of art, yes, it could easily be sold, but for very little of its true worth.'

The detective drank some more of his coffee and thought for a moment.

Then, seemingly having made up his mind as to how much to reveal, said to Samuel, 'Nothing else was stolen ... this,' again referring to the sheet in his hand, 'is the only thing missing, and, according to them, they had only recently come into possession of it. Not many people knew it was even there. You, of course, are one of those people.'

Samuel thought about this for a moment, frowned, then looking at the detective, said, 'Mmm, now that's interesting.'

'In what way?'

'It could add weight to the fact that this item is the real thing. If it was the only thing stolen, then someone knew what it was, and possibly stole to order. With items like these, rare pieces, more people know about them than you would think.

Mrs Wagenaar, who I dealt with, had said that her husband had researched the item, realising its potential value, hence the suggested auction price. Believe me, in the world of art, this kind of information gets around.'

'Well, that's very helpful Mr Price, thank you. We'll circulate this around the antique shops in the area and in the big cities. You never know, we might get lucky.'

The detective finished his coffee, stood up and headed for the door. Then, turned and said, 'As this is an on-going investigation, please do not contact the Wagenaars yourself. Any questions, or suggestions or thoughts, please call me,' handing over one of his business cards.

'I will continue research the item. If anything relevant pops up, I'll be in touch,' Samuel promised, taking the card as he let the detective out.

Closing the door, he walked over to the coffee table, picked up his mug and finished his drink.

Taking both mugs into the kitchen, Sam walked over to the desk and opened up his laptop. An interesting twist, he thought to himself, and for some reason memories of all those years ago, when he left the auction house in Paris, came to mind, a day he would never forget for it was the day his wife had passed away …

He was already on board the train back to Rotterdam that day when his phone rang.

'Monsieur Price?' it was the director of the Auction House.

'I have taken a look at the provenance of the Gauguin. As you know, it did not sell today, in fact, it did not come close to its reserve.

But I find, that the painting was purchased in 1898, in Copenhagen and sold in 1908 in Paris, by a Monsieur Samuel Price?'

Of course! Sam thought, as the train sped through the flat Dutch countryside. His great-grandfather was a diplomat, an ambassador, travelled far and wide, and, was an art lover.

'My great-grandfather,' Sam explained on the phone. 'He wrote comprehensive journals, and had a collection of paintings of which he had photo's. That's how I know the painting. I didn't realise the connection, I will go through his journals, find the pictures, and I'll get back to you.'

'Tres bien, thank you,' answered the director.

A conversation and a discovery that had led to him working as an assessor for the company now ...

He fired up his laptop, then reprinted the copy of the brochure layout of the item and looked at it.

An interesting turn of events, he thought.

MEANWHILE AT AROUND THE SAME TIME; ANTWERP BELGIUM

In an office of the 'Zwart-Wit Verzekeringen' an insurance company situated in central Antwerp just beyond the cathedral, Samantha Price thumbed through a folder, then pulled out and handed a form over to the woman who sat opposite her and said, 'This is it.'

The female detective, also from the Amersfoort Division, and having liaised with the Belgian authorities as a matter of courtesy, took the form, 'So, this is the updated policy, including the item you saw last Tuesday? Ah, yes, I see it here. Is it really worth that much?'

'Apparently, it is a rare find, an item that was deemed lost for centuries. I did a little investigation on it. If it is indeed the real thing, then yes, it would be worth at least that much,' Samantha answered.

Only moments earlier, Samantha's boss had knocked and entered her office, asking her to get the Wagenaar file and see a detective who had been placed in one of the other offices. She had grabbed the file, followed her boss out and was introduced to the detective.

'You dealt with the Wagenaars? How did they seem?' asked the detective as she looked up from the form.

'I didn't see Mrs Wagenaar. I dealt with her husband. He was not very talkative, more business-like, but he seemed fine. Why, what is all this about?'

'He wanted this item,' looking at the form, 'put on his insurance schedule, is that why you went there?' the detective asked, ignoring Samantha's question for the moment.

'Yes, we had a call. They wanted a valuable item added to their existing policy. It was something they acquired recently and wanted insured.'

'This couldn't be done by phone? Or online?'

'Not with such a high value item. I wanted to check it out, see it physically, photograph and document it, and determine whether or not the valuation was reasonable.'

'It was stolen,' the detective said, watching Samantha for any reaction.

'Goodness, did they have a break in? Are they alright? As far as I'm aware, we have not been notified, when did this happen, was much taken?'

The detective absorbed the barrage of questions, then, looking down at the form still in her hand, said, 'The only thing stolen, was this item.'

'That's ...' Samantha began ...

'Suspicious?' filled in the detective, 'I agree.'

'Strange, I was going to say, but, suspicious, yes. As you can see, we are talking a high value item. Still, strange as well. They are a valued customer, have been with us, for,' Samantha flicking through the file, 'over nine years.'

'Have they ever claimed for anything?'

'No, never. I'm guessing they will be claiming for this, and, you say nothing else was stolen? They have only recently obtained it, that is suspicious.'

'Indeed, and only a few people knew this, you included, of course,' the detective said, again, watching for any reaction.

It was Samantha's turn to sidestep the inference, 'We will need a full police report. We will also do our own investigation. Company policy when it comes to such large claims.'

'Who will be in charge of that?'

'That will be me,' Samantha answered, taking the form back from the detective.

'Are you related to a Samuel Price?' was the next question, as Samantha put the form back into the file from whence it came.

'No, not that I'm aware of, why?'

The detective stood up, 'I'll make sure you get a full report Miss Price. Thank you for your time, and, whatever you might find in your investigation, make sure you keep us informed, and, oh, until we tell you otherwise, you cannot directly contact the Wagenaars. Standard procedure with ongoing investigations.'

'Of course,' Samantha answered, also standing up and opening the door of the office to let the detective out.

'Good' she said as she left the room. Both women looked each other in the eye briefly, each with a clear message that suggested, 'Don't get in my way.'

THE PAST;

PERIOD 2

DECEMBER 1612

Pietro Esposito sat upright on the single bunk bed in the officer's quarters, one of two, on the old three-master. A Spanish built galleon.

He could see and hear the rain lashing against the porthole. One moment all he could see was water as the ship went down into a trough, then, as she rose, he could make out the sky, barely a different shade to that of the sea, briefly before the ship went down into another trough.

The swell was high, but nothing the old ship couldn't handle. They were on the Atlantic Ocean, not far from the French coast, heading north for Amsterdam. Normally Pietro wouldn't mind being on deck, in fact he loved it, especially in fairly rough conditions as it was now. But this wasn't his ship. He wasn't part of the crew on this occasion, so, when the wind increased and the rain came, he decided to retreat to his appointed quarters.

The galleon belonged to his uncle, the brother of his father. He was also the master of the ship, and from him Pietro had learned practically all he knew about shipping, trade, cargo distribution, navigation and a host of other marine-related skills over the past twelve years. Pietro was now thirty-two.

He was considered a handsome man, standing a little under six foot. His skin was tanned, his brown eyes set in a chiselled face, clean shaven, with prominent cheekbones, a Roman nose and a square jawline. He was a contented man and almost always smiled. Though he had had several romantic relationships, he had not, as yet, he kept telling his mother, met the right one.

The ship rose out of another trough, and through the porthole Pietro noticed the sky was getting brighter. The rain began to ease.

His father had passed away just three years ago. As the eldest son, Pietro had received a substantial legacy, including the family house and estate. Though the family owned vineyards, and were one of the main wine producers in Monaco, his heart belonged to the sea.

He wanted to be the master of his own ship one day, and that day was nearing.

He achieved his master's ticket, a little over a year ago. Using some of his legacy, together with his earnings over many years, he had set about to purchase his own galleon. He'd looked to the Dutch. Not just because of the connections he and his family had, but they were also considered to be the best shipbuilders at that time.

He was now on his way to Amsterdam, to take possession. The ship, a three-masted galleon, at least a quarter bigger than the ship he was now on, was nearing completion.

The seas calmed, the swells reduced, and the sky became brighter. More light poured into the cabin and Pietro walked over to where a three-drawer cabinet was secured to the wall. He opened the top drawer. A stack of papers and documents filled the space. These were navigational charts, mainly sourced from the Portuguese, upon which were various trade routes to the Far East, the Philippines, Indonesia, Java, Central Persia, as well as a few to the West Indies and South America.

Once in Amsterdam, Pietro hoped to secure a few more maps from the Dutch.

He closed the drawer again, stood by the porthole, dug deep into the pocket of his trousers and pulled out a black soft leather pouch. Undoing the cord, he opened it, slipped the item into his hand and looked at it in the light from the porthole.

He admired the artistry, loved the feel of the object, such a fine item, and very dear to him. He thought back to only a few months ago when he had first seen it when it had been given to him.

His mother, Viana, had arrived in Monaco in early April of the year 1578. Before the end of that year, she had been courted, had fallen deeply in love, and had married. She gave birth to her firstborn, a son, in the year 1580. Pietro.

Her quest of finding her father had already come to an end, for it hadn't been long after her arrival in Monaco that she found out that he had died some years earlier, in 1569, even before she had set out from Rome that February morning.

Pietro recalled his mother telling of this quest, this story, several times, but then, recently, when he was at home after nearly a month at sea, she asked him to come with her to the garden pavilion.

A rectangular building set in the grounds of their estate, it was made of mainly glass panels.

Inside were several white painted wooden benches, a few cast iron round tables, a bunch of chairs and many rows of shelves upon which were a huge variety of plants, some of which he had brought home from his travels.

He liked this place, loved the smell, a humid, hot and musty smell, a bit like being in Java, a place that he loved.

When he was home, which wasn't often, this was the place he would go to the most, just being in there, looking at the plants, drinking in the atmosphere, reflecting on the memories that came to him.

As he walked beside her that warm and sunny day, late in the month of August, he wondered what was on her mind. She was quiet as they strolled along. Still a very striking woman, almost as tall as he was. He was very fond of her; she had been the one who had taught him to speak fluently in Italian and adequately in English.

They arrived at the pavilion and, upon entering, Pietro noticed several items spread out upon two tables.

Viana explained. This was an inheritance, given to her by the artist Giulio, and they were all pieces of art painted by a man who had been her mother's lover, a man who was, according to her mother, her father, therefore his grandfather.

There were three sketches, each signed, that had, by the look them, been rolled up for some time. There was a wide red ribbon by the side of each of them. Then there was a painted miniature depicting the Colosseum, this one not signed, a larger oil painting on a wood panel, which was again signed, and, finally, his mother pulled from her pocket a leather pouch containing the most precious piece, a miniature oil painted on ivory. It was not signed. She showed it to him. He too thought this was very special.

'They are for you' she had said, 'all of them. Take them with you when you go to Amsterdam. Then they will at least have travelled the journey I was going to make. Do as you please with them. Sell them, you'll probably need extra funds to hire a crew.'

Pietro had taken his time to look at all the pieces, especially his mother's favourite. Hugging her, he said, 'Thank you mother. I will sell them, all except this one. This one I will keep with me always.'

Pietro broke from his reverie. He took another look at the precious miniature, then slid it back into the pouch and into his pocket.

They would be sailing into Amsterdam the following day.

On board with him were four men, four trusted men, four capable men. These were his officers. Their responsibility would be to hire the crew, to thoroughly check out the new ship, to organise obtaining the sails and, once ready, to purchase and load provisions. Pietro himself would negotiate cargoes and deal with all the necessary documentation needed to take possession of the galleon.

AMSTERDAM

It was cold and frosty. But the sky was clear and blue. Pietro and his men disembarked, having said their goodbyes to the master and crew.

As they walked along the dock, heading for an assortment of buildings that housed the customs people and dock operators, they were a little taken aback.

Whilst they had all been to ports in France, Italy, Spain and the Far East, never had they been here in Amsterdam, and they were in awe of the immense hustle and bustle of the place. It was exciting. Many ships berthed, and were being loaded or unloaded, horses and carts were moving about, dogs barking, men shouting, laughing and even singing. What an atmosphere! Pietro felt it and was wrapped in its intensity. He loved it.

They would be staying here for a little while. Although their ship was nearly ready for them to take possession, much still had to be done before they could set off on their maiden voyage.

The five men entered one of the port buildings. Pietro sorted out their registration and then the group set about to find lodgings, from several options they'd been given.

They made their way along narrow cobbled streets, each carrying their own personal belongings in tote bags, and settled on the second address on their list. Pietro, not only their natural leader but also the only one who spoke a number of languages, including a smattering of Dutch, secured their accommodation for the next couple of months.

Stashing their belongings, the five then went along to the dry dock and shipyard to see their new ship. They had a rudimentary map of the city and only took one wrong turn before they reached their destination.

Again, they were amazed at all the activity.

By the look of it, three ships were currently under construction and a further two were undergoing repairs.

Pietro led the way and reached their new vessel. After showing some papers to a man in a small wooden shack, they proceeded along the dock and stopped by the bow with 'Serenus Venti' painted in white and gold near the tip. The name, meaning 'calm winds' had been chosen by Pietro.

They all stood and looked up together. The galleon looked absolutely splendid in the afternoon sunlight.

It was dark by the time the excited men returned to their lodgings.

The Weeskamer was an auction house, a reputable one, run with efficiency and by men experienced in all manner of goods, including fine arts. One such person looked over the five items that Pietro brought in to sell.

It was by now the middle of January, and much had already been sourced in the way of provisions, crew and sails for the three-master.

It was time to sell the items given him by his mother, all, of course, except one.

The goods were accepted, and a good response was expected, with the auctioneer very happy with the pieces on offer. The next auction was to be held early February.

THE PRESENT;

AMSTERDAM

11.30AM WEDNESDAY 13TH MARCH

Samuel Price had been searching through the relevant archives at the Maritime Museum for just under half an hour when he found what he was looking for.

He was in an office not accessible to the general public. He had the files that he had asked for around him on a table. Furthermore, he had been supplied with coffee and biscuits and was left to it.

For a little over three and a half years now, Sam had worked for the Paris Fine Arts Auction House.

Over the years he had built up a detailed list of museums and private collectors so that if he should come across paintings by certain masters, sculptures of Greek mythology, or anything relating to maritime, or animals, or royal connections, or a host of other specialities, then he would contact the relevant interested party.

This had a dual benefit for Sam. Firstly, it increased the probability of obtaining a better price at the auction, which, in turn, meant a better financial reward for him for he had, from the very beginning, negotiated a contract whereby he would receive one percent of the total sale of any item or items that he was involved in, either through referrals from the Paris office, as was the case for the Wagenaars, or ones he had secured personally. Though perhaps a seemingly low return, in the first year alone the sale of thirteen items he had secured, reached over five million euros, bringing in over fifty thousand for him.

Secondly, it had gained him the gratitude of those interested parties for keeping them informed about what had surfaced, and what was about to be auctioned.

Sam had in this way informed the Maritime Museum, as well as quite a few others, of several items of interest over the years. This was usually reciprocated with comments that went along the lines of, 'Thank you Sam, I owe you one.'

Hence, when he called yesterday he was assured of access to whatever he needed. The coffee and the biscuits were a lovely bonus.

From the archive, he read the top, or first, copy, the one retained by the auction house, checking this against the photograph he had taken showing the second copy, the one retained by the customer.

The date, February 1613, was clear, but the actual day was illegible on both copies, so a check for that.

The item listed, an oil painted miniature, Rome, check, the seller, Pietro Esposito, Rome, check, the buyer, Nicholas v Struyten, Leiden, check. The price paid was smudged too much to be read on both copies.

Studying both copies very carefully, Sam determined that the bill of sale belonging to the Wagenaars, at least, was the real deal.

Did it really pertained to the item they had shown him? Of that he wasn't convinced.

Deciding he wanted to know more about the seller, Pietro Esposito, he delved more into the archives and searched the internet for further information.

Who was this chap? How did he come by the item, which, if it was the genuine article, would have been painted, according to Sam's research, some sixty years earlier, around 1553?

After some time, and after a kind member of staff brought a replacement flask of coffee, he had found several entries.

First he had found two more sales documents showing Pietro as the seller, one for three sketches signed by the artist and authenticated by the auction house, and another for an oil painted on a wood panel with the inscription, 'Scene of Italy', this one also signed and authenticated.

Samuel took pictures of both these documents and put them back in the files.

Second, the name Esposito came up again, though in a different area altogether. Sam found out that Pietro had purchased a Galleon. He found documentation about this ship, the builders and the launch date, which was shown as March 1613.

This all tied together the presence of this, obviously quite wealthy person, in Amsterdam at that time, and, the likelihood that the items he had brought to auction, were indeed the real thing.

However, he discovered an interesting anomaly.

On the documents relating to the purchased galleon, Esposito was listed as being from Monaco, whereas on the auction room documents he was shown as being from Rome.

Finally, Sam put the archive folders back where he had found them, made a few more notes on his laptop, then shut it down.

Though he had found that first document within half an hour, it was now four hours later.

He was hungry, despite having eaten half a dozen biscuits.

Further research needed to be done.

Samuel Price left the room, and the building after saying his goodbyes and thank yous, and headed for the railway station.

On the way as he was running through all that he had found in his mind, one thing in particular puzzled him.

He had studied many of the sales documents from the auction house the Weeskamer, and noticed that there were certainly people working there who were quite knowledgeable about art and artists, hence their ability to authenticate the paintings that Pietro had brought in, yet, the item that had been unsigned and described as an oil painted miniature, Rome, wasn't Rome at all, nor was there any mention that it was painted on ivory.

It was pretty clear to Sam that the bill of sale shown him by the Wagenaars did not relate to the item that had been with it.

Something wasn't right.

Samantha Price, armed with her file on Mr and Mrs Wagenaar, including the photographs she had taken at their house, had travelled up by train from Antwerp to Leiden, changing at Rotterdam. She also had with her a copy of the police report about the break in. She reread this on the train.

The report stated that the house had been entered via the back door. This was only accessible through the back garden. A gate opened up to an alleyway that ran behind the row of houses.

A door-to-door enquiry had not been fruitful. No one had seen a thing, and no one in that row of houses in that block had ever been burgled. The report also stated that the alarm system had been rendered inactive, and the word, 'professionally', was highlighted.

No prints were found anywhere.

Gazing out of the window of the high-speed train on her first leg out of Antwerp, Samantha had a few things on her mind. Who knew the item was in the house? Who knew, when coming in by the back door, where the alarm box, which she knew from her files was well hidden in the front hallway, was situated?

It was all rather suspicious, but, as she had been clearly told she couldn't talk to the Wagenaars at this point, she had to gather information some other way. Hence her trip to Leiden.

She wanted to follow up on the purchaser of the item listed on the bill of sale back in 1613, this Nicholas v Struyten, and how he was related, if their story of an inheritance was to be believed.

The insurance documents she had sent with the new cover and premium costs had been duly signed and returned.

The claim came in on Monday, arriving shortly after she had spoken with the detective.

The policy agreement stated that the cover amount would be paid out within thirty days of any incident, which was on the 9th.

It was now Wednesday, she had a maximum of twenty-six days left to challenge the claim, and she would need solid proof to claim fraudulence, for she was in no doubt that this was a case of fraud.

THE PAST;

PERIOD 3

THE YEAR 1617

He stood there, beside the grave. He stood there, still, like a statue.

He stood there, looking out to sea.

He was well over six feet tall, broad shouldered, blond hair that was almost white in sharp contrast to his skin which was tanned a deep brown.

Blue eyes.

He stood there, beside the grave he himself had dug. Almost all the others had already returned to the village, which lay to the south about half a mile away, after the short funeral service which he had conducted.

Almost all.

One remained, a young woman. She stood about ten feet away.

Quietly watching the young man, quietly waiting.

Karel Maas was only eighteen years of age. His facial hair was only just beginning to thicken out into a blond beard and moustache. The day was beautiful, only a whisper of a breeze, not a cloud in the deep blue sky. It was hot.

The sea was calm, a gentle swell, and the waves rolling on to the beach hardly made a sound at all, as if in respect of the moment.

Five weeks earlier, this Sea of Java, was not so calm. It had been wild and turbulent.

The young woman, her dark hair long, her eyes brown, was about the same age as Karel.

As she stood there watching him, she thought back to when she first had seen him, back when the first of two storms had battered her coastline village on the northern coast of Java, around ten miles west of Surabaya, a large town and main port where many vessels called.

Such had been the heaviness and density of the rain, she didn't see the ship, not at first.

Karel took a long slow breath, inhaling through his nose, then exhaled slowly.

He took a last look at the grave beside him. The man, who had taught him so much, the man to whom he would forever be grateful, was now at rest.

By the sea he loved so much, yet, the sea that had taken so much as well.

Karel moved away, walking towards the young woman who stood waiting.

Out at sea, less than a hundred yards away, one mast stuck out. One mast, marking the place where the ship, broken, now lay.

The storm had come just before the break of day. Suddenly the wind increased; the rain came. For a few brief moments it fell gently, lightly, then, in the next instant it intensified to a roar. With the lightning and thunder, the sea grew wild and the ship began pitching and rolling.

Men emerged from below deck to assist those who were on duty above. A bolt of lightning zigzagged down, its light blinding, and with a loud crack that shattered the air, it struck the forward mast. The mast split, splintered and crashed to the deck. Sails came down.

In that moment five men had been swept overboard and three men lay dying or badly injured on the deck. The rain kept up its intensity. The ship lost steerage, turned broadside, and a huge wave smashed into the side.

The ship shuddered and floundered. It rolled heavily to port then, creaking and groaning, the galleon struggled back upright.

Men were losing their footing. There were more casualties, either swept away into the turbulent sea or crushed on the decks.

There was shouting; instructions yelled to be heard above the noise of the storm. The captain appeared on deck, between the middle and aft masts, struggling to balance as the ship, so far battling well, had come upright again.

But it was still broadside to the wind and a second wave hit. Several crossbeams on the main mast, cracked, broke and came hurtling down. A jagged piece struck captain Pietro, gashing his thigh.

He fell to one knee, then was struck again by a second piece of beam and tumbled backwards, down some steps onto a small deck.

Young Karel, who had not been far behind his captain, managed to cushion the fall, preventing his master's head from crashing on the deck, but even so, he could see the captain was in a bad way, dazed, bleeding from a cut to his face, but, more seriously, the young lad saw the damage to his master's thigh.

The ship shuddered as it again tried to struggle upright, the last wave having almost capsized it.

Karel knew he had to stop the bleeding.

For him, nothing else mattered, not the rain or the wind, not the shouting or the men scrambling around, or the heaving deck. He focused solely on his master. Ripping his shirt off, he somehow managed to keep his balance despite the rolling deck. He gripped the shirt with his teeth whilst tearing his master's trousers open to expose the gashed thigh, then tied his shirt around the wound, stemming the flow of blood.

Karel realised that the captain was semi-conscious. He also knew that the ship was losing its battle with the elements. He dragged himself and his master over to the railing on the port side, securing a tight grip on the captain, and watched and waited in the growing light of daybreak.

The rain was still intense; the wind still howling.

But the shouting had stopped. It seemed everyone knew the end was inevitable.

The battle with the sea was lost, the fight was over, and as the ship rolled again, Karel knew, it wouldn't roll back.

He clung to the railing with his free hand, waiting, waiting and then, as the ship capsized fully, he dragged himself and his master over the railing and into the water, kicked out and swam.

One arm wrapped securely around his master's waist, with the other pulling through the water and his feet kicking in the turbulent sea, he made progress.

Karel was immensely strong with a natural strength he had since he was very young.

He swam on and saw the coastline, thankfully not that far away. He heard his master splutter a few times, relieved to know he was still alive and then, just as quickly as the rain, wind and storm had come, they went. The light grew brighter. The sea eased a little and for several moments it was eerily quiet.

Then, when it seemed time was standing still and it felt like he had been in the water for a lifetime, he heard shouts, he saw the beach, saw people there, and saw help coming.

Two hundred and forty-eight crew had been on board when the ship had left Surabaya late the previous day.

Forty-one perished that morning, a further seventy-four were injured, of who nine died that same day.

The people of the nearby village worked tirelessly to help the crew, attending and caring for their needs as best they could.

The day after the storm, one hundred and fifty-three men set off for Surabaya.

There they would be able to further tend to the wounded, and find passage on other ships.

The rest stayed, tending to those unable to walk, and to the burial of those who had perished.

Karel tended only to his master's needs, rarely leaving his side.

The captain's injuries were severe. At first, he seemed to recover, but then his condition worsened day by day.

At the age of fourteen, four years ago, Karel had stood by the ship in one of the docks in Amsterdam. He had walked up and down, admiring this brand-new ship.

'Serenus Venti' was the name of the galleon. The young lad had observed several men working on the deck and preparing the sails. Then, standing by the bow, he saw a man coming. He asked in his native Dutch, pointing to the name, 'What does that mean?'

The man smiled at the boy, and, having lived in Amsterdam for these past three months, understood his question and answered in Dutch, 'calm winds'.

Pietro took a liking to this lad. In his broken Dutch, mixed with French, and the odd Italian word, he asked the lad why he was there, where he was from, and why he was interested in ships.

The boy had come from Rotterdam, and had left home to find work here as a ship's boy, but, so far had not been picked.

Most boys his age were much smaller in stature and more suitable for the work they were to carry out in the small confines of a ship.

It hadn't taken Pietro long to make up his mind. He said to the boy, 'come with me' took him to the docks administration building, duly registered the boy, and took him on.

In his last days, as he lay ailing in a cane and straw bed in one of the village huts, Pietro was glad that he had taken the lad on and comforted by him. The boy proved to be hard-working, loyal, and a sponge for knowledge. He had seen the lad grow and mature, and was humbled by the helpful nature. He had never seen the lad angry or upset. He had always been ready to do whatever was asked of him.

Four days after the first storm a second hit the coast. It battered the little village, tearing down trees and destroying several huts.

Karel had worked as hard as he ever had, shifting rubble, pulling three elderly people to safety, and then leading these villagers in re-organising and rebuilding the damaged huts, all the while never forgetting to keep an eye on his master.

The remaining crew had left the previous day, only he and his master remained.

Three days after that Pietro's condition worsened. He struggled to a sitting position, then beckoned Karel over, who at that point stood looking out the small window of the hut.

With difficulty Pietro spoke at length, then produced the leather pouch, the one his mother had given him, the one he always had with him, deep in his trouser pocket. Even on the morning of the storm, it had survived the swim ashore.

Karel had seen the item contained within the pouch before. Had thought it a thing of beauty.

He recalled the day his master had first shown it him; he had spoken Italian that day. It was a teaching game they had had between them for a few years now. Whatever language his master used first thing in the morning was the language they would converse in that day.

He listened as his master spoke, not ashamed of the tears that welled up and rolled down his cheeks ...

Karel took another deep breath before he reached the young woman.

Salee was her name. She had been around him from the beginning. It had been her who had first seen the ship battling the storm that morning. It had been her who had gone for help.

In those first days, Karel recalls, there had been three other young women who had shown an interest in him, trying to catch his eye, but this one, Salee, stood out.

She showed defiance, her stance, her piercing brown eyes, her long, almost black, hair and the fact that she was taller than the others.

The others had, wisely, given up the contest.

She stood there now, quietly, waiting.

During these days she had not spoken much to him at all. When she did, it was in her native tongue, a dialect that he knew a little, though he did not let on to her that he understood some of what she was saying. Her voice was soft, yet strong and reassuring. He had observed her, was drawn to her, had acknowledged her presence, and had spoken the odd word to her.

She had smiled at his shyness, was grateful for his strength, and moved by his gentleness and care, that which he showed others, that which he showed his master.

There were tears in his eyes as he stopped before her. She raised her arm, softly placed the palm of her right hand on his cheek, said nothing, but looked into his blue eyes.

She then took his hand and they walked back to the village.

She threw him a sideways glance, this was her man now, and she was his woman.

THE PRESENT;

BAARN

4PM WEDNESDAY 13TH MARCH

Wouter Wagenaar and his wife, Mies, sat by the dining table.

Eight days ago, he had unwrapped and shown the item to the lady from the insurance company, Miss Price.

Eight days ago, she had unwrapped and shown the item to the auction valuer, Mr Price.

Mrs Wagenaar was holding her phone. They had just finished speaking with their daughter, briefly, all too briefly.

'Mum, dad, hang in there okay,' her voice had come through the speaker phone, 'all will be well, it will be alright, okay ...' Her voice sounded a little strained, a little tired, then a male voice spoke, 'Just do as your daughter says. Everything will be fine ...' then the call was ended, the connection broken.

They looked at each other for a moment, neither saying a word.

MEANWHILE IN LEIDEN

In the University Library, Samantha had spent the past few hours going through the genealogy of Nicholas v Struyten.

Quite a task. It had taken her along an incorrect branch of the family twice, but finally she had all the details she needed.

Putting all the information into a folder on her laptop, intending to print it out when she got home, she readied herself to leave. Shutting down her computer and putting on her coat, she stood up and whispered to herself, 'They lied'.

WHILST;

On a train heading back to Rotterdam, Samuel sat in the first-class compartment checking something on his laptop.

There was something nagging at him about the bill of sale, the one regarding the item that Pietro Esposito had sold and that Nicholas v Struyten had purchased.

When Sam arrived in the museum earlier and saw the many archive folders that had been placed at his disposal, he had first quickly taken photos of several of the documents pertaining to the Weeskamer Auction House, covering a five-year period.

This meant that if he ran out of time, he would be able to double check these at a later stage, in case he had missed something.

Scrolling through these copies now, he struck lucky, a bill of sale, four years later. In 1617 Nicholas v Struyten sold the very item he had purchased. Reading through the details, Samuel realised something very interesting, two things in fact.

The train slowed pulling into Rotterdam Central.

Standing up and gathering his gear, he whispered to himself, 'Well, well, it's definitely not the right item for one thing.'

Then, as he exited the train, 'They lied.'

THE PAST;

PERIOD 4

THE YEAR 1668

The day wasn't new. In fact, the sun had already been up for several hours, but had, thus far, failed to fully penetrate the fog. It created an eerie scene that gave virtually no indication at all as to what time of the day it really was.

A tall, slim young woman walked up the narrow, cobbled path leading to the front door of a stone cottage.

She had olive skin, very dark brown hair that reached the small of her back and green eyes. Her leather boots made hardly a sound as she walked. She wore a very long dark green woollen coat and carried a small bag in her right hand.

Her name was Bibiana.

She was well-schooled, spoke four languages fluently, had extensive knowledge of the shipping industry, and knew about trade, cargo handling and finances.

She reached the door to the cottage, close to the Haringvliet district of Rotterdam, knocked twice on the door, then opened it and entered.

Two weeks ago, she had married a prominent citizen of Middelburg. A wealthy man in his late thirties. Bibiana was twenty-three.

He was part of a group of businessmen in the province of Zeeland who had clubbed together and financed a fleet of ships to set out and conquer Paramaribo, in Suriname, South America. This venture had been successful.

Subsequently a fort had been established there to protect their conquest and the lucrative trade that could be set up there, in particular in sugar, a highly desirable commodity.

Bibiana Maas, though her married name was now De Reder, walked into the small room and greeted her grandfather with a huge hug and many kisses.

Karel Maas, now nearly seventy, still stood very tall, and still looked formidably strong. His hair, what was left of it, was very white and his eyes still a vivid blue. He hugged her warmly and smiled.

'How is grandmother?' she asked, almost in a whisper.

'A little better. She's in the scullery. Go and see her,' he answered and sat down again.

The scullery was the second room in the stone cottage. About half the size of the main room, it too had a stone floor.

An iron tub placed upon a wooden bench served both for washing clothes and themselves. The opposite wall was lined with shelves upon which were placed a variety of items, a selection of flour, spices and currants and a range of vegetables, such as potatoes, beets, cabbage and carrots.

At the far end of the room was the hearth, an open fireplace where the cooking was done.

In the main room, Karel pulled some tobacco from a pouch and set to fill his old pipe, a habit he had acquired when in his forties. He heard the ladies talk in the next room and looked around him.

So different from what they had experienced in the past, but it was home.

This room too had a fireplace, some occasional tables and a very nice Persian rug which occupied most of the centre of the room, bringing colour and warmth to the place. Against a wall was what looked like a large wardrobe, but was in fact, where they slept.

Karel got his pipe going and took a few puffs as they came into the room.

Bibiana helped Salee, who was quite frail, into her chair. Sadly, neither of them had been able to attend Bibiana's wedding.

The aroma from the pipe began to fill the room.

Bibiana sat down.

Karel thought back, a long, long way back ...

After the burial of his master, Karel spent the next four months in the village. He continued to help with the rebuilding, learned more about their customs, their lifestyle, their dialect.

He also set about to try and recover what he could from the sunken galleon. He was a strong swimmer, and, with the help of a couple of the local men, he made a wooden raft which he floated over to where the centre mast rose, like a monument, above the water.

Diving, sometimes up to ten times in succession, Karel brought back item after item, some small, some quite big, some that crumbled into nothing, but in the main he found salvageable goods. He recovered spices, tea, herbs and reams of silk.

He also managed to pull some tools to the surface, a few small chests, and a handful of gold sovereigns that were inside an ornate wooden box he found.

In a ceremony conducted by the village elder, Karel married Salee, the woman who had captured his heart and whose heart he had captured. Then they left the village behind, setting out for Surabaya and taking with them a cart full of goods.

With his skills and knowledge, Karel set up a trading post at the port and it wasn't long before he built up a relationship with the many trade ships, Portuguese, Spanish, French and of course many Dutch vessels, that docked on a regular basis.

Trade was good.

Not only did the business grow and grow, but so did his family.

Five years later it was the biggest trading post locally, and Karel and Salee had four children, two boys and two girls.

Karel never forgot his master. Every year he would make the journey back to spend some time at the graveside. He would pull out the pouch and bring out the item Pietro had given him.

A treasured possession, he would hold it, look at it, all the while talking to his master. As in life, sometimes he would speak in Dutch, other times French, or Italian. Every time though, tears would come; every time he would feel that great sense of loss.

Many years passed.

Then came a time that he made the journey with his wife, Salee.

It had been thirty years. Thirty years since that storm. Thirty years since he had dug the grave. It would be the last time he called.

The family had grown up and left home. Their eldest son had gone to sea, the second son was going to carry on the trading post. Their daughters had both married and moved to another part of Java.

They had decided, he and Salee, that they would leave the island. He was longing to return to his homeland.

'I'm so very fond of you, grandfather' Bibiana said, settling herself down on the Persian rug beside his chair. Her voice broke through his thoughts and he looked at her, sensing she was about to say more ...

'I have come to say goodbye,' she said, her green eyes like emeralds, looking up at him, glistening with coming tears in the dim light of the room.

He looked at her, looked into those eyes, nodded slowly, and smiled caringly and lovingly, 'I have told you many stories' he said.

'I know grandfather, and I remember them all,' she answered, quickly wiping away a tear that had begun to roll down her cheek.

'Well, the time has come for you to make new stories, to live new stories, with your new man.' Reaching out, he placed the palm of his hand on her cheek.

He glanced at Salee, who, he recalled fondly, had placed her palm on his cheek, all those years ago.

Bibiana grabbed his hand and pressed it tight against her skin. She thought back to her wedding day. How it had saddened her that grandmother had been so ill, and they couldn't travel to make it. They were the only close family she had left.

Her father, Karel and Salee's eldest son, had, like his father, become a seaman and had travelled many oceans.

One time, when he had been in port in Persia, he met the woman who was to be her mother, in a place called Bandar Abbas, this was in the year 1637.

He chose to stay when his ship sailed. A romance began, a marriage ensued and a year later he took his new wife to the old country and they made a home together in the town of Middelburg. Then he went back to sea.

Sitting there, next to her grandfather and her frail grandmother who was dozing off in her chair, Bibiana clearly remembers what happened some years later.

It was the year 1655, she was ten years old. She had no siblings.

Her mother took her and a bag of her clothes, and travelled by horse and wagon to Rotterdam and to this very cottage.

She recalls the many tears, and then her mother left. Her father, she was told later by grandfather, had perished at sea.

Her mother never returned.

'You have told me, and taught me so much, grandfather,' she said, wiping away another tear, her voice little more than a whisper, 'and I love you both so much, but Johan is taking me to Paramaribo. He has a plantation there. It will be our new home.' she paused for a moment, then continued, 'We sail in four days'.

A few more tears rolled down her cheeks, and she let them.

Karel took a couple of puffs on his pipe, then got up from his chair, crossed the room to a small sideboard, took something from a drawer, and returned to his chair.

He noticed Salee was fast asleep now.

He opened the leather pouch, slid out the item and showed it to her. She took it from him and looked at it. It was beautiful.

'There is one more story to tell,' he said.

It had been Karel's intention to relate this story and to give her the item as a wedding gift on the day.

He now told it, and Bibiana once more listened to a story from her grandfather.

The fire in the hearth crackled, the smoke from the pipe swirled around the room, and Bibiana, holding the item from the pouch, took in every word as she sat beside her grandfather as she had so many times before.

Later, Bibiana stirred her grandmother to wakefulness and kissed her goodbye. Her grandfather put on a heavy coat.

She and her grandfather walked down the cobbled path, then he turned to her, hugged her warmly and tightly one last time, and said, 'Take care, and, keep that treasure to yourself. Don't show Johan.'

She frowned, 'You don't like him grandfather?' she asked, concern in her eyes.

'Just be careful,' he smiled at her, planted a kiss on her forehead and released her.

'I will,' Bibiana managed to answer, then turned and walked away, more tears now flowing from her eyes. It wasn't until she had walked some thirty yards that she stopped. She turned around and gave a last wave to her grandfather.

She could see his smile as he waved back.

THE PRESENT;

AMERSFOORT

8.30AM THURSDAY 14TH MARCH

It was raining.

Detective Martijn Vogel sat at his desk, a steaming mug of coffee waiting to be consumed to the right of his computer. He watched the rivulets of rain racing down the windowpane for a moment, then, hearing his colleague arrive, turned towards the door.

Behind him, on the wall, hung a colourful Piet Mondriaan picture, a framed print by the artist who was born in this very city.

An old city, the first wall built around it after completion of the city was finished in 1300, then, as the city grew, a second wall was started, which was completed around 1450 and incorporated, a now famous landmark, the water and land gate, called the Koppelpoort.

The first wall was then taken down to make room for more housing.

Currently the population of this city in the Province of Utrecht in the central area of the Netherlands, is around one hundred and fifty thousand.

Froukje Boersma, his colleague, entered and took off her raincoat. She said good morning and noticed the mug of coffee in readiness on her desk directly opposite his.

'You got here early' she remarked, flicking her long blond hair back over her shoulders as she sat herself down and switched her terminal on.

'Got some news on the Baarn case last night' he said, carefully taking a sip from his mug.

'Really?' she answered, as she typed in her password.

'Had a call last night' Martijn said.

He was the senior detective, had just turned thirty nine, and, together with the thirty-two-year-old Froukje, headed the burglary division from their base in Amersfoort, covering the North East of the Province.

'An antique dealer in the Spiegelkwartier in Amsterdam called. He had a young man in his shop, late yesterday afternoon. This guy had a shawl of some sort, which he unwrapped, revealing an assortment of items that he said had belonged to his grandmother, there were earrings, a watch, a broach and ... a miniature, according to the dealer, the one in the photo we circulated.'

'Did he buy them?' she asked, reaching for her coffee.

'No, the young man just wanted to know a value and whether or not to take them to an auction.'

'What did the dealer say?'

'Well, he told this chap that, as a job lot, it might be worth around two or three thousand, thinking that offering such a high amount would tempt the chap to part with it, but the guy just said thanks and left.'

'Any CCTV?'

'Yes, someone is running the tape down, though it may not help much. The guy was wearing a rain jacket, with the collar up, and had an American style baseball cap on his head obscuring most of his face, anyway, we'll take a look and see' Martijn answered, drinking some more coffee.

The phone on Froukje's desk rang.

'Hello detective, this is Samantha Price,' a voice said.

'Miss Price,' Froukje answered, looking across to her colleague. 'Good morning, how can I help you?'

'I was wondering if there had been any developments? I really would like to speak to the Wagenaars, get a little more information on how they inherited the item.'

'We are in the process of following some leads, but, no, you cannot see the Wagenaars at this point. I realise what is at stake for your company, but any, let's say, confrontation, from you, could harm our investigation; not to mention that they might file a grievance against you,' Froukje said.

At home in Antwerp Samantha knew very well that this would be the case. Her boss had already suggested not to question the Wagenaars, but to look for proof of fraud via a different route.

She asked the question, expecting a negative answer, to then ask another hoping for a favourable response. 'I understand, I had to ask, but, tell me, you asked me if I was related to a Samuel Price. How is this man related to the case?'

'Wait one moment please. Let me get the file' Froukje answered, then spoke to Martijn, 'She wants to know how Samuel Price fits in.'

He nodded in affirmative across the desk.

'Yes, here we are,' Froukje said, speaking to Samantha. 'Okay, I will give you this information. On the day you visited the house and dealt with Mr Wagenaar, a man also called at the house, his name is Samuel Price.

He is a valuer for the Parisian Fine Arts Auction House, and he was asked to view the item in order to place it up for auction. I can't give you his address or phone number, but I'm sure you can get that from the Auction House in Paris, I have that number here if you want it.'

Samantha was pleased with herself, and excited about the response she got, but in a calm voice said, 'Thank you, yes, that is helpful, I have a pen ready.'

Froukje gave her the number, then said goodbye and hung up the phone.

It was still raining in Amersfoort.

MEANWHILE IN ANTWERP

Samantha, phone in hand, paced her living room, a spacious, fully-carpeted room, and looked out of the large panorama window of her fifth-floor apartment on to the river Scheldt below.

It was overcast but dry and as she waited several barges went past.

'Yes, I'm here.' She spun around, heading for the low coffee table, 'Go ahead.' She scribbled a number down, said, 'Thank you,' and ended the call.

She immediately punched in the number she'd been given and continued her pacing as it rang.

'Sam Price,' a man answered.

'We need to talk,' Samantha said, her voice curt and crisp.

'Err, okay, and ...you are? '

'Sam Price' she answered.

THE PAST;

PERIOD 5

THE YEAR 1729

The young man sat, sort of sideways, at the round table. He was scribbling on a jotter pad, every now and then looking across at the man he was interviewing.

There was a cup of tea on the table of which he had only taken one sip since the housekeeper had brought it in.

Most of the time he had been writing. Listening and writing.

The man sitting in the chair by the fireplace was Doctor Robert Ward.

He was ninety.

This was his cottage in Plymouth, England.

The old man was his mother's uncle, the brother of his maternal grandmother.

'I wasn't a doctor then of course,' the old man said, his voice calm and strong. His dark blue eyes staring reflectively as he spoke, 'but I knew quite a bit about medicine, knew how to set broken bones, treat various illnesses, that sort of thing. You see, young Thomas,' he said, glancing at the man at the table, 'I wanted to be a doctor, but then I also wanted to go to sea, to travel, to visit other lands. For me, it was all about the adventure.'

'Did you consider you might be caught up in battle?' Thomas asked

'I heard stories, of course, skirmishes with other ships, pirates even, but mostly I heard about the power of storms and how much damage they could do, to the ship and to men.'

'Was this, part of the adventure, that you were seeking?'

'Yes. It was hearing stories like that, that made me think about the need for a doctor on board on journeys like that, I was studying medicine, but at the time, I was helping my father out in the store. We supplied farming equipment, feed, tools, machinery and so on. He, my father, wanted me to eventually take over the business, but my heart just wasn't in it.'

'So,' the young man asked, looking at the old man 'You left?'

Robert, looking directly at the him, frowned for a moment, recalling the event in his mind, then answered, 'I had a row, another one, with him, my father, upshot is he told me to just go, so, I walked into town, couple of miles away ...'

'This was here? In Plymouth?' Thomas, who had been taken on by the New York Gazette a little over three years ago as a reporter, interjected.

'Yes. I loved coming into town, to the port. Loved watching the ships come and go. Got to know several folks on the docks. Well, that particular day, when I had the row and left the store, I headed straight for the harbour. Just wanted to be where I knew I could be ... relaxed, and happy, with my own thoughts and dreams, not my father's, if you see what I mean.'

He paused to take a sip of his tea, then continued, 'I hadn't been there long when there was an accident. One of the mates had slipped and fallen off a gangplank on to the dock, had fallen awkwardly.

'I rushed over, saw at once that he had broken his leg, so, I set about it to fix him up. I knew what to do, what I needed, so, even ordered a few men who had gathered to get what I required, and that was it, I knew then what I wanted to be, what I wanted to do.'

The reporter remembered his own cup of tea, took a quick sip, then asked, looking at his notes, 'So, then what happened?'

'A first mate of that ship, the one off whose gangplank the dock worker had fallen, pulled me aside afterwards. Wanted to know if I would be interested in joining the crew as the ship's doctor,' Robert answered.

'And you did?'

'Told him I wasn't a qualified doctor, but he said, that I knew enough and that they didn't have anyone with medical knowledge onboard, so he said, how about it?'
Robert recalled.
A day that would change his life. He sighed, remembering so very clearly.
'I said yes,' Robert continued, 'there and then. Went back home, passed by the store straight to the house, packed a few things, kissed my mother goodbye. Never called in to say goodbye to my father, something I regret very much ...'

After a little pause, the reporter, taking another sip from the now tepid tea, and making a few notes said, 'You sailed that very day?'

'No,' Robert answered, putting the cup of tea down. 'No, I walked back into town carrying two bags, I remember struggling with those. I had a few books on medicine and they were rather heavy. But I was excited, though a little apprehensive, as to what might lie ahead.
'Anyway, got to the ship. The first mate took me on board, showed me to a cabin which was where I was to receive the sick and wounded, but also, in a slightly set off part of that cabin were my personal quarters. I recall the scent of wood and the very atmosphere of that place. It felt good, it felt as if this was where I belonged.
I was happy, really happy.' Robert smiled at young Thomas, loving reliving these thoughts, and the fact that he was in the company of such a good listener.

'So,' the old man went on, 'he left me to it. Told me if there was anything I needed to ask, and he would try to obtain it, then said we were to set sail the following day. He took down my particulars and went to register me.'

Thomas scribbled some more on his pad and was about to ask something, but Doctor Robert spoke again.

'You know, I didn't meet the captain until we were a day out at sea. Likeable chap. James something or other, can't recall ...'

It was the year 1665 when the then twenty-six-year-old Robert Ward set out from Plymouth. They set sail towards the West Indies.

Robert was constantly on the go, dealing with everything, from toothaches to splinters, bruises, cuts and a variety of gastric ailments.

He found, much to his relief, that he could cope well with the sea.

Five weeks later, and off the coast of South America, everything changed.

No more fair winds and fine weather. No longer just the sound of the wind in the sails and the sea as the bow sliced through the waters.

They sailed into a battle.

A battle with a fleet of Dutch ships. A battle for control of Guyana and the port of Essequibo.

A battle that didn't last very long at all.

They were outnumbered, outgunned, outmanoeuvred.

It all happened so quickly, a lapse of concentration, the low sun a hindrance.

Two shots.

Two cannonballs, first the sound of the powder igniting, the blast sending the shot hurtling across the water, then, the sound of splintering wood as they struck the ship.

There were casualties, one man killed instantly, four men badly injured.

The forward mast was badly damaged. They couldn't turn and run as they found themselves suddenly surrounded.

They had no option but to surrender.

Two Dutch vessels came in closer and escorted the stricken ship into the port at Essequibo.

All the while, Robert worked tirelessly, tending to the wounded men. All else that was happening around him he blocked out, totally focusing on his duty with the wounded.

The Dutch, realising that the English ship was a trader, not a war ship, were amicable and helpful.

They were pleased, of course, that they had easily protected their stronghold, but negotiated with the captain, and repairs began on the ship.

Robert was unaware of all this.

After he had the wounded transported ashore, he had been given a large room in one of the buildings at Essequibo in which to work, and had also been given extra medical equipment, including a variety of medicines and salves.

On top of all this, he discovered that some of the natives were ill. He began to negotiate with the Dutch to treat them, which they readily accepted as, at that time, they had no medical person of their own ashore.

Robert worked almost without stopping to eat or sleep over the next four days. At one point he treated the master of one of the Dutch ships who had suffered a badly damaged arm due to a mishap on deck, for which much gratitude was shown.

The natives, those he had treated, became better, and it was at this point that Robert knew his days at sea were over.

This place, Essequibo, this was where he wanted to stay.

The English galleon was mended and sailed away with no cargo, for it wasn't in the interest of the Dutch to supply their potential enemy with a cargo that could bring in funds, which in turn could be used to fund warships.

Robert thanked the first mate for his support and stood on the pier waving goodbye …

'So, there you were, suddenly the doctor of this, town, this place called Essequibo?' The reporter asked, remembering the tea and taking another sip, realising as he swallowed that it was by now stone cold.

'Yes, there had been a doctor in town for a while, an elderly Dutchman, but I learned that he contracted an illness from which he died, and no replacement had thus far been organised, so, yes, there I was.' Robert answered, then continued, 'the native people accepted me straight away. They were lovely folk, very kind and supportive.

The Dutch had a large trading post there and quite a few men worked and lived in town. They too became my patients. As well as the room which I was given to work in, they organised a small cabin adjacent to it, which became my home.

Over the years I divided the large room into several, more private rooms and was soon delivering babies as well.'

Thomas smiled at the man in the chair by the fireplace.

His mother had informed him, in a letter sent, about this man, this Robert Ward, and had said, if he wanted a great life story for his American readers, then to come over, seek him out and talk to him.

At first he had wondered if this was a ploy to get him to come home so that she could see him, and it was sure nice to see his mother, but she had been right about this man, and his life story, it would indeed be good reading.

'That's some adventure you found for yourself' he said.

'Mmmm, not at all as I had envisioned it, but, interesting nevertheless, though, the best was yet to come …'

Thomas waited expectantly, thinking to himself that this had certainly been worth the journey.

Nearly a month it took to come back to England, another month of travel still to come when going back to the Gazette in New York.

Prior to his current post, he had been a reporter for the Shrewsbury Chronicle, since 1719.

A founding member of that paper had been contacted by a relative who worked in New York in the hope of securing a reporter for the Gazette.

Thomas was sent over and taken on in the year 1726. It was his first time back since then.

'Well,' Robert continued, 'it was about five, no, six years later, the year 1671.

A ship was coming into port, a Dutch schooner, a two-master.

'I remember this very well; it was a hot and humid day. I had longed for a drink and the trading post was a cool place to just sit for a bit. The surgery, or hospital if you like, was quiet. By then I had trained, let me think, yes, seven women and two men in various nursing skills, so, all was in control.

'Anyway, this ship was coming in. Someone informed me it was coming from Paramaribo, in Suriname, so, I decided to stand in the doorway of the trading store, watching.

Seeing it being moored, observing the folk coming off.'

The old doctor paused for a moment, then, again looking straight at Thomas, a definite sparkle in his eyes, said, 'And this is why I recall this day so very well for there she was, a young woman, a beauty.

She stepped on to the gangplank, then stopped to take in the scene. She was tall, had very long, almost black, hair. Her skin, very smooth and a soft brown in colour. Even from that distance, I could see that her clothes were of the finest quality.

I could also tell from the way she stood and the way she moved that she was a lady of breeding, confident, self-assured.'

The old man paused again for a few moments, then re-adjusted his position in the chair and continued, 'Well, she spotted me, caught me staring at her. She smiled at me. Then walked down the ramp.

'Behind her, two young lads carried a few cases and a third lad struggled with a small trunk.' ...

Bibiana stood for a moment at the top of the gangplank.

She surveyed her surroundings, then spotted the man standing in the doorway of the trading post.

She noticed him looking at her and gave him a smile. Even at this distance, she knew he blushed.

He had light brown curly hair that was rather ruffled in appearance, in fact his whole look was slightly scruffy.

There was a lovely demeanour about him. And as she walked down the gangplank and over the dock towards him, she saw he had a friendly face.

Her gaze was interrupted, when one of the lads behind her called, 'In here, Miss,'

She turned and was pointed in the direction of the port's arrival building.

Bibiana duly followed the instructions and entered.

Inside she met the master of the schooner, and again thanked him for his assistance and discretion. Two more young lads appeared and together with the other three escorted her outside, through part of the town and to a small cabin.

As she passed the trading post entrance she noticed the man had gone.

Twenty minutes later she was alone.

The lads had gone.

Her luggage was on the floor.

The cabin was a wooden structure, two rooms, very basic. But it was dry, and it was clean.

It had all she needed right now. A far cry from the luxury of her house on the plantation in Paramaribo.

But here she was safe and free.

She sat on the single wooden bed and recalled her grandfather's words to be careful.

She pulled the leather pouch from a pocket in her long skirt, slipped out the item it contained and held it in her hand.

Gratefully she looked at it. She admired its beauty, mindful of what it meant to her grandfather, what it meant to her.

'Thank you for your advice, grandfather,' she whispered.

It had all started so well, that journey to Suriname, to Paramaribo. All well and good.

The settling in at the large plantation villa, all very nice, very luxurious. A handful of staff seeing to all her needs.

Getting pregnant, also fine, she was happy and content.

She wrote to her grandfather and grandmother, relating all the news.

But then, it all began to fall apart. She recalled it all, this as she began unpacking her cases and trunk, wanting to create a sense of new normality as soon as possible.

Her reverie was cut short, however, as there was a knock on the door.

She opened it to find the somewhat scruffy young man standing there.

'Er, I speak a little Dutch ...' he began.

'You are English,' she said, picking up his accent through his attempt at her language, 'I can speak English quite well.'

'Ah, yes, well yes, you speak it very well, ehh, I am Robert, Robert Ward, I am the ... nearly a doctor, here, so, er, if you need ...'

'Well, Robert, nearly a doctor, very nice to meet you. If I get sick, then you can fix me, I am Bibiana'.

Not really knowing how to proceed, Robert nodded and turned and left.

Bibiana closed the door and smiled to herself.

Then, carrying on with unpacking, she returned to her previous thoughts, her recollections.

She felt strongly that she needed to think through all these things again, having done so a few times on board the schooner that had brought her here in order to clear her mind, to ready herself to move on.

She briefly paused and closed her eyes ...

The day came for the birth of her first child.

It didn't go well. It didn't at all go as it should.

The baby, a boy, died almost immediately, and she, herself, was quite ill for some time, nearly two weeks.

Her husband did not react the way she thought he should or would. He didn't seem to be saddened, and showed no emotion for the dead child, no compassion for her.

He was angry. He blamed her.

On top of all that, it was likely that she would not be able to have any children at all.

This left him even angrier. He became moody and remote.

Then he became violent towards her, hitting her on two occasions for no reason, though in her mind there should never be a reason to hit a woman.

This was unacceptable.

And so, after that second time, she began to plot her escape.

That had been over a year ago now. Thankfully her husband had sailed back to the old country during that time and had been away for nearly seven months.

She spent the time getting fit and strong, regaining her confidence and her state of mind. It was a time spent in setting new goals.

During this time, she received a letter from her grandfather telling her grandmother had passed away. She wrote back and told of the loss of her son and her illness, but that she was recovering well and missed him. She did not mention her situation and her plans, but silently thanked him for his wise words.

On the plantation she had already forged some friendships, and these bonds she strengthened while creating new bonds with people at the port, her knowledge of shipping helping her in conversations.

Her husband came back with a young woman in tow. He openly doted on her. This was fine by Bibiana; he would leave her alone.

It also made it easier to put together the last details of her plan. It would soon be time to take action.

She slipped away from the plantation very early one morning, and reached the port by daybreak. Here she had already stashed and secured what she was going to take with her.

She boarded the schooner, an arrangement made weeks earlier with a payment of silver coins taken from a hiding place that her husband was unaware she knew about.

As she made the final payment to the master, she smiled at how her husband would react once he missed the coins.

Her possessions on board, they set sail and left the harbour not long after the sun had released itself from the horizon.

She spent many hours standing on the deck near the bow of the ship, feeling the wind in her face and blowing through her hair.

A new life lay ahead.

Gripped tightly in her hand, the leather pouch and the item it contained which her grandfather had given her.

'So, who was this woman then?' Thomas asked the doctor, breaking into his thoughts, 'And what happened next?'

THE PRESENT;

ROTTERDAM

FRIDAY 15TH MARCH

Samantha got off the train from Antwerp, took the stairs down to the concourse, then walked along a wide corridor with hundreds of commuters and entered the vast foyer area.

She looked for the Feyenoord Fanshop outside which he should be waiting.

She spotted him. A little over six foot she guessed, slim built. He was older than she'd thought he might be, probably around mid-forties. Short cropped blond hair, glasses, and had a short beard and moustache.

He wore a green jacket over a checked shirt tucked into dark blue jeans, and brown shoes with a thick rubber sole.

In his left hand he held a small leather satchel.

He had stood for a little while outside the Fanshop, a place he had suggested for their meeting point, watching the people come and go.

He recalled the old central station building, a classic of its day which he loved, but this new structure was growing on him.

Earlier he had left his apartment, in the Schiebroek suburb of Rotterdam and taken the tram. He wondered what this Sam Price might be like and pondered the situation that they were finding themselves in.

Whilst awaiting the arrival of his namesake, his mind also took him back to Paris, to the events of the Gauguin, the subsequent phone call the director had made to him when he was on the train back home and the information of the provenance that mentioned his great-grandfather's name.

Arriving home that evening, he recalls the feeling he had as he entered the apartment. A realisation hit.

There was no-one home.

Yet he was surprisingly relieved to know that it had been her that had made all the preparations.

Preparations for the funeral, all arranged to the smallest detail, preparations for the insurance, for the bank, all the administration, in fact. She had printed out a checklist list for him, which, and she had stressed this point, he had to follow, and all would be well.

All would be well.

Well it certainly didn't feel like it, having escaped the reality, for a while, going to Paris, the confrontation with the French woman, the thoughts on the painting, the auction, the phone call, his great-grandfather, all distractions.

But as he had entered the apartment, it had suddenly hit him.

Sonja would not ever come home again.

It had been only that very morning that she had so calmly spoken to him, so lovingly, so reassuringly.

For some time that evening, he had paced about, had cried, had stared into space, had felt such a loss.

But at some point he made himself focus. Focus on finding those books, those notes that his grandfather had passed onto his father who had, as he had little interest in them, passed them straight onto his son, onto Samuel.

Journals and notes that belonged to Samuel Price, the first, in the family tree, his grandfather was the second, though always referred to as Samuel Junior, and he himself, the third.

It took only minutes of flicking through the books containing notes and photographs, that he found it.

Samuel Price the first, had been an ambassador, had travelled extensively and had been a keen art lover and owner of several dozen fine paintings. All catalogued, with notes of when and where purchased or sold, all also photographed, although only in black and white.

He found the Gauguin.

Studying the photo and reading the description in the notes led to the only conclusion.

He had to go back to Paris ...

His eyes had picked up a movement. He spotted a woman coming directly towards him; she had obviously seen him first.

She was lovely, he thought, quite tall, slim, her light brown hair touching her shoulders. She wore a greenish coloured coat which had a blue check pattern running through it over dark trousers and black ankle boots with a small heel.

A handbag, dark green leather, was slung over one shoulder. He caught her eye and smiled.

She smiled back.

'Sam Price?' she asked, extending her hand.

'The one, but not only,' he replied, and shook her hand. She had a firm grip.

He recommended a place adjacent to the station for coffee and it wasn't long before they sat down at a table by the large glass windows and someone came over to take their order.

'So, 'she began, 'you went to the Wagenaars and valued the item. They wanted to sell it?'

'Yes,' he answered, taking his jacket off as it was nice and warm inside. 'They contacted the office in Paris, who, in turn sent me to check out the item.

The office was told by the Wagenaars that they had inherited a piece of art that they believe is a missing Breughel, with a potential value of around two million.

So, I went to asses if it was as valuable as they suggested it might be, and, of course, if it really could be a missing piece of art by this artist.'

'And?' she prompted, wanting to keep control of the conversation.

Just as he was about to speak, the waiter came and brought them their drinks.

Ripping a sugar sachet open and pouring it into his black coffee, Samuel continued, 'Well, before I went there I did some checking. As the item in question was a miniature painted on ivory, I discovered that such a piece indeed existed, likely painted about mid-sixteenth century, so that was a good start.

'When I saw it, it was indeed a great piece. I photographed it, along with the bill of sale they had, in preparation for the auction catalogue.'

Samuel paused, watching the woman opposite him as she took off her coat, revealing a soft mint coloured blouse, and waited for the next question.

'So, do you think it's genuine then?' She asked, picking up her latte and taking a sip.

'Do you?' he asked, smiling at her.

'Well,' she answered, 'when they contacted me, they too told of an inheritance, of a piece of art, a miniature, believed to have been painted by Breughel the elder, and, after having done some research, felt it could be worth as much as two million euros, and, they wanted it insured as soon as possible.' Taking another sip of her drink, she looked at him, then continued, 'Like you, I did a little digging, decided, that their story rang true, so I went along to view it, and, like you to take photos.'

'I'm an assessor, not an expert,' Samuel said, taking up the conversation. 'I sent all the details to the head office in Paris. But, in answer to your question, I have a fair knowledge of art in general. The item itself looks good, but the bill of sale does not relate to that miniature.'

'Really? Why? What do you mean?' she asked, sitting herself more comfortably and trying to gain some insight into this man opposite.

He looked at her, thought for a moment, then spoke, 'Well, initially the story they told seemed plausible, so, I was quite pleased. Figured that if it checked out okay, this would be a good sale.

Then the police came knocking at my door telling me what had occurred. Well, two thoughts went through my mind.

'One, this was rather suspicious as it was the only thing stolen, along with the document, so was this then a scam?

'And two, a lost item of this importance may well attract attention. For the Wagenaars to have come to this value, they must have done some research, spoken to people. Word gets around, so therefore its theft could add weight to the fact that it was indeed the real thing.'

Sam paused for a moment, watched the woman opposite him sip her drink and obviously thinking things through.

Continuing, as she was sitting quietly, he said, 'As for me, personally, the theft means a loss of commission, not so good, so, I did some research, found out that the document is genuine ...' here he paused, took a sip of his coffee and looked at her. Her turn he felt, watching her and waiting.

She took in all that he had said, took another sip, then, looking directly into his eyes, which she noticed were dark green, said, 'But it doesn't belong to the miniature?'

He put his cup down, and smiled at her. 'I assume your company is facing a big insurance payout, something that you would naturally investigate, particularly as this theft is rather suspicious. I'm sure you haven't been sitting still. You found out about me for starters, so, have you found anything of use?' He asked, sidestepping her question for a moment.

'It's my job to check out the genuineness of all this. As the police gave me your number, or rather I should say, your office number in Paris, I'm sure they rule you out as a suspect.'

'What I would like to know,' she continued, 'seeing as I am not able to talk to the Wagenaars at present, is, what did you think of them, what was your impression of them, who did you deal with, was it him?'

'No, it was the wife. She was polite, didn't say very much, showed me the item, and I did my thing, but as I said, I found the story of how they obtained it certainly plausible.'

'I dealt with him,' she said, drinking some more of her latte. 'He told me most probably the same story she told you, that they had recently discovered it amongst some things they had inherited. But you are right, I haven't been sitting still, this is a big claim, and I found out that they can't have inherited it from a family member.'

'You followed up on the original purchaser, Nicholas v Struyten,' he surmised.

'Yes, turns out his family died out over the next 120 years, no descendants. '

'Mmm, that's interesting,' he said, pausing briefly, 'however … he sold it four years later.'

Samantha sat back and blew out her cheeks. Fool, she thought to herself.

Why hadn't she even considered that.

She looked across at the man opposite, beginning to see him in a different light.

Then, after a few moments, she leant forward a little, and asked him, 'Who to? Do you know?'

'That,' Samuel answered, reaching for his satchel and retrieving something from it, 'is no longer relevant.'

'Because,' and he laid out two sheets of paper on the table, facing towards her, 'on your left there is the original bill of sale, the one you also saw at the house. Now, on the right there is a bill of sale four years later when Nicholas v Struyten sold it. Look closely at the description of the item on both copies.'

Samantha studied the two sheets closely, then sat up and looked at him.

'Oh, my goodness,' she said, 'I see what you mean now. These documents relate to a different miniature, not at all to the one they had.'

'Exactly, though this still might not be of help to you,' he said.

She thought about what he said, and came to same conclusion, 'No, whilst it may prove the document doesn't relate to the item, the miniature they had, it could still be the genuine article.'

'And I guess you would need strong proof to prove otherwise, especially as both of us, and I assume you do as well, agree that it might be a genuine article and you've insured it as such,' he said, sitting back and finishing his drink.

'Yes, the item was breathtaking, and, as you say, I had no reason to doubt it wasn't real, so, again yes, it's insured as such,' she answered, sitting back and glancing out the window. 'The only way to know is to test the item, but unless it turns up soon we can't do that, and we'll be forced to pay out'

'How much time have you got,' he asked, 'before you have to pay out?'

'Thirty days, and I have only got twenty-four left' she answered.

'There is, possibly, another way' Samuel suggested, looking at her, a smile appearing on his face.'

'Go on,' she said.

'Well' Samuel began, leaning forward and locking his eyes with hers, 'the item, that both you and I saw is a piece of art that is recorded as having existed, but, it's deemed to be missing. Now, look at the bill of sale they showed us,' placing his finger upon the sheet of paper still on the table.
She leaned forward and looked.
'The seller' he continued, 'as you can see, was a chap named Pietro Esposito. Now, I delved into who he was.
Turns out, he was quite a wealthy man, from a respected and influential family, good credentials.
According to the records I found, a total of six items, all by the same artist, all by Pieter Brueghel, are recorded as having existed, but are missing.
This man Pietro, and here again I found all the relevant documents, sold five of them, so, it made me think, what if he also had the sixth, but kept it?'

Samantha sat up again, taking in what he had said, and thinking how much he had uncovered already.
Having first decided to just hear what this man had to say, and how exactly he was connected to the case, it had been her plan to then move on to further investigate on her own.
Now she began to think differently.
'Okay, let me see if I get this straight. This, Pietro guy, had the right connections and wealth to have in his possession the genuine articles, sure, that makes sense.
You say he sold five items that are listed as having existed, along with a sixth, by the same artist, so, how is it all connected?
How do you know these are the same as the items listed, and what happened to the five items this man sold?' she asked, trying to get her head around the sequence of events.

'Okay,' he answered, 'let me backtrack a little. First of all, let's begin with the miniature, the one you and I saw. Now, I investigated this in order for me to confirm, first of all it's possible existence, and second, to then get a provenance of the item, previous owners and so on, because the better the provenance, the better chance of realising a good sale.

Whilst searching, I discovered a description of a total of six items that Breughel painted whilst visiting and staying with a close friend in Rome, including the ivory miniature.

Now, these items are recorded as missing from Rome, no mention of them since, so we're talking around 1550, or thereabouts.'

Samuel paused and noticed that Samantha was taking in everything he said.

'My first aim,' Samuel went on, 'was to check out the seller that was on the bill of sale, Pietro Esposito, which I did, and so found information, that I guess no-one else has found yet, or connected the dots from.

The five items he sold, match the description, and, as I said, he would have had the connections to have these items. Even though we're talking some sixty years later, they could well have been in his family for that time, so there is a connection to Rome.'

'I get the picture now' Samantha said, 'and yes, I agree, for him to have had five of those items, it does seem very likely that he would have possessed the sixth, but, if he didn't sell it, where is it now, and how can this help us?'

Before Samuel answered, Samantha continued, 'after all, they could still be one and the same item. The one the Wagenaars had, could still be the real thing.'

'I don't think so,' Samuel answered.

'Firstly, they lied as to how they obtained it, and secondly, the bill of sale does not match the item. They, or someone, is going to a great length, to convince us it is the genuine article, and, therefore, very valuable.'

After a brief pause, Samuel went on to say, 'We should try to trace the trail from the beginning; find the real miniature'

Samuel looked away from her and out of the large window.

Outside the trams were coming and going, the people to-ing and fro-ing.

With its population of over six hundred thousand, he loved his city.

Momentarily, his mind wandered while watching the scene outside as across the table from him Samantha was also pondering.

'We, Mr Price?' Samantha asked, attracting his attention, 'What is your interest?'

Before Samuel could answer, a pinging sound came from within her bag.

'Excuse me, let me just check this.' She retrieved her phone.

It was a text. With a frown she read it.

'That,' she said, looking up and at him, 'was a text from the detective. A man went into one of the antiques shops in Amsterdam. He had a number of items, including the miniature, and was looking for a valuation. The dealer recognised the item from the notice the police had distributed, and offered to buy it, but apparently the man just left.'

They both sat quietly for a while, each with their own thoughts.

Samuel caught the eye of a passing waiter and ordered another round of coffee, after catching Samantha's eye for confirmation.

'Earlier you asked how this might help us when I told you what I had found out. Us, you and me. You have your reasons, obviously finding proof to counter this, which must surely be an insurance scam.

'For me, well, there's a loss of commission on the sale for one, but, more importantly, I'd like to find this miniature, trace its journey, track its whereabouts, and find out for sure if the one we saw is fake or genuine. To find a piece of missing art by a famous artist is a big thing.' He paused briefly, 'So, how about we, you and me, work together. Two heads are better than one, Miss Price. How about it? Shall we tango the dance floor of intrigue in the art world?'

She smiled.

She didn't hesitate at all with her reply, and leaned forward, extending her hand, 'Cue the music, Mr Price.'

He took her hand and they gave each other a smile as they shook hands.

The waiter brought their drinks at that moment, and they both leant back in their chairs.

'Go and find someone to love,' his late wife's words came to him.

He hadn't thought about that for the past few years.

Could this woman, be right? No, he thought, she was very attractive, and quite a bit younger. Still ...he pondered, watching her, studying her face, or the profile of her face as she was looking out of the window, seemingly in deep thought.

Samantha looked out the window. This day wasn't going at all as she had thought it would go.

Coffee in hand, she reflected.

Surprisingly, she felt quite at ease. Earlier, when she was on the train heading for Rotterdam, she had felt annoyed.

Annoyed with herself, for her company was facing a two million euro pay out, and she blamed herself; felt she had been duped, had been played.

Now, having met Samuel Price, no relation, she had a clearer picture of what had seemingly happened; a well planned and executed insurance fraud.

She had agreed the price and had insured the item. Samuel had agreed the price for his auction, and the Wagenaars had two witnesses who had not only seen but photographed the item.

They would need very strong proof to counter the Wagenaars claim, yet, she felt more at ease now, and also ever more determined to find the truth.

She still couldn't quite understand how Mr Wagenaar, by appearance a nice man, as well a valued customer, was involved in this.

THE PAST;

PERIOD 6

THE YEAR 1752

Lady Evangeline Powell-Hunter sat in a chair placed by the sash window of her bedroom.

The chair, a silk covered gilt wood armchair, was one of a pair in the room and she would often sit, as she was now, by the window to read.

The room was on the first floor of their manor house in the county of Shropshire.

It seemed unfair that it should be such a sunny and glorious day as she looked out over the countryside; their estate, consisting of nearly two hundred acres of woodland, farmland, two small lakes and several outbuildings as well as a large farm.

Spring was turning into summer.

Two men on horseback had arrived earlier.

They delivered sad news.

The parlour maid had bundled up the stairs to wake her mistress, tears rolling down her cheeks as she had been the one to open the doors to these men and had refused to wake her mistress unless told what it might be about. Hence, the maid received the news that her master had died.

She woke her mistress, sobbing.

The lady of the house, calmly and reassuringly comforted her maid, before dressing and meeting these men.

They gave her the details of what had occurred.

She thanked them, invited them to have some refreshments before setting off again, which they graciously declined.

They left.

Now, several hours later, she sat in her chair.

Now, she allowed herself time to grieve.

Now, tears rolled down her cheeks. In her lap lay her husband's diary and notebook that the men had brought with them, along with a small travel case.

Despite her tears, she thought back to when she had first met him …

It was fourteen years ago.

It was at a celebration party, in this very house. It was her thirtieth birthday.

The year 1738.

The house was full of folk, neighbours, friends of her parents, her own friends. There had been a man who played the piano, who had brought with him a singer. She recalled a West Indian lady with a lovely voice. They were the entertainment.

Then there was him. Then there was Thomas, though she did not know his name then, nor who he was.

She had noticed him, because he was scribbling something in a little book.

Not the sort of thing a guest would do. She figured that he was a local reporter, a gate crasher, an uninvited guest.

She approached him. She was going to have some fun with him, embarrass him, and make him wish he'd never come.

Through her tears she smiled at the memory …

A plan formulated in her mind as she reached the intruder.

'Well, 'she said, smiling broadly, 'and what do you think of the Rembrandt Daddy purchased last month?' indicating the large painting that adorned the wall where he stood.

He looked at her, his eyes meeting hers and he didn't waver, then, broke contact and turned to look at the painting, studying it for a moment.

Turning back to her, said, 'Happy birthday Miss Evangeline,' and smiled. 'It's a lovely party. It's also a great painting, but, it's a Vermeer, not a Rembrandt, though I think you know that'. Then he turned and walked away.

Taking a lace handkerchief from her sleeve, she wiped her eyes.

It hadn't gone to plan for her that day, but she liked him, liked the sound of his voice, and his eyes were warm and kind.

She closed her eyes for a moment. She would miss him so much.

After a while, she stood up from her chair, drying her eyes once more she pulled herself together, said aloud to herself, 'Right, come on. Things to be done,' and left the room.

Lady Evangeline spoke to all her staff. They all seemed to be in shock and uncertain as to what to say or do in her presence.

She spoke words of encouragement to them.

Then she organised her carriage to be brought around to take her to where their twin daughters were at boarding school, some fifteen miles away.

Once on the road on this far too glorious day for marking such a sad occasion she sat back and reflected some more on how they had met.

As she knew that he was a reporter, it hadn't taken her long the following day to find out where he worked and what his name was.

Then she did some research on him.

Thomas Powell, who was born at the turn of the century, had worked at the Shrewsbury Chronicle from 1719 through to 1726.

He had then set sail for America where he was appointed reporter for the New York Gazette. Here he worked until returning to England in 1737.

Evangeline found out that he had married whilst in New York, a young woman he had met whilst reporting on a theatre production, the first of its kind in the city, which was called 'The Recruitment Officer'.

They had a son, who, when they came to England, was three years old.

Sadly, Thomas's wife died from tuberculosis soon after their arrival. Thomas had a sister who, thankfully, offered to raise the child.

Thomas himself then travelled back to his roots, back to Shrewsbury, and worked again for the Chronicle.

Evangeline, having unearthed all this information about him, was intrigued and wanted to know more, so, one day, she stepped into the offices of the Chronicle and said to him, once she they were out of earshot of others in the office, 'You know a little about me. I know a little about you. How about we get to know each other better?'

She clearly visualised that moment, as the carriage bumped over uneven ground. The two-horse vehicle had already nearly covered half the distance to the school.

He had blushed, looked her in the eyes and had only been able to nod.

Lady Evangeline received her title along with the manor house and estate only a few years ago when her father passed away.

Her mother had died a year earlier and she was an only child.

She took on running of the estate and loved it.

Thomas took the decision to leave the Chronicle to help her with the estate and to write his memoirs.

On the odd occasion, he was called in to cover a significant event or situation. As there were few journalists of his calibre around, he was happy to do so.

Then, two months ago, he was asked if would consider going to Yemen to a place called Mocha, as it was a turbulent time there. A hotspot of trouble.

The adventurer in him couldn't resist, and Evangeline, seeing the sparkle in his eyes, gave her blessing.

The carriage slowed, entered the gates and pulled up to the front of the school. She closed her eyes for a moment.

Then, exhaling, readied herself.

A full hour passed before she returned to her carriage.

She nodded her thanks as one of the men opened the door, and she gave instruction to head back home.

She leaned back on the leather upholstered seat. The sun was still shining brightly and the sky was a vivid blue.

She had wanted to tell their daughters immediately to ensure they received the news from her, not through hearsay.

Afterwards the headteacher took the girls to the large conservatory where, she assured Lady Evangeline, she would stay with them in this time of need.

Now onto her next mission.

She would arrange to travel to Plymouth, to see her sister-in-law, to speak with the boy, her husband's son, John Robert, who was now a young man, eighteen years of age.

And then she could begin to make all the arrangements for the funeral.

Tears flowed as the carriage passed through the gates of the school and headed for home.

THE PRESENT;

STILL ROTTERDAM

STILL FRIDAY 15TH MARCH

One name, just one name.

That's all they had to go on, that's all they had to continue their search with.

One name, that of Karel Maas.

On the tram ride, and walk, en route to his apartment, Samuel told Samantha about the ship that Pietro Esposito had come to Amsterdam for, a-three masted galleon, that he had commissioned to be built.

So, going on the assumption that Pietro had retained the sixth item for himself, and very likely had it in his possession, where did he go.

The ship was called the 'Serenus Venti,' so, following this path. Samuel had discovered that it had sunk off the coast of Java due to a violent storm.

He also found some written reports. In these he found out that the master, Pietro, had been rescued by a cabin boy servant, that Pietro had been badly injured, and that he had eventually died from his wounds.

According to reports, the boy buried his master then stayed on in Java where he later married and set up a successful trading post in the port of Surabaya.

He ran this business for over two decades.

His name was Karel Maas.

Samuel figured that, as this cabin boy was obviously close to the captain, it seemed possible that at the end the master, if he had the item with him, would likely have passed it on to his faithful servant, unless of course it had been lost at sea.

This was the only lead they had to go on, a single name.

Samuel's apartment was on the top floor.

A corner dwelling on the Peppelweg, a local shopping precinct, it had a large rectangular lounge leading to an open-plan kitchen and dining area. The apartment had two bedrooms and a further sizeable room in the loft.

Samuel sat himself at his desk against the right-hand wall of the lounge and opened his laptop.

Samantha sat herself on the two-seater couch and opened hers.

They began the search. Scrolling, reading, hunting.

At some point, Samuel got up, retrieved a pizza from the freezer and baked it in the small oven, serving it twenty minutes later along with a drink.

At another point Samantha got up from the couch, stood by the window and arched her back in a stretching exercise to relieve some stiffness.

They hardly spoke. Outside the world carried on. The sound of cars, bicycle bells and trams were to be heard faintly over the music that Sam had playing softly on his stereo.

It was late afternoon and the sun was well on its way towards the horizon when Samantha, exclaimed loudly, 'Yes!'

Samuel looked over. Samantha was totally absorbed reading what she had found.

He waited and waited.

Finally, she looked up and across at him, smiled, and said, 'This is it,' then, frowning a little, said, 'though, not totally it, but, the next step. Come over and read this. It's an article in the New York Gazette from 1729.'

He came across and she scooted over a little to make room for him, then they both read the article that was on the screen of her laptop.

'A tale of many tongues' by Thomas Powell.

We live in a great city, New York City. Peoples from near and far live here.

From Scandinavia, England, Scotland. From Western Europe, Eastern Europe. From Africa and South America. From North America and from Asia.

From near and from far, we live here, we work here, we live and work side by side. We have a common language and we have our own language.

We abide by a common law and share in common customs. We have our own traditions and our own customs, but we live together in a city that is great and destined to be even greater in future days.

But this is not always so today, this was not always so in days gone by and, sadly, this will not always be so in times to come.

Let me share with you a tale told me by a man. A tale about an artefact that touched the lives of many; an artefact that portrays the creating and scattering of tongues, yet a tale that tells the possibilities of gathering tongues together again.

The Holy Bible has this story, in the eleventh chapter of the Book of Genesis, and it reads thus;

> *Now the whole earth had one language and one speech. And it came to pass as they journeyed from the East, that they found a plain in the land of Shinar, and they dwelt there. Then they said to one another, 'Come, let us make bricks and bake them thoroughly.'*
> *They had bricks for stone, and they had asphalt for mortar. And they said, 'Come, let us build ourselves a city, and a tower whose top is in the heavens, let us make a name for ourselves, lest we be scattered abroad over the face of the whole earth.'*
> *But the Lord came down to see the city and the tower which the sons of men had built. And the Lord said, 'Indeed the people are one and they all have one language, and this is what they begin to do, now nothing that they propose to do will be withheld from them.'*

'Come, let Us go down and there confuse their language,
that they may not understand one another's speech.'
So, the Lord scattered them abroad from there over the face
of all the earth, and they ceased building the city. Therefore
its name is called Babel, because the Lord confused the lan-
guage of all the earth, and from there the Lord scattered
them abroad over the face of all the earth.

In my hand I hold an artefact.

It is small, and, it depicts the scene of the building of the Tower of Babel.

It is beautifully painted in oil upon a piece of ivory.

Various artists have painted such a scene as this, but the one I hold is deemed to be by Pieter Brueghel.

Let me tell you the tale of its journey, how it too, has travelled over the face of this earth, how its journey has brought people together in the past, how it connects people in the present, and how it will continue to do so in times to come.

Join me tomorrow for the next and concluding part of this tale.

Thomas Powell.

They finished reading at the same time. Samuel looked at Samantha,' Did you find the next part?'

She smiled at him, 'Yes, it was actually the next part I found first, for it contains the name Karel Maas. Let me pull it up. '

Then, whilst she did so, she said, 'Must find out more about this guy, this Thomas Powell. To be writing a serial in a newspaper in those days can't have been a common thing … here we are, the next instalment.'

'A tale of many tongues' by Thomas Powell.

The artefact on the desk in front of me depicting the scene of the building of the Tower of Babel, an oil painted miniature on ivory, was, according to my source, painted by Pieter Brueghel sometime around the year 1553 when he was in Rome.

The story of its beginnings were told to a young man whose name was Karel Maas.

He was a young Dutch lad who had wanted to go to sea.

An opportunity to do so was given to him by a man who became his master, Captain Pietro Esposito.

They sailed from Amsterdam in a newly built galleon in March of the year 1613.

The miniature was given to Pietro in Monaco by his mother, who in turn had received it from an Italian Cardinal in Rome.

And so, the tale of this artefact begins.

It travelled from Italy to Monaco. It touched the hands of those speaking Latin, Italian and French. The scattered languages it depicts are gathered together.

Captain Esposito journeyed with it for several years plying the trade routes to the Far East.

Then, one day a severe storm destroyed his ship off the coast of Java.

Many hands perished, but the captain survived, his life saved by the young lad he had taken on as a cabin boy four years earlier.

Sadly however, he did die several days later from the wounds he sustained, but not before he showed the artefact to young Karel, told of its history, and pressed it into his hands.

Karel stayed on in Java, married a local girl and established a trading post in the port of Surabaya.

Dutch and Javanese languages were added to the connection with the artefact.

My source, Doctor Robert Ward, had written these accounts down, told to him by his wife Bibiana, who was the granddaughter of Karel Maas.

A long time later, in the year 1668, the artefact was given to her.

Her mother came from Bandar Abbas in Persia and had taught her daughter the Persian dialect, Bandari, and so another tongue was added.

The good doctor, from England met and married Bibiana in Essequibo, Guyana, where she had fled to from the country of Suriname to get away from her abusive husband. English was added into the mix.

The artefact that describes the scattering of the people and the creation of many languages is, I believe, a challenge, set by God.

This was now connecting people and languages back together.

It was the doctor himself who spoke with me at length, whose notes I was given, and who gave me this artefact now on my desk before me.

Where will it travel next? Who will it connect in future days? Who knows. I leave you, my readers, with this;

In this great city in which we live, let us bring our languages, our cultures, our heritage, together that we may live side by side and bring about the foundations to make this great city the greatest city on the face of this earth.

Thomas Powell.

'Wow,' said Samuel, 'well found. Quite some article, plus, now we have another lead to follow.'

'Yes, we have, this Thomas Powell, though it still doesn't rule out that what we saw was the genuine article.'

'No, you're right, it doesn't.'

THE PAST;

PERIOD 7

NEW ORLEANS

THE YEAR 1763

It was raining. Not hard, but a miserable drizzle, and although it was very early in the morning, it was hot.

The man, lying prone on a wooden sidewalk, was dead.

These were bad times in the city. A city once described as a place of a hundred wretched hovels in a malarious wet thicket of willows and dwarf palmettos, infested by serpents and alligators.

That was about forty years earlier. Change was slow. These days of colonial rule brought, in the main, an influx of undesirables creating a tense and dangerous scene.

The man had been stabbed, had bled out and died. As the drizzle continued the dirt street became thick and sticky. Two men, approaching with a wooden two-wheeled cart, struggled to move through it. They reached the body, and together they picked the dead man up and unceremoniously dumped him on to the flatbed cart.

It was quiet in the streets as the men pulled the cart through the city grid system towards the building behind the town hall, the morgue.

Not far from there the Mississippi river flowed to the sea.

Here he was deposited for someone later to do a rudimentary autopsy and check for the identity of this victim.

They covered the body with hessian, to form some sort of protection against diseases.

Later that day the body was stripped and hosed down, the cause of death determined and noted. The clothes were checked.

At first it was thought he was just another nameless victim, but some papers were found in the lining of the jacket he had been wearing. The documents recovered were almost totally blood soaked. One was a form of sales docket, another was made out to be a document for passage, and on the third, and here they had more luck, they could determine a name and a place.

John Robert Powell from Plymouth.

SIX WEEKS EARLIER; PLYMOUTH, ENGLAND

He arrived in Plymouth late afternoon, made his way to the dock area, and wandered around for a bit. He then chose a local pub where he ordered a beer and settled himself in a quiet corner near a window from where he could see the street clearly.

It wasn't very busy as yet, but he knew it soon would be for it wouldn't be long before the men working on the docks would be finishing their shift and come bustling in, downing several drinks after a hard day's work, before heading home, often with a merry song and a shaky step.

His aim, as he slowly sipped his beer, was not to be noticed. He was a wanted man.

Known by some as the 'Oxman' for two reasons. He was originally from Oxford, and he was built like an ox, only five and a half feet in height, but with a barrel chest, legs like tree trunks, a thick neck and arms like clubs.

He couldn't read or write, spoke very little, and supported himself either by collecting winnings from prize fights or by simply robbing folk.

Beginning to be recognised too easily, and wanting to avoid the law, he had left his hometown of Oxford some years ago. He was in Winchester for a spell, but had to leave quickly for one of his robbery victims had tried to fight back, but one savage blow from the Oxman had rendered him unconscious, and the man had died from his wounds a few hours later.

On the run once more he had headed south. This time his aim was to reach a port and flee the country for, if caught, he would be hung.

By the time he had reached Plymouth, he had formulated a plan of sorts which was to, by some means, board a vessel to anywhere.

He had arrived to find several ships in port, wandered around to get the layout of the dock area, worked out which pub would be the most likely to be frequented by the workers, and spent some time watching the unloading and loading of cargo. In all that time he had spoken to no-one, but had picked up several snippets of conversation.

He took another small sip of his beer.

Tonight, was not for getting drunk.

Tonight, was for staying sober, alert, watchful. To find a target, an opportunity.

The day was ending, the evening beginning, and the pub was filling up. The sound rose by several decibels, and beer flowed.

Chatter and laughter rang throughout.

Then a young man entered.

The Oxman noticed him immediately. This was not a dock worker. His clothes were of good quality, his skin was fair and smooth, his hair combed and tidy.

Not one who worked on the docks, not a labourer, but one who had means.

He was a little taller than the Oxman, and quite lot slimmer.

As he came closer to the bar area, the newcomer spotted someone he knew, they greeted each other, then managed to obtain drinks from the bar and make their way towards where he was sitting, still sipping his first beer.

The well-dressed newcomer, the Oxman noted, was rather excited as he and his friend sat themselves down at a table close by. Trying to filter out all the background noise of laughter song and chatter, he tried hard to focus just on what these two men were talking about, and as he picked up snippets, a plan was forming.

This was it; this was the opportunity; this was the chance for escape that he had hoped he would find.

And when the young man left, less than an hour later, the Oxman followed.

It was almost noon the following day when the Oxman boarded an old galleon.

Smiling, trying to be and look relaxed, trying to act with confidence.

He had already shown papers at the customs hall, hoping that they were the right papers he needed for he could not read. He did not speak but gave an occasional grunt now and then.

The papers were handed back, he was wished a good journey and waved on his way to the gangplank.

He tried to breathe normally and felt beads of sweat on the back of his neck. His thinning hair was plastered back slickly.

His clothes weren't new, but looked clean, he had done the best he could with his own boots to make them look presentable. Carrying two satchels he stepped on to the gangplank where at the top he was asked for his papers.

The Oxman obliged, then after the ship's mate had handed them back, followed him below.

The mate explained about meal times, about where he could and could not go, to be always aware of the ship's crew and never get in their way, and what to watch out for on the decks whilst taking him to a small cabin.

Finally, when he was left alone, he set the luggage on the floor, sat down on the bunk and exhaled.

So far, so good. He was on board and the ship would soon be setting sail for America, to Philadelphia.

No-one had questioned him; no-one had doubted the papers he had shown.

He was now John Robert Powell.

THE PRESENT;

ANTWERP

SUNDAY 17ᵀᴴ MARCH

Samantha, in her dressing gown and fluffy slippers, was tucking into a pot of yoghurt as she stood by the window in the lounge that overlooked the river below.

Early Sunday morning. She heard the bells of several churches in the distance. Taking another spoonful, she thought about church. She hadn't been for some time and, right now, she needed a miracle for the deadline for the payout would come around soon enough Time was not on her side.

A mug of steaming tea stood cooling down on the kitchen bench. She dipped the spoon into the yoghurt pot again, and ran through the events of the past couple of days in her head.

Friday had not at all gone the way she thought it might.

She had, after agreeing on the meeting point, gone to Rotterdam to meet with Mr Sam Price. She had wanted to meet him, to check him out, check his credentials and involvement in the case, and then move on.

To her surprise, and slight annoyance, she found him to be a charming man, obviously well-educated, and he had uncovered more on this case than she had.

Going back to his place had not remotely been part of her plan, but it had proved useful. Following the clue he had found about a young man named Karel Maas had led to the next clue in their search, a new lead.

Samantha placed the spoon on the kitchen bench, then replacing the top of the yoghurt pot and put it in the fridge.

She smiled to herself as she collected her mug of tea, went back into the lounge, and recollected the events on Friday and how easily, and surprisingly quickly, she had bonded with him.

The new lead they had found was the journalist and reporter, the Englishman called Thomas Powell. It was already late afternoon by then, she politely declined the offer of dinner, and he had escorted her back to the railway station.

Yesterday she had sent an e-mail report to her boss, and had also sent the full police report that she had been given to Samuel as he had asked to see it when she mentioned it. She then set about searching for all she could find on Thomas Powell, a task she was going to resume today.

MEANWHILE

Samuel was on the road. He had two assessments to do, the first near the city of S'Hertogenbosch, more commonly referred to as Den Bosch, followed by another in Veenendaal.

It wasn't unusual to have these assignments on a Sunday, often it was the only day people were at home. Both were paintings offered for auction.

In a service road that ran behind the apartment where he lived was a row of garages. It was here that he housed his car, a classic 1968 Citroen DS, his favourite car, and he had finally been able to purchase it a little over two years ago upon receipt of a sizeable commission.

He smiled to himself as he drove, thinking back to Friday, and to her question at one point of the proceedings, an innocent question, she had asked while they were enjoying the pizza break, 'So, how did you get into this work, and with a Parisian company?'

An opportunity, to speak about that day, the day his wife had died, the day he had lost the love of his life. The day he had left her side for the last time and had taken himself off to Paris.

An opportunity to voice his feelings perhaps. But he couldn't. For a moment, whilst chewing a piece of the pizza, he had quickly looked around his apartment. There was not a single photograph on display, of her, or him, or anyone. Several paintings, some pop art, but no photos.

He couldn't speak to her about that day, at least not at this time.

'I walked into the auction house one day,' he began, 'about three and half years ago, perhaps a little more. They had this gallery where you could view the paintings or pieces of art that were to be auctioned that day, a preview, if you will.

Well I noticed a Gauguin, and, somehow, it felt that I knew this painting.

And yet, it seemed different. Anyway, to cut a long story short, turns out my, great-grandfather, who was a British ambassador, had, at one time, owned this very painting.

Except, it wasn't the same, so, having gone through his notes and the photographs he had of all the paintings he had purchased and sold, and his very clear descriptions and notes on what he bought and sold them for, well, I discovered, they had a fake painting on their hands.

This knowledge was gratefully received. The Auction House is a long-established company, with a reputation to uphold, so, the director offered me a job as a private assessor. We made a deal that very day, and well, here we are.'

'Wow, what happened to the real Gauguin, the one your, great-grandfather had?' she asked.

'A mystery, much like this one. I did look into it, of course, following a weak trail, but, so far, it still remains a mystery.'

He finished his pizza, turned and went back to his laptop thinking back to that time he had returned to Paris. bringing the notes and the photographs with him, to compare them to the Gauguin.

The director and the French woman, whose name was Sophie Louise Pontiac, and who wasn't her fiery self but rather subdued, were most apologetic when they together realised that the painting they had, was not the real thing.

The frame was totally different and, upon inspecting the photo and comparing it to the painting, it was deemed not the same.

All the provenance they had to go along with it was now hugely in doubt and needed further investigation.

He had readily accepted the offer of this job. New beginnings. The deal for one percent of the sold price of any item that he was involved in meant that a particular sale had netted him just under twenty thousand euros with which he had purchased this car.

The weather was reasonable, the traffic was light, and he made good time.

The ride was smooth. He had replaced the old radio cassette with a CD player that had USB ports, and he listened to a selection of music from the sixties which he had loaded onto a drive.

He felt content as he drove.

He shook his head slightly as he reflected back to when he had called upon Mrs Wagenaar in Baarn. Normally pretty good at sensing any tension, or reading people, why had he not picked up anything unusual that day?

He reached his first port of call and was back in his car forty minutes later. Driving on towards Veenendaal he looked for and found a place to stop for coffee where he also typed up the notes he had made at his first call.

Driving once more, he thought back to yesterday, to when he had received the police report from Samantha which she had agreed to e-mail him.

He had read it through twice, then, after a while of pacing up and down in the living room, he made a decision.

Thomas Powell was the obvious lead they had found, but Samuel decided to leave that to Samantha at this stage. He, himself, settled behind his desk, then proceeded to scroll through social media.

His aim was to find out as much as he could about the son and daughter of the Wagenaars.

His next call took just over half an hour; a set of two limited edition paintings the owners had purchased eight years ago, and which were now valued at almost four times the original cost. They agreed on the valuation and to proceed with the auction. Another satisfied customer Samuel thought as he pointed the Citroen towards home.

BACK IN ANTWERP

Samantha smiled and sat back into her comfy couch. It was the middle of the afternoon. After her yoghurt and tea for breakfast, she had showered and dressed and then had set about another concentrated search.

The first couple of hours, however, had brought no success.

She took a break, had a light lunch, caught up with her work e-mails and then took another stab at her effort to find out more about Thomas Powell.

Now, the afternoon giving way to the evening, stretching and giving her neck a massage, she was pleased.

Very pleased.

Leaning forward she took her pen and wrote on a pad just one word.

Philadelphia.

THE PAST;

PERIOD 8

PHILADELPHIA; AMERICA
THE YEAR 1763

Christoffer Rosenborg was an astute man, an observant man, a learned man.

Born in Copenhagen, Denmark, into a wealthy family, he was well schooled, but, at an early age decided that, as the youngest of the children and certainly unlikely to inherit any of the family estate or fortune, he wanted to be an adventurer.

He wanted to discover the world. But not just discover, to journal his travels, write about the things he would see, the people he would meet, the different cultures and different peoples.

In his early teens he would frequently be found in the dock area.

Watching, observing, taking notes, speaking to the dock workers, to the customs people. He could get about easily, and people knew the lad and that he was from an important and influential family, an observation that didn't go amiss for Christoffer, and he used it well.

Over the next couple of years, he befriended several Dutch merchants, learned about their vessels, their cargoes and their trade routes.

When he was seventeen, he sailed away on his first journey, to the port of Amsterdam.

With finances at his disposal and family backing, he stayed in the Netherlands and continued his studies at the University of Leiden.

Founded by William, Prince of Orange, in 1575, this university is still in the top one hundred academic institutions in the world.

So it was that three years later, at the age of twenty, he joined the VOC, better known as 'The Dutch East India Company'.

He had knowledge of trading and bartering, knew about cargo and weight distribution, had a grasp of trading routes, map reading and navigation, and he spoke several languages, for as well as his native Danish, he now spoke Dutch fluently and could comfortably converse in French, English and Spanish.

He was taken on as a negotiator, with responsibilities for the loading and unloading of cargo.

Furthermore, he would journal his voyages, document procedures and contacts, in fact, be a correspondent for the company.

Now, some sixteen years later, he stood in the large trading post in the port of Philadelphia.

Never before had he seen such a set up as this one.

Not only was there a vast array of goods, from food and ingredients to clothing, from leather goods to woollen blankets, but there was also riding gear, and you could buy a horse, purchase a cart or wagon, or even hire one complete with drivers.

The man who ran this little empire was a short fellow. His name was Zecheriah Strauss, and as well as being able to barter or purchase any goods, he also dealt in gold and silver, copper and jewels to be bought or sold.

He had a crew of over twenty spread across the several buildings he occupied in the busy port.

Christoffer, having taken it all in, was now looking at the leather wide brimmed hats that were displayed against a far wall, next to the saddles, riding gear and boots.

He had arrived in Philadelphia a few hours ago on a French schooner after having spent three weeks in the Canadian province of Nova Scotia, mainly in the towns of Halifax and Dartmouth, journaling the situation there, and the conflict the French were engaged in with the natives, as well as with the English.

Having sailed many journeys to Java, the Philippines, China and Persia with the Dutch, giving them over thirteen years of service, Christoffer had decided to concentrate on freelance writing, visiting troubled areas as a neutral, documenting wars and skirmishes, but also documenting how towns and peoples were re-established under new rule, or how new trade deals were made.

For the past couple of years, he had found passage to various parts of South America with English and Spanish ships, and to North America with the French.

Still giving some thought to the headwear he was looking at, Christoffer noticed a man who entered. Ever observant, he studied this man as he, after briefly glancing around, made his way to where the silver-haired Zecheriah stood behind a large wooden counter, beside which stood a glass encased display unit.

Zecheriah was busy writing in a big ledger book.

Already, in the short time he had been inside the trading post, Christoffer had seen the little man at work, going about his business, and had found him a likeable man.

He was witty, had a sense of humour, his blue eyes behind his horn-rimmed glasses were bright and quite piercing. He was a sharp operator, with a knowledge of many things.

The man who had just entered, Christoffer presumed off a ship that had docked about twenty minutes ago, headed for the counter.

The jacket the man wore was of good quality, but seemed a little tight, the trousers were a much poorer quality, as were the boots he wore, Christoffer noted.

The two satchels he carried were again of good quality, but the cap he wore over his ruffled and unkempt hair was old. Certainly, a strange mix of clothing, and the man was somewhat nervous.

Deciding to keep an eye on this newcomer, he took the hat he was holding and headed for the counter, circumnavigating several racks and boxes of goods, to where the man was now placing the bags on the floor, and heard him say to Zecheriah, 'You buy things?' his voice low.

'Sure, what have you got my friend?' Zecheriah replied, studying the man before him, who was not much taller, but very thickset in build.

Christoffer stopped by a rack of denim jeans and pretended to look through them, all the while watching the scene by the counter not far away as he was a little suspicious of this rugged looking newcomer.

Just then two men came from another part of the store, chatting amicably in French, nodded a greeting to Christoffer as they passed by, and one of them, noticing the hat, asked him if he was going to be a cowboy now.

He smiled and replied in French that he felt the hat would appeal to the ladies, recognising them as seamen on the ship he had come in on. They both laughed and carried on.

Turning his attention back to the counter, he saw Zecheriah hand the man a few silver coins.

Pocketing the coins, he then picked up his bag and walked out of the store.

Little did this oddly dressed man know, or even imagine, that a week later he would be dead.

Zecheriah Strauss was studying the item he had just purchased, nodded approvingly and muttered a few words in his native Hebrew, then placed the item in the glass display unit and looked up as Christoffer approached, placed the hat on the counter and looked at what the old man had just placed in the cabinet.

It was a painted miniature, and, even at a glance, he saw that it was beautiful.

THE PRESENT;

ANTWERP

SUNDAY 17TH MARCH

Her phone rang. She noted the number on the screen, and recognising it, answered, 'Sam Price.'

'Yes, it is,' he said, 'how did you know?'

'I tried to call you earlier' she said, smiling. 'It went to voicemail, but I wanted to speak to you, so, glad you rang.'

'I had a couple of jobs today. Been driving, just got back in. How did you get on; find anything?'

'Made progress, eventually. I have a new possible lead, what about you?'

'Have to confess here, Samantha, I got side-tracked yesterday. Got to read that full police report you sent me, it bothered me, so that took me in a different direction. Shall I explain?'

'The report bothered me a little as well. Go ahead, what are your thoughts?' she said, settling herself comfortably on the large couch.

It was good to hear her voice, he thought, recalling the time they spent together and how, though after an initially tentative start, they had felt comfortable in each other's presence. There was no tension.

He liked her, but quickly pushed any other thoughts aside. This was work. This was a professional situation, keep it so.

'It's the daughter, Elsa. Can't get my head around the fact that there she is, a brainbox, a lecturer at the university. She has a master's in art and one in philosophy, and, she doesn't know about the miniature her mum and dad have?

I don't buy it, and she's out of the country and they want to sell it?

No, I can't see it, unless she has had a major falling out with them, but I don't believe that either. If they, as they said, inherited this item, surely, the first person they would come to would be their daughter who has an art degree! Don't you think?'

'Wait, what? She has a master's in art? I didn't know that; all I knew from the police report was that she was a lecturer, currently out of the country.'

'Sorry, I'm getting ahead of myself. I took some time to find out more about her. I am also guessing that the police will do the same, if they haven't already done so. They too will be suspicious for sure.'

'Absolutely. Goodness me, I agree, they would surely have told her, unless, as you say, they had a falling out. After all, by their own admission they had a falling out with their son, according to the police report. Still, you're right, I can't see it; she has to be involved, but as you know, I can't contact the Wagenaars, but, I sense you have a plan?"

'Yes, I'm going to Leiden tomorrow. Want to check out whether she really is out of the country. The police may well be checking, but how thorough are they going to be? Now, what about you, you say you have another lead?'

'I have,' Samantha answered, still taking in what Samuel had told her, 'I got side-tracked too.

I was well into researching Thomas Powell, then came across the fact that he married whilst in America. Not only that, but that they had a son.

They left to go back to England. Lost track of them for a while, but then, in searching for the son, whose name was John Robert, I got lucky. A John Robert Powell sailed for America in 1763, to Philadelphia, but that's as far as I got.'

'That's a good lead. This John Robert Powell, as eldest, possibly only, son is likely to have inherited the item. The timeline you've discovered seems to fit, also. I guess that as his father had been in the States it seems likely he would want to go there. Well done you, so what's your plan?'

'I'll make some calls tomorrow, will check with my boss, but it's likely I'll have to fly to the States to get any further.'

'Two million reasons to do so. Good idea. I think I might also look into the Wagenaars' son, Erik, who, according to the police report you sent, has a police record and possibly lives in Mexico.'

'Sounds good, coming at the trail from two directions. Thanks by the way, for your help.'

'My pleasure, take care, goodnight.'

'Goodnight' Samantha said, ending the call.

Getting up from the couch, she walked over to the window.

Two million reasons, Samuel was right, but, yet, they were not even close to having concrete proof and she only had three weeks left.

She sighed, then turned and headed for her bedroom. It was time to pack.

Philadelphia here I come, she thought to herself.

THE FOLLOWING DAY; LEIDEN

Samuel had set off early, caught the tram to the station, then travelled by train to Leiden. The best time, he figured, to be mooching around the university campus, would be before nine, before classes.

Checking online on the layout of the university grounds, he decided to head for the main lecture hall.

He walked onto campus a little after eight thirty and entered the lecture hall a few minutes later. Whilst searching through social media, he had found over a dozen pictures of Elsa, and downloaded three that showed her face clearly and were the most recent.

He studied the various noticeboards in the foyer area and found a couple relating to Elsa Wagenaar.

He then found two brochures about a seminar by her, a senior lecturer, the first one, also corresponding to one of the notices on the board, mentioned the upcoming seminar that she titled 'My big fat Greek ...', and underneath the main title was written, '... marriage of art and philosophy'.

The brochure had a photo of her on the back.

The second leaflet was all about her lecture classes on the arts, times, administration and so on.

With these brochures in hand, Samuel wandered around looking for students to question. With so many men and women now studying at a later age, he wasn't out of place.

Disappointed, Samuel left the university grounds forty minutes later. Having approached several students in that time, he had found out nothing new, just confirmation that she was currently away in Greece.

As she had rooms on campus, Samuel figured, it was unlikely that if she hadn't gone to Greece, and she was still around, she would be staying here.

Wondering what his next move might be, he headed back to the centre of town. A coffee was what was needed.

A cold wind was blowing, but it was a dry day, and a frost was forecast for that night.

Heading towards a cafe near the station, his eye caught sight of a bag, a bag which had the logo of the university emblazoned on the side.

He looked up to see over whose shoulder this bag hung.

The woman was talking on her phone. She wore dark glasses, had very blond hair, and was dressed in light blue jeans and a sweater underneath a light jacket.

Samuel was almost at the door of the cafe, when he spotted something.

Underneath her chin, on the left side of her neck, there was a birthmark, a light brown line, about an inch in length and less than a quarter of an inch in width.

This he had seen before.

The woman finished her call and entered the cafe in front of him, not even noticing him.

Samuel stopped, decided not to enter, and instead took his phone from the pocket of his coat and flicked through to where he had stored the photos of Elsa.

Then he also took another look at the photo on the back of the brochure he had taken.

No doubt whatsoever.

This woman was none other than Elsa Wagenaar.

Her normally light brown hair was now a vivid blond, dark glasses, unusual on an overcast day, were no doubt to hide her light blue eyes. She was clearly hiding her identity, however, she'd forgotten her noticeable birthmark.

Sam checked for traffic, then crossed the road, turned and waited. Was she in the cafe to meet someone, or was she just picking up a coffee?

It was the latter, for she reappeared, drink in hand.

Phone at the ready, Sam took two pictures in succession, then checked the screen of his phone, enlarged the shots and was well pleased.

He had captured her face, birthmark and all, as well as the cafe. He had proof of where she was, and when.

She walked away from the centre of town, heading north; a different direction to that of the university.

Hoping she wouldn't catch a bus, Sam followed.

Less than five minutes later, after a left and right turn, she walked up to the lobby of an apartment block.

Holding her coffee in her left hand, with her right she fished out some keys from the pocket of her jacket, then unlocked and entered the lobby.

On the opposite side of the street, Sam watched.

The stairwell had a window on each floor. He saw her walk up to the first, then lost sight of her briefly before seeing her walk up to the second floor. She didn't go up to the third and top floor of the building.

Sam took pictures of the lobby area. With two apartments leading off from the stairs at each level, he now knew that she was living or staying in one of two apartments.

Walking slowly on, he looked to see if he could narrow it down further, but he could see no movement beyond the windows of either apartment.

Deciding not to linger, Samuel walked on, took a photo of the street name, then circled back to the town centre. He was really gasping for a coffee now.

Not much later he was sipping his Americano, back on the train, heading home.

Very pleased indeed.

Elsa Wagenaar was not in Greece; she was in Leiden and he had proof.

He was looking forward to informing Samantha and wondered where she was right now.

Samantha, had earlier stopped by her office, and with her boss' backing, had booked her travel and was just entering the check-in line.

She would fly to Washington, stay one night, then the following morning would board an Amtrak train at Union Station to 30th Street Station in Philadelphia, about a two-hour journey on a train called 'The Crescent'.

She had also contacted, and made an appointment with, the curator of the Maritime Museum for later that day.

She checked in a small suitcase then took her boarding card and proceeded through security.

After that she wandered around the shops for a while, and sat down for a bit, her flight was just over an hour away.

She took a sip of water and wondered what she might find out in Philadelphia.

THE PAST;

PERIOD 9

THE YEAR 1802

Sofia Camille Argent had mixed emotions. She sat in a cane chair on the veranda of an old colonial plantation house.

The floorboards, once a light green in colour, were chipped, scuffed and faded from the sun.

Beside her, her baby son, almost ten-months old, lay sleeping on a brightly coloured woollen blanket. The afternoon sun was bringing warmth to them both.

Mixed emotions because it had been hard to leave her ailing father behind. But he had insisted.

Sofia was born with one eye blind; it was a few shades lighter blue than her good eye, but she had never known any different. Her brain adjusted perfectly, and her good eye had incredibly sharp vision. She would often be able to spot things at a distance that others with both eyes struggled with.

She was born in Caracas, Venezuela, almost thirty years ago.

Growing up in a well-to-do family, she had good schooling through private tutors, though had learned most by far from her father.

She loved her father very much. Her mother had passed away when she was twenty years of age, and since then her father had stopped travelling, which he had been doing through much of his life, to spend time with her, their only child.

Mixed emotions because in the morning they would continue on their way to France. She was excited about that.

She had married Renee Franck Argent a couple of years ago.

She recalls her father, Christoffer, despite his already failing health, immensely enjoying the moment when he walked her down the aisle of the large church. Walking arm in arm.

She smiled again at the thought. He was so proud, and stood so tall.

A smile never left his face, though later he had been quite emotional as it would have been wonderful to have had her mother there.

Sofia, smiling at the memories, glanced down at the item she held in hand.

A beautifully painted miniature on ivory depicting the building of the Tower of Babel which her father had given her on the wedding day.

She closed her eyes. Felt the warmth of the sun on her face.

Mixed emotions.

Had she done the right thing, she wondered, agreeing to move to France. Had she done the right thing, taking her son away from his grandfather.

Clasping the item tightly, she thought about all that her father had taught her over the years. All the stories he had told. Fascinating tales from lands far away, and she had always been so excited whenever he had returned from somewhere, to sit with him and listen to another story, another adventure and she imagined she would herself, one day, go with him.

That day would never come.

He was ailing; his health would only get worse.

But he had been adamant.

Had said to her to remember him as he was, had said to her that it would be harder on them both if she stayed. Had told her that Renee was right in moving back to France.

Sofia opened her eyes, and checked on her son. He was still asleep; he would not remember these days. She would tell him.

Her husband, Renee, was a quiet and lovely man. He was concerned for the safety of his wife and son. Already there had been some skirmishes in the city. The situation was tense. It was likely to get worse. It was the right time to move.

Though she had been pursued by several young men during her late teenage years and well into her twenties, most of whom would have been considered as 'good catches' she did not have any, 'special' feelings for any of them.

In fact, she found most to be arrogant, self-centred and with egos way beyond their capabilities.

It was at a dance, four years ago now, that she met Renee. He was the younger brother of one of the men who had, some years, earlier pursued her.

Renee was different. He was somewhat shy, had a slight stutter at times, but when Sofia had for the first time looked into his eyes, as they bumped into each other on the dance floor whilst dancing with other partners, she knew, just knew.

He was the one.

The courtship had been fun. She recalls the first time he called on her, having been invited to do so as she felt she needed to encourage the first move due to his shyness.

He had arrived, looking smart, looking nervous. Had brought her flowers, then, as he entered, had tripped on the threshold and had stumbled through the door.

Sofia had caught him, her smile cutting through his embarrassment, and they had laughed.

Now they were here, in a place called Essequibo, in Guyana.

They had packed and taken as much as they could, and had boarded a ship belonging to a cousin of Renee.

There was freight on board destined for Essequibo and fresh cargo to be loaded once there, bound for France.

The treaty of Amiens had just been signed with regard to Guyana, so hostilities had ceased. Even so, Renee would be glad to be on the way again. They had docked in the harbour the previous afternoon and were due to set sail early tomorrow.

Good contacts meant they had been given the run of an old colonial house that stood less than half a mile from the port.

Sofia sat on the comfortable cane chair and took a deep breath.

Sad and happy, happy and sad, mixed feelings. Mixed emotions.

She looked again at what she held in her hand, and thought of the story surrounding it, how her father had acquired it.

'I purchased this' he would say, as he had told the story a few times already, 'way back in the year 1763, in a place called Philadelphia.

I was there, having just arrived from Halifax, in Nova Scotia,' and here he would sometimes digress and tell her why he had been there, before returning to the story, 'I was there, in this, quite remarkable trading post, run by this great character called Zecheriah Strauss,' and again, at this point he would often digress and tell of all the wonderful things one could buy there, before once more returning to the story.

'He, Zecheriah, had just bought it from an Englishman, a rather odd looking fellow. Well, I saw the item. It was beautiful. I just had to have it, so I purchased it then and there and it has travelled with me ever since,' and at this point of the story he would get quite philosophical and say, with his voice taking on a dramatic tone for effect, 'Many lands, many tongues,' would be the opening line, his eyes wide …'who knows how many have handled this piece of art before; who knows how many more in the future, for it will be yours one day.'

Sofia smiled again at the memories, then, putting it back in the leather pouch, she tucked it in the pocket of her skirt.

She couldn't possibly know, or even imagine, that another woman, whose name was Bibiana, had held and had looked in wonder at the very same painted ivory miniature, sat on a single wooden bed, in an old cabin, over a hundred and thirty years ago, not fifty yards from where she now sat on the veranda in the afternoon sun.

She heard the sound of voices, looked up and saw her husband coming up the dirt road along with the master of the ship, his cousin Antoine, who was also lodging in the house.

The following morning Sofia busied herself getting her and the baby ready.

Cousin Antoine had already departed.

Two young lads came to help carry the luggage and they set off for the harbour.

It was already warm and humid. Renee led the procession, carrying two large bags. Sofia followed; she was thinking about Paris. She had heard much about this city, heard people speak highly of it, and was looking forward to seeing it for herself.

She held her son in her arms as she followed behind her husband.

The baby was awake, and, as babies do, was searching for something to grab. Something to sniff, something to bite and explore, as babies do.

Somehow, he got hold of a leather pouch, he brought it to his mouth, tried to bite it, then, dropped it.

Nobody noticed. They walked on.

The two lads in the rear, carrying more luggage, hadn't noticed the pouch falling to the dirt road.

Their feet scuffed up the dirt on the road, and the pouch was kicked to one side, partly covered up already.

A devastated Sofia would hunt in vain later that day, already many hours from port.

There was no going back.

Sofia would later write and send a letter to the trading post but would never hear back.

THE PRESENT;

PHILADELPHIA

TUESDAY 19TH MARCH

'Hello, Sam speaking.'

'Hey, this is also Sam speaking.'

'Hi, how are you? I take it you're ringing from the States?'

'I am, didn't ring you yesterday because of the time difference, but got your e-mail which said, "call me". I take it, that means progress?'

'Indeed, it does, Elsa Wagenaar is not in Greece. She is in Leiden. I saw her, photographed her, found out where she is staying. She was definitely trying not to be recognised, wearing sunshades, her hair either dyed very blond, or she was wearing a wig, but it was her, for sure'

'Wow, that's great work. Something's going on for sure. I'll have to give some thought as to how to proceed with that information,' Samantha answered, scribbling something down on a pad. 'That's some sleuthing.'

'I got lucky actually,' Samuel said. 'Got nowhere at the university, everyone there believed her to be in Greece, but on my way back to the station, literally bumped into her.'

'How did you know it was her?'

'It was the bag she carried over her shoulder that drew my attention; it had the university logo on it. Then, when I saw her, initially I dismissed her, but then, something caught my eye.

She has a birthmark on her neck, and I remembered it from photos I have of her. It was her alright, a break really, but a good one I feel.'

'Absolutely, it's something in our favour,' Samantha answered, smiling at the thought of recognising that they were working as a team.

'I'll leave that info with you, and I will see if I can track down the son, Erik. Who knows, maybe he and sis are in it together. I'll see what I can find, so, now, how about you, across the ocean, what news m'lady?'

She smiled at his impersonation of Parker from the Thunderbirds and said, 'Well, as you know, the only lead we had left was the son of Thomas Powell, and, this John Robert, as the eldest, would be the most likely to inherit. However, this was put in some doubt I feel, for I discovered that the wife he married in America had died when the boy was about three, so, it's quite possible that Thomas married again. Still, as we had already found out that John Robert sailed for Philadelphia in 1763, here I am.'

A slight pause, then Samuel asked, 'And ...? I sense you have more to tell, I can hear it in your voice ...'

'Mmmm, I guess I'm not very good at suppressing my excitement. Yes, yes, I have indeed found out more. Yesterday I spent several hours with the curator of the Maritime Museum here, very accommodating chap. Finally hit pay dirt. Listen to this. A John Robert Powell landed here in 1763 from Plymouth. On the same day, I found his name on a ledger from the trading post at the port, that was run by a Zecheriah Strauss.

It shows, that he sold an item, an oil painted miniature on ivory, depicting the Tower of Babel, all written very clearly, no mistake. It has to be our item.'

'Hey, that's fantastic, you're right, that can only be our item, but why do you think he sold it upon arrival in the States?'

'I wondered about that. Surely his father would have told him the significance of the item, but, who knows, maybe he just needed funds.'

'Very possible' Samuel said, then, 'is there more? I think so.'

'Aah, you're right again, there is more. Listen, on the same day that very item was also sold, to a Mr Christoffer Rosenborg, however, all I have been able to find out so far is that he was from Copenhagen, Denmark, and had recently arrived in Philadelphia, actually, on that same day, from Halifax, Nova Scotia.'

'Mmm, Christoffer Rosenborg, you say? Strange, the name rings a bell. Can you spell that for me?' Samuel asked.

Samantha spelled out the name, then, after chatting some more, she hung up. It was time for breakfast.

ROTTERDAM

Samuel looked at the name he had written down on his pad. Why, he wondered, did it ring a bell?

He let the thought wander around his mind for a bit as he paced the room. His stereo system was playing a selection of music, currently *Suzie Q* by Creedence Clearwater Revival was on in the background.

He always liked to have music on. It helped him in his work.

Rosenborg. It definitely was a name he had come across. Was it when he was doing his research at the maritime museum? Pacing some more he entered the kitchen and grabbed a biscuit, he was forever eating biscuits, then stopped by the large window in the lounge and looked outside.

Below was the shopping street, busy, pedestrians, bicycles, mopeds and cars.

Then something clicked, He remembered where he had come across the name before.

He went into the second bedroom, A smaller guest-room it held a single bed, a small wardrobe, a chest of drawers, and here Samuel had placed a bookcase. It was an old antique oak piece of furniture, two cupboards on the lower half, then two glass doors behind which there were three shelves, all lined with books.

He opened the right-hand side glass door, pulled out a thick book, then headed back to the lounge where he sat down on the couch and began flicking through the pages.

THE PAST;

PERIOD 10

THE YEAR 1802

Four months.

For four months the sandy dirt road that led to the port of Essequibo was travelled upon.

The feet of men and women and children. The hooves of horses and oxen. The wheels of carts and wagons.

Not to mention dogs and chickens.

There it lay, the leather pouch. In the hot sun, in the cool night, in the dry and in the wet.

Four months the pouch lay tucked up against a chunky weed.

Many feet and hooves and wheels had come close to it.

But there it lay, untouched.

A ship was in port. A Spanish ship, a large galleon. The sky was a vivid blue; a haze lay over the water.

A treaty, the treaty of Amiens, signed by the French, English, Spanish and Batavians, later to become the Dutch, was in force and peace reigned in the area. For now.

Cargo had been unloaded, fresh cargo, sugar in the main, was now being taken aboard. Hot work on a hot day.

A large cart was heading towards the dock on the dirt road, pulled by two horses. One man, a native Guyanese, walked and guided the big horses along. Another man, a Spanish crewman, walked alongside him.

Behind the cart, which was loaded with sugar, unrefined brown sugar in jute bags, four young boys ambled along. Ship's boys.

They had helped with the loading and would soon be working with others to unload the cart and get the cargo onto the galleon.

One boy, though the same age as the others, thirteen, was much smaller in stature. He was lagging behind. His bare feet kicking up the dust on the dirt road.

He had a nickname. They called him 'Ardilla' meaning squirrel, as he was quick, nimble and a great climber.

Though at times seen working on the sails way up high on the crossbeams, he was mainly to be found in the galley.

There he cleaned the floor, washed out the pots and pans and from time to time helped in the preparation of food. It was there that he was happiest.

His bunk was cramped into a space with six others. He didn't bond with the others so much, though was not at odds with them either. He had seen to that early on this, his first voyage.

Being small, he figured he would have to be smart to survive and, as he was ideally suited to work in the narrow and tight galley, this was where he was placed, and he loved it. This also gave him opportunities to occasionally secure some extra titbits of food for his bunkmates. In turn, they didn't pick on him, tease or bully him, but just let him be.

Young Ardilla, as he was soon known to all, quickly established a bond with the rotund and jolly cook.

The men, horses, cart and boys passed by the old plantation house where Sofia, her husband and their baby son, along with Renee's cousin had stayed for two days, four months ago.

Ardilla, now even further behind as he daydreamed along, suddenly noticed something. He investigated, bent down and picked up a leather pouch.

He looked up. The three other boys, now well up the road, were chatting among themselves. They weren't looking. They did not even notice that Ardilla was that far behind.

The young boy looked all around, then, sure that no-one was about, quickly tucked the pouch, which he felt contained something, into a pocket of his well-worn trousers.

His heart was beating a little faster, what had he found? what could be inside that pouch?

He picked up his pace, almost to a run, to catch up with the group ahead.

Working in pairs, the four boys helped a group of four men with the loading. Ardilla was quiet, pre-occupied, but no-one noticed or cared.

When he was done, he quickly made his way to the galley, pleased to find nobody there.

He delved deep into his pocket, drew out the pouch, then making sure the coast was clear, opened it, and slipped the contents into his little hand.

Mouth open, he was astonished at what he saw. Never before had he seen anything this beautiful.

Even in the dimness of the galley with only four small portholes bringing any light into it, the item in his hand shone.

He forced himself to put it back into the pouch.

What to do with it?

This was a problem.

He couldn't show it to anyone, as he would lose it for sure.

This was his, he had found it, and he was determined to keep it.

But, where to hide it?

It couldn't be anywhere near where he and the other boys slept. That would not be wise. He looked around the galley. This was his place, his domain. He knew every corner of it, furthermore, only a few people ever came in here.

He knew the answer.

Ardilla had created for himself, a 'resting place' in the galley. This was a tight space, reached via a low shelf onto a narrow space behind one of the wooden benches that ran along, up against the outer hull of the ship.

He would sometimes, when no one saw, slip in there, just to rest a while.

Often the cook would be confused as to where the lad had suddenly disappeared to, and would then, just as suddenly, appear again, much to Ardilla's amusement.

Listening out, the coast was still clear. No-one was coming.

Ardilla moved quickly, slipped into his secret place, then took the pouch from the pocket of his trousers. In the narrow confines with a bit of a struggle, then, twisting around and feeling with his free hand, he came across a bent iron nail, sticking out just enough from the back of one of the bench legs.

Ideal.

He hung the pouch there, checked it was secure, then, hearing voices coming nearer, he quickly slipped out again.

He leant against a bench, hoping they wouldn't hear his thumping heart as the cook and two other galley workers entered.

Four months it had lain in the dirt road, now it hung on a makeshift hook in the galley of a Spanish galleon. It was intact; it was undamaged. It had survived, rescued by a little Spanish boy named Ardilla.

THE PRESENT;

ROTTERDAM

WEDNESDAY 20ᵀᴴ MARCH

Samuel had his notes ready, had a coffee ready, was tucking into one of his favourite treats, a 'gevulde koek' a type of almond filled biscuit cake, and was ready for the call.

Checking the clock on the wall, he figured she would be ringing soon.

What would her thoughts be regarding Elsa, he wondered, and what, if anything, had she found out about Christoffer Rosenborg?

He realised the pressure that must be on her, for this was assuredly a case of fraud, but she had approved the insurance details, just as he had approved the details for the purpose of the auction, so proof was needed, solid proof, and as yet they had none.

His phone rang.

'Good morning, Miss Price,' he said, knowing it was her.

'Good afternoon, Mr Price,' she answered, 'well, that's enough of the pleasantries, got anything?'

'Ladies first,' answered Samuel.

He realised his heart was beating a little faster as he heard her voice. He also realised he was picturing her in his mind. Once again the words of his late wife came to him, 'Go and find someone to love' ... once again he dismissed the idea; shook the thoughts away. She was very attractive and much younger. Focus. Focus on what needs to be done. He listened as she spoke.

'Okay, well, I have nothing. All I have come up with is a Rosenborg Castle, in Denmark, a few Christoffers, but not our Christoffer,' she said, sounding a little resigned and deflated.

'Sometimes that happens. So much is out there, it's just finding that right connection, and that is not only time consuming, but could often lead nowhere, but don't lose heart. I know the clock is ticking, and I have come up with a possibility, however, I need to discuss something else first.'

'Okay,' Samantha answered, sounding wary, 'that sounds ominous. You want a finder's fee or something?'

'No,' he said with a little laugh, 'no, of course not, but tell me, about Elsa. I don't know what you have decided about her yet, but I was thinking, it might be, well, worthwhile perhaps, if we could get a better insight about the family, about the daughter?'

'Go on,' she said, 'what's your idea?'

'I said I would look into the son, Erik. Well, I found him.'

'Seriously, you found him?' Samantha, ringing from her hotel in Philadelphia, said, her voice a lot more upbeat now.

'I found him; I'll tell you how.
    Now, I'm going to blow my own trumpet here. You see, I felt, that, as he had supposedly left home under a cloud and with a police record, he may have changed his name, so, I looked at the name Wagenaar, then anglicized it, and came up with the possibility of Wagner. Well, and you can say, well done my good man. I found him that way,' Samuel paused.

Samantha smiling said, 'Well done my good man,' and laughed.

'He is now Rico Wagner,' Samuel continued, 'and runs a successful coffee house in Acapulco. I will, in a moment, send you all the details. My thought is this. Whilst you are there across the Atlantic, go and see him.'

She sat in her dressing gown, in a chair by the window of her hotel room. The city was awakening. Below she could hear the morning traffic.

She thought for a few moments, about his suggestion.

She was checking out of the hotel later this morning, was already booked on a train back to Washington and had her return ticket from there to Amsterdam also confirmed and had already checked in online.

She would have to try to postpone her return, then get a return flight to Acapulco from Washington. It would be possible, but would it be worth it? Would it, in any way, be helpful to her investigation, with time already beginning to run out?

'You think it might be worth it?' she said at last.

He had patiently waited. Could almost hear the cogs in her brain whirring, it was an extra expense, and would cost extra time, would it, or could it pay dividends?

'Yes,' he answered, 'yes I do. I've given it some thought since I found him, and I really think it would be worthwhile. You could, of course, also call him, but I really feel to meet him in person will be best,' Samuel said, again pausing briefly, then continuing, 'and I have found another lead on Christoffer that I could follow.'

'You found a lead?' she asked, still thinking through which would be the best way forward in the investigation.

'Yes, remember I said, when you mentioned his name, that it rang a bell. Well, I finally recalled where I had heard it before. In my great-grandfather's notes, he was a British ambassador, and, it had been when in Copenhagen, which is where he purchased the Gauguin, that he made connections with an influential family there called Rosenborg. So taking that info and doing some family tree research, I found out about a Christoffer Rosenborg who studied, would you believe, at Leiden University in the early seventeen hundreds, and he worked for the VOC, the Dutch East India Company, for many years.

He was later a correspondent and covered wars and skirmishes. One of the places he went to was Nova Scotia. You mentioned that he had arrived from Halifax, Nova Scotia, so that dovetails in nicely. I have him married and living in Caracas, Venezuela, in 1770, so, I'll continue to see if I can follow that trail further. What do you think?'

Samantha was in thought, then, again after a few moments, said, 'Okay, that's the best move, I agree. You carry on with Christoffer, I will go and see this Rico. Send me the info straight away please. I will re-arrange my travel, and thanks, well done. I'll be in touch.'

'I'll send you the details straight away. Good luck and take care.'

'You too' she replied, then ended the call. Breakfast would have to wait.

THE PAST;

PERIOD II

THE YEAR 1803

Young Ardilla had not counted on one thing.

He was still growing.

The voyage north, across the Atlantic, to the port of Cadiz had been uneventful.

Regularly, when the coast was clear, little Ardilla would check out his prize item. He would slip on to the small lower shelf of the bench, twist himself behind the unit into the narrow void beyond the bench, then, would carefully unhook the pouch from the iron nail, smell the leather and feel its soft touch, then very gingerly would slip the item from it, hold it in his hands and admire it.

Even though the light wasn't great, he would stare at it in wonder, fascinated how someone had been able to paint such a tiny scene with such detail. He wondered who it might have been who had made this item. How long ago? How did it end up where it did on the dirt road?

Equally carefully he would put it all back and twist himself out from his secret place.

They had sailed into the port of Cadiz around mid-morning. A very old city, it had been first established by the Phoenicians, around 1104 BC.

On arrival by sea, the many towers could be seen; well over a hundred and fifty of them.

Most housed dwellings for merchants, and the view from the top of these towers afforded the scene of the coming and going of many a vessel.

Christopher Columbus had sailed from here on his second and fourth journeys.

Cargo was unloaded.

Another load was bartered for and the galleon would set sail again in three days.

Her destination this time, Caracas, Venezuela.

The master would be happy once they were on their way again. The treaty of Amiens was holding, but the Napoleonic war was a threat.

It was on this voyage, about a week out of Cadiz, when young Ardilla experienced something he hadn't given any thought to.

He had a growth spurt.

And so it was, that one afternoon, the sea calm, a light breeze and a quiet spell in the galley, that he slipped onto his shelf, twisted around and behind into the void, as he had many times by now, set to view his prize possession.

He got the pouch off the hooked nail, then, as he twisted himself to a different position, he got stuck.

This was crazy, how could he be stuck?

He knew how to get in and out of this space with precision and ease. What had changed?

But, no matter how he wormed and twisted, he was stuck. He just couldn't move, couldn't get out.

The cook came back in the galley. Ardilla heard him.

The rotund and jolly man, in his late forties, also had a nickname, they called him 'Morsa' meaning Walrus. This was because he had an enormous moustache that was a great feature on his round face.

He drank much beer and frequently used copious amounts of it in his cooking.

'Morsa' the boy called out.

The cook investigated, and after the boy had called out a second time, he found the young lad.

A puzzle solved, for he had many times wondered where the boy had suddenly disappeared to.

He studied the situation, then set about to help the lad from his tight predicament.

He got on well with the boy. The lad worked hard and was always helpful to him.

After some struggle, Ardilla managed to get out.

Now he stood there, red-faced, a scratch on his leg that was almost bleeding, in front of Morsa, the leather pouch in his hand.

'Found it,' Ardilla said, handing the pouch to the cook.

Morsa took the pouch, looked at the boy, then at the pouch, opened it and slid out the contents.

He too was taken aback by the beauty of the item that he held in his hand.

He looked at Ardilla again.

'Found it,' the boy said again, 'on the ground, sugar place.'

Morsa frowned, then understood, 'You found it in Essequibo?'

'On the ground, sugar place,' confirmed the boy.

Morsa thought some more, looking at the item, then, said to the boy, 'We sell it when we get to next port, or trade it, maybe clothes, maybe boots,' looking at Ardilla's bare feet, then went on to say, 'for you, not for me, for you.'

Morsa held out his big hand, and the boy shook it. He nodded and smiled up at the cook. Tried to speak but couldn't.

Morsa noticed the boy's eyes welling up. He ruffled the lad's hair and said, 'We work now,' and put the item back into the pouch, which he stuck in his pocket, then turned and began preparations for the evening meal.

Ardilla was relieved. Morsa was his friend. He could trust Morsa.

A little over two weeks later the ship sailed into the port of Caracas.

It was early October of the year 1803.

Christoffer Rosenborg walked slowly with the aid of a stick.

He was at the port.

He was often at the port, he would come and sit, and watch the vessels coming in, and going out.

He would think of his daughter, Sofia.

It was well over a year ago now that she and her husband Renee and their little boy, his grandson, had sailed from here.

He had received no news from them as yet.

He knew he would not see them again. Would not see his grandson, who they had named Christoffer Junior, grow up.

But he had resigned himself to that fact.

He himself had left home to go travelling when he was just seventeen.

He had, in all these years of journeying, never returned home, never seen his parents again.

He sat down on a low brick wall which was his place, his seat.

A Spanish galleon was arriving.

He thought about the many lands he had visited, the many peoples he had met, the occasional confrontation with pirates, and the numerous and varied trade deals he had been part of.

Why, he wondered, had he never ventured back home?

He knew nothing of the lives of his two brothers and a sister. Had they married? Did he have a score of nieces or nephews he knew nothing about?

Was there a reason he had left that day; was there a reason he had never returned?

He was dying.

He knew he was dying.

Each day it got a little harder.

It was perhaps why he had all these questions in his head.

It was why he gave them, his daughter whom he loved so much and her husband and their child, his blessing to leave, to live in France, his son-in-law's home country.

He had heard news of the war in Europe. He prayed that they would be safe.

He sat, as he did most days now, on that low brick wall, right in the port, right in a place he could view the harbour, see the ships coming and going, and watch the loading and unloading of cargoes.

To the right of him the open sea, to the left, the dock buildings, the customs hall, the trading post and, beyond them, lay the city of Caracas.

It was relatively quiet in the harbour. Most fishing vessels were out, a couple of large coastal schooners were anchored, an English galleon was already docked, and a Spanish galleon was coming in.

On board the Spanish galleon, Morsa was giving instruction to his two galley assistants, a list of produce, meat, poultry, fruit and vegetables and various spices and herbs to be sourced which he would later check out and barter for.

He himself took young Ardilla with him to the trading post.

Henry Hopkins had spent the last ten years working in the tin mines in his native Cornwall, England. Usually from early morning to early evening.

His fair skin had not often been exposed to the sun.

He arrived in Caracas, about as red as a lobster and with much of his sunburned skin peeling away.

Despite his discomfort, Henry walked into the port's trading post in a good mood. The voyage across had been reasonable though he had been seasick on a few occasions early on in the journey.

It was good to feel solid ground beneath his feet.

Henry was not much taller than five foot six but had a muscular build. His hair was quite long, touching his shoulders, and dark brown in colour.

He also sported a dark brown moustache and whiskers.

His eyes were dark blue.

He was in a good mood, not only because he was on dry land, though this was only temporary as he was to journey on to Cartagena, Colombia, in two days' time, but also because he was here; here in South America.

A place he had heard others speak of, with tales of huge jungles, strange creatures and hot, very, very hot weather.

A place he had longed to go to for the past five years.

Henry had, while working in the mine, studied, as best he could, mining procedures, about the type of equipment that was available, geology and minerals, and about silver and gold.

One thing he had not learned was Spanish, but figured he would learn the language once he lived and worked in South America.

His destination was a mining region that lay between Cartagena and Bogota.

He figured and hoped, that he would secure a job there because of his many years' experience.

He looked around the large store, spotted a rack of hats on display and headed for them.

Morsa and Ardilla entered the store. The cook, having been here before, knew where to go and who to speak to. The boy followed in his wake.

There were several folk milling around the store, mostly seamen from the English galleon, and about a dozen or so from the Spanish ship were just entering. Lively chatter was ringing around the trading post, which had all manner of goods for sale.

Henry selected two hats, both wide brimmed, as he surely wasn't about to get such sunburn again. He sauntered around for a bit, picking up a few other items and then made his way to one of the three sales counters.

He was quite wealthy by local standards. He had with him eight silver coins and even two gold sovereigns.

He placed his items on the counter just as a man and boy were leaving. Another customer was next to be served. Henry waited.

Now in another part of the store, Morsa was helping the boy to select boots and clothing. The young lad was bright-eyed and excited. Never before had he seen such an array of goods in one place.

One of the assistants in the trading post opened a glass topped case that was right beside where Henry stood, and placed an item inside, making room for it on the top shelf to display it and closed the case. He returned to his position.

Henry watched with interest as he was still waiting to be served. The item on the shelf was a thing of beauty. He stepped a little closer to the glass case and looked at it closely.

A beautifully painted scene, so small, yet so clear, painted upon what he could see was ivory.

What's more, he recognised the scene.

He had faithfully attended his village church every Sunday since a very young age, and he recalled looking at a picture of this very scene on one of the pages of a large book he had seen once.

It was his turn to be served. Without hesitation he pointed to the item on the shelf in the glass case.

And so, Henry Hopkins from Cornwall became the thirteenth possessor of the item, not counting the Spanish cook who sold it on behalf of the young boy named Ardilla.

Christoffer had been in the sun enough. He got to his feet and walked slowly towards the port's trading post.

He would often have a wander around the place.

As he was about to enter, a man, quite seriously sunburned, came out, noticed him and held the door open for him.

Christoffer nodded his thanks, and it would never occur to him that in that man's possession was the same item he himself had purchased, in Philadelphia, forty years ago.

THE PRESENT;

ACAPULCO, MEXICO

THURSDAY 21ST MARCH

Samantha Price was thirty-four years of age. She stood five foot seven inches in stockinged feet, had a trim figure, light brown hair that reached to just below her shoulders and blue eyes set in a lightly tanned face.

She had been through two serious relationships that had petered out, and several short-term flings that were never going to lead to anything substantial.

Though she did not, at present, have a significant other, she was happy, content, and confident in herself. She enjoyed life, and enjoyed work.

She found the times she had been involved in the investigation of potentially fraudulent or suspicious claims especially satisfying, and had thus far solved five cases saving the company several hundred thousand euros.

She was well liked and respected at work where she had now been for over twelve years. She had her own office, and her own portfolio of customers to look after, and was the senior investigator in cases of suspicious claims.

She sent an e-mail to her boss explaining her change of plans and diversion to Acapulco. She knew he would back her decisions and, having sent the message, set about re-arranging her travel.

Two hours later, after successfully re-scheduling everything, and after she enjoyed a lovely breakfast at last, she checked out of the hotel.

A taxi, a train journey, and another taxi took her to the airport in Washington. Then it was a flight to San Francisco, which looked to be the best route, with just one change to take her to on to Acapulco.

Samantha entered her hotel room and flung herself upon the king-size bed. She was worn out.

It was a little before ten o'clock in the evening.

A little later, after a refreshing shower, she read the information Samuel had sent with regard to the son of the Wagenaars, now known as Rico Wagner.

It was a lengthy report.

Hi Sam, hope you are able to re-arrange your travel and head down south to Mexico.

I was in Acapulco once. Though a long time ago, I remember going up to the cliff and watching these divers jump from it and into the sea far below. There was a little shrine, sort of carved into the cliffside. Here they would pray before jumping. Crazy. Memories, memories. Anyway, to business.

First then, please find attached a couple of photos I found of Rico Wagner.

Also attached is the info on his establishment, called CafeCasa.

I believe a visit to him could be helpful, so I hope you are able to make it.

Just to confirm my findings on Christoffer Rosenborg, after many years with the Dutch East India Company, he became a freelance writer, a journalist really, spent much time in the West indies, and, as you yourself found out, he had arrived in Philadelphia from Halifax. He ended up in Caracas, and, as I said, the last date I have on him is living there in 1770.

So, you are now as up to date as I am. 'Well done my good man', you must be saying right now. I will continue my search on Christoffer. Hope you get to Acapulco and, if you do, have fun. Sam.

Smiling, Samantha opened the attachment and studied the information and the photographs. Then closing her laptop down, said in a soft voice 'Well done indeed, my good man'.

Once in bed, she fell asleep in seconds.

It was a little after nine-thirty in the morning. Already the sun was hot and the sky blue. Not even a wisp of cloud to be seen.

She walked along at a leisurely pace, with the Pacific Ocean to her right, the slight breeze coming from it very welcome, and headed for the cafe.

She entered CafeCasa. It was refreshingly cool inside. Very nice.

It wasn't busy. Only two customers sat at a table by the window chatting amicably in their own language.

Samantha caught sight of the man behind the counter. She approached and felt herself blush a little. He was handsome.

Over six feet tall, very tanned, short cropped curly blond hair, a clean-shaven face and green eyes that were already fixed on her.

'Ola,' he said, his voice deep and friendly.

Samantha smiled at him, then tore her eyes away and looked at the clearly stencilled menu on the wall behind him.

Feeling she now had control of her voice, she said, 'Hi, I'll have a latte please,' in English.

'Drink here or take out,' he asked, also now in English.

'Here please,' she answered and prepared to get her purse from her handbag.

'Please, find a seat; I'll bring it to you. Pay later,' he said, smiling at her, then turned to prepare her order.

She chose a table by the window, though on the opposite side to where the other customers, both women and both still chatting, sat.

She sat herself down, not quite sure how to open the conversation.

She had rehearsed in her mind what she might say, but right now her mind had gone blank.

She looked over to where the man was preparing her drink. There was no mistake; this was Rico, the man in the photos that Sam had sent.

She liked him instantly. He had a kind face, sincere eyes, and his voice was warm. Not to mention she thought him handsome, and she had already noticed that he wore no rings on his fingers.

He came over.

'Thank you,' she said, smiling up at him as he placed her latte on the table, 'are you Rico?' she asked, knowing he was and that the photos Sam had sent didn't do him any justice.

He looked at her, his eyes meeting hers, 'I am.'

'Do you think we could talk,' she held his gaze and added, 'please?'

He turned and called to the kitchen area, 'Chita,' and when she appeared, he spoke to her in Spanish asking her to watch the counter for a bit.

'Thank you,' Samantha said, then invited him to sit with her.

Rico Wagner sat down and looked at her expectantly, his face and demeanour calm, his green eyes focused, and a slight smile on his lips.

'I would like to ask you, about your parents,' she began. Then before he could react or respond, continued, 'My name is Samantha, Samantha Price. I work for an insurance company based in Antwerp, Belgium, though I'm sure you know that. Antwerp being in Belgium I mean; I sound a bit like an American now. They often connect a city with a country when they talk, like, I'm going to Paris, France, or Rome, Italy.

Anyway, the thing is this. Your parents, Mr and Mrs Wagenaar, have an insurance policy with us, and, about twelve days ago they were burgled. Oh, they weren't hurt or anything,' she quickly added, then, his eyes still totally focused on hers, she continued, 'but an item was taken. It was the only thing that was taken. Potentially, a very valuable item which they told me they had inherited.' She paused briefly, then said, 'Now, it's company policy when it comes to a large claim that it needs to be investigated, and so, that's why I'm here,' she finished. Tearing her eyes way from his, she took hold of her cup to drink some of her latte.

He sat back, his eyes never leaving hers, tilted his head ever so slightly to one side and with a frown, asked, 'So, first, how does that involve me? And second, how did you find me?'

'Oh, no, you're not under suspicion or anything, it was just, well, I need some more information on your parents.

They seem nice folk, but I can't speak to them directly as it is an ongoing police investigation, I just need to, well, get a better idea as to what they are like. You see, with just the one item stolen, and it being an incredibly valuable one, it is a suspicious claim, so it's my job, to investigate.'

'Well, I see, it must be quite a claim then, for you to come all the way over here, and find out about me.

I'm still unsure how I could help, I left home a long time ago. I'm still puzzled though, as to how you found me.'

Samantha studied the man for a moment, he sat, very relaxed, still a little smile on his face and his eyes still locked on hers.

His command of the English language was very good. She was sure that they could very well continue this conversation in Dutch but stuck to English for now.

'Two million euros' she said, 'and yes, I know you left home over ten years ago, but my search for answers took me to the

States, and my partner in this investigation, he is the one that tracked you down, suggested it might be worthwhile to talk to you, whilst I was on this side of the Atlantic.'

A group of people came into the cafe.

'I shouldn't keep you away from your work, I have time, so ...'

Rico stood up, looked at the counter area, then back at Samantha, said, 'I will get you a piece of my famous Dutch apple cake, with cream of course, and another latte, on the house, then we can talk later, yes?'

'Absolutely,' she answered, 'thank you,' and as he moved away to help with the customers, she felt a tingling in her body and a tightening in her stomach. Feeling herself colour, she realised she was attracted to him.

The Dutch apple cake with cream and a second latte came, delivered by Chita, who gave her a friendly smile.

More customers entered the cafe and it was about half an hour later, when Rico returned to her table, 'Come,' he said, we'll go upstairs, where we can talk more privately.'

She had enjoyed the cake, noticed there was now another assistant helping Chita and stood up, grabbing her handbag, then followed Rico.

He took her through a door, through the kitchen area, then up a flight of stairs, along a narrow corridor, then through another door which led to a small balcony.

There was a table in the centre, a round table made of cane, with a glass top and four cane chairs around it.

There were also several pots with plants dotted around and a small electric fridge sat upon a low table in one corner.

Samantha took in the view. They were above the cafe and the scene was wonderful. A direct and uninterrupted view of the harbour where several small boats lay moored alongside a wooden jetty. Further out in the harbour two ships lay anchored. To the left she could see the large fort, and to the right the street she had earlier walked along.

He invited her to sit, went to the fridge and took out two cans of coke. 'Would you like one?' he asked, holding them up for her to see.

She turned her head, 'Yes please,' then walked over to the white painted stucco wall that surrounded the balcony and took in the view. It was warm, the sun high in the still cloudless sky. It was nearly noon.

Rico placed the cans on the table and studied the woman standing by the railing. He found her rather attractive.

He thought about his parents, though he would think about them from time to time, he hadn't considered going to see them. Nor had he considered, after all these years, that someone would find him, and of all people, that someone would be such an attractive woman.

He had been through several relationships over the years, but nothing serious enough for him to reveal the truth about who he was. He wouldn't allow himself to seriously consider a relationship without stating his real name, or how he came to be in Mexico.

He was still looking at her when she turned and their eyes met.

He invited her to sit at the table and she walked over and sat down.

They both opened their cans with a fizz and drank straight from the can.

He waited.

'Okay', she said, the tightness in her stomach was still there, but her voice sounded firm and secure, 'the story is this. The item in question, the item your parents said they had inherited, is alleged to be an oil painting, a miniature, painted on ivory, and likely to be by Pieter Brueghel, the elder, and the scene depicted is that of the building of the Tower of Babel.

Now, this piece of art, is known to have existed, but, is deemed lost.

I went over to your folks' house, to view this object. This was because they had contacted my insurance company and wanted it insured, but, as it was a very valuable item, or deemed to be, an estimated value of two million euros, I had to see the item for myself, to confirm its existence.'

Samantha took another sip from her can, then continued, 'So, I did, saw it, took pictures, and it was indeed a fine piece of art with a sales certificate from 1613, which also looked genuine.

All seemed to be in order to my satisfaction, so this item was added to their existing policy.

'So far, so good. Then, four days later, it was stolen. Furthermore, it was the only thing, that was stolen.

As I said, for such a big claim, it needed to be investigated.

The police did their thing. They confirmed the back door had been forced and the alarm had been tampered with, but I was suspicious.'

Rico took a sip of coke, then said, 'I would be too. Go on, I sense there's more.'

'There is,' Samantha answered. 'There was another witness who saw the item. As well as wanting to insure the item, they, your folks, also contacted an auction house in order to sell the item. An assessor came to their house, actually on the same day as me, also to verify the item and its potential worth.

After the theft, the police visited him as well as me, and I contacted him. He, like me, was also very suspicious and knowing more about the art world and its dealings, we decided to work together. You see, though he had also valued the item, he and the auction house still needed to verify the document and the item's provenance in order for it to realise the best price, which he agreed, could be in the region of two million.'

After another sip, with Rico listening attentively and waiting, she went on, 'So, we found out a number of things. As I said, we couldn't question your parents as the police would not allow it.

First of all, we discovered that the sales document, though genuine, did not relate to the item, and secondly, that your folks did not inherit this item as they said,' and after a brief pause, Samantha continued, 'I don't believe your parents are, well criminals, it seems unlikely, but ...' and here she stopped.

Rico took a few sips, placed the can on the table, got up and went over to the wall and looked out to sea, then said, 'I take it, you've spoken to my sister?'

Samantha got up and joined him. She noticed his voice had changed a little, and sensed his mood had changed a little.

She waited until he turned his face to look at her, then spoke, 'Actually no, she was, supposedly, away in Greece for a couple of months doing research for her lectures.

Sam, he's the auction house man, found it odd that your parents had not told your sister about the item, given her art degree, and even more suspicious that they would sell it without her knowing. All this was told to the police and is in the report which I received a copy of. Well, Sam found out, that your sister wasn't in Greece at all.

Both he and I feel she could be involved ...'

Rico nodded, but said nothing and looked out at sea again.

The mighty Pacific Ocean stretched as far as the eye could see. A gentle swell, and the sunlight bouncing of the water.

Samantha could see he was in thought, so she waited, also taking in the view from the balcony.

'Let me tell you about my sister,' he said at last, still looking out, then he turned his head to look at her 'She was the brains of the family, high grades at school, very talented at art, Mum and Dad, naturally, proud.

Then, one day, she rings me. She was in distress, crying, sobbing.

She had been taken to a police station and charged with dealing in drugs and pills. Well, I went over. She then pleaded with me to do something. If she was charged, there would be no university entrance for her, and Mum and Dad would be devastated. So ...'

'So ... you took the blame?' Samantha guessed.

He nodded.

She sensed his hurt.
    Wanted to just hug this man right now but restrained the urge and waited.

Rico took a deep breath, then stood up straight having been leaning on the balcony wall, 'We never got on. My sister is involved, I'm sure of it. She always could get anything from Mum and Dad.

'I mean, to contact you, the insurance company, and to contact an auction house, all in the same day, and then the theft, she is involved, of that I'm sure. Moreover, she has dragged Mum and Dad into whatever she's up to. This is not good.' His eyes locked onto hers, 'What can I do to help?'

Samantha placed her hand on his arm, just above his elbow, her eyes never leaving his, which she noticed were slightly moist, and said, 'I have a call to make. We'll sort this out, I promise,' her voice soft and caring.

She turned away from him, went over to her bag and took out her phone.

'Hang on,' he said striding past her, 'there's something I want to show you. I'll be back in a minute'

Samantha exhaled, she felt quite emotional.
    Phone in hand, she walked back to the balcony wall, and waited.

Her emotion turned to anger towards a woman she had never met; towards the daughter of these people, who she felt were nice people; towards the sister of the man who had taken the blame for something he had not done and, consequently, now had a police record. Was this why he had left home?

She exhaled loudly, spoke to herself to compose herself, to be professional.

Rico reappeared.

'Like I said, never got on with my sister. She had a mean streak at times. Didn't quite trust her either that day at the police station. So I spoke with her, I got some paper and a pen, and made her write a confession of all that she had done, that she was the guilty party, before I would agree to take the blame.

'She wrote it, I kept it, I have it here.' He handed Samantha the note.

Samantha took the note, read it, then asked, 'Do you have a scanner? And a printer?'

He affirmed he had.

THE PAST;

PERIOD 12

THE YEAR 1821

Captain Jan de Lange stood on the port side of the poop deck. He leaned on the weather-beaten railing of his Dutch built 'East Indiaman' a three-masted galleon and surveyed the scene around him.

The sun was well on its way towards the horizon. It had been a very hot day and he longed for the cool of the evening.

He had stood at this same spot for the best part of two hours now. His longboats had been going to and fro unloading and loading cargo. He had watched with interest as the local fishermen had gone out to sea and come back in their precarious boats they called 'Cabalitto de totora' which means 'little boats of straw'.

He had been fascinated to learn that these boats had been made as early as the third century, and the skill of making them and sailing them had passed from father to son over generations.

Seeing them bringing in their catch, gave him an appetite. He would secure some fish for dinner tonight.

It was December in the year 1821. Captain Jan again let his gaze roam from left to right, taking in the whole panorama, the forests and mountains of the South American continent.

A truly magnificent view. Neither he, nor any of his crew, had ever set foot here before.

They were anchored in the harbour of Puerto Chicama, northern Peru, some fifty miles to the north of Trujillo.

About seven hundred miles to the south, Simon Bolivar and his armies were fighting a decisive battle against the Spanish royalists.

Under the commanding general, Antonio Jose de Sucre, the battle of Ayacucho was in full swing, and their victory would mean independence.

Captain Jan was well aware of the war that was raging. His Spanish was excellent and he had gathered a great deal of information when in their last port.

Standing six foot tall, sporting a now greying beard and whiskers, with what hair was left on his head matching in colour, he was an imposing man.

Lean in build, he had a wiry strength that was greater than his size or age would suggest, and that many had underestimated over the years, particularly when he set about to pull his crew from local pubs and bars.

He had been Master of the 'Willemstad II 'for over sixteen years now. Built in 1748 in Middelburg, Zeeland, the ship was wearing well for its age.

He repacked his pipe, lit it, and looked over to the wooden jetty. There weren't many crates and boxes left to load.

He spotted the young Peruvian, an adventurer, an opportunist. Surprisingly well-educated he had found out. The Peruvian had been there in the morning, as they anchored and came ashore in the longboat.

Three officials had greeted them, and as the captain walked with them to the ramshackle collection of timber huts, stone buildings and a couple of stone and tin sheds that represented the port and customs, the young Peruvian had been standing there, arms crossed, just watching and waiting, with an air of confidence about him that made him even more noticeable.

A little over half an hour was spent with the officials, bartering and agreeing on the price of goods he had brought from Mexico, and setting a price for the cargo he would be taking back there, which consisted mainly of sugar.

Coming out of one of those ramshackle buildings that had been designated as the shipping office, the young Peruvian he had earlier spotted walked across and approached him.

He introduced himself in Spanish and asked how much it would cost to take him, together with his cargo, pointing to several boxes and crates that stood in a row on the jetty, to Mexico.

At this point he explained, that he had been waiting for a little over two weeks now for a ship to call on the port and, as he had also discovered whilst the captain had been in with the officials, this ship would be heading for Mexico. That then was where he wanted to go.

An agreement was soon established to take the young man and his cargo to the port of Acapulco.

The master returned to the ship, gave the orders to commence the unloading, then set about to write up the documentation for both the off-loaded cargo and the new consignment.

Now the day was coming to an end. The sun almost touching the rim of the vast Pacific Ocean.

The last crates were coming on board. These were the ones belonging to the young Peruvian.

His name was Zoltina Huanca, he was twenty-two years of age. His hair was short and almost jet black, his eyes very dark brown and his skin a light brown in colour.

He wasn't very tall, but well-built, and though his appearance was a little rough, he spoke well, not only in Spanish and his own dialect, but he had a good grasp of the English language as well.

He could also read and write.

The cargo he had with him, in the various crates, was in the main mining equipment.

Though Zoltina would have been fully prepared to pay whatever fare the captain would set, he negotiated, offering his skills in carpentry and metal work.

The captain, taking a liking to this young adventurer, agreed he could work for the passage, but would charge a small fee for the shipping of his goods, explaining that any profit from the transport of cargo would be divided up amongst the crew.

And so it was that he was shown to a small cabin on the orlop deck.

This deck ran above the hold and housed the galley, the surgeon's cabin, the sick room, the steward's room, and the quarters for the petty officers.

The carpenters cabin lay in the forward section and Zoltina was pleased to have his own space available.

Throwing his personal belongings inside, he immediately sought the captain and asked who to report to.

The captain had a list of work to be done. He summoned the first mate, who spoke Spanish, and instructed him to show Zoltina around and where to find equipment and so on.

It was a timely coincidence for the Peruvian to have arrived on the scene.

Six weeks earlier, the previous carpenter, along with seven others, had perished in a violent storm. Severe winds, heavy rain and a high swell had battered the old galleon.

The ship had weathered the storm very well, almost, at times, becoming one with the ocean itself as it rode through the troughs, lifting with the swell to the top of peaks of more than twenty metres in height, before plunging down again, a motion that brought discomfort to even the hardiest sailors.

Then, two massive gusts, bringing with them a deluge of water, had swept across decks, in quick succession.

The first knocked several men, working on tying down the sails and securing hatches, clean off their feet, and before they even had a chance to regain their balance or find something to cling to, the second gust and deluge swept them overboard.

The following day, in serenely calm waters, a service was held for the eight crew who had been lost.

Two more days it took for the ship to be once more seaworthy and continue on its journey.

In the light of a half-moon, the Willemstad II weighed anchor and set course for Acapulco, Mexico.

The VOC, which stands for 'Verenigde **O**ostindische **C**ompagnie' more commonly known as the Dutch East India Company, operated from the early 1600s to almost the turn of the eighteenth century and is regarded as the first ever global company.

Captain Jan de Lange, had served as first mate and master on a number of vessels, brought a number of business friends and associates together and they purchased a VOC vessel, the Middelburg II, in 1804.

He was thirty-three at the time and over the next sixteen years he plied the routes to the Far East, shipping French and German wines, copper pots and pans, paper and hand tools to the east and returning with fine silks, porcelain, exotic herbs and spices, tea and ivory.

The large and powerful ship was well manned and well-armed.

The senior crew were all Dutch. Of them only three spoke Spanish. The Master and one other also spoke French and English.

Captain Jan de Lange had a crew of fifty-one soldiers. These men solely responsible for the defence of the ship against marauders.

They had available to them a selection of arms, as well as sixteen cannons and enough gunpowder and cannonballs to fend off the most resolute of pirates.

There were ninety-four other crew members, though this had at one time been as high as a hundred and twenty-three. These were mainly Dutch and Indonesian, with a further mix of Portuguese, French and Greek.

Then, lastly, there were twenty-eight officers, of which nine were senior, bringing the total to one hundred and seventy-five, including, now, the young Peruvian.

Zoltina, in the dim moonlight, familiarised himself with the ship, courteously greeting any and every crew member he came across as the ship sailed on calm seas.

Later, by lamplight, in his cabin, he studied the list of work to be done.

When he lay down on his bunk he fell asleep almost instantly, the movement of the galleon on the water soothing.

The master, now standing on the starboard side of the poop deck, smoked his pipe and watched the mountains of Peru slip by slowly, the moonlight reflecting on the water.

Eight weeks earlier, two weeks before the storm that had taken the lives of eight men, an event took place that would bring this ship and its crew to the waters off the coast of South America.

They had just sailed out of port and were in the waters south of Java, heading for home, when a typhoon struck.

The big old ship coped well. There had been no loss of life, but some cargo that had been lashed on deck had broken free and was lost at sea.

Amidst the fury of the storm, another ship had been spotted.

It was a Spanish galleon, a smaller vessel than theirs, and it was in deep trouble.

The centre mast had snapped cleanly off, the ship was floundering, struggling to remain upright in the high swell.

Captain Jan, squinting through lashing rain, sized up the situation. He could see that it wouldn't be long, before the ship would succumb to the storm and sink.

He made a decision, a hard one, a dangerous one.

Shouting his orders above the wind, which was, thankfully, easing a little, he ordered they come about and draw alongside the Spanish galleon, now only some two thousand feet away.

His crew worked hard, battling the wind and the seas. But slowly they managed to draw nearer the stricken ship. They heard shouts coming from the other ship, perhaps there was a fear that they were about to be boarded.

Captain Jan, using a bullhorn now, shouted in Spanish, as they were within a thousand feet now, informing them of his intention to take them off their foundering ship.

Seven hundred feet, five hundred feet, they manoeuvred closer.

The wind calmed down a little more, the swells still high and the Spanish ship keeled heavily.

The master of the Spanish ship responded, advising he would get his crew ready to cross.

Captain Jan was proud of his crew. Their expertise was great, their courage even greater. They were totally focused on what needed to be done.

Two hundred feet.

Then a large swell lifted both ships and suddenly the gap was less than fifty.

More shouting, more manoeuvring.

Both Captains now shouting orders.

One in Dutch, the other in Spanish.

The rain still lashing down.

When the two ships came together, amazingly, it was a gentle kiss. Then they were side by side.

The next few minutes were all action as the crew from the stricken Spanish galleon, via many ropes, crossed from their ship to the other.

Only when the Spanish master was sure that all the crew was safely across, did he make the crossing himself.

Captain Jan shouted new orders. The ships clung to each other for some moments, then they separated.

It was less than five minutes later, when the Willemstad II was already more than a thousand feet away, that the Spanish ship slipped broadside, then, it's stern sank down, and in the easing rain and calming seas, they watched as it slid completely into the sea.

They rode out the storm and when the seas had calmed, they made for port.

After checking on his crew and thanking many of the Dutch seamen, the Spanish captain was brought to the master's cabin. He thanked the Dutch captain profusely, then, reaching inside his drenched great coat, he pulled out a leather-bound roll of documents.

These, he handed over, explaining what they were.

In gratitude he had given the Dutch master a navigational map of the coasts of South America, along with details of harbours, several ports, and even a few companies which would be helpful in establishing trade deals.

Furthermore, he explained, once in port, he would write a letter of introduction, as well as detailing what had happened and how he and his crew had been rescued despite severe weather conditions.

He suggested to Captain Jan that Acapulco would be a good place to start.

A meeting was held. Captain Jan speaking with his senior officers about the new opportunity that was theirs.

All agreed to set off on this new venture.

Whilst they replenished the lost cargo of silk, Captain Jan wrote a letter of intent to the co-owners back in Middelburg, documenting what had occurred and that their plans now were to establish new trade deals.

Three days later they set sail to head across the vast Pacific Ocean.

Destination, Acapulco, Mexico.

A new crossing, a new route.

Days and days of vast ocean. A maiden journey for the Dutch vessel as it sailed towards the east.

Though the voyage was marred by the storm that took the lives of eight men, upon arrival in Acapulco they were warmly welcomed as the Spanish captain had predicted.

The letter of introduction also proved enormously helpful, for they sold their complete cargo for a vast sum, on top of which they secured a great load to be taken down to Peru with the possibility of bringing a consignment back to Mexico.

Captain Jan had been well content.

Zoltina Huanca performed his duties admirably.

He mixed well with the petty officers and was delighted to be on board.

He had never set foot on a ship before, but had often watched them as a young lad when he and his father and mother and sister lived in Trujillo.

Now, here he was on this old, but still magnificent, galleon.

It was early evening.

The sea was calm, and a cool breeze kept the heat down.

He stood on the top deck, on the starboard side and could just make out a shadowy landscape on the horizon.

He unbuttoned the pocket of his cotton jacket, fished out a leather pouch and slid the contents into his hand. In the evening light provided by the moon in a clear sky, he admired it.

Such a fine painting, such great detail and so small. A beautiful piece of art.

It had been another busy time and he had worked on various tasks throughout the day. Now, after having had a good meal, he had come up here, to this upper deck, in the quiet of the evening to reflect.

What a day it had been; his third full day on board.

His carpentry skills had been well used in several repairs, but he had also helped out a little in the galley and had assisted the doc, who had collared him as he was passing, to help hold down a big fellow who needed a tooth extracted.

Life on board ship sure wasn't dull.

Studying the item he held in his hand he thought back to how it was he now possessed it.

He put the miniature back into its leather pouch, put it back into the pocket of his jacket and leaned on the weather-beaten wooden rail, with the wind in his face. He closed his eyes …

It was four years ago. He had just turned eighteen years old.

He and his dad had moved to live in an old stone building that had once been used for storage.

It had a roof made up of many strips of tin, most of which were covered in rust.

Together they had cleared this structure, and cleaned and scrubbed the floors and beams and posts and rafters.

They'd thrown out the rubble and other bits of odds and ends that had been left there.

Then, three men had arrived from Trujillo with two wagon-loads of material, including sacking, wood, woollen blankets an assortment of tools and a cooking stove, along with food supplies.

The old building was on land that his father had purchased some months earlier.

Situated some eight miles inland from Puerto Chicama, this land parcel contained the reason why he had bought it.

A mine.

A silver mine, though it hadn't been worked for quite some time and had been abandoned.

The price, he convinced his family, was too good a bargain for him to turn down.

His mother and older sister stayed in their home in Trujillo. He went with his father. This was an adventure, and Zoltina loved adventure.

In the first three months, after establishing a place to sleep and eat, and clearing and sorting through the equipment that had been left, together with the three men who had been taken on as labourers and who slept outdoors, they cleared the entrance to the mine.

A further nine months later, when they had been there for almost a year, they had successfully mined a little silver, enough to cover the initial costs, pay the workers and have a little left over for themselves.

This was much to the surprise, but relief, of his mother.

Halfway into their second year, however, the situation in the land changed.

The three labourers left to join the army to fight for their independence.

His father was too old to serve and Zoltina didn't want to leave him on his own, so, the two of them continued to work the mine by themselves.

But not for long.

Four days after the three workers had left, a man appeared. His name was Henry Hopkins.

He was alone. Just him and his horse. He approached and greeted them cordially in Spanish.

Zoltina looked over to his father and sensed that he was somewhat wary, but the man smiled, seemed to be very relaxed and dismounted.

He then took out a map from one of the leather satchels that were strapped on the horse and explained who he was and what he was doing here.

He said he had worked in the mines in Colombia for over ten years.

He had subsequently travelled to Ecuador, spent a few years there and it had been whilst there that he had picked up information and a map on a mine, a silver mine. Their mine.

The newcomer had quickly put them at ease and soon all three were looking at this map.

Zoltina's father then spoke at length as to how he acquired it, how it had been abandoned, and how over the past two years they had worked it.

Henry told them of his success in Colombia, and told them that, not far away, a team of four men, three wagons and six horses were following with some new equipment that would increase the yield of the mine several times over.

He said that it had been his understanding that the mine was abandoned and that no-one owned it, but he reassured them that a deal could be made to benefit all of them, and so, after only a brief negotiation, a deal was struck.

For the next two and a half- years, they worked the mine.

The new equipment that Henry had brought along was fascinating. It was a steam pump designed by fellow countryman, Richard Trevithick, who was also in South America at the time.

Young Zoltina was very interested, and spent many hours with Henry, learning about mining, listening to the many tales of his exploits in Colombia and Ecuador, and also hearing about the man's homeland, England, and the county of Cornwall where Henry was from and where his mining career had begun in the tin mines there.

But, most of all, he learned skills, carpentry skills, metal working skills, how to dismantle and reassemble the steam pump, about its workings and, on top of all that, Henry taught him English.

The pump worked well. Silver was mined at a rate previously unthinkable.

The team of seven worked well together and bonded over the years.

Then, one morning, coming out of the sun. Bandits.

Word had gone around about roaming bands of marauders.

Henry was always vigilant, had been from the very start, as his times in the other two countries had taught him that.

He had with him two long-barrelled shotguns.

Fully loaded and ready at all times.

Unfortunately, three of their team weren't present, having gone to Trujillo for supplies the previous day. It seemed likely that the bandits had been watching and waiting for the right moment.

There were six of them, on horseback. By the time they were less than forty yards away, two of them had been shot dead by Henry.

This confused the remaining four, having perhaps not expected such a quick resistance. But two of them leapt from their horses and came in with knives at the ready.

Zoltina's father stood firm, pickaxe in hand.

Henry had hold of the second shotgun. Two more shots, one more dead bandit on the ground, another wounded.

Zoltina and the other man in their company had still been asleep when they heard Henry call out the warning.

By the time the two of them came bundling from the stone building they now shared as a house, Henry had fired his second and third shot.

Zoltina noticed his father was under attack by two marauders and ran towards the scene.

The other man, spotting the remaining, but wounded horseman charging towards Henry, stopped, aimed his pistol and fired.

Henry reloaded. He ignored the horseman coming towards him, and noticed that Zoltina's father had wounded one of the attackers, but was himself wounded and falling to the ground.

From the corner of his eye, Henry saw help coming from the house, then, heard the shot and quickly glanced to his left to see the wounded horseman thrown from the horse to collapse on the ground.

The remaining bandit saw the youngster coming towards him. It had all gone horribly wrong. He realised he was the only one still standing.

He quickly scanned around him for his horse, but it was nowhere to be seen.

The young lad was nearly upon him, but was unarmed.

Just to the left of him, the old man and his cohort, lay wounded and moaning on the ground.

He stood firm, knife, blood dripping from it, at the ready.

Another shot rang out …

Zoltina wiped a tear away that had begun to roll down his cheek.

He looked around, but there was no-one else, and took a deep breath. It was getting darker, but it was nice just to be here, on deck, the wind in his face, and the sound of the waves as the bow of the ship sliced through them; the ruffle of the sails as the wind pushed the ship through the calm waters of the Pacific Ocean.

Another tear appeared and he wiped it as he continued his reflections of the events that brought him to this point ...

The remaining bandit was blown clear off his feet and died instantly.

Zoltina knelt beside his father, took him in his arms, but realised that there was nothing to be done.

The bandit that lay close by, lay still barely alive.

For some moments Zoltina sat there, holding his father.

By the time Henry had come over and laid a hand on the young man's shoulder, both the bandit and the old man had died.

Henry Hopkins took control of all the arrangements.

It was time to move on.

When the three men came back from Trujillo later that day, he laid out his plans to everyone.

He himself would travel with Zoltina to Trujillo, along with the body of the old man, and take care of all the funeral arrangements. The rest of the team would work two more days in the mine, then, when he returned, they would pack up and leave.

The tension in the country was increasing and the Spanish Royalists were a threat.

On the way to town, riding alongside Henry on the wagon with his father's body in the back, Zoltina spoke little, but was formulating a plan.

The funeral was well attended.

Thanks to the success of the mine, his mother and sister would be well provided for and secure.

After the funeral, he said goodbye to his mother and sister, said it was too dangerous, as a young man, to stay here, and that he planned to travel north.

He travelled back to the mine with Henry.

Henry then set about placing explosives around the mine. Nobody was going to benefit from their hard work, especially not the enemy.

Zoltina set about dismantling the pump and sorting out various tools which he then began to put in crates. Henry had told Zoltina that all the equipment would be his now.

Early one morning, having placed the explosives, and ready to move on, Henry gave Zoltina the honour of pushing the plunger.

The four men said their goodbyes, then rode off, taking two wagons and four horses with them.

Henry Hopkins mounted his horse, then, taking a pouch from his saddlebag, said, 'For you,' handing it down to the young lad.

Henry turned his horse and galloped away after his associates, not once turning to look back.

Zoltina stood and watched until he could see Henry no more. Then, and only then, did he take a look at what was inside the pouch.

Later he mounted his horse, to guide the horse and wagon to Puerto Chicama.

That had been three weeks ago.

He had stored the crates and boxes in one of the customs buildings, sold the wagon and remaining horses, found accommodation and waited.

He was financially secure, had a plan of sorts, and waited …

… It was time to get some sleep. Tomorrow would be another busy day.

He took another deep breath, then left the deck to head for his cabin.

Three more days and they would arrive in Acapulco.

THE PRESENT;

LEIDEN

SUNDAY 24TH MARCH

They rang the doorbell at a little after seven o'clock in the morning. The detectives from Amersfoort, Martijn Vogel and Froukje Boersma.

Downstairs, a local police officer had gained them entry into the lobby area of the block of apartments, and research had identified which apartment they needed to be in.

The door chain rattled; the door opened. A sleepy woman looked quizzical for a moment, then realisation set in, her eyes opened wide, her jaw dropped slightly, and all the colour drained from her face.

Elsa felt herself transfixed. She couldn't move for a moment. Her brain was ticking over, she was desperate to find words to speak, wanted to just slam the door shut, but she just couldn't move.

She could see the confidence on the faces of the two people who stood in the doorway. Her brain slowly registered the words they spoke as they showed their ID cards.

This was it. The game was up. She was caught.

Finally, her feet responded, and she stepped back as the detectives entered.

Finding a voice of sorts, she asked, 'Can I get dressed?'

The female detective said she could and escorted her.

Still struggling to comprehend it all, still struggling for her brain to work properly, she wondered what had gone wrong. How had they found her? Had her parents contacted them?

But even they didn't know where she was. Had it been her accomplice?

The young man, a student of hers, whom she had paid and paid well to force the lock and tamper with the alarm; to travel to the antiques quarter in Amsterdam in the hope of creating the impression that it had been a random burglary, had it been him?

But how? Even he didn't know where she was staying.

So how did they find her?

She dressed, still trying to find something to say, but words wouldn't come.

She suddenly felt cold and scared. All this planning. All this effort. All the details she had so painstakingly planned.

What had gone wrong?

Some minutes later, Martijn walked her down the stairs and into a waiting unmarked police car.

She was still in somewhat of a daze, and other than asking if she could get dressed, she had not spoken a word.

Detective Boersma stayed in the apartment and was joined a minute or so later by the local policeman to search the place.

MEANWHILE IN ROTTERDAM

Samuel was having his breakfast and keeping an eye on the clock on the wall.

He calculated that it would be nearly one o'clock in the morning in Acapulco.

She would be flying out of Mexico late morning for a connecting flight mid-afternoon that would take her to Washington, then a late evening connection would see her fly over the Atlantic to land in Amsterdam early Monday morning. Tomorrow.

He hoped he would receive news in the next few hours, news he hoped was all good, that he could tell her about when she landed.

After breakfast, he listened to the Gotan Project and began pacing the room.

He couldn't concentrate on anything.

He wanted the phone to ring.

Samantha had rung him Friday evening, had brought him up to date on her meeting with Rico, had thanked him profusely for suggesting the idea, and had told him she would e-mail some information on Elsa.

She told him it was most probably Elsa who was behind the whole scam, but, as yet, there was no concrete proof, just suspicious circumstances.

Samuel had listened, heard the emotion in her voice and read the e-mail she sent, which was a copy of a letter; a letter written by Elsa confessing to the crime she committed, the one which Erik, now Rico, had agreed to take the blame for, all those years ago.

Samuel had told her to leave it with him, and then taking down all her flight details, said he would meet her at Schiphol airport on Monday.

He paced around his living room, every now and then stopping to take a look at the world outside. He hoped the phone would ring soon.

Over these past years as an assessor for the auction house in Paris, Samuel had made many connections. The curator of the Maritime Museum in Amsterdam was one of those, and had been all too pleased and ready to assist in his research only the other day.

Another such connection was a man who was the chief of police in Rotterdam.

Time for a return of a favour.

Late Saturday morning he made contact with the man, outlined the whole scenario, his and Samantha's findings, Elsa's letter of confession, his identifying her in Leiden, and the location of an address along with the names of the detectives in Amersfoort who were handling the case.

Leave it with me, the chief of police had said.

Four hours later he called back to explain what would be happening early the following morning, and to wait for a call.

It was the following morning, and he was waiting for a call.

Samuel blew out his cheeks, stopped pacing and checked his e-mails, then made himself a coffee.

The phone rang a little before ten. It was detective Martijn Vogel and he spoke at length.

THE PAST;

PERIOD 13

THE YEAR 1922

Zeta Huanca was both excited and apprehensive, both happy and sad, for she was about to leave home. Not only leave home, but leave Mexico, leave Acapulco, where, just over a hundred years ago, her great-great-grandfather had settled, having arrived there from Peru ...

... It had been a warm and bright morning, when, for the second time, the Willemstad II dropped anchor in the harbour of Acapulco.

Zoltina had been up since the break of dawn and watched the land comes closer and closer. He surveyed the scene from the upper deck, from the place he had often stood in the evenings, and saw the town.

This, he knew, was to be his new home. It felt right; it felt good.

He insisted that he help with the unloading of all the cargo, before finally standing in a stone-built hall that served as the custom hall, with his own selection of crates and boxes.

Captain Jan had been so impressed with the young Peruvian and his hard work that he took him aside later that morning after all the documentation had been done, and gave him a share of the profits from their cargo.

Zoltina thanked him warmly and wished him and his crew a safe voyage as they were to sail for Java in a few days' time.

When that day came, he stood on the dock and watched the ship sail away until he could see it no more.

Within a week he had sourced a buyer for all the mining equipment he had and demonstrated the workings, the opportunities and the work rate of the steam pumps.

The Pachuca Mining Company, which operated a silver mine several miles inland from the port, bought the lot.

Zoltina travelled by wagon with the new owner and spent four days at the mines, showing and teaching the operating system of the steam pump.

Back in town he lodged in a house with several harbour workers, a contact made through the captain, and lived there for almost two months.

With the proceeds of the sale of all the mining gear together with other funds he had, Zoltina set up a small fishing equipment business, and bought an old building right on the harbour front.

He also purchased a small boat, which could be hired out, and bought a house in town, a little uphill from the port.

A very nice house with a great view over the harbour and ocean.

He worked hard and it took time, but slowly the business grew, and he soon integrated into the community and was well liked.

With his carpentry skills and his knowledge of metal work, he was able to supplement his income, and it was on one such occasion that he met the daughter of a prominent citizen whose house needed some attention.

A little over a year after his arrival, he got married.

They had a son, and named him Eduardo, after Zoltina's father who had been so brutally murdered by marauders that fateful day.

They also gave him a second name, Henry, in honour of Henry Hopkins, who had not only been instrumental in the defeat of those bandits, but who had been a huge influence on Zoltina, had taught him so many things, and, had so generously, given him that pouch on the day he left, a pouch containing that most beautiful miniature.

Such a generous gift.

Eduardo got a sister a couple of years later. The business grew, the family grew.

Time passed.

At the age of fourteen, Eduardo began to help in the store and learn the business.

Seven years later he got married and had a son in 1852, who they named Zoltina II.

At this point the business was handed over to Eduardo.

By then, they had purchased another building adjacent to their existing business and set up a fresh fish stall, which quickly attracted a steady trade.

More time passed.

Zoltina II married in 1878 and produced a son, Carlos, who was born two months before Zoltina passed away at the age of eighty-two.

Carlos also carried on with the family business, and by the time he was in charge, they owned seven houses, had a positive influence in the town and were well-liked and respected.

Carlos married Maryanne, an American girl, in 1901 and the following year they had a daughter, Zeta.

Zeta wanted to travel, wanted to see the world, but most of all, she wanted to run.

She loved running.

As a young girl she would run to school, and back, would run to the shops, or to where her father worked in the store.

On a number of occasions, they held running races in the town for the school children. She won them all.

She really could run very fast.

She was excited and apprehensive; she was happy and at the same time, a little sad.

She sighed as she boarded the sturdy three-master.

Two young lads walked behind her, carrying her luggage, an officer walked ahead of her, guiding her to her cabin.

The Huanca family not only had great influence in the town, but over the years they had built up many contacts, particularly in shipping.

One of the houses they owned in town was specifically used to accommodate seamen when on shore leave.

She reached her cabin and the lads deposited her luggage and left. The officer, slightly awkward around this young and attractive woman, explained about the workings of the ship, the facilities, dinner arrangements and such matters, then excused himself and left her to it.

She smiled her thanks which caused him to slightly misjudge the door frame with which he collided on exiting the cabin.

She walked over to the large porthole and looked out. The waters in the harbour were calm.

She spotted the boat that had brought her from the shore as the port was too shallow for larger ships to dock at the pier.

She had said her goodbyes.

To her mother, her father, to her grandparents, to her little brother, who would one day carry on in the family business.

Would she ever see them all again, she wondered?

The previous evening, her father had taken her aside, into his study.

A room which her great-great-grandfather had also used as his study, so long ago.

A large Persian rug was on the wooden floor, covering almost the whole room. Despite its age, the colours were still vibrant shades of red and green, with lines and curves in shades of maroon and gold woven throughout the pattern.

Upon the rug stood a solid oak desk and chair, a small table and a further two chairs. A large bookcase filled most of one wall.

Zeta loved this room and had often sat in one of those chairs to read one of the many books that were on the shelves.

Her father asked her to sit down, went to his desk, opened a drawer and retrieved something from it, then walked around to sit opposite her, a leather pouch in his hand.

He told her a story, a story his father had told him, and had been told by his father before him.

A story about a little painting. He then slipped it from the pouch and showed it her.

She looked at it in wonder as he told the story.

It had been a gift, from an Englishman, whose name was Henry Hopkins.

As she held the small ivory painting, she listened to the story of the mine, the bandits, and of how her great-great-grandfather had left Peru to come to Acapulco.

It was time now, her father had said, for this item to travel once more. Take it, treasure it, and be reminded of home and of your roots.

Zeta came away from the porthole, wiped away a tear and looked around her cabin. She began to sort out a few clothes.

Keep yourself busy, she thought to herself.

And so, just as Zoltina Huanca had arrived from Peru by sea, over a hundred years earlier, Zeta Huanca left by sea.

Her destination was San Francisco.

Later that day, after coming out on the open deck to see her hometown disappear, she returned to her cabin and sat down on her bed.

From a small satchel, she retrieved two things: one was a well-worn bible, the other was the leather pouch.

After she'd heard the story of the painted ivory, she had looked up the relevant passage in the Holy Book and read it through whilst the ivory lay on her lap.

She would not have thought that this very item that lay on her lap as the ship gently moved through the water, had crossed thirteen oceans and seas over the last three-hundred and forty years, and that she, Zeta, was its seventeenth owner, and only the fourth woman.

Time, as it does, marched on.

Three years after her arrival in San Francisco, and having worked in a hospital and continued with her studies, she qualified as a physiotherapist.

An opportunity arose, and she accepted the position offered by a hospital in Seattle.

It was there where she met the man she would marry.

His name was Jonathan Bell, and he was an athletic coach for the Canadian Olympic Team.

Zeta loved running.

While working and studying in San Francisco, she would run nearly every day in a park that was near the hospital. When she moved to Seattle, and here a list of names that she had been given by her father for shipping contacts proved useful as she was able to secure passage on a coastal schooner at no cost at all, she joined an athletic club and began to run on a track.

It was at a friendly Vancouver–Seattle track meet, when one morning, early, before the actual competition began, she was running. She thought she was all alone when, out of nowhere, a man appeared by her side and ran with her.

He said nothing but kept pace with her for two laps.

He then waited for her to finish her run and as she approached, slowing down, he smiled at her.

She smiled back.

They married in Vancouver in 1927.

Zeta attended the Olympic trials later that year and was picked to participate in the 1928 Amsterdam Olympic Games, representing Canada.

Quite an achievement.

She enjoyed the travel, the experience, the camaraderie and, of course, the running.

Zeta ran second fastest in the heats, but, suffering from some pain in her left leg, came fourth in the final. So close to a medal, but proud, nonetheless.

Not long after their return to Vancouver, Zeta was offered a senior post in a hospital in Halifax, Nova Scotia.

Her husband, Jonathan, with his background, qualifications and experience, secured a position as athletic coach of a large school, and so the couple moved from one coast to the other and set up home there.

Sadly, Zeta had a miscarriage and was unable to have more children.

Eleven years after they were married, Jonathan became very ill with cancer.

An operation was necessary, and funds were needed.

She took her husband to Boston for specialist care and, in order to raise money to cover the costs, she made the decision, a hard and tearful decision, to sell the precious ivory miniature.

This was done through the Boston auction house of Franck Huysen & Son in 1938.

The operation was successful, and Jonathan made a full recovery.

THE PRESENT;

SCHIPHOL AIRPORT, AMSTERDAM

MONDAY 25TH MARCH

Forty-seven-year-old Samuel Price had, just over an hour ago, taken his orange and black Citroen out of the garage and driven to the airport.

He was upbeat, longing to tell Samantha all that had happened the previous day. The traffic was heavy coming into Rotterdam, but it was flowing well out of the city, for Samuel, heading north.

There was just a bit of congestion coming into the airport, but he parked the car and was waiting in arrivals in plenty of time.

Checking the board, he saw her flight was due to land in fifteen minutes.

Fifty-seven minutes after landing she appeared, and they spotted each other almost simultaneously. They greeted each other with a hug and the customary three kisses.

'Good flight?' he asked as they walked through the terminal.

'Flights, plural,' she answered, smiling. 'Acapulco to San Francisco, then on to Washington, and finally, the last leg, to here, but, yeah, good flights, all of them.'

Samantha dug her elbow into his ribs, 'Come on, I know something has happened. You're dying to tell me; it's written all over your face.'

He raised his eyebrows and smiled, 'Let's wait till we get in the car then I'll bring you up to date. It's too noisy here, and the car's not far away. You'll just need to be patient.'

As they walked through the busy terminal, Samuel sensed that something had changed. There was an air of confidence in her steps as she walked beside him.

He smiled to himself as he began to realise why there was a change in her. There was a glow to her skin, a sparkle in her eyes.

He figured that she must be in love.

As they walked up the wide ramp towards the car park area, his thoughts went to his late wife, and her words.

Speaking to her in his mind, he said, 'no, my dear, it is not going to be this one.'

Samuel paid at the machine and then escorted Samantha to his car and placed her luggage in the boot.

It wasn't until they had left the multi-storey car park and were on the highway heading for Rotterdam that he began to speak.

'Okay then, here goes.' he said, glancing sideways at her, noticing that, despite her many hours of flying and that she was undoubtedly feeling tired, her eyes were wide open and she was eager to hear the story.

'Early yesterday morning, the police went to the apartment where Elsa is staying. Together, you and I, we had enough circumstantial evidence to warrant an arrest and search.' He again glanced across at her. 'They took her in for questioning, but, as was related to me, Elsa knew that the game was up. The apartment was searched, and they found several paintings.

All copies of pieces by lesser-known artists, though they could still be quite valuable, and ... and I know you must be thinking, "get on with it man", so, yes, they found the miniature.'

He looked at her yet again, smiling broadly.

'Wow, fantastic. What a relief! And? Is the miniature also a fake?' Samantha asked, as she sat back and relaxed in the plush seat of the car driving smoothly along the highway at just over hundred and ten kilometres an hour.

'Yes, it is. Elsa is quite the artist, very talented. She broke down completely, apparently, confessed to all. She has an addiction, gambling, and had gotten herself into a lot of debt.

The odd copy she had painted and sold brought in some money, but not nearly enough, so, she had come up with the idea of an insurance scam,' Samuel said, slowing down a little as traffic was building up as they drew nearer Rotterdam.

'She had, some years earlier, found this old sales document in a market sale, knew it was genuine dating to 1613, and it was this document that gave her an idea.

'So, in her research into art over the years she discovered information about a missing piece of art by Bruegel and decided that this was ideal for her plans.

She had in her possession, a miniature painted ivory, but done by an unknown sailor and worth very little, so she used this, painting over it, and creating the item that we saw.'

'Obviously a very good artist. What a waste of talent! Tell me though, her parents, how did they figure in all of this?'

'Sadly, she led her parents to believe that she was being threatened and held captive, that she had to tell everyone that she was in Greece doing research, and that she needed them to help her, to do as she asked, and, of course, not to reveal this to the police.

She told them a package would arrive, which was the item. They were then to go out one Saturday evening and leave the alarm off.

'Elsa then tempted one of her students, with a cash incentive, into gaining entry, damaging the back door lock and tampering with the alarm in some way.' Samuel slowed right down to eighty kilometres an hour as they approached the outer suburbs of the city.

'Also, it was at her idea to send this same young man to Amsterdam with the items and some other bits, to create the idea of a random theft. Clearly she had put a lot of thought into it,' Samuel said.

'And to contact me, and you, all her idea?' Samantha asked.

'She did her research. She obviously knew her parents' insurance company, so that was easy, then chose my auction house, likely because of its dealings with top-end pieces of art. Apparently she had written very clear instructions that came with the item in the package she sent.' Samuel replied, taking the off ramp from the highway, then said, 'Listen, we'll go to my place first, have some lunch, and you can freshen up, even have a sleep if you want to as I have a guest room available.'

'Okay, sounds good, but tell me more. So, what was her plan?'

'Well, the idea was after you and I had seen and valued the item for it then to be stolen. The instruction was to leave the item on the dining room table.

'Elsa's student accomplice then gained entry to house. By the way, he was given a back door key and was told where the alarm box was and, of course, that it was deactivated. He did his thing with the back door and alarm, creating an impression of a burglary and took the item to Elsa.

After that, it was a matter of waiting as the insurance would have to be paid out within a month.

Elsa had set up a separate account, in which her folks had to deposit the money when they received it.'

'Although Mr and Mrs Wagenaar didn't tell the police about the abduction, and went along with what Elsa had asked them to do, they kept the letter that accompanied the item which had the instructions and the account number in which to deposit the money, which the police now have; another nail in Elsa's coffin really,' Samuel concluded.

He took a moment whilst slowly driving through heavy traffic then continued, 'So, what happens next is that Elsa will go to jail, all her fake paintings are being catalogued, and they will then be destroyed. Others that she has already sold will be tracked as well. They found a ledger describing the various paintings she has forged over the years. As for the young student who assisted her, well, I'm not sure; maybe just get a fine. As for our item, well, unfortunately, but rightly so, it will also be destroyed.'

They drove in silence for a while, getting closer to Samuel's apartment.

Then Samantha spoke, 'Her poor folks. I guess they must be distraught right now.'

'I know, they're decent folk, really.' Sam glanced in her direction, smiling, and said, 'Anyway, tell me, how was Acapulco?' as he drove on.

Noticing his smile, she answered, 'It was a good idea to go there. It helped in the case.'

'Samantha Price,' he said, 'there is more to tell. It's written all over your face!' He noticed she was blushing slightly.

'Samuel Price,' she answered, 'you are a rotter. Yes, there is more. Rico, well, he is a very nice guy. Poor guy, taking the blame for his sister's actions all those years ago, and his parents practically throwing him out. Neither he nor his parents are in a nice place right now.'

Then after a pause, Samantha continued, 'But I'm going to see if I can fix that.'

'That sounds good. Sounds like you have a plan,' said Sam, finding a space for his car not far from his apartment.

'I have. Just thinking it through at this very minute. First though, I'm going to ring my boss, tell him the good news, then I'll take you up on your offer of lunch and, if I may, take a shower and change, so I'll need my case, please.'

'Sure,' Sam answered, shutting off the engine and getting out of the car.

Samantha pressed some numbers on her phone as she got out, and then spoke at length as Samuel took her case from the boot, then walked towards his apartment. Samantha, still talking, walking alongside him.

They walked around to the back of the building, went through a door and got into a small elevator taking them to the first floor.

Samuel was thankful for not having to take the stairs and wondered why it was that women seemed to need so much stuff for a few days. Her case was quite heavy and she had a second piece of carry-on luggage as well as a handbag.

He unlocked the door to his apartment and gestured for Samantha to enter.

She finished her call.

He wheeled her case and carry on bag to the guest room. She followed, deep in thought.

He got towels out for her, then said he would make some lunch.

Sensing she was thinking through some things, he smiled at her and left her to it.

What he had sensed, what he had thought might have happened, was surely true. Samantha had fallen for Rico, and no doubt vice versa.

He sighed.

'Can you take me to Baarn this afternoon?' she asked, appearing in the living room, towelling her hair with one towel, whilst a larger towel was wrapped around her.

'I don't suppose you've got a hairdryer?'

'Yes, of course I can take you to Baarn, and there's a hairdryer, top drawer, left-hand side dressing table.'

She thanked him and disappeared.

Reappearing twenty minutes later, she looked refreshed and every inch the business woman in an A-line knee-length grey skirt, a silky white, long-sleeved blouse with tiny grey dots here and there, a pair of very light tan stockings and her shoes were deep maroon. She had a jacket in her hand, maroon in colour, matching the shoes, which she draped over a leather chair in the lounge, then walked on through to the kitchen-diner area and sat herself down at a small table.

There were bread rolls, various toppings, some cheese and a small bowl of salad, as well as an assortment of condiments.

'Coffee, or juice?' he asked.

'Juice please. Thank you, this looks great.'

Samuel poured two glasses of juice, sat down as well and said 'Tuck in.'

'Well?' he asked after a few moments, his eyebrows raised and a smile on his face as he looked into her eyes.

She looked at him, finished chewing her mouthful then said, 'Rico is a nice man. I, well, I really like him. He was hard done by early in his life. He was hurt.

Thinking that his sister had somehow tricked their parents into some scheme or other infuriated him, poor guy. I want to send him an e-mail, as soon as possible, now I know the full story, then I'll ring him later.

But I also want to visit his mum and dad. I don't know if the police have informed them of the letter his sister wrote, that admission, but I, well, they need to know ...'

'I'm not sure how much they have been told. They must be, as you said earlier, pretty devastated at this time. Talking with them is absolutely a good idea. You've met with their son, who they haven't had contact with for a decade, so it's time to put some wrongs right,' Samuel answered.

She nodded, and he spoke again, 'So, listen, your case is closed, no massive insurance payout, but I still intend to follow any information that may lead to, what we now know for sure, is the real miniature. Interested in helping?'

'Mmm,' she answered. 'It is intriguing, that's for sure, but haven't we hit a dead end? Or are you holding out on me?'

'Yes, and yes again,' Samuel said, smiling at her across the table.

'Yes, we did hit a dead end with Christoffer Rosenborg. I haven't found out any more on him that could be of help, and yes, I have been holding out on something.

I tried to come at it from a different angle. I couldn't do any more about the Elsa side of things, and had to leave that with the police, so, I googled a bit, sort of randomly. I put in details of a miniature, it's original date of around the middle of the sixteenth century, then put in the word auction to see what would come up.'

Samuel got up from the table, went over to his desk, pulled something from it and returned to place it on the table.

'I came across this,' he said, then walked around the table and sat down again, watching her as she read the piece of paper.

'As you can see,' he said, after she had read it and looked up at him, 'it's an auction advertisement from 1938, from an auction house in Boston, called Franck Huysen & Son, and what is listed there is an oil painted miniature, on ivory, possibly attributed to Giulio Clovio, depicting an Italian tower, circa 1600.

'Now, I'm wondering if they simply mistook the scene, didn't recognise it as the Tower of Babel, and that they assumed that, as Giulio was well known for his miniatures, that it might be by him. I think, Miss Price, that this could possibly be our item.'

Samantha read through the note again, then looked at Samuel, 'It certainly sounds like it could be, but how did it suddenly turn up in Boston, Massachusetts, and how many years is it, between this and the last known whereabouts of Christoffer? Any thoughts on that, Mr Price?' she asked, smiling at him.

'Two things,' Samuel answered, 'firstly, that auction house still exists, so I can hopefully follow up on that advertisement. Secondly, I did look at the timeline, the gap. I had Christoffer in Caracas in 1770. This advert was placed in 1938, in Boston, so that's a hundred and sixty-eight years, and a lot of miles geographically, but think about what we have uncovered so far, how far it has travelled, and also keep in mind, that both are seaports, so I feel, rather optimistic.'

'Mmm' Samantha answered, then finishing her mouthful, said, 'or maybe you are clutching at straws.'

'Maybe I am. Still, it's the only straw that's poking out, so have to grab it.'

THE PAST;

PERIOD 14

THE YEAR 1938

Professor Edward Small, known better as Eddie, wandered around the auction room. A rectangular room, with dark wooden beams, high ceilings, three windows on one wall which had been shuttered closed.

Overhead lamps, three rows of four, shone light upon the many things displayed on counters, in glass cases, or placed upon the wooden floor, set up in sections so as to be more easily accessed and viewed by a fairly large crowd of in excess of a hundred people.

The forty-five-year-old professor had been drawn to come here for one thing only. The advertised miniature, possibly, as stated, by the classical artist of miniatures, Giulio.

He had already taken a look at it, displayed in one of the five glass cabinets.

It looked good, but it was not a signed piece, hence the statement, 'possibly by', listed on the card.

Also written on the card was an estimated date of circa 1600, which, Professor Eddie knew would be in the right region for it to be by Giulio.

Not a great provenance at all on this piece. All it had was the name of the seller, Mrs Zeta Bell from Halifax, Nova Scotia.

He walked around the room some more, looking at some of the other pieces that would be auctioned off shortly, but kept an eye on the item he'd come for to see if anyone else might be showing an interest.

He wondered who this Mrs Bell from Halifax was, and what else she might be able to say about this piece.

Professor Eddie was a well-liked and respected lecturer in the field of science at MIT. He was a small man, with a wiry frame, a mop of grey hair, blue eyes behind horn-rimmed glasses, and, inevitably, he wore a tweed jacket over a checked shirt tucked into corduroy trousers with brown shoes.

He settled down for the auction in an adjacent room, where five rows of benches were placed in three sections facing a wooden rostrum.

Forty minutes later, he had purchased it. There had been another bidder, but only briefly. He was pleased with his purchase as he had been prepared to go quite a bit higher.

Initially it had been his intention to find out as much as he could about the piece. He had contacts in the art world both in the Netherlands and in France. However, the situation in Europe was tense.

He was able to obtain an address from the auction house for Mrs Zeta Bell in Halifax, but he never received a letter in reply to his.

Then war broke out.

The Second World War had begun.

Professor Eddie placed the item, wrapped carefully in one of his tweed scarves, in a drawer. He was determined not to have it on show until he found out more about it, but he would have to resume investigations at a later date.

For one reason or another, in the drawer it remained until 1946.

Then, one summer's day, Professor Edward Small flew out of Boston and travelled to Amsterdam.

There he spent a few days with a friend and colleague before journeying on to Rome, Italy.

Prior to leaving, he had done a little research and had found a gallery in Rome whose owner was a renowned expert on the works of Giulio Clovio.

Eddie had written a letter to the owner with regard to the item he possessed and of his intentions to travel and see him.

Eddie Small flew from Amsterdam to Genoa. But he never made it to Rome, never made it to the gallery, nor was he ever heard from again.

THE PRESENT;

BAARN

MONDAY 25TH MARCH

Samantha knocked on the door. It was late afternoon and although it had been overcast all day, it had not rained thus far. The wind was fresh, however, and she felt it as she stood on the doorstep.

She said she would prefer to go in on her own after Samuel asked if she wanted him to come with her. He remained in the car.

Her heart was beating a little faster, and she felt a little apprehensive, but this was a talk she needed to have with them.

The door opened.

Mr Wagenaar looked several years older.

His face was drawn and pale, and his eyes looked tired.

'Oh, Miss Price, er ...' he began.

'Please Mr Wagenaar, I would really like to speak with you and your wife. I am fully aware of what has happened, please,' she said.

'Yes, yes of course, please come in,' he answered, and stood aside to let her inside.

From his car, Samuel saw that they had let her in, 'Good luck Sam,' he whispered to himself, then set about selecting some music to listen to while waiting.

Mr Wagenaar took her through to the dining room, a route she had taken before, one day short of three weeks ago, when she had come to view the item.

He introduced her to his wife.

Samantha shook Mrs Wagenaar's hand and gave her, what she hoped, was a comforting smile.

Like her husband, she looked tired, her face drawn and her eyes a little red.

He invited her to sit down, asked her if she wanted a coffee, which she declined. He then sat beside his wife.

'Let me state, first of all,' began Samantha, looking at each of them in turn across the table, 'that you are in no way to blame for any of what has happened.

I am so sorry for what you have been through, I can't even begin to think how you must feel right now.'

'Thank you, that is very understanding and kind of you,' he replied, his voice a little ragged and broken.

Then, looking at his wife, said, 'The police informed us that you were, well, instrumental in, eh ... resolving this matter?'

'Well, a little. It is my job to investigate when it comes to substantial claims, and, well, under the circumstances, I was rather suspicious of what had occurred. Now, you know the man who came here, the assessor for the auction house, Sam Price?'

'Yes, I remember him, I showed him the piece' Mrs Wagenaar answered.

'Well, we ended up working together, as both of us had suspicions after having been contacted by the police. To be fair to him, it was actually him who was more instrumental in solving this case.'

They sat quietly for a while before Samantha broke the silence, 'You are probably wondering why I have come today; why I wanted to talk with you. It's not about your policy, or your claim, you are still valued customers, and, as far as your policy goes, it will revert back to the original one, no problem there whatsoever.

It's about something else, something the police may not have spoken to you about,' Samantha paused for a moment, again looking from one to the other.

'I met your son,' she said.

They both stared at her, eyes wide open. Mrs Wagenaar's jaw dropped and it was her found her voice, 'You met Erik? Is he, is he alright?'

'He has something to do with this?' Mr Wagenaar asked.

His voice a little harder and his eyes showed a flare of anger, an action confirming to Samantha that the police had not told them of the letter that their daughter had written all those years ago, the confession of the crime that their son had taken the blame for.

Samantha reached over the table and placed her hand over the hands of Mrs Wagenaar, 'Yes, he is fine,' then she looking at Mr Wagenaar, 'No, your son is not involved in any of this.'

'Now,' again looking at both in turn, 'I don't know how much you know about all that has occurred. You obviously didn't know that we had made contact with your son, so, let me tell you.' She released her hold on Mrs Wagenaar's hands.

'As we were investigating this case, Sam, Mr Price, no relation by the way, felt it might be beneficial to talk with your son, hopefully to gain an insight into you. Anyway, Sam searched for, and found, your son, living in Mexico, in Acapulco.'

At this point Samantha reached into her handbag and pulled out an envelope, from which she drew a photograph.

This she placed before them.

'Here is your son' she said.

They both stared at it for some time, almost afraid to pick it up.

Samantha noticed Mrs Wagenaar's eyes welling up and tears dropping onto her cheeks.

'You know, it might be a good idea, to have that coffee, and then I'll tell you more. How does that sound?' Samantha suggested.

Mrs Wagenaar looked up at Samantha and nodded, then got up from the table and set about preparing the drinks.

Mr Wagenaar picked up the photo and just looked at it, not saying a word.

After Samantha had helped serve the drinks, and they were all sat down again, she continued her story, 'He changed his name. He is now Rico, Rico Wagner. He has his own business, a cafe, a lovely little cafe that he calls CafeCasa. It's right on the harbour front, and he lives upstairs. It really is a lovely place.

Though Sam found out where and who he was now, it was me who went to see him. I was in Philadelphia at the time, so it made sense for me to go.'

Samantha paused briefly, looked at them each in turn. They were totally focused on what she was telling them.

'I have to say, I am so glad that I did. Your son is truly a lovely man, furthermore, he was able to help us with the case, and what I am about to tell you next, well, it's quite sad really, but I feel strongly that you should know. I wasn't sure whether the police might have informed you of this, but I know now that they haven't. 'So,' she looked at them both again and took a deep breath, 'well, you know now that your daughter, Elsa, has a gambling addiction. It is why she went to great lengths to think up this insurance scam.

'She was deep in debt, well, Elsa had been in trouble before, but a long time ago. Again she was in debt through gambling, and she was arrested for trying to sell drugs and pills. What happened then is that she called Rico, I mean Erik, and, because she was so afraid of losing out on a university place and did not want to disappoint you, she made a deal with your son, pleaded with him, to take the blame, and, as you know, he did.'

She paused, drank some of her coffee, and let the truth of it all settle in.

Finally, it was Wouter spoke first, 'He never explained. He never said, even when we ...well, told him to leave ...he never said ...'

Mies broke down and sobbed, tears streaming down her cheeks.

Samantha stood up, walked around the table and knelt beside her, placing an arm around her, comforting her, 'What,' Wouter began, 'what was the deal he made, with Elsa?'

'For her not to gamble again,' Samantha answered, looking across at him, 'he also got her to write, in her own words, what she had done, and a promise not to gamble again. It was this letter, this note, that she had written that day at the police station, that helped in obtaining a warrant for her arrest,' Samantha explained, still comforting Mrs Wagenaar.

'In fairness to her though,' Samantha said, 'she didn't gamble for many years, however, apparently about four years ago, she got hooked again. Have you spoken with her yet?'

Again, it was Wouter who spoke, Samantha was still knelt beside Mies, still with an arm around her, 'The police knocked on the door yesterday, spoke to us at length as to what Elsa had done, and why. They also said to us that she did not want us to see her.'

'And Erik?' Mies asked through her tears, looking at Samantha, 'Do you think he'll ever want to speak to us again?'

Samantha looked into her eyes, smiling. 'Oh, I think so. I think he will, he is a good man, and, I have a plan ...' she said, standing up.

'Do you really think he will?' Wouter asked.

Then his wife asked, 'You have a plan?'

'First,' Samantha answered, 'may I suggest one more thing. Don't think that I'm being awful or anything like that, but you need to be there for your daughter, okay?'

Mies Wagenaar stood up, went over to Samantha and gave her a huge hug and a kiss on the cheek, 'We will. Truly, we will, thank you so, so much.'

'Right then, let me tell you my plan,' said Samantha.

THE PAST;

PERIOD 15

THE YEAR 1997

Edward Small was born in the year 1893, in Boston. He had married young and they had a son, born in 1922.

The marriage did not last, they divorced, and he moved back to live with his mother.

He was a qualified teacher and decided to continue studying.

His mother died in 1935, leaving him financially secure, and, as the only child, the house became his. At around the same time, his son, with whom he had little contact, suddenly came back into his life when his ex-wife died in an accident.

Edward hired a housekeeper, organised a child minder, and brought the boy, now a thirteen-year-old, up as best he could.

He got his professorship in 1936 and was appointed as a science lecturer at MIT that same year.

In 1944, at the age of twenty-two, the boy, Carl, joined the war effort in Europe.

He returned in 1945.

In the summer of 1946, his father, Edward, set off on a journey to Rome, but went missing and was not heard from again.

Carl, after a hearing the court ruling, and after seven years had passed, inherited the house in Boston.

He married at the age of thirty-six and they had two children, both boys, early on in their marriage, then a late comer, a daughter, was born to them in 1972 ...

It was now the year 1997.

Christina was twenty-five years old, and in a short space of time a lot happened. Her older brothers were married and both had recently moved away, one to Dubai, the other to Australia.

She had never been close to either of them, probably due to the age difference.

Then, not long after they had left to their respective destinations, her mother had packed her bags and left her father, moving to Florida.

She had not been close to her either, and quickly lost contact.

Then her father died suddenly, and Chrissie, as she preferred to be known as, was devastated.

What was even harder for her was that neither brother made the effort to come to the funeral, nor was her mother there.

When she stood by his grave, the last person left, she wondered, through her tears, how a family of five had so quickly disintegrated, leaving her now quite alone.

Three days after the funeral:

Chrissie had taken some time off work. She walked up the path, then up the steps to the door, unlocked and opened it, and stepped inside what was now, her house.

Closing the door, she stood still for a moment. She loved this house; had been born here; grew up here.

It had only been recently, less than two years ago, when she had left home and moved into an apartment on the other side of town, but she had regularly spoken with her father on the phone or called in to see him.

Yesterday, at the solicitors, she had been given all the paperwork, the documents. The will had been read to her. Her father had left everything to her.

Nothing to her brothers or their family. Between them they had three children, her niece and two nephews, but nothing was left for them.

There was nothing for her mother either; everything came to her.

She figured that something must have happened in the family that she knew nothing about, hence the non-attendance at the funeral.

She had called her brothers a few hours after he had died, and the conversations had been brief, and both asked for her to e-mail the details of the funeral, which she did. But there had been no communication since.

More or less the same happened with her mother, a sympathetic response, but she had said she would not come to the funeral before hanging up.

Chrissie now stood in the foyer. The house felt empty and cold.

Taking a deep breath, she composed herself. She looked up at the wide staircase.

It was a substantial house. It had a high-ceilinged entrance from which the first door on the left led to the dining room which in turn led to the kitchen, the first door on the right directly opposite led to a very large front room, or lounge, which occupied the total area of that side of the house, with double doors leading to the back garden.

Straight ahead a staircase curved slightly to the left, and beside it to the right a corridor ran further into the house from which were doors to a cloakroom, a cupboard, another door to the kitchen, and another door that entered the back of the lounge.

Upstairs were five, good-sized bedrooms and three bathrooms.

Chrissie thought for a moment about where to begin. There were so many thoughts running through her mind now: what had happened to her family?

Why had the others just left?

What had happened between her father and mother?

She decided to go upstairs first.

Another thought came to mind as she climbed the carpeted staircase.

When younger, she had, on several occasions, asked about her paternal grandfather who had lived in this very house, but, for whatever reason, she was not given much information.

All her dad told her was that he had gone to Italy shortly after the war, and had never returned.

Though this had made her curious, she had been unable to unearth anything further. Maybe the house might give her some clues.

She was surprised to find the house in a sad state upstairs. The master bedroom and en suite bathroom was clean and tidy, but the other rooms were dusty and messy, with lots of stuff, clothing, books, ornaments, tools and various lamps, strewn all over the floors and beds.

Chrissie set about sorting things out, beginning with what was once her own bedroom. This she intended to use straight away. She worked tirelessly for a day and a half, sifting through what to keep, what to throw away, and what to give to charity.

She thoroughly cleaned the second of the three bathrooms, for herself, and used one of the bedrooms for storage leaving the master and en suite untouched.

It was towards the end of the second day in the house. She rummaged through a large cupboard in the hallway, which held a couple of old vacuum cleaners, several boxes of cleaning equipment, a box of tools and a box with old towels and aprons and stuff. As she moved the last box out and began emptying it, she came across a wooden box.

Her eyes opened wide in surprise as she pulled it from the large cardboard box.

This was beautiful. It had an ornate lid, was about thirty centimetre in length, around eighteen centimetres in width and some eight centimetres deep.

Never before had she seen this box.

Excitedly, she took it through to the lounge, sat down and opened it.

Inside were two old diaries, a couple of old coins, a small notebook, several certificates, and a couple of letters.

She noticed one of the letters had an Italian stamp on it, and noticed the date stamp across it, 1946.

On the back of the envelope she read that it had come from an art gallery in Rome.

Her heart was beating noticeably faster as she opened the envelope and began to read the letter.

It stated that they were looking forward to meeting him, this being her grandfather Edward, and to examine the item he was to bring to ascertain if this was indeed a miniature by Giulio Clovio.

Chrissie read through the letter again.

At last, she thought, a clue as to what may have happened to her grandfather, but what was all this about a miniature, and who was Giulio Clovio?

Two weeks later, Chrissie moved into the house.

She had sold her apartment, a sale that happened very quickly, had disposed of the rubbish, given heaps to charity, and had totally revamped the master bedroom which she now used for herself.

Furthermore, she had a company come and deep clean the whole house.

Then, with the help of one of her grandfather's diaries, she contacted a housekeeper who had previously worked here, who had worked for her grandfather for over ten years, and asked if she could meet with her.

Chrissie found out that the housekeeper was living in a residential home not far away and was now eighty-four years of age.

She would ask her if she knew anything about the ornate wooden box.

A week later, she took more time off work and booked a flight to Rome.

THE PRESENT;

ROTTERDAM

MONDAY 1ST APRIL

A week ago, he had collected Samantha from the airport; had brought her up to speed with all that had occurred the day before.

A week ago, he had driven her to Baarn in the afternoon, where she spent some time talking with the Wagenaars.

A week ago, he had taken her, with all her luggage, to the central train station in Rotterdam in the evening, where she had boarded a high-speed train to Antwerp.

When saying goodbye, she had thanked him for everything, told him that she would be in touch, told him that she would be interested in the further search for the item, but that, in the meantime, she had another affair to sort out, an affair of the heart.

And with a beaming smile had waved goodbye.

That evening, upon returning home, an e-mail was awaiting him.

He had, the day before, sent a request to the auction house in Boston, for further information on a sale, dating back to 1938.

He read the response.

Sitting relaxed in the comfy leather chair by the window, sipping his last coffee for the day, he thought about his next move, though found it hard to concentrate as he also thought about Samantha.

He had, at one point, wondered, about her, about the possibility of a romance. He liked her, she was attractive, though quite a bit younger, but, they, whoever they are, say that love knows no boundaries.

Still, he sensed there was no such feeling from her, and he could very well see that she had truly fallen in love with a man he had found and who he had strongly suggested she visit.

So, he said to himself, that was that. She was not the one for him. But what of the continued search for the lost miniature? He had another lead, in Boston.

Finishing his drink, he got up and sat at his desk. Time to organise some travel.

Just as his boarding card was printing out, for a flight the next day, his phone rang.

AMSTERDAM

Sophie Louise Pontiac was running.

Well, not quite running, half running, half walking fast. Every now and then slowing to a normal walk, clutching her side.

She was scared. She was lost. She was wounded.

Not badly though, a scratch, a cut from a knife. The blade would have cut in a lot deeper had she not reacted as quickly as she did.

Her situation would be a lot worse, had she not quite acrobatically manoeuvred away from her assailant and had managed to escape.

She knew she was somewhere near the Ajax football stadium, but had taken several turns and had lost her direction.

The street she was now in was quiet. It was a wide street, tram rails running through the middle, but, at a little after eight thirty in the evening, on a Monday, there were few people around.

She finally slowed completely to a walk.

A tram trundled by and it startled her. She hadn't even heard it coming.

Her right hand clutched her left side.

Earlier, she had stopped briefly after her escape to ram her scarf under her blouse to stop the bleeding and had ever since had kept her hand in place.

It was hurting, but she knew it wasn't deep.

She had a phone, but she didn't want to call the police, or an ambulance.

She had to get away and think.

The tram ahead turned, and she saw it enter a large building. A depot.

Possibly a place to seek refuge she wondered as she walked on.

She had her phone, but had lost her handbag. They had that, along with her passport, her house keys, and her credit cards.

Two of the three big sliding doors to the large depot were open. Though she could see quite a number of trams, as she walked past the doors, she saw no-one.

She stopped, turned back, then just walked inside, slipping around to the left, and took in her dim surroundings.

She heard voices, but still saw no-one. Somewhere music was playing.

Ahead of her were stairs up to what she assumed would be offices.

Taking the steps, her heart now audibly pounding in her ears, she stopped on the landing, chanced a look over the railing down below, but could not see anyone.

So far, so good. The first of the three offices along the landing was in darkness, the second had a light on, but as she strode past the window, she noticed it was empty. The third was again in darkness, she tried the door. It opened.

She sat herself on the floor below the window.

Gaining control of her breathing, she released her grip on her side and reached for her phone. The screen lit up as she pressed a button and she hurriedly bent forward to diminish the glow it was emitting in the office.

Scrolling for a while, she found the right number, and dialled.

After the call, she re-applied pressure on her wound, then tried to relax, and hoped that no-one would come into the office.

She waited.

Thinking back to the very first time she had met Samuel Price. Nearly four years ago now, in Paris ...

His casting a doubt on the Gauguin she was sure was genuine had drawn a vehement argument from her, in no uncertain terms, stating her qualifications and reputation and challenging his.

When later he had come to Paris with documents and photographs, and the Gauguin, after a fresh re-examination, had indeed proved to be a fake, it had left her shaken, angry and embarrassed.

But thinking back, he, Samuel, had been quiet spoken, and had not been in any way arrogant or smug.

He had left that day, and she had not seen or spoken to him since.

But, one thing she wanted to do was to follow through. Who faked the Gauguin, and where was the real one, the one once in the possession of his great-grandfather?

Right now, wounded, hunted, and feeling more than a little apprehensive, she was glad that, before her trip to Amsterdam, she had put his number in her phone.

Glad too, that he had been home, and even gladder that he was on his way.

She closed her eyes. In the vast depot, she heard music, voices and machinery. Since she had been there, three more trams had arrived to be housed and cleaned overnight, ready for another busy day tomorrow.

Traffic was reasonably light, and the Citroen easily touched a hundred and thirty kilometres an hour as he drove smoothly in the fast lane.

The call had lasted barely over a minute.

The French woman had sounded anxious as she whispered her predicament. Being chased, wounded, and hiding. No police, could he come and get her.

He knew where she was, knew this particular tram depot.

207

He himself had, in his late teens, worked at the very place for a few weeks, picking up extra money cleaning the trams.

He turned off the main highway, decided to go through Amstelveen and reach the depot from that direction, assuming the traffic would be lighter.

Chased, she had said, by whom? What had she got herself into?

Wounded she had said, how bad? And no police, what was she up to?

Reaching the depot, he parked close by, and noticed that one of the three main sliding doors was still open. He sent her a text message.

Sophie's phone lit up, in the dark room she felt it was blindingly bright and hoped no one would notice. She read the text. 'I'm outside.'

She put her phone away, got up and was about to exit the office when she heard talking. Close by and getting closer.

Daring to take a peep through the window, she saw two men climbing up the stairs, towards the offices.

Holding her breath, she waited.

Exhaling audibly, she was relieved as they had entered the office next door.

She opened the door; all clear.

Walking swiftly by the other two offices, praying no-one would spot her or come out at that point she reached the stairs. Her shoes made more noise on the metal treads than she wished, but so far, so good.

Then her heart stopped as a man appeared from outside. He turned and spotted her.

Again, she exhaled audibly and quickened her steps towards him.

It was the Dutchman; it was Samuel.

Sam moved towards the woman, put his arm around her and steered her from the building. She was extremely pale and as he held her, he felt her tremble.

Saying nothing he walked her to the car, opened the door for her and helped her into it.

Seeing her clutching her side and noticing the bloody hand, he secured her seat belt before quickly moving around the car to the driver's side. He got in, started the engine, secured his own seat belt and drove away.

Glancing at her, he said 'No police, what about a hospital?'

She looked at him. A little colour was back in her cheeks, her brown eyes looked large, like a startled deer in the headlights. 'No' she whispered.

Sam drove on, heading back more or less the same way he had come. She would tell him what it was all about in due course he figured.

He look across at her again.

She sat almost motionless, and he noticed tears on her cheek.

Sophie finally began to relax. She was safe now. Tears had appeared and were rolling down her cheeks. She let them. She was relieved and grateful. He was quiet and drove on. She appreciated his silence.

She thought back to just over four years ago, when she had first met him.

The Gauguin, the wretched painting that she had deemed genuine, the painting that had now placed her in danger.

When they had first had the painting re-examined by another expert, and it had been judged a fake, the first thing the auction house needed to do was to contact the seller …

Sophie was tired. She felt safe, she fell asleep as Sam cruised homewards.

'Come on Sophie, we're here,' Sam said. He had opened her door and was leaning over to release her seat belt.

She stirred with a start, was momentarily disorientated, then recognised him and smiled.

Sam helped her out of the car which he had parked back in his garage, then, after turning off the lights and locking the garage, he walked her up the path towards his apartment.

He persuaded her to show him the cut, which was on her left side, a gash of about two inches long, but, thankfully, not very deep, and it had stopped bleeding.

'Go and have a quick shower,' he said to her, taking hold of her ashen face with both hands, looking into her eyes. 'It will possibly bleed again, but that's okay, it is not a deep cut, so I'll get bandages. Come, I'll get the shower ready for you.'

Sam took her to the en suite of his bedroom, left her to it, and went to the other bathroom where he kept an assortment of plasters, bandages and various ointments.

Selecting what he needed he returned to the bedroom just as she appeared.

A quick shower indeed.

Her dark hair framed her still pale face and she stopped before him, a large blue towel wrapped around her waist and a smaller towel she held against her upper half, leaving her midriff bare.

The cut, though looking red and sore, had not started to bleed again.

'Sorry, this will no doubt sting a little,' he said, as he took a cotton ball and dabbed antiseptic over the wound.

She winced a little and he saw her stomach muscles tighten.

He stood upright again, looked into her brown eyes and said, 'Just stand straight, then I'll put a plaster on it, then a bandage which I'll wrap around.'

She nodded ever so slightly, and Sam set about to do what he had said, thinking about this French woman he was attending to. She was a little taller than he remembered, around five foot seven, also, he noticed, she was pretty fit.

The last time he had spoken to her, she had been angry, and somewhat subdued, and the first time he met her she had been so fiery, so defiantly stubborn, and, he remembered at the time thinking, that she was so typically French.

Now, as he placed the plaster across the nearly two inch cut, and proceeded to bandage her, he felt more compassion towards her. She was rather attractive, had gorgeous brown eyes and her face was so much nicer than he recalled.

Sophie had closed her eyes. The antiseptic had stung more than a little. But she felt his hands as he placed the plaster. They were warm and she sensed a tender touch and as he wrapped the bandage around her, totally absorbed in what he was doing, she felt him close, felt his breath. The man she had vented her anger and rage at had become her knight in shining armour.

He had come; he had asked no questions; he had been caring and patient.

Sam finished, 'So, that's done, now. I'll get you a robe, then make you a hot chocolate. How does that sound?'

It was nearly midnight.

Dressed in a bathrobe, Sophie sipped from a mug of hot chocolate and, looking at Sam, who sat expectantly across from her.

'Tell me everything', he had asked her, after she had completed drying her hair and dressed in the robe he had produced, arriving in the kitchen as he was preparing the drinks.

'Well,' she began, 'when you came that day, with the papers, the journals belonging to your great-grandfather, and the photos. Well, after you had gone, we brought in another expert to look at the painting. At first he was really quite indecisive, but in the end did think that it was most likely a forgery.

So, then I contacted the owner. Needed to speak with her with regard to the painting, to further establish its provenance.

211

She said she was away the following day, but that I could see her the day after.

So, I went there.

'But there was no-one home. I looked through the windows. Now I was getting suspicious.

I checked with neighbours. The small house was in a quiet residential area, people notice things. Found out the house belonged to an older man, though he was often away to visit with his sister.

Then there was the blond, much younger than him, kept much to herself, but had left the previous day. A holiday it was thought, as she had packed several cases in the car. But, not having enough proof of any wrongdoing, I could not get a search warrant, so, a dead end.

The papers she had signed and the painting ownership papers had her as a Miss Steffie Baertjens, but as no other information was found about her, again, a dead end.'

Sophie took another sip of her hot chocolate. Her face not quite so pale any more, but she was looking tired. She then continued, 'It was not until two days ago, as I was beginning my holiday and I was tidying up, I found the notes which I had made at the time and all of a sudden, I began to wonder.

Your ancestor purchased the painting in Copenhagen. This part I feel checks out perfectly.

Gauguin painted in Tahiti at the time, sent his work to his wife in Copenhagen, she was involved with the diplomatic circles and so was you great-grandfather, so, that ties in correctly.

'He, your great-grandfather, buys the painting in 1898, then sells the painting in Paris in 1908. Again all the details are correct. I do not know how long he was in Denmark, or when he came to Paris, but the paperwork is correct. Now I have the name of the person who purchased it in 1908, a Mr Jan Smettens.

Then the picture is sold, in Amsterdam, many many years later in 2015, to the now missing lady, this Miss Baertjens.

I should have explored deeper at the time, but I was, well, a bit arrogant. I thought I knew it all, so, though the early provenance is good, I should have delved deeper as to where this painting was from 1908 through to 2015. That's well over a hundred years.'

Again Sophie paused, drank a little, closed her eyes briefly as she felt where she had been cut when she moved slightly.

'So, to recap then, the painting your great-grandfather sold in 1908, was, no doubt, the real thing, however, I'm sure now that the painting sold in 2015 was not.

I told myself to do my work properly, and decided to investigate again.

Yesterday I came to Amsterdam. I brought your phone number with me, from the records in the office, in case I needed your help in translation.

Good thing I had it.'

She looked up at Sam. Sighed deeply and was beginning to feel very tired indeed. The warm drink was helping to relax her.

Samuel had listened, had taken in all she had said, and had looked into those brown eyes.

Her voice had been soft and calm, her demeanour relaxed, and she had spoken all this time with a certainty and a confidence which was far from her outburst and vehemence in the Paris office that day, over four years ago, the day his wife had passed away.

'So,' she continued, 'I went to the auction house, got access to their records. They were very helpful, and I found an address.

This evening I went there, stupid I know, to go there by myself.

I rang the bell and a young man answered. I asked to see Miss Steffie and he let me in. Then it all went wrong.'

Sam waited, whilst she paused and drank the last of her hot, though probably not so warm by now, cocoa.

'I was escorted into a room, a large lounge. Next she appeared, spoke in Dutch briefly, then walked right up to me, grabbed my head with her hand and with her face this close,' Sophie placed her hand inches from her nose, 'said, "How did you find me?", she didn't wait for an answer. Said, "You are a problem," then she spoke to the young man in Dutch, and left the room.

'I was pretty scared then. This guy, about early twenties I think, came up to me, so, I kicked him, hard as I could, then ran towards the nearest door, I had put my handbag on a nearby table, but couldn't go that way. I reached the door, but it was locked. I turned and he was coming towards me again. This time he had a knife.

'I moved forward then, towards him, and, as he slashed with the knife, I jumped back. I could feel he had cut me, but he was off balance, so I kicked him again.

'This time I connected much better and he crumpled to the floor, cursing and yelling. I then ran for the other door, the way clear now; still couldn't get to my bag. I opened the door wondering if she was right behind it, but she wasn't.

There was a corridor straight ahead. I ran down it, then saw a small kitchen through a door on the right, saw a back door, saw a garden beyond, turned and headed for that.

The door was locked, but the key was in it. I turned the key, thinking that the guy must be just about right behind me now.'

Sophie looked quickly at Sam, her face flushed as she was reliving the experience.

'Then, as I was about to go through this back door, I noticed a sort of wallet on the bench. I took it, having no money now and no way to get back to my handbag, a spur of the moment thing. Amazed I was even able to think about it really, then ran through the garden, climbed over the fence and ran and ran for a little while.'

Sophie closed her eyes again briefly, then continued, 'Then I stopped, dared to turn, but no-one was behind me. I now felt that my side was bleeding, used my scarf to hopefully stop it. 'Then I discovered what it was I had picked up from the kitchen bench,' Sophie said. Reaching into the pocket of the bathrobe, she drew out the wallet, and handed it over to Sam who opened it.

Sam saw, it wasn't a wallet, it was an ID, a badge, with a photograph showing a man's face, name and details. The badge of the Amsterdam police force.

'I see your reason for not going to the police,' he said, holding the ID in his hands and looking at her. She was paler again, looking very tired.

'I continued to run, as best I could, then entered this tram depot, hid in one of the offices up the stairs you saw me coming down, and, that's when I called you'

Sam was quiet for a moment. Thinking.

Sophie, finding it harder to stay awake now, waited.

'Okay,' he said a last. 'Come on, I'll show you the guest room. You need to sleep. Let me think this through and we'll make a plan tomorrow, or actually, today,' looking at the clock on the wall which told him it was a quarter after midnight.

Tuesday 2nd April

It was late afternoon.

He had arrived in Boston.

He took cab to his hotel and, after a refreshing shower, had set off to locate the address the auction house had given him.

The address of a Mr Edward Small, who had purchased the item about which he had enquired.

A computer search on Edward Small had been fruitless, so to Boston he had to go, and after listening at length to Sophie, and already having booked his travel, he made a plan for her.

215

Unable to sleep yet, and still mulling over what had happened to Sophie, who was now fast asleep in the guest room, he made up his mind as to what to do next.

The buzzer for his apartment rang. Sam headed for the communication phone on the wall, and, having identified the caller, buzzed the lobby door open.

Moments later he opened the door to let Detective Martijn Vogel in.

He had called him at home, just before seven thirty this morning, and had quickly outlined the situation. The detective told him he would come over straight away and left his home in Amersfoort fifteen minutes later.

'Thanks for coming so quickly,' Sam said, shaking his hand. 'Coffee is ready, come on in. She will be through soon; just in the shower at present.'

Martijn took off his coat, opened his leather satchel and withdrew some papers, saying, 'Thanks by the way. You and Samantha gave us what we needed to close the Wagenaar case.'

Sophie entered the lounge from the hallway and stopped as she noticed the newcomer.

'Morning Sophie' Sam said, 'this is Detective Vogel.'

'Good morning,' he said, standing up and extending his hand, 'please, call me Martijn. Sam rang me early this morning, and told me what happened to you yesterday. Please, take me through everything.'

An hour and a bit later, they said goodbye to the detective.

Sam then produced an old laptop for Sophie to work on, gave her a some cash so she could purchase some clothes as it was deemed safer for her to remain in his flat for the time being. After handing over a spare set of keys to the apartment, Sam grabbed his travel bag, already packed, and set off to catch his flight.

She had, before he opened the door, walked up to him, placed her arms around his neck and drawn herself up to him, kissing him on the lips.

Sam boarded a flight just before 1pm, and arrived in his hotel just after 4pm after a nearly eight hour flight.

Flying high over the Atlantic, Sam thought about his late wife; thought back to the day she had passed away; thought back to the events at the Paris Fine Arts Auction House that day.

Again, recalling those words she had said to him, her last words, when she had said to him, 'Go and find someone to love'.

And how he had thought that day, with the French woman berating him, that it sure wasn't going to be her.

He smiled, as he thought about her so differently now. Still savouring that kiss she had planted on him this morning.

Map in hand, Samuel left the hotel and set off. It was a cloudy and quite chilly afternoon and as he walked along. He wondered who might live at this address today, and would they know of a Mr Edward Small who had lived there way back in 1938.

He turned into the street, which he had noticed wasn't that far from the hotel on the map the receptionist gave him.

It was a well-established wide avenue, with a row of mature trees along one side.

The houses were substantial in size, well-kept and, without a doubt, would be rather expensive.

He estimated, judging by their style, that they had been built in the early twenties.

Finding the correct number, he walked up the short path and up the steps.

He pushed the bell.

Somewhere inside he heard a bell chiming.

Waiting, taking a quick look around the street, he hoped that someone would be in.

He heard footsteps.

Moments later, the door opened. A woman stood there, 'Yes?' she asked.

She would be in her late thirties to early forties, Samuel estimated quickly sizing her up. Blond hair tied in a ponytail, glasses, obviously for reading as they were perched on her forehead. She had a pleasant face and green eyes that were focused on him expectantly.

'Er, hi, 'Sam began. 'I have this address as that of a Mr Small, who, used to live here, I mean, way back, in 1938. I wonder, I know it's probably a long shot, but do you have any knowledge of that family?'

She tilted her head, ever so slightly to one side, her eyebrows knitted together for a moment, then asked, 'What is it in connection with?'

He liked her voice, liked her accent.

He noted that she wore jeans, a floral blouse under a knitted pullover, and her feet were in a pair of casual shoes.

'I am trying to track down, a piece of art that Mr Small purchased at an auction, here in Boston, in 1938.' Samuel saw no reason not to tell of his intentions.

'After all these years?' she asked, frowning slightly. 'Was it stolen or something?'

There was something in her voice, in her eyes, eyes that he found rather lovely, that triggered the thought, 'You know him, don't you, a relation?' he asked, looking steadily into those green eyes.

She too, having summed him up and going on instinct, decided on the direct approach, 'Professor Edward Small,' she answered, 'was my grandfather, and the piece of art you refer to, would it be a miniature oil painting on ivory?'

It was Samuel's turn to raise his eyebrows, and simply answer, 'Yes.'

'Come in' she said, stepping aside to allow him to enter, then she gestured for him to go through the door on the right, closed the front door and followed him.

He sat down at her request, in a comfortable-looking plush armchair, as she perched herself on the edge of a two-seater couch, looking intently at him, then said, 'Okay, spill, what's this about?'

'It's quite a long story, but here goes ...' and Samuel spoke at length.

He told her everything from the moment he had valued the item for auction, an item that in the end proved to be a fake, to a trail of the real item, the written proof that they, and here he mentioned the insurance investigator Samantha, had found, right up to the moment he had discovered an account of the auction house, here in Boston, where, her grandfather he now knew, had purchased it, and he had got this address from them.'

She listened attentively, fascinated by the whole story.

When he had finished, she blew out her cheeks, and sat herself back on the couch. 'Wow,' she said, 'where were you twenty years ago? I could have used your help.'

Sam looked quizzically at her. She elaborated, telling her own story about finding the letter from the art gallery in Rome, that her grandfather had been headed there, along with the miniature, which he thought was by an artist called Giulio.

Apparently, the man at the gallery was a renowned expert on this artist.

So, I flew there to check it out, now this was back in 1997. The gallery still existed, they rummaged through their old correspondence and found the letter my grandfather had sent, as well as a copy of their reply, which I had with me.

But there was a notation that he never arrived there.'

Then, after a brief pause, she said,' In fact, he totally disappeared, and was never heard from again.'

'Goodness,' Sam replied, 'and no clues at all as to what happened to him?'

'Sadly, no. I flew back home, disappointed as you can imagine, but there are no clues at all as to what happened to him.'

Samuel thought it all through: her story, the gallery, the letter.
Then asked her, 'Your grandfather, you said he was a professor, what did he do? What was he like?'

Deciding she liked and trusted this man, she stood up, moved towards him and extended her hand, 'Chrissie, Chrissie Small' she said.

Taken a little by surprise at her movement, he scrambled out of the comfy chair to stand and shake her hand. 'Pleased to meet you, I'm Sam, Sam Price.'

She slightly tilted her head to one side again, and asked, 'Your English is very good, but, you're not English?' then sat herself back on the edge of the couch.
Also sitting down again, 'Dutch,' he answered, 'born in the Netherlands, Dutch mother, English father.'

'Dutch?' she asked, then suddenly stood up again. 'Goodness, I've just remembered, Grandfather knew a Dutchman, from his MIT days, I recall reading about him in one of Granddad's diaries. Let me find it.' As she headed for the door, she added, 'won't be long,' and left the room.

It was in fact almost ten minutes later when she reappeared.

She was flushed with excitement, 'You'll never believe it,' she said, a little breathless as she had bounded down the stairs, and sat herself down on the couch again, 'I just found this letter. It was inside this diary, and slipped out as I grabbed it. Can't believe I never saw it before, look,' she reached over and handed him the letter.

Reaching forward, Sam took the letter as she said 'It's from that Dutchman I mentioned, but this letter says, well, read it for yourself, I read it upstairs.'

Chrissie, sat forward, elbows on her knees, hands clasped, and watched as he read the letter. Her mind was whirring. Would she be able to find out what happened to her grandfather after all? With the help of this man, perhaps.

Sam read the brief letter. Aside from some pleasantries, it stated that he, his name was Adriaan Molenaar, was looking forward to meeting Eddie, that he would be at the airport to greet him, and it gave a date in 1946.

The letter was posted in Amsterdam.

'Okay,' Sam said, handing the letter back to her, 'and you are excited, why exactly?'

'Because I assumed granddad went to Rome directly. He never got there, but now I know he must have flown to Amsterdam first. Hang on, back in a minute,' and again she leaped up from the couch and left the room.

She was back within a minute with her laptop. She sat down and opened it, and after a moment, began typing.

Samuel watched her. He liked her and studied her as she was focused on the screen, scrolling through whatever she was looking at.

She would be around five foot six, and wore no rings on her fingers.

Her face was still slightly flushed, and he smiled as he noticed she had kicked off her shoes and her bare toes were curling and uncurling on the soft rug.

'Well I never, 'she said, pushing her reading glasses back on her forehead and looking at Sam, her green eyes bright and almost sparkling with excitement. Then sitting back a little, said, 'You asked me earlier who my grandfather was and what he did. Well, he was a professor of science, a lecturer at MIT, and he was almost always reading one book or another. He quite liked art, but was specifically interested in ivory. Loved the Japanese carvings, what are they called again? Netskis, or something?'

'Netski, or Netsuke, Japanese miniature carvings, very nice,' Sam replied.

'Right, there's about a dozen or so in a cabinet upstairs,' Chrissie continued, 'so, it made sense that he was drawn to this painted miniature on ivory. Well, this chap, this friend of his in Amsterdam, he was an art expert specialising in old Dutch masters. He has several books of his findings to his name, and a catalogue of those findings. He died in 1966. I think granddad must have wanted to show him the miniature before going to Rome. That would make sense, don't you think?'

'Absolutely,' Samuel responded, 'more than you think. Your grandfather obviously was drawn to miniatures, Japanese or otherwise. Now the artist Giulio was considered one of the best in painting miniatures.

The advert in the paper that he read, about the auction, mentions that there was a piece there, probably by Giulio, so no doubt he was drawn to that, and, we know, he purchased it.'

'However,' Sam continued, 'we feel, that this piece might be a missing Brueghel, who worked with Giulio whilst in Rome at that period.'

'So,' Samuel went on as Chrissie listened intently, 'seeing his friend in Amsterdam, this art expert on old Dutch masters, well, it is possible that he identified the piece as being more likely to be by Brueghel, and maybe your grandfather didn't travel to Rome at all. Well, we know he never got there.'

Chrissie closed her laptop and sat in silence for a bit.

Samuel studied her for a moment. Crazy, he thought to himself. Not all that long ago, a woman had walked up to him and kissed him. A woman, who, when he had first met her, wasn't at all the kind of woman he could possibly have feelings for, and now, sitting here in the lounge of a woman he had met only a very short while ago, he seemed to have feelings for her. Crazy.

Maybe he was suffering from jet lag.

He spoke 'I'm on a flight back to Amsterdam tomorrow. I will follow up the information you have given me, if that is okay with you?'

She turned her head to look at him.

Then, raising her eyebrows, said 'Absolutely, yes, but I would very much like to follow this through with you,' and before Sam could answer, she continued, 'You are chasing a piece of art, I'm trying to find out what happened to my grandfather. I failed before, but now, well, there's a chance ...What do you say?'

Then, again before Samuel had a chance to answer, she stood up, and asked 'Would you like a drink?'

'Thought you'd never ask. Coffee please, black, one sugar' he answered smiling up at her.

Smiling, she turned and headed towards the back of the lounge, then slipped through a door towards the kitchen.

Preparing the drinks gave her a moment to think.

Here was an opportunity to find out what had happened to her grandfather.

Why had he gone missing. Was it anything to do with that miniature he had with him?

Would going to Amsterdam give her answers?

She took the drinks through to the lounge.

MEANWHILE IN ACAPULCO;

A little over three thousand miles to the south, and an hour's time difference, Samantha landed at the airport in Acapulco.

She emerged from customs with her bags and looked around.

But he had already spotted her and came up from behind, startling her with a deep 'Hello.'

She smiled, turned around and allowed him to embrace her.

Then she drew back a little, took hold of his face with both hands, looked into his eyes and planted a kiss on his lips.

His response was instinctive and immediate.

It was natural.

For several moments, the airport announcements faded into nothingness.

The noise of the passengers, the sounds of squeaky wheels on suitcases, the hurrying and scurrying all around them ceased to be.

They kissed.

The undeniable attraction they felt for each other, surfaced.

Time they had previously spent together had been almost business like.

It had taken Samantha all her will power to stay focused on the case to ensure the best possible outcome for his parents, to ensure, that his sister, the culprit in all of this, was caught and convicted.

She had felt his sorrow, his anger. She had seen the hurt in his eyes. But she had stayed at a distance, though comforting him as much she could, whilst really wishing that she could just hold him and hug him.

After he had given her the letter that Elsa had written; her confession, which she then e-mailed to Samuel, there had been little in the way of conversation.

She had stayed a while longer, but then felt it wise to return to her hotel, promising him she would call around the following day, as her flight wasn't until the day after.

He had been a perfect gentleman, though obviously still much in thought. He had showed her around the town. They spent most of that Saturday together, often each with his or her own thoughts. But it wasn't uncomfortable, in fact, it was rather relaxing.

For him it was perhaps because he felt a burden had lifted or was thinking about the possibility of seeing his parents again.

For her perhaps it was because the case was reaching a successful end, or was it that she was falling in love?

When the time had come for her to fly back to Amsterdam, she had insisted he didn't come to the airport, but that she would be in touch with news as soon as possible. A hard call to make from her hotel room, but she felt she needed to be professional at this point.

The terminal announcements returned. The noise of the people and their suitcases once more became audible.

She drew back, looked into his eyes which were shining brightly, at his tanned face which was beaming with delight.

'Sorry I was a little cold when I left,' she apologised.

'Don't be silly, 'He answered, still smiling broadly. 'Now, Mum tells me, that you have a plan?'

Samantha smiled and they walked arm in arm out of the terminal building into the bright sunshine.

THE PAST;

PERIOD 16

THE YEAR 2005

She turned the key, and the engine of her battered VW Beetle chugged to silence.

Looking across the street she saw the offices of the law firm.

Stratford, Strauss & Helpin.

Yonkers, New York.

She checked the time on her watch. Ten minutes to ten. Her appointment was at ten o'clock. She had made good time travelling from Hoboken to come here as requested.

Two days ago she had received a letter. A letter from this law firm asking her to come and meet with them at her earliest opportunity and to contact them for an appointment.

This she had done, but despite asking what it was to do with, she had been told this could not be discussed over the phone and that she had to come in person. Furthermore she was also to supply them with proof of identity.

She got out of the car and fed the parking meter. Then, checking for traffic, crossed the street and entered the building.

'Good morning, may I help you?' the lady behind the reception desk enquired.

'Hi, I'm Tamara Wilson, I have an appointment.'

'Yes, Miss Wilson, please take a seat. Mr Stratford will see you soon,' and she pressed a button on her console and spoke briefly.

Tamara Wilson was twenty-two years of age. She was no more than five foot three and slim in build, wearing a brightly coloured top, tucked into faded blue jeans.

Her denim jacket was too long in the sleeves, which she liked, and she wore brown, short boots. Her ensemble was made complete by a pair of dangly green earrings and a green leather handbag slung over her shoulder. She wore little make-up and had a pretty face topped with shortish blond hair.

'Miss Wilson?' a voice from behind said, as she was standing by the window looking out onto the street, wondering what all this was about.

She turned and smiled. The man was about fifty, she guessed, wore a dark suit, white shirt with a navy and maroon tie. His shoes were shiny black. 'Please, come this way' he said, smiling at her, then turned.

She followed him through a door into a corridor and then into a large office. She again let her mind wander as it had done so often these past days.

The only thing, that she came back to, time and again, was that this must be something to do with her adoption.

Maybe a biological mother or father seeking to re-connect.

She had also thought about what her response might be, should this be the case.

Beside an ornate desk, behind which was a large leather chair and two more chairs, there was an area where four cosy chairs surrounded a low oval table.

He invited her to sit in one of these.

'Thank you for coming so promptly Miss Wilson' he said, also sitting down.

Tamara, though her friends called her Tammy, felt her heart beating in her chest and she had a dry throat. She slowly exhaled and looked at the man sat opposite her in expectation.

Would it be as she thought?

Her adoptive parents were both gone, her father in an accident, over six years ago, her mother more recently, ten months ago through illness.

She had no brothers or sisters, at least, none that she knew off.

'Do you know a Rosemary Quinton?' he asked and opened a large folder that he had taken from his desk.

She frowned, and thought, but the name didn't ring a bell. 'No, I don't.' Wanting to know why she had taken the day off to come here, she said, 'Why am I here? what's this all about?'

Robert Stratford, senior partner in Stratford, Strauss & Helpin, said, 'Miss Wilson, did you bring proof of your identity? '

She rummaged in her handbag, pulled out a passport and a few other documents and handed them over. Her heart was still thumping quite rapidly.

'Thank you, these are perfectly in order. I will need to take photocopies of these for our files. All will become clear soon. Now, before we get started, can I offer you a drink?'

Seven minutes later, documents copied, and originals returned, drinks and biscuits on the table, Mr Stratford, was ready to explain.

Outside, on this March day, it began to rain lightly.

'Rosemary Quinton,' he began, 'was eighty-three years old when she passed two months ago. She was your biological grandmother, on the maternal side of the family, your real mother's mother.'

Tammy knew it. It was all to do with her biological roots.

But now what? She didn't speak, she waited.

'Your grandmother has given you a commission,' he said. 'Let me explain. First, your biological mother passed many years ago, and of your biological father there is no record, but your grandmother tracked your life, followed you growing up. She could do this because it had been her that had organised for you to be adopted by the parents that you have known.'

'Wow,' Tammy said, 'so, how come she never ...'

'Never made contact? Well, until the death of your mother, your adoptive mother, she was legally not allowed to, those were the conditions of the adoption which she herself had stipulated.

'Since your adopted mother's passing, it had been your grand-mother's intention to meet with you, but she became quite ill, bedridden, and decided to contact you in this way instead.'

'You said something about a commission?' Tammy asked. She drank some of her coffee and was beginning to feel more relaxed.

'Indeed,' was his reply. 'Now, I don't know the details of this commission, this task or challenge if you will, it is all sealed for your eyes only.

I can tell you the following. Should you agree to take this on, you will be well funded. You will have travel and living expenses paid for, in fact, you will have a credit card at your disposal, with considerable funds to use as you wish.

You must, however, share with us your findings. We ourselves have a sealed envelope that we can only open once you have agreed to undertake this commission. Furthermore, we are to be at your disposal if there are queries or matters in which we may be of assistance.'

It was a lot for Tammy to take in.

She liked the idea of travel. She had obtained for herself a passport some time ago, with the intention of travelling, but thus far had not been in a position to do so.

And living expenses, this sounded very attractive. She currently worked as a waitress in a fancy restaurant, as she'd not had a great time of it at school and had dropped out when she was seventeen.

A commission, what did that mean? What would that entail? Was this a test, a challenge?

She was curious, a little apprehensive, maybe, but this all sounded very exciting.

'So, this is something that my grandmother wants me to do? It sounds very, mysterious, and what if I don't succeed? What if I can't, whatever it is, what if I can't do it?' she asked, feeling it was the right thing to ask.

'That is a good question Miss Wilson,' Mr Stratford replied, 'and one that your grandmother anticipated. The answer is that the details you will have, once you accept the request, will be able to clarify your, mission, if you will, and we too will have a better understanding of what that means, and will know to what extent you are successful.

'Remember, the funds you will have at your disposal are substantial.

I can tell you though, Miss Wilson, should you succeed, the reward will be even greater, for Mrs Quinton was a wealthy woman.'

Taking another sip of her drink, Tammy thought it through, but the decision was already made. A chance to travel, a mysterious quest, what an opportunity!

'Any other stipulations?' she asked, before giving her final answer.

'Only one,' came the quick reply. 'You may not tell anyone, or ask anyone for help with this, other than ourselves here. You have to do it on your own.'

'Okay, where do I sign?' she asked.

Eight days later she stood by the window of her Hoboken apartment keeping an eye out for the cab that she had ordered to take her to the airport.

Her suitcase and carry-on bag were ready by the door.

She was smartly dressed in a very dark green trouser suit, comfortable brogues, a lightweight long brown coloured raincoat and a multicoloured scarf around her neck.

She had resigned from her waitressing job.

Her luggage was new. Her outfit was new, at least half of the clothes she had packed, were new.

She had spent more on make-up and cosmetics than she had ever thought was possible, and as she stood awaiting the taxi, she felt great, albeit a little nervous about her new adventure.

Eight days ago she had read through and signed a number of documents and was made clearly aware of the conditions of the commission she was about to undertake, including a time frame of one calendar year.

In turn she had received a large bulky envelope which had her name written upon it, presumable, Tammy figured, by her grandmother, the late Rosemary Quinton.

Furthermore, she was given another envelope which, she was told, contained her credit card and its security pin number.

She was advised that an account had been set up, and that, if needed, she had up to fifty-thousand dollars that she could spend, an amount that staggered her when she was told this.

On top of that she was also given a new cell phone, the latest model, and a small but high-quality laptop.

It was like all her Christmases had come at once.

Everything was then put into a leather case and she left, driving ever so carefully, back home.

It was just after two o'clock on that, still rainy day, back in her apartment, when she opened the case, and opened the bulky envelope.

The taxi arrived and its horn beeped.

Tammy slung her handbag across her shoulder, grabbed her luggage and took the elevator from her fourth-floor apartment down to the lobby.

She was on her way.

Passport and boarding pass in her bag, check.

Travel and insurance documents in her bag, check.

She was mentally re-checking she had everything with her, having already gone through that procedure several times.

She had never flown before. And she was going to be flying business-class.

She was both excited and nervous.

The flight took off from New York's JFK airport on time, and was soon crossing the Atlantic en route to Paris. She had longed to go to Paris one day.

That day had come.

Her window seat was comfortable, she had no-one beside her as the business-class section was only three quarters full, so that was good.

She felt exhilarated after, what was for her, a breathtaking take-off.

Outwardly though, she, as much as possible, tried to reflect that this was a regular occurrence.

An hour into the flight, she dared to unclip her seat belt and went to the restroom. She then resettled in her seat and took an envelope, containing the letter from her grandmother, out of her handbag.

She had left the leather case behind as she found it too bulky to carry everywhere. Her new laptop was stowed in her carry-on case.

She opened up the letter and began to read it once more, having done so four times already.

'My dear Tamara,' it began …

Whilst the big jet flew smoothly through the skies over the Atlantic, Tammy once more read the letter, and once more was drawn into the story it told.

It was as if she was living it herself, the tension, the drama, the adventure …

The noise of the jet engines faded away. No longer was she thirty-six thousand feet, but there on the ground, living in her grandmother's world ...

It was 1946.

Twenty-four-year-old Rosemary Quinton was travelling on the road leading away from Rome, heading for the port of Civitavecchia.

She had arrived only a week ago. Had come to Italy, had come to Rome, the eternal city, to see the sights, to see the Colosseum, see St. Paul's, see the Sistine Chapel. But though the war had ended a year ago, the signs were still very visible. The scars that marked the ravages of war were still healing.

There was tension; there was suspicion; there was poverty.

Walking through the streets she was aware that the clothes she wore were expensive. She was made aware that, as an American, she would receive mixed reactions, adoration, suspicion and even dislike. She was made aware that, as an attractive woman, she could find herself in difficult situations.

Her father had just given her the money. He was a wealthy man. He had organised her flight to Rome, had told her to have a great time, but also that she needed to make the money last, for he would be away on business for the next three months.

Now, she sat on a bus, having with her just a large holdall and a handbag.

It was a warm day in July, and she was happy to be leaving the big city.

She had seen the sights she had come to see, but in her various walks had to almost constantly, brush off the many young men that seemed to be just hanging around the city and making passes at and suggestions to her and other young women.

Maybe it was their past-time, their sense of fun. She found it annoying and a little worrying.

Earlier, she had packed her suitcase with the clothes she didn't want to lug around and had given this to the concierge of the hotel to give to some shelter or other, an offer he was surprised and grateful for.

When she had asked him for the cheapest way to get to Paris, for she had spent more than she thought she would in accommodation and meals, he suggested she go by boat to Genoa, and from there, by train.

He said he could arrange for her to obtain passage by boat for free, as he had a brother who owned a cutter that plied to and from Genoa regularly.

She gratefully accepted ...

Tammy's reading was disturbed when on board the flight, lunch was served.

She put the letter down, looked out the window to see the clouds below, and noticed that the estimated time of arrival in Paris was just over four hours away.

She enjoyed her lunch and thought about how different her circumstances were to those of her grandmother who was also heading for Paris.

Lunch over, she shifted her tray over to the seat next to her, took up the letter and continued to read. Again, her mind and imagination quickly took her back to the time and place where her grandmother was ...

... The small cutter, laden with an assortment of freight, left the port of Civitavecchia late in the afternoon.

The sea was calm, the sun shone brightly, and Rosemary felt more relaxed than she had done for some time.

She stood on the deck and felt the breeze in her face.

Little did she know then that she would soon have a connection with a woman who had taken this voyage three hundred and sixty-eight years ago.

It was late afternoon of the following day when they arrived in Genoa.

The skipper, brother of the concierge, suggested a small hotel at the harbour front, and gave her directions.

It wasn't far, and though the sun was well on its way to-wards the horizon, it was still quite warm and she was pleased to reach the hotel.

She paid for a room, dropped her luggage inside, then set about to arrange train tickets.

On the way back she had a run in with three prostitutes who saw her as competition and were shouting, what must have been some colourful language, at her, which she ignored as she walked past.

She got back to her hotel, all the while thinking about her situation.

Having purchased the train ticket for Paris, which had cost her more than she had anticipated, she was fast running low on funds.

After a basic, but very tasty, dinner, she went to the bar area of the hotel and saw a man.

A man who, going by his accent as he tried to speak to the bartender, was an American.

He was in his fifties, she guessed. He wore a nice suit and good quality shoes. He seemed a little out of place here in this, rather run down, hotel.

A plan formed in her mind.

She walked up to the bar and sat herself down beside him.

'Buy an American girl a drink mister?' she asked, smiling at him.

Rosemary drank slowly, and thought and thought about a plan that was formulating in her head.

All the while, this man was talking and drinking.

Pleased, she supposed, that he had someone to converse with.

She wasn't listening that intently but picked up on the fact that he was awaiting a voyage to Rome.

He hadn't been able to find a flight, the trains were severely disrupted and going by ship was a good option.

He was a nice man, but she had made up her mind. She was going to seduce him, which wasn't going to be difficult, then, come early morning, take his money and disappear, head to the station and board the train set to leave at just before six o'clock in the morning.

He should still be fast asleep by then, she figured, as he ordered another drink.

When she sensed that he had had enough to drink, she took him to his room. So far, it was all going to plan.

He was still chatting when they entered his room. She sensed he was perhaps a little nervous in her company.

She smiled at him, then came up to him, flung her arms around his neck and embraced him.

He kissed her on her neck, then extracted himself from her, went over to his suitcase, opened it and took out a parcel.

He told her he wanted to show her something and unwound a woolly scarf to reveal a paper parcel. This he unwrapped to reveal what it contained.

Rosemary was taken by this miniature painting.

She picked it up from the bed where he had placed it, and studied it for several moments. 'It's beautiful' she said, then put it back.

He rewrapped the item, and placed it back in his suitcase ...

Tammy took a deep breath.

She knew what was coming next.

She sat in thought for a while. The jet engines droned on and, taking a look through the window, she noticed the sky was clear and she could see the ocean below.

Paris was now a little under three hours away.

THE PRESENT;

AMERSFOORT

WEDNESDAY 3RD APRIL

Martijn Vogel sat behind his desk going through all the notes he had made the previous day and checking his e-mail for any response from his counterpart in Amsterdam.

When Samuel Price had rung him at home and had briefly explained why, he had no hesitation in driving over to Rotterdam to see him.

He and the insurance lady, Samantha, had been most instrumental in obtaining the information needed for them to get a warrant and make the arrest of Elsa Wagenaar.

Furthermore, the Chief of the Rotterdam police was a friend of his.

Arriving back at his station he had briefed his colleague Froukje on his visit to Samuel and the French woman.

Dividing their tasks, Froukje had made contact, first, with the French police who agreed to check out Miss Pontiac's address.

Secondly, she had spoken to the director of the Paris Fine Arts Auction House, Mr Emmanuel Sauvonne, explaining the situation and assuring him that Miss Pontiac was safe and well.

She then contacted Interpol in France, sourced a contact to whom she would send all the information they had pertaining to a forged Gauguin, an address in Paris and the name of a person of interest, Miss Steffie Baertjens.

Meanwhile Martijn had contacted a friend of his in the Amsterdam police force, relayed the info he had and the address where Miss

Pontiac had been attacked, along with the details of the police ID found on those premises.

He then spoke to Sam's friend, Chief of Police in Rotterdam, again outlining the case, mentioning the police ID, and telling him about Steffie Baertjens and the need to alert border patrol.

A matter, the Chief had said, that he would deal with himself.

Now it was the following day.

Froukje arrived, again to find a coffee ready at her desk.

'Anything new?' she asked, settling herself down behind her desk.

'Yes, there is, 'Martijn answered, reading an e-mail that had just come in. 'The police ID that Miss Pontiac took from the house, is, as I suspected, fake, though a good one.

The Amsterdam police went to the house where she was attacked, arrested a young man, who's description matches the one given by Miss Pontiac, but Miss Baertjens had gone, flew out to Florence on Tuesday morning. I'll copy you in.'

'Okay, I'll send the info on to Interpol. Do you think it would be safe for the French woman to go home now?

'I'll speak to the Chief shortly, get his take on it, then I'll ring Miss Pontiac.'

MEANWHILE IN ROTTERDAM

Sophie had, after saying goodbye to Sam the previous day, gone to the shops in the street below, purchased some clothes, underwear, cosmetics and toiletries, picked up a few groceries, and headed back to his apartment.

Making a note of what she had spent, she had then used the old laptop he had given her, along with his great-grandfather's journals, set about to hopefully discover a better provenance on the Gauguin.

She woke early this morning, having slept reasonably well thanks to a call the previous evening from the detective, Martijn. He informed her that her house in Paris had not been broken into and that surveillance was in place. He also said that her boss, Emmanuel, was fine and aware of the situation, though he recommended not exchanging any phone calls at this time in order to keep her whereabouts secret.

She had thanked him and agreed.

After some breakfast, she was reflecting on how relieved she was at hearing Sam's voice when she had called him and how thankful she had been when he had arrived to rescue her.

She realised she really knew very little about him.

What she found had brought her to tears.

The day he had come to Paris, the day he had questioned the Gauguin, the day she had torn a strip of him, in her anger and arrogance, was also the day, that his wife had died.

The Gauguin, which had no official title but was listed in the records as 'Woman on the shore,' had been painted in Tahiti in 1898, and was sent, along with several others, to Gauguin's wife in Copenhagen. It was here, in the same year, that Sam's great-grandfather, also Samuel Price, purchased it.

Sophie was wondering, as she once more, focused on recording the full provenance of the painting, how did it get to Paris where it was sold in 1908?

She began reading through Sam's ancestors journals, while also pondering how this Miss Steffie Baertjens fitted into the picture.

Who was she?

THE PAST;

PERIOD 17

AMSTERDAM
6ᵀᴴ JANUARY 2015

Sitting in the third row from the front, Steffie Baertjens was anxiously waiting for the right lot number.

The auction house was packed, the fine arts sale well into the second half and her eye was on a painting coming up in three lots time.

Dressed in a smart trouser suit, her overcoat folded and laying on her lap, she held the auction paddle at the ready.

Her hair was a very light blonde, almost white and cut short. She wore diamond earrings and her fingers were adorned with numerous rings. Her watch was large, a diamond encrusted Cartier.

The current lot was sold, the next one brought to the stage. Not long now.

Three years ago, she was working in a bank in Cape Town, South Africa.

Three years ago, she was somebody else altogether ...

One day when she was in charge of the safety deposit box area, in the basement of the bank, a woman walked in, and an idea began to form.

She was tired of her job, tired of her life.

Her husband had walked out over a year earlier with a new woman in tow, taking all their savings, leaving the country, and leaving her pretty much penniless.

The woman who had entered was well dressed. She was also arrogant, dismissive and demanding.

They had a few customers like that. She knew several, and tolerated them. This was her job, her income, her life.

She had been at the bank for over eight years.

This woman, though, she had not encountered before. But what struck her, what had begun to form an idea in her mind, was that she was physically, very similar to her. Even her hair, light brown in colour, was cut in almost the same style, she listened to the woman's demands and got her to sign a form, then observed her more closely. She was wearing very high heels, so would probably be about an inch shorter than herself, but, her facial features were remarkably similar.

She could easily pass for a sister, possibly even a twin who had walked into the bank that Friday afternoon.

She had with her a small cabin bag, which she left on a table. Once she had signed the form, she produced a key and waited as the safety box was retrieved from a bank of them in a wall and placed in a cubicle.

She closed the curtain and let the woman get on with it, all the while her mind churning over a plan that was fast developing.

She took a look at the cabin bag, noticed the tag, noticed the name, and an address.

Why come in with it? She must be going somewhere, flying somewhere. Today.

She looked at the clock. Half an hour before the end of her work day. The weekend lay ahead. It couldn't be better she thought.

The woman came out of the cubicle; judging by the sounds, she had emptied the contents of the box.

She came out with not only her handbag, but also a small vanity case.

This she put on the table next to her case, then opened the case and placed the box inside before closing it again.

It the meantime, her handbag lay open and a ticket had half slid out.

She was indeed on a flight, leaving early evening, bound for London

The idea in her mind, grew more and more. A plan began to form.

The woman left and she went up with her in the elevator, and noticed there was a taxi waiting, no doubt heading straight for the airport.

No time to lose, the plan had to be put into action now or never.

She left work, making an excuse that she was unwell. With only ten minutes to go before the end of her shift now, that was no problem.

She hailed a cab to take her to the airport.

The two women arrived at almost the same time. She watched the other woman, who hailed a porter, go inside to the British Airways counter.

Also noting that she had two cases with her, plus her cabin bag.

She took a few pictures with her phone of the woman, of her luggage.

Next thing, to get through security.

The flight to London was still nearly two hours away.

She always carried ID with her, and purchased a ticket, to Johannesburg, having noticed a flight listed on the board.

Trying to keep an eye on the other woman, she managed to get to and through security, only about seven people behind.

Passing by a chemist, she quickly stepped inside.

Prior to working in the bank, she had been a practice nurse. She knew what she needed, and quickly sourced and purchased it.

It didn't take her long to spot her prey once again, and an opportunity came less than fifteen minutes later.

The woman entered the ladies' restroom.

She followed right behind.

A woman was coming out, and, as luck would have it, a quick look ascertained no-one else was there.

She was fit. She was strong. She was desperate.

In two quick steps, she reached the other woman, swung her around, and with the edge of her hand she struck a blow on the woman's throat. Then, all in a swift and flowing motion, dragged her into a cubicle.

The woman was gagging and struggling for breath. She tried feebly to resist, but to no avail.

She was forcible placed upon the seat, then held in place securely forced to swallow the pills that had been taken from the boxes.

The struggle continued for less than half a minute, then the woman went limp.

She placed her so that she wouldn't slip, then, locked the cubicle.

Taking the woman's coat and handbag, she replaced it with her own.

She then slipped athletically beneath the door of the cubicle, and entered the one next door to it.

Just in time as someone entered.

She put on the coat, and left the cubicle. After checking herself in the mirror, she took the cabin bag and left the restroom.

Ten minutes later she sat down by the correct departure gate, checked through the handbag and retrieved the other woman's boarding pass and passport.

She smiled to herself as she realised, she was flying first class.

No longer was she Lucie Van Doorn, bank employee but was now Petra Leyland, by all accounts a pretty wealthy lady.

That was three years ago ...

Her lot came up.

It was a Gauguin. She purchased it.

THE PRESENT;

ROTTERDAM

THURSDAY 4TH APRIL

Samuel entered the lobby, used the lift, then had the key to his door at the ready. But it opened as he approached.

Sophie must have heard him coming, or kept an eye out for him, for she greeted him with a beaming smile and, once again, flung her arms around his neck.

'Welcome home' she said, then planted a kiss on his lips.

'Well, that's a nice welcome. So, did you miss me, or have you got good news to share?' he asked, untangling himself from her and entering his apartment.

She smiled, closed the door behind him, then said, 'Get yourself sorted, I'll make you a coffee. I'm sure you won't say no to that. Then, I'll tell you, so yes, I have some news, but I also missed you.' She threw him a smile as she entered the kitchen.

Five minutes later, a steaming black coffee on the table in front of him, Sam sat on the two-seater and watched Sophie as she paced up and down, obviously quite desperate to tell him what she had found.

He noticed her outfit that she had purchased from the shops below. A two-tone pair of leggings, a form fitting skirt over the top, all topped with a floral blouse.

She had a fine figure he thought, as she began to speak.

'First of all, your detective friend rang yesterday. He did want to talk to you, but I told him you were still in Boston and due back today. He told me that it was okay for me to go home again, and he gave me a contact number to ring in case I saw something or someone suspicious, so, that was that. Then he told me the guy who attacked me was under arrest and helping the police with their enquiries.

My handbag and my credit cards and stuff were found. They'll be sent to my home. I have another number to ring, so I can arrange that and sign for them.

Then, lastly on that, Miss Baertjens has flown, apparently she boarded a flight to Florence on Tuesday.'

'Okay, well, that's good news that you're able to go home, and about your handbag and stuff. I'll give Martijn a ring later, but I sense there's more you want to tell me, pacing up and down like that, so?'

Sophie sat herself on the two-seater next to him, looked directly into his eyes, 'I ...I did a little research, on you, and, well, found out that on that day in Paris, when I was so rude to you, your wife ...' she stopped, not knowing quite what to say.

Sam gently, using his thumb and forefinger, took hold of her chin, then leaned forward and kissed her lightly on her lips.

'It's okay' he said, 'it was actually a distraction from the events of that day, and you have nothing to be sorry for. It's okay, truly.'

Sophie, feeling as though her heart had stopped beating, remembered to draw a breath, then leaned forward.

They kissed.

Suddenly Sophie drew away, smiling. She looked at him, then said, 'but there's more!'

She got up again and once more began pacing the lounge floor.

Sam took hold of his mug of coffee and sipped as she spoke.

'I read through your great-grandfather's journals. Found exactly what I was looking for.'

Sophie went over to Sam's desk, retrieved a sheet of paper and continued speaking.

'Samuel Price, the first' she said, smiling at Sam, 'was a British ambassador, he was appointed, his first appointment, to Copenhagen.

Here, we know, he bought the Gauguin, 'Woman on the shore' from Mette, Gauguin's wife, in 1898.

And, as she was involved in teaching French in those circles, that all fits in perfectly.

Gauguin sent her this painting, along with others, most likely earlier in that same year.'

Sophie paused for a moment, reading through the sheet, then went on, 'So, Samuel Price, the first' again smiling at Sam, 'was then appointed to be the British ambassador in Cape Town, South Africa. This was in 1901. He was there through to 1904 and was then posted to Paris.

Four years later, just prior to being posted to The Hague, he sold the painting.'

'And this is at that time, the correct painting you think?' Sam asked.

'Absolutely. I'm sure of it. Now the man who bought it in Paris was Jan Smettens, so, I followed up on that, something I should have done at the beginning,' Sophie continued. 'Anyway, he was from Delft, but, get this, he was also in Cape Town at the same time as your great-grandfather.'

'Really?' Sam interjected, 'That could be significant.'

'I agree,' Sophie said, 'but I don't know how, anyway. I did find out that the painting seems to have remained in his family for the next century.

It was sold in a house clearance in 2015, the house having belonged to a Miss Steenwoude, who, I discovered, was a relative, so that all looks to fit, making the provenance correct.

However, at some point, after 2015 when it was purchased by Miss Baertjens, the painting was substituted, which bring me to two things that stood out for me in my research,' Sophie said, and stopped pacing.

She sat next to him again.

Sam looked at her and asked 'First?'

'First, the fact that this Jan Smettens was in Cape Town.'

'And second?' Sam prompted.

'And second, Miss Baertjens has a distinct South African accent.'

THE FOLLOWING DAY;

PARIS

FRIDAY 5TH APRIL

Sophie Louise Pontiac studied herself in the long mirror on the wall of her apartment hallway.

Thirty-eight. Not married.

Had she been too ambitious, too focused on her career, too demanding of any suitors that had come her way?

She had a trim figure, her dark hair cut short, she knew she drew attention from men, and women, which did secretly please her.

But had she left it too late?

She wanted children, didn't she?

Was she falling in love?

The kiss on the couch had been more than nice.

For a few moments there, she had felt, sort of lost, lost in time, lost in space.

The moment had carried her away.

But he had suggested that she should go home.

Had taken her to the train station and had purchased her ticket.

She had promised him she would pay him back all her expenses.

He had briefly kissed her as he said goodbye.

Did he feel the same about her?

Was he too much of a gentleman to ask her to stay another night?

She tore herself away from the mirror.

She had placed a call to the number she had been given, late afternoon when she arrived home, and twenty minutes later a courier had arrived with her belongings.

She had phoned Emmanuel and filled him in on what had happened, and that she was still on holiday and would return to work in a week's time.

She had paced her apartment.
She had prepared a meal for herself.
She had gone to bed early but had not slept well.
Come on, she said to herself, focus.
But she returned to the hallway and to the mirror.
Looking at herself once more, she told herself, 'You will have to take the lead on this'.

Just over an hour later, she leaned back in her desk chair and whispered to herself, 'now that's very interesting.'

MEANWHILE IN ROTTERDAM

Sitting at his desk, Sam was thinking.
He thought back to the previous day, when he had taken Sophie to the train. Should he have asked her to stay one more night? Had he insisted too strongly that it was better for her to go home? Had he perhaps been worried that things might go too far?
And what would be wrong with that?
Was the woman, whom he had dismissed as someone of no interest on that day in Paris, now the woman he could fall in love with? Or had he already fallen in love with her?
And what about the American woman, what about Chrissie?
He had, once he returned from dropping Sophie off at the station, followed up on the lead he had with regard to the man whom Chrissie's grandfather was to meet.

Sam spent some time searching for, and locating, relatives of Adriaan Molenaar, the friend to whom Edward Small had written, way back in 1946.

The friend who had been a renowned art expert, specialising in old Dutch masters.

It hadn't taken long to find the right connection.

Sam rang the number he had found which was answered by a man named Adriaan.

Samuel explained the situation, and found out that the man who had answered the call had been named after his grandfather and was in possession of the man's diaries.

Must be a thing he thought, as he had in his possession, his great-grandfathers' journals, and Chrissie had diaries belonging to her grandfather.

Whilst still on the phone, Adriaan searched for the relevant dates and information, a task, he explained, which was made easy as the diaries were meticulously written and he, the grandson, had placed them in date order upon the bookshelf.

'Yes, here we are,' the man said, 'my grandfather met his friend, Eddie. Collected him from the airport.

'It says here,' the man continued, 'that due to post war restrictions he had only been able to find a flight to Genoa, and from there he would have to find transport to Rome. But ...' and there was a pause for a few seconds. Sam heard the man turn some pages, 'no, there is nothing here, no mention of a painted miniature, sorry.'

Sam asked if there was a date for that flight to Genoa, which there was and he was given. He thanked Adriaan for his help.

So, Sam was thinking, he definitely made it to Genoa, but not to Rome. There was nothing else for it, they, he and Chrissie, would have to go there and continue the search.

After spending some time finding flights and connections, he e-mailed Chrissie in Boston and suggested she fly to Paris and from there on to Genoa where he would be waiting, giving her the flight and transfer details.

Sitting at his desk now, he thought about Sophie, and about Chrissie, as he read Chrissie's e-mail response confirming she had booked her flights as per instruction and would see him on Monday.

Snapping out of his reflections, Sam began to type. Sophie had done some research on him. Time to look into what he could find out about Sophie.

During lunch, still scrolling through information whilst eating a sandwich, he stopped in his tracks. Putting the sandwich down for a moment, he typed and scrolled some more, then sat back in his chair and said to himself, 'Now, that's very interesting.'

Genoa Italy
Monday 8th April

Chrissie Small stood, with arms folded, on the small wooden boardwalk and gazed out over the Mediterranean Sea.

Behind her a restaurant and a bicycle hire business now stood where once there had been a seafarer's hotel.

Her eyes welled up as she gazed over the water.

This was the first opportunity she had to let her emotions surface.

This was as far as her grandfather had travelled.

This was where his travels, and his life, had ended.

Behind her, on one of the four benches that lined the board-walk, sat the man, who, nearly a week ago, had knocked on her door in Boston.

A man who had re-ignited her quest to find out what had happened to her grandfather in 1946.

She took a deep breath, quickly wiped a tear away and watched as a large ferry sailed out of the harbour from the busy port that lay a few miles to her right.

Genoa, Italy.

Samuel Price sat quietly on the bench. It was late afternoon. It had been a mild day, but now, as he sat and waited, he could feel a cool breeze coming off the sea.

What they had found out today had not been pleasant, nor had it been, perhaps, what either of them had suspected, or even considered, may have happened.

Chrissie turned and gave Sam a smile.

He had been such a help, and she would never forget this day.

He had been at the airport this morning, as promised. They had then taken a taxi to the hotel where he had booked two rooms and then, at his suggestion, they had gone to the library in the city centre, which was just opening.

'I wonder why there was no mention of the miniature in that man's diaries?' she asked as they climbed an ornate staircase to the second floor of this beautiful library.

'I wondered about that myself,' Sam answered. 'I figure it might possibly have been identified as a Brueghel, but in order to make certain, your grandfather still needed to go to the expert in Rome.

Also, as it was very possibly a missing and important piece of art, maybe they felt it better not to mention it at this stage until they had more proof.'

'I see what you mean. It makes sense I guess, so, tell me why are we here? In the library I mean. You've not shared any thoughts so far, been very quiet in fact, have you already found something?' Chrissie asked, giving him a sideways glance.

'Your grandfather made it this far, so something must have happened for him not to have gone to Rome,' Sam answered, turning left at the top of the stairs.

'We have a date, a date of his arrival here. Due to the post war disruptions, as I mentioned, he could only secure a flight to Genoa. He had limited options from here: by train, also still at the time suffering from long delays, or by ship, the latter seemingly the most likely. In order to, hopefully, find out what happened next, we read the newspapers.'

'Can you read Italian?' she asked.
They reached the old newspapers archive section.

'No, 'he answered, 'but before I left Rotterdam, I googled, then rang this library.
A lovely receptionist explained that they have a huge archive of newspapers, and where I would find them. She also said that there would most likely be someone around to help with any translation. Very helpful indeed she was.'

'You're such a charmer,' she said, smiling.

Fifteen minutes later, they were both staring at an article from a daily newspaper dated four days after Edward Small had arrived in the city.
They both saw it at the same time, looked at each other, then back at the article.
Sam looked around, saw a couple of young students not far away and walked over to them, asking if they could help to translate an article for them. They gladly agreed and came back with Sam.
The students, both girls of around seventeen or so, read the article through, then, between them, they read and translated the story.
Sam thanked them very much.
He looked at Chrissie, she had paled slightly.

The story told of an American man who had been found dead in a hotel room on the harbour front, told of how any identification papers and money had been stolen, that the man's watch had been stolen, and that a leather holdall had been stolen.

It told of an American woman who had been seen with the man the previous evening, a woman who had disappeared but who had been seen buying a ticket for Paris the previous day.

It told that the man had died of a suspected heart attack.

As much as the article was a shock, particularly for Chrissie, what was most strange was that someone had, some time ago judging by the faintness of the mark, circled the item.

Sam placed his hand on her upper arm, 'Sorry,' he said, his voice soft and warm.

Chrissie nodded 'I feared something had happened, but, here, in black and white, no mistake, it has to have been him'

'Very likely, but we can follow it up. The best we can do now is go to the police, and hopefully check their records. More information may have been found,' said Sam, closing the newspaper archive books and returning them to the shelves.

'Okay,' Chrissie answered.

As they headed down the stairs to the exit she asked, 'Why was it circled? Do you think someone else was searching?'

'It sure looks that way, but who, and why?' Sam answered.

The police proved very accommodating. They were taken to an office, then a young sergeant, who's English was very good, eventually came into the room armed with some files.

He opened a folder, flicked through several pages, then, finding what he was looking for, read through the contents of a report.

'Yes,' he said at last, looking across at them, 'this is the report that you tell me about from the newspaper. Not very much here, it was 1946, not much man power. The American woman was not found. The man who died, died from heart attack.

The man's coat was American make, and hotel keeper say that the man was from America and waiting to travel to Rome by ship. No more.'

Then after a pause, as the sergeant turned a page, 'This interesting,' he said.

'A woman came to ask of this case. This was in 2005, a Miss Tamara Wilson, from New York. No more information. Came here in July 2005.' He then paused again for a moment, and spoke in rapid Italian to one of his colleagues across the room. A reply came back, and the sergeant explained, 'One of my colleagues remembers this lady. Says she was small lady, about in her middle twenties, blonde, very pretty, maybe this helps?'

They thanked him for his helpfulness and exited the police station.

'That's who must have circled the article in the paper,' Chrissie said, once outside.

'Absolutely, but who is Tamara Wilson from New York. Any idea?'

'None, 'Chrissie replied, 'and why was she, this little blonde, looking into the death of my grandfather?'

'Let's go and find this hotel where it all happened,' Chrissie suggested.

Sadly, the hotel had been torn down quite some years ago, back in the late sixties, they found out.

Chrissie walked back towards Sam on the bench, looking at the restaurant and bicycle hire place that now stood where once the hotel had been.

Where her grandfather had died.

Sam stood up and together they walked back to their hotel.

One search was over. Chrissie now knew what had happened to her granddad. Another search was still ongoing. What had happened to the item, and who was Tamara Wilson?

Sam glanced at Chrissie; she was deep in thought.

He liked her. He liked Sophie too.

His thoughts were, once again, rather jumbled.

Thinking of Brueghel's miniature, thinking of the Gauguin, thinking of the words his wife had spoken, thinking of Chrissie, thinking of Sophie.

Two pieces of art. Two women.

He was looking forward to travelling home tomorrow. He had, very briefly, spoken to Sophie on Sunday morning, before flying out to Genoa.

He had told her about Chrissie from Boston, about the miniature, and about searching for the answer to what had happened to the American Professor.

He also said that he had found something rather interesting and would tell her when he got back.

She, in return, had said she had found something interesting too and would tell him then.

THREE DAYS LATER

NEW YORK
THURSDAY 11TH APRIL

Chrissie had found Tamara Wilson.

She stopped outside the restaurant and looked at the menu on the window.

It was a quarter to five in the afternoon on a cloudy and cool day.

Chrissie was dressed smartly in a knee-length grey and purple skirt, a dark pink lightweight sweater over a patterned white blouse, black shoes with a two-inch heel, a light grey overcoat and a black leather handbag slung over her right shoulder.

Her blond hair was neatly in a bun at the back of her head. She entered.

The establishment was a block away from Central Park; a small, but well-established place, quite pricey, serving classic dishes, mainly French cuisine.

The young woman behind the reception desk greeted her with a friendly hello and smile, and asked if she had a reservation.

'I'm here to see Miss Wilson,' Chrissie said. 'It's of a personal nature,' she added as the young woman was about to say something.

'Oh, okay, one moment please,' and she slipped away into the restaurant area leaving Chrissie in the small foyer and cloakroom.

Chrissie slowly exhaled, looked out of the window and waited.

She had, a little reluctantly, said goodbye to Samuel.

He had been wonderful, a true gentleman, kind, charming, considerate.

If he had not come knocking at her door, she would likely never have uncovered the truth surrounding her grandfather's disappearance.

They had enjoyed a quiet dinner that evening at the hotel. He'd not spoken a lot, but she had found the company not uncomfortable, in fact, she had felt quite relaxed and at ease in his presence.

The following day he had returned to Amsterdam by a direct flight, and she had flown, via Paris, back to Boston.

Her thoughts were broken when a voice behind her said, 'I am Tamara Wilson,' then as she turned to face her, 'you wanted to see me?'

Chrissie sized up the woman before her. About an inch or two shorter than her, she was slim and had a pretty face, little make-up, and short cropped blond hair.

She was smartly dressed in a grey skirt, similar to that of her own, but several inches shorter, a white silk blouse and a matching grey jacket.

Her silky stockinged legs were tucked into a pair of expensive black shoes with a small heel.

She presented a very smart and professional appearance.

Chrissie walked towards her and said, looking directly into her eyes, 'Hi, I'm Chrissie Small, and I believe you were in Genoa, Italy back in 2005.'

'Aaah, yes, yes I was ...' Tammy answered, but before she could say anything else, Chrissie spoke again,' and you circled an article in a local newspaper from 1946'

There was a moment of silence between the two women, each thinking about the other.

It was Tammy who reacted first, 'Okay,' she said, 'this is interesting. Please, let me make a call, and then we can talk.'

Chrissie nodded approval at this suggestion and listened as the other woman retrieved her phone from the pocket of her jacket, pressed a few buttons, then spoke softly and briefly, 'Hi, it's me, I have to go, family matter. If you need extra cover, get someone, okay,' then listened briefly and ended the call.

'Okay. You here by car?' she asked.

'No, I've flown in from Boston,' Chrissie replied.

'All right then, follow me. We'll go to my place, it's close by,' and with that she turned and headed into the restaurant with Chrissie following on her heels.

Tamara stopped briefly in what Chrissie assumed was her office, to pick up her coat and bag, and they left via a back door.

'I can't just tell you about it, 'she said, looking across at Chrissie by her side, 'I have to show you. Goodness me, after all these years ...'

They continued walking in silence for two blocks, each with their own thoughts.

Tamara brought back to mind that day when she had excitedly circled that article in the old newspaper, nearly fourteen years ago.

Having spent three amazing days in Paris, walking all around and taking in the atmosphere of the city she had often dreamed about visiting, she set of for the Italian city of Genoa, deciding to go by train.

Her mind once more on the mission her grandmother had given her, to find the hotel that she had stayed in, the hotel where he had died, and, the main reason for her visit, the commission she had been given to hopefully find out if ever they found out who this man had been.

She thought it clever of her to check the library for possible news articles about the event and was pleased with herself when she found it.

However, even after checking the police records later that day she had not found what she had come for. No-one had subsequently found out who the man was.

She did ask, and was told, what happened to the body. It had been buried with an unmarked stone, in a graveyard to the south of the city.

She had visited, taken a few photographs, and had left, sad that she had not been successful.

Chrissie was deep in thought as well, thinking about this woman beside her. What is her connection? what is it, she wants to show me? She sensed no suspicion from this woman, but more a sense of relief.

'This is me,' Tammy said turning, and entered the lobby with a key. She nodded hello to a man behind a counter, the doorman, Chrissie assumed, then headed for a bank of elevators.

Moments later they rode smoothly to the twenty-eighth floor.

'Well, I can't tell you what a surprise this is. Can't even think about where you fit in, but I sense a personal connection, I'm intrigued, fancy a glass of wine?' she asked, throwing her coat off and onto the back of a leather couch.

'Sure,' Chrissie answered, also taking her coat of and placing it next to the other one, 'White?'

'Absolutely, please, make yourself at home.'

Chrissie walked over to the large window which offered a panoramic view of the city, across Central Park no less, prime real estate, she was thinking. This woman was obviously financially very well to do.

Tamara came, from the kitchen area, and brought two glasses of wine, handing one to Chrissie.

'Well,' she said, looking at the other woman, 'here's to mysteries and their revelations'

'I'll drink to that,' Chrissie answered, and they chinked glasses.

Then they both sat down, Chrissie spoke first,' The man, in that article, the man who died in that hotel, he was my grandfather, Edward Small.'

'Wow, finally, a name, Edward Small,' then after a brief pause, 'I'm sorry, I guess you have only recently found out. A shock I'm sure,' Tamara answered. 'By the way,' she went on, and extended her right hand, 'please call me Tammy.'

Chrissie shook her hand, 'Chrissie, and yes, it was a shock, although I had expected something had happened. I found out three days ago, found out you had been to the police station, a note to that effect was on the crime file, hence, here I am. What was your reason for being there?'

Tammy took a sip of wine, then said, 'The woman, the American woman, was my grandmother' then followed on, 'sorry, but I want to show you a letter.'

She placed her glass on the small table in front of her, then got up and left the room, coming back almost immediately with a bulky letter in hand.

'Read this first,'she said, offering the letter, 'then we'll talk, okay?'

Chrissie nodded, took the letter, placed her glass on the table, and began to read.

It wasn't long before she was totally absorbed in its contents, and the world around her ceased to be.

Across from her, Tammy watched and waited.

It was several minutes later, when Chrissie looked up, looked at Tammy.

'This, this is how Sam found me ...' she said, then clarified, 'Sam is an auction assessor, the item your grandmother mentions here, the painted miniature, well, he's been following a trail. Long story, but the thing is, his research led to the point where my grandfather purchased it at auction in, let me think, yes, in 1938.

This led Sam to my door, and subsequently, together, we worked out that grandad had travelled to Genoa, and so ...'

Tammy nodded, then said, 'Better read on ...'

Chrissie returned to the letter, to the part where he had shown Tammy's grandmother the item, to the part where he had re-wrapped it and put it back in the suitcase.

Again, the words in the letter, transported her. She imagined the scene, imagined the place, the words took her there, to that hotel, to that very room, that very evening ...

> *I smiled at him, started to take my clothes off ... in the hope*
> *he would do so too. I wanted him asleep. I wanted it all to be*
> *over. I wanted it to be morning.*
> *But then, something happened that I hadn't foreseen.*
> *Standing there, in my underwear, I noticed he had stripped*
> *down to his boxer shorts and was hovering near the bed, but*
> *he didn't look well.*
> *He had gone red, and sort of blotchy, though the light in the*
> *room was not great, I could see, he was not at all well ...*

... Rosemary watched, unsure as to what to do, as the man suddenly clutched his chest, then half sat, half collapsed on the bed.

Next thing he lay down, still clutching his chest with one hand. All colour had now drained from him and he was almost white.

Standing there, frozen to the spot, she heard a small gurgle in the man's throat, then he stiffened, and went, sort of limp.

He lay still. His eyes were closed, His mouth was closed.

She could see he wasn't breathing.

Rosemary finally found movement in her feet, and quickly walked around to his side of the bed. Gingerly she bent down and felt for a pulse in his neck.

There was no pulse to be found.

'Oh, my goodness, oh my goodness, 'she muttered to herself.

'Breathe girl, breathe,' she then said, standing up, 'think, think.'

She slowly got herself dressed and began to think things through.

The hotel had no register, it was a cash up front service only, very well suited for the prostitutes, for earlier she had spotted two of the three that had verbally abused her down there at the bar.

This was good, no record of this man.

She was going to keep it that way.

She took off the watch he was still wearing, then checked through the room for any sort of identification or papers. She found his passport, some letters, an aeroplane ticket, a book and, happily for her, quite an amount of cash in a worn wallet.

She emptied the leather holdall he also had with him, and placed all the identifiable items in there, along with the parcel containing that fine painting he had shown her.

She also took a number of clothing items from the room and from the suitcase, stuffed these into the holdall, then, satisfied she had left nothing that would identify him, she took the key from the lock, listened for a moment, then opened the door, locked it, and pushed the key back under the door.

She quickly made her way to her own room.

She stayed awake, sat on her bed, and waited.

Slowly the sounds of talking and laughter downstairs grew softer, until, after some noises in the corridors and adjacent rooms had ceased, the hotel fell into silence.

Rosemary waited a full hour, and just after four o'clock in the morning, taking with her her own holdall and the acquired black leather one, she left her room, locked the door and crept downstairs.

She left the key on the desk in the lobby and left the hotel.

Fifteen minutes later, she walked into the waiting room of the railway station and once more waited.

Her heart was thumping noticeably and her stomach was tight with tension.

Her train was less than an hour and a half away.

She hoped it would be on time ...

Chrissie pulled herself away from the scene created by the letter, reached over to take a sip of her wine and looked across at Tammy.

Mixed emotions were flooding through her.

The callousness of that woman, the intent, the deception.

She was angry at her.

Poor grandad.

'I'm so sorry' Tammy spoke, almost a whisper, sensing the emotion and anger in the other woman.

Chrissie gave a slight nod, then, taking another sip and a deep breath, resumed reading the story ...

Of course, initially I had only wanted to take some money, but then, in order for me to get away, I just had to take anything that could identify him.
There could be no trail for the police to follow. I needed time to get away ...

... Dawn was breaking as the train departed, on time.

Rosemary placed both holdalls on the seat beside her, and sat by the window, watching the train roll out of the station.

She felt a little bit relieved, a little more assertive, a little more herself.

No-one would be up yet at the hotel she figured, and no-one would check his room for some time yet.

The train rumbled on the tracks. There were not many passengers on board.

Whilst waiting in her room for the right time to leave, she had transferred all her stuff into the better-quality black leather holdall, and his stuff into hers, with the aim of discarding it at some point it.

She had decided she would get rid of everything, with the exception of the parcel containing the painting, the watch and the book he had with him, and of course the money. The wallet, the passport, and everything else, had to go.

The train pulled into Turin.

Rosemary sat, hopefully looking relaxed, but inside she was in turmoil as the train stopped, hoping not to see hordes of policemen descending upon her.

It didn't happen. The train pulled out again. A conductor walked by and checked her ticket, all was well.

Next stop Lyon, France.

It was there, where French officials boarded the train and checked passports.

She was American, she was welcomed, they smiled at her. She smiled back.

She was in France ...

Again, Chrissie pulled herself away from the story.

Taking another sip of wine, she realised that Tammy had gone, though at that moment reappeared, bottle of wine in hand, plus, what looked like some photographs.

She topped up the glasses, put the bottle down, then asked, as she sat down, 'So, where are you up to?'

'About to reach Paris,' Chrissie answered.

'I don't know if you did,' Tammy said, 'but when I was there, I found out where they buried ...your grandfather. Well, I took some photos,' and handed Chrissie several prints.

'Gosh, I should be ashamed of myself. I didn't even think to ...' taking the photographs and studying them for some moments.

Feeling embarrassed and cross with herself, Chrissie looked at the photos and promised herself that she would go back and get his name put on the marker.

'I didn't do it, for, sentimental purposes,' Tammy admitted.

'Because of my grandmother's, wishes, I needed to supply proof that I had, well, tried to find out who he was, hence the photos and I wrote a report to go along with it as well. That is all at the lawyers, the ones dealing with grandmother's estate.

I printed a couple of them off for myself, though I don't know why really. Oh, and, well I don't know if you want to know, but here's a picture of my grandmother, though much more recently, about seven years ago, she was about seventy-five or -six here.' Tammy explained and handed Chrissie another photograph.

Chrissie took it, looked at the woman.

Though still feeling raw towards her, in the photograph she looked to be a kind person.

She handed the picture back.

'How, did you feel, when you read this?' Chrissie asked.

'Well, obviously like you, I was transported, to that time and that place. The words just took me there, so, when it came to the hotel and to this man, your grandfather, I was upset, I guess. I was also, perhaps, embarrassed, felt, guilty. Now, knowing a name, knowing that this was your grandfather, well, I'm so sorry ...'

'It's not your fault,' Chrissie reassured her, giving her a brief smile, 'and, well, this was a different time. I have no doubt, that your grandmother was pretty scared.'

'Carry on reading.' Tammy stood up, and as she moved away, said, 'I'll fix us something to eat.'

But Chrissie did not hear the last part, as she was already engrossed once more in the letter.

> *I remember how I felt, as I walked through the station.*
> *My legs were trembling, I was feeling weak, almost nau-*
> *seous, but, to my relief, there were no Parisian Gendarmes*
> *heading my way.*
> *I reached the exit and walked into the streets of Paris ...*

... It was approaching mid-afternoon on a warm and sunny day, when Rosemary arrived in the French capital.

Throughout the countryside, and here in the city, the scars of war were still visible. She turned off into a side street, and just walked, her intention to seek a small hotel somewhere.

An opportunity arose early on, when she saw a truck in the street, a refuse truck. Three men were walking along, picking up trash cans and emptying them in the low open bed truck.

Without hesitation, Rosemary walked up beside the vehicle, then quickly, placed the black leather holdall on the ground and, using both hands, flung her old bag into the lorry.

Picking up the other bag, she walked on. Nobody had noticed.

Fifteen minutes later, in a busy street near the Opera, she walked into a bank and changed all the Italian money she had for French.

Less than five minutes after that, she booked herself into a hotel.

Once safely in her room, she threw herself on the bed, broke down and cried.

Rosemary Quinton had started in Rome, Italy, the eternal city, and it had always been her intention to finish in Paris, France, the city of romance.

But as she walked through the streets over the next three days, despite the music that permeated through the air from the many bars and cafes, despite the joy and laughter she encountered, the smiles of the people, despite the invitations she had on several occasions to join a party here or there, despite the beauty of the fabulous buildings all around, despite the smile she placed on her face, she was unhappy, felt sad and lost.

She felt guilty and alone.

Three days after her arrival, having cried herself to sleep every night, she checked out and took a train to Antwerp.

She wanted to go home, but felt security at the airports would be greater than in a port.

Antwerp had a port; she would seek a passage to New York.

It was there, in the Flemish city of Antwerp, that she would find change, would find relief from her guilt, would find happiness, laughter and love …

Chrissie looked up as Tammy placed two plates of food on the table.

She looked down at Chrissie, 'I'm hungry,' she said, smiling.

Chrissie smiled back, looked at her watch, time had flown by, 'Now that you mention it, so am I. This looks fabulous, so, are you a chef then?' she asked.

Tammy sat down. 'So,' she said, avoiding the question for the moment, 'how did you find me?'

'Through social media,' Chrissie answered, 'I had your name, and also had a brief description, from a police officer who had been there when you came, a pretty blonde, he called you'

'Really? Of course, I could have changed the colour of my hair,' Tammy replied between mouthfuls.

'Sure, it took some searching, but when I found some photos of you online from when you were in Paris, in the year 2005, well, I figured you to be the best bet.
   I mean, I had your name, the pictures showing a pretty blonde, and the right year, it just had to be you.'

'Mmm, good detecting, and in answer to your question about me being a chef, I used to be a waitress at that restaurant. As it happened when I returned the previous owners wanted to sell, and so, thanks to grandma, I was able to buy it.
   Then I took myself on a course, trained to be not only a chef, but also got myself a degree in hotel and hospitality management. '

'Well done you,' Chrissie said, 'and this is truly lovely.'

'Thanks,' Tammy replied. 'So, you must be near the end of the letter?'

'I think so, currently in Antwerp.'

THE PRESENT;

ANTWERP

SUNDAY 21ST APRIL

Samuel arrived at the Antwerp Central Station.

He was casually dressed in a checked green and black shirt tucked into blue jeans, brown shoes with a solid rubber soul and a short green rain jacket.

Hands in pockets he strode along the Keyserlei, took the underpass beneath the N1 and then down the Leystraat, into the shopping street, De Meir.

It was still early on Sunday. It was quiet.

Overcast, rain was forecast, and a cool wind blowing. Samuel walked on.

A little while later he wandered around the antique and flea market, then made his way to where he had arranged to meet with Samantha, not that far from where she lived.

He had contacted her two days ago. She had just returned from Mexico.

He asked her to meet him here and despite her questions, he had not told her why, just to come.

The meeting point was the entrance to the St. Anna tunnel, a pedestrian and bicycle tunnel that ran beneath the River Scheldt.

It was opened in 1933 and its main feature was the wooden escalators, deemed to be the oldest and longest in the world.

He saw her arriving.

They greeted. 'Good morning Miss Price' he said, and they embraced and kissed in the customary way.

She smiled at him, 'And good morning to you too, Mr Price.'

'Well, you are positively beaming Samantha,' Samuel said.

'Observant of you,' Samantha replied. 'I guess I can't help but smile at the moment.'

'Now, I'm guessing it's not because you don't have a two million euro claim to pay out is it, or even because of seeing me,' Sam said, then went on, 'must be a man in your life.'

'And that, Mr Price, 'she answered, 'is all because of you.'

'Has to be Rico.'

She smiled at him, 'Rico it is. We just, well, clicked, you know,' she answered, a slight blush on her cheeks. 'Anyway, enough of that. You wanted to meet me here, so, spill, why are we here? How did you get on in Boston?'

Samuel smiled back, then said, pointing, 'See that house over there, on the other side of the market, the one on the corner with that little dormer?'

'Aha, I see it'

'Well, our miniature, was once in that very house, back in 1946,' he said, then turning, 'we are going for a little walk, down through the tunnel, and I will explain all.'
   In a little while they stepped onto the wooden escalator and rode down.

'Boston.' Samuel began, 'I got the address from the auction house, of the man, this Edward Small, who purchased what we believed might be the Brueghel miniature, in 1938.
   I went there, and, low and behold, the woman who answered the door was this man's granddaughter, her name is Chrissie.

I told her how it was I was there, and then she proceeded to tell me an interesting story. Turns out, her grandfather had written to a gallery in Rome. He did this after the war, as he couldn't travel to Europe during war time. Anyway, this gallery, apparently, was owned by an expert on Giulio miniatures.

Edward had purchased the item that day, at the auction, thinking it might be by this artist, whereas, if you recall, I was thinking that it might be our missing Brueghel.

So, he went to Rome, according to the granddaughter, but, and this is where it gets interesting, he disappeared,' Samuel said, pausing and looking across at Samantha.

They reached the bottom of the escalator, and began walking along the tunnel.

'Disappeared?', she asked, 'as in, never heard from again?'

'Correct. So, years passed, and when Chrissie's father died, she inherited the house, found some diaries, and, as she had heard stories of her missing grandfather, felt this might be an opportunity to investigate.'

'So,' Samuel continued, sensing that Samantha was hanging on to his every word, 'back in 1997, she flew to Rome, taking with her the reply letter from the gallery that she had found, and visited the gallery, which still exists. They confirmed that they had expected Mr Small, but that he never arrived. Chrissie, not being able to find out anything else, flew back home disappointed.'

'Wow,' Samantha said, then turning to look at him, said, 'but then you came along.'

'Ah, yes well, what can I say? Anyway, when telling her my story, or I should say, our story, and she telling me hers, she went to fetch her grandfather's diaries. To her surprise a letter slipped out, and this was key. It was a letter from a friend of her grandfather saying he was looking forward to meeting him, and would collect him from the airport, in, wait for it ... Amsterdam!'

'Really?' Samantha asked, 'So, he didn't go to Rome at all?'

'I'll come to that. Now, this friend in Amsterdam was also an art expert, so, I guess Edward wanted to show him what he had purchased and get his opinion on it.

When I got back from Boston, I contacted the family, the man himself had passed away in 1966, but I spoke to his grandson and he was able to confirm that Edward had indeed arrived in Amsterdam, back in 1946, and, had, a couple of days later, taken a flight to Genoa, in Italy.' Sam explained, as they casually walked the five hundred and seventy-eight metres length of the tunnel.

It was quiet. An occasional pedestrian and a couple of cyclists had passed by.

'So, Genoa was the next clue then?' Samantha asked, keen to find out more of this story.

'Yes. I contacted Chrissie in Boston and we arranged to meet in Genoa.

Knowing the date of his arrival in 1946, we checked the local newspapers and found an article. An American man had died, in a hotel on the harbour front, but all was not straightforward, though it was suspected that the man had died from a heart attack, they had no idea who he was. The hotel manager had confirmed that he was an American, but they found no identification. No passport, no wallet, no money, and concluded that he had been robbed.

The only other clue the police had was that he was seen with an American woman the night before.'

'So, you think whoever stole from him, possibly this woman, also took the miniature?'

'No doubt about it,' Sam answered, giving her a smile. 'We found out from visiting the police there that someone else had been investigating this event. There was a record on file that in 2005 an American woman made enquiries, a certain Tamara Wilson, from New York.'

'Okay, do go on. This is fascinating, and getting more interesting by the second,' Samantha observed.

'The rest is Chrissie's work.' Sam explained. 'She searched for, located and spoke with Tamara Wilson, and, who is she, you may well ask ...' Sam paused, looking over to Samantha.

'Okay,' Samantha said, smiling, 'who is she?'

'She is the granddaughter of the woman who was in Genoa in 1946.'

'The American woman? And? Did she kill him? Did she steal the miniature?'

'No, and yes.' Samuel answered. 'It's a bit complicated, but the upshot is, that this Tamara, who likes to be called Tammy, so I was told, received a letter from her grandmother,who had passed away in 2005, in a will.

'In this letter she tells the whole story and she asks her granddaughter to see if she can investigate, and, hopefully, find out who this man was that she met at this hotel on the harbour front, for no, she did not kill him, but, yes, she stole from him, including the miniature.'

'Wow,' this is, like a movie or something. What a lot of turns and intrigue. So, come on, do we know now the whereabouts of the miniature?'

They had reached the other end of the tunnel.

Samuel stopped, then spoke again, 'Tammy had done a search, back in 2005, but she was unable to find a name for the man who had died. Although the American woman, Tammy's grand-mother, had taken the man's passport, she had never looked at it, before discarding it, and other items, in Paris.

Also, although she would likely have known his name, during the time she spent with him, this knowledge was gone, likely due to what had happened, a sort of repressed memory.

It wasn't until Chrissie met with Tammy that the whole story came out.

She was shown the letter, which was very detailed, about what had happened in Genoa in 1946. How she had taken a train from there to Paris where she had thrown away, all the things that she had taken that could have identified the man, everything with the exception of these three things, the man's watch, a book he was reading and, yes, the miniature.'

'Now, she didn't stay in Paris for very long, only a few days,' Samuel explained, as they started to make their way back along the tunnel.

Three young ladies, in their early twenties walked by them, chatting away and only briefly casting them a glance.

'She went from Paris, to Antwerp,' Samuel said.

'Of course, you told me, the house on the corner,' Samantha exclaimed.

'Indeed. Now, she had intended to seek passage to head back to New York from here, but she fell in love ...'

'This can happen,' Samantha interjected, smiling.

'Indeed,' Sam smiled back at her, then continued, 'now, this chap, who she fell in love with, and his name was not mentioned in the letter, was a bricklayer. He worked for a team that was involved in restoration work.

Mainly getting war damaged buildings back to how they were.

Now, the letter tells, that one night, in the middle of the night, she, that is Tammy's grandmother, who's name, by the way, was Rosemary Quinton, came down here, into this very tunnel.'

Sam stopped at this point and gestured with his hands, 'you see, parts of this tunnel were also being repaired after suffering damage in the war. Well, the chap, her boyfriend, the bricklayer, scraped away a cavity in the wall then, according to the letter, Rosemary placed the miniature into this cavity, and he sealed it, placing a tile on top.

So, Miss Price, in this tile-lined tunnel, how many tiles would there be?' he asked and started walking again.

'Goodness, thousands,' She answered, looking up and down the tunnel.

'Thousands indeed, and, behind one of these', again gesturing with his hand, 'lies our miniature.'

They were both silent for a bit, then she asked, 'And no sign, of which tile? Or what area of the tunnel? Any clue at all?'

Then, looking at Samuel and detecting half a smile, she cocked her head slightly to one side, and looked him in the eyes, 'You know, don't you?'

'Mmmm, not exactly, no, but I've had this information for a couple of days now and I have been thinking it through,' Samuel replied, and as they stood there, he looked to his left and to his right, the tunnel was void of anyone at that moment. They were alone.

'I dug through some archives of works carried out by the council here in Antwerp, not a lot of help, but I did narrow it down. Come with me, back this way.'

Sam walked back along the tunnel for about forty metres, looking at the ceiling, then stopped.

'Okay,' he said, looking at Samantha, 'it's got to be in this area,' then, indicating with his hands, 'it could be three metres or so, in either direction, and, it could be on either side. I don't know, but this is the area, where work was carried out in the week prior to when Rosemary Quinton, left to go back to America.'

They both looked around for a bit, letting two more cyclists whizz past, but saw no noticeable signs.
    'There must still be over a thousand tiles in this area alone,' Samantha said.

'I'm guessing more than two thousand,' Samuel answered.

After a moment, Samantha looked at Samuel and said, 'Of course, it may not necessarily still be here.'

You're thinking, maybe the guy, this bricklayer boyfriend, might have come back and taken it out?' he asked, half smiling.

'Okay, you're doing that grinning again, what else do you know? Come on,' she said, and was slightly startled, when another cyclist shot past them.

'Come on, let's go, and I'll tell you,' he answered, and they began to make their way back.

'Also, thanks to the information Chrissie sent me, I was able to find out how Rosemary Quinton returned to America. She sailed from here to Boston. I found the ship's manifest, and, though I can't be a hundred percent certain at this point as I still have to comb through other documents, she did not travel back alone.'

'He went with her?' she guessed

'That's my assumption, though why he wasn't mentioned in the letter, I don't know, but there was a name directly above that of

Rosemary Quinton, that of a Bastiaan Bouten, but I can't really be sure, and as she didn't name him in the letter, well who knows.'

'You don't seem to be too concerned, not finding it I mean,' Samantha asked, glancing at him as they neared the wooden escalator.

He looked at her, then said, 'As I said, with the information I had, all that Chrissie had found out, there were no details, no markers, no specific reference points, so, I didn't think it would be as simple as just walking up to where x marks the spot, and, even if that was the case,' he continued as they rode up the first stage of the escalator, we can't just hammer and chisel and start taking tiles off!'

'No, of course not. So, what are you thinking? Leave it be?'

'Maybe, for now at least,' he answered as they walked across to the second section of the old wooden escalator that would bring them to street level.

'But I did consider, that there might be, a reference, a clue, a marker, and, that made me think as to what that might be. It came to me in the middle of the night, last night in fact, so, I got up, checked what Chrissie had sent me, then something clicked.
   This Rosemary, back in Genoa, had taken identifiable items from Chrissie's grandfather. She then discarded all but three, his watch, a book, and the miniature.
   Why? I mean, why keep the watch and the book?'
   They reached the top and exited the building.
   Once outside, Sam stopped and looked at Samantha, 'What are your thoughts on that?'

She pondered for a moment, then said, 'Perhaps the watch had an inscription? Maybe she, one day, wanted to give the watch to someone?'

'Possibly' Samuel answered, 'I did think of that too, but what puzzles me more, is the book.'

'I guess that is rather odd,' Samantha agreed.

Samuel led them to a nearby basketball court, and they sat down on a bench. The nearby market was getting busier.

'The story however,' Sam said, 'has another twist, but I have talked far too much and for long enough. It's your turn. Tell me all about Rico. I recall you telling me you had a plan?'

'Well remembered. Yes, I had plan, which was for Rico and his mum and dad to be reunited. Also, I wanted to see if I could help get a new passport for him.

Once he had arrived in Mexico, he set up the business, changed his name, and was happy to be there, but, as he had no official documents he could not travel. He managed to register as Rico Wagner in the city, in order to set up his business, but, as I said, no passport.

'Anyway, with his mum's assistance and the help of the detective from Amersfoort, Martijn, who had the right connections, we were able to sort a temporary travel document.

So I went back to Acapulco, and, well, he is the one for me,' she said, pausing and again looking slightly flushed as she smiled at Samuel.

'I am back here to finalise some things, but, thanks to the internet, I can work from home. I will still be working for the same firm, still also as the senior fraud investigator. Of course for that I will no doubt need to travel back at times, but other than that, I'll be working from, my new home, from Acapulco.

His mum and dad are there right now, catching up and mending broken bridges, so that is going well.'

'That's really great Samantha, I am so pleased for you.' He gave her a broad smile, then said, 'Well, to finish then. The end of the story.

'This Rosemary Quinton was a wealthy woman. Now, she not only left her granddaughter, Tammy, the letter, which, in reality, is a confession, I suppose, a very detailed report of the events of that time, but she also left her a New York apartment, according to Chrissie, a fabulous pad, overlooking Central Park, on top of which she was left a substantial amount of money as well.

'But this still isn't all to tell,' Sam continued, with Samantha listening closely.

'She also left, with her lawyers, an envelope to be given to a proven relative of the man she stole from, from Professor Edward Small, so Chrissie, with Tammy, together went over to see this lawyer, and Chrissie was given an envelope, which contained, the watch and a book.'

'That must have been, I guess, a little emotional, for the granddaughter, perhaps even both granddaughters,' Samantha said.

'I think so too,' Samuel agreed. 'As well as those items, there was also a legacy, if you will, a sum of money, so, to that end,' and Sam fished in the pocket of his jacket, and drew out an envelope which he gave to Samantha, 'this is for you'.

Samantha frowned at him briefly, accepted the envelope and opened it.

She drew out its contents and gasped. Her jaw dropping wide open.

'This ...this can't be right? Can it?' she managed to ask, still looking at the slip of paper in her hand.

'It's right, and very real,' Sam answered. 'It's a banker's cheque. It is in American dollars, but, a reasonable amount, don't you think?'

'A reasonable amount? It's for a quarter of a million dollars!

'Indeed. This is your half,' Sam said.

Then he explained, 'Chrissie is now a very wealthy woman. The total of the legacy she received is in excess of nine million. She wanted to give me a million, but I declined. I settled for half a million, and for you to have half of that. Its' only fair. If it had not been for us, she wouldn't have had any of this'.

Samantha flung herself at Samuel, 'Thank you! Thank you so much, you are such a gentleman.'

They hugged for a few moments.

It had been less than six weeks ago when they first met. It now seemed like they had known each other much longer.

They got up from the bench

She asked him, 'So, are you going to pursue the search for the miniature?'

'I think the book might have a clue. I will contact Chrissie about it, and find out what might be so special about this book for Rosemary to have kept it.'

Samuel then leaned forward, kissed Samantha on the cheek and said, as he walked away heading back towards the centre of town, 'I had better receive an invitation to the wedding when it happens Miss Price.'

'Count on it, Mr Price' she answered. Then seeing his wave in acknowledgement, smiled and headed for home.

EPILOGUE;

ROTTERDAM

SUNDAY 21ST APRIL

A little after eight in the evening.

Sam was tidying up in the kitchen, having prepared for himself another meal.

His mind aimlessly wandering, from one thing to the next.

How many meals had he made for himself, these past years.

How many times had he eaten alone.

These moments still ached in his heart. These moments he still missed her so much.

Keeping his mind on his work, or certainly trying to, was a relief, an escape from the reality of it all.

He stood at the sink, thinking about an early Eagles song, from memory he recalled it was their first single, back in 1972.

'Take it easy.'

The opening lines of the song, 'Well I'm running down the road, trying to loosen my load, I've got seven women on my mind ...'

Seven!

He was only thinking of three. His late wife, Sonja, the French woman, Sophie, and the American woman, Chrissie.

As well as that in his mind, unable to focus on just one thing, flitting from one thought to the next, there was the miniature, the Brueghel, most likely behind one of thousands of tiles in the tunnel in Antwerp, the Gauguin, what happened to the original, when did it get switched.

Also, the book. This book that Rosemary Quinton had deemed important to keep.

He had spoken to Chrissie, asking her about it. Was it unusual? Were there any notations, any marks?

There were none. The book was by C.S. Lewis, titled *The Screwtape Letters*. It was published in 1942. Why had she kept it?

And the watch, it too had no markings.

Sophie had found out about the purchaser of the Gauguin in 1908, a fellow by the name of Jan Smettens, who, she discovered, had also been in Cape Town at the same time as his great-grandfather, ambassador there at the time.

Chrissie, Sophie, Sonja.

Sam finished placing the dishes in the dishwasher.

Then there was the fact, that Rosemary never revealed the name of her boyfriend, the bricklayer from Antwerp, who had helped her hide the miniature, and, who it was who presumably sailed with her to Boston. Was it indeed this Bastiaan Bouten?

Why?

He himself had taken a quick look through his great-grandfather's journals and had discovered an interesting fact, having also done some genealogy work on Sophie. She was related by marriage to Gauguin. How amazing was that.

He had spoken to her about that. She, in turn, was silent for a few moments taking that news in, and had then told him of something she had discovered.

Jan Smettens had been a diplomatic courier for the British Embassy, and as such would have known Ambassador Samuel Price personally.

A very interesting connection indeed.

Sam made himself a coffee, took it into the lounge and stood by the window. It was dark outside and he watched the traffic below for a while.

His mind was still jumping all over the place.

Again, seemingly unable to just focus on one thing.

His thoughts returned to the song. 'Take it easy'

Well, he could, in fact, take it easy. Financially he was very secure.

But then his late wife's words came back to him.

Those final words she had spoken, that morning in the hospital.

'Go and find someone to love'

Chrissie? Sophie?

Blowing out his cheeks, he sat down in the lounge chair and carefully took a sip of his coffee.

Two trails, one chasing the item, chasing the Breughel miniature, and two, looking for what had happened to the genuine Gauguin?

Then there were two women, occupying a place in his heart.

Chrissie and Sophie.

'It isn't that easy,' he whispered to himself, 'but I will keep trying.'

BOOK 2

THREE DIRECTIONS

PROLOGUE

PRESENT DAY, ANTWERP

MONDAY 1ST APRIL

She brushed her long auburn hair. Not her natural colour, a new colour.

Well, not exactly new, but a colour she had settled on about three years ago.

It seemed to go well with her green eyes.

As she brushed, she took in what she saw in the mirror.

Forty-seven years of age.

Fifty seemed to loom closer ever so quickly.

She studied her face as she continued brushing. Her green eyes were set in a tanned face.

A brief smile appeared as she acknowledged how much she had changed. So different now to the person she had been.

For she had been, and she recalled the words her, now ex, husband had once used, a stuck-up arrogant bitch.

He had been right. How had she become like that? How had it all happened, why had she changed?

She closed her eyes briefly, remembered that at the time, she had felt like the queen bee, the cream of the crop. At that time she felt sure that the world turned around her. She had flirted, had strayed, had left men in her wake.

Opening her eyes she stopped brushing.

A lifetime ago.

In the mirror she saw the box that was on the bed.

A jewellery box. Containing a diamond studded necklace with matching earrings and bracelet.

She had them back. Once again they were hers. She put the brush down.

Her cream silk set of pyjamas swished with a whispering sound as she got up from the dressing table stool and sat herself on the edge of the king-size bed.

Leaning over she moved the box closer to her, opened it and once more studied the sparkling contents.

She was pleased with herself. They were once again hers.

Everything changed. That day. That fateful day.

She got up from the bed, placed the jewellery box in the safe, then adjusting the curtain and taking a quick peek out onto the Groeneplaats below she got into bed.

Once again she brought to mind that day, seven years ago, as she regularly did. She wanted to keep reminding herself of that event, to remain focused, remain determined to put a wrong right.

Then, and only then could she, she felt, truly move on.

Adjusting the bed sheet, snuggling down, she closed her eyes and thought back …

It had been a Friday. Cape Town, South Africa.

Her husband had flown over to the States.

She knew their marriage was over, but was adamant to escape unscathed and on her terms.

She had purchased a one-way ticket, first class, bound for London.

She had packed two large suitcases, plus a carry-on case, and had, late that afternoon, set off for the bank where, in a safe deposit box, she kept her precious jewels and a bundle of cash.

All was going splendidly and she was feeling upbeat and ready for new adventures and conquests.

This was, however, her old self. Arrogant, selfish.

Then it had all gone wrong at the airport.

She had checked in, gone through security and wandered around the various duty-free stores for a bit. She had then visited the ladies restroom.

The attack had been quick.

Next thing she knew, she was stirring and coming around in a hospital room and the nurse was calling her Miss Van Doorn.

However much she tried, she couldn't speak, couldn't seem to move her arms or legs. Her mind was a whirling mixture of confusion.

It wasn't until sometime later that she regained some sense of control, then, having gestured that she wanted some paper and a pen, managed to write down, her hand quite shaky, that she had been attacked at the airport and that she was not this Miss Van Doorn.

The police were called.

She had been discovered by a cleaner and it was assumed that the woman had suffered a heart attack; therefore an ambulance was called and she was taken to hospital. No foul play was even suspected at that time.

Her voice finally returned and the doctors, having now done some different blood tests, confirmed she had been given a concoction of drugs that rendered her vocal cords and muscles very weak.

By this time however, the woman who had assaulted her, taken her identity and her place on the flight to London had already landed and passed through customs.

The police quickly worked out a likely scenario. This Miss Van Doorn, first name Lucie, was an employee of the bank, in fact the very same woman who had helped her with her safe deposit box that day.

The detective who had come to her hospital bed the following day explained what they surmised must have happened. This woman from the bank, who, and the detective showed her a photograph, looked remarkably similar to her, had taken that fact as an opportunity, a spur of the moment chance, to create for herself a new identity, and a new life for herself.

That event changed her.

Later the detective had returned to escort her home and had written up a report that she would need for her insurance.

Once alone in her house, the realisation of what had occurred hit her.

She could have been killed.

Time passed. The police investigation petered out. No trace was found of the woman, no trace of her jewels.

Her husband never returned from the States and filed for divorce.

The house was sold, and the proceeds split.

Insurance paid for her hospital bill, for the loss of her jewels, suitcases and clothing.

A handsome settlement as she was well covered.

Petra Leyland returned to her maiden name and ordered a new passport.

A new life, a new start with her old name, Petra Stevens.

Three weeks later, the day her new passport arrived, she stood in front of the mirror in the hallway of her new apartment.

She made a resolution to once again become the woman she used to be. A better person. Discarding the old ways, the old her. She was fuelled and focused by a promise she made to herself, that she would not rest until she found this woman and would do all she could to retrieve her jewels.

Seven years ...

Reaching over, she turned off the light.

Seven years, though some of her jewellery would be very difficult, more likely impossible, to relocate, her prize possession was the necklace, diamond studded, with the matching earrings and bracelet. This was a unique set.

It was an heirloom, having once belonged to her grandmother.

Scanning the internet, following the websites of auction houses, particularly in London, Amsterdam, Paris and Antwerp, and regularly checking well-known jewellery stores in the big cities in Europe, Petra, at last, found them.

In Antwerp, opposite the railway station, a large outlet placed her items on their website.

The day after locating them, Petra walked into the store, saw her pieces on display, and insisted on seeing the manager.

A man duly came out from his office and Petra showed him a photograph of herself wearing the very same set, showed him the full police report, then, as she had been reimbursed by the insurance company, offered to buy them back, but, she suggested, at the best price he could do.

Also, as she felt she was on a roll with this man, a jovial chap who was certainly showing her much concern, she asked him to give her the details of who had sold them to him, in order to pass that information onto the police back home.

Petra turned on to her side.

She was pleased with herself.

Taking in a deep breath, she stretched, then curled up and closed her eyes.

She had her jewellery back.

The concerned manager had been very sympathetic and had given her a good price.

Such had been her confidence in dealing with him, she also had the details of the person who had sold the items to the store.

She had a name.

It was a woman who had sold the set just over a year ago, but, as they hadn't sold as quickly as they had hoped, they placed the item on their website.

Her name, according to the ledger, was Miss Steffie Baertjens, from Amsterdam.

Furthermore, she had an address.

Was it real? Did she really live there? was she still living there? She would find out tomorrow.

A few moments later Petra Stevens was sound asleep.

What she would find out, upon arrival at that address, was that the police were there, that a woman had been assaulted there, and that Steffie Baertjens had flown to Florence.

THE PRESENT;

PARIS

TUESDAY 30TH APRIL

Sophie Pontiac returned to work two weeks ago, after an eventful couple of weeks.

It had been a trail that had led to danger, the beginning of a romance that had not taken root and a mystery that had not as yet been resolved.

After a brief catch up with her boss Emmanuel, she entered her own office, switched on her computer terminal and got her bottle of water from her bag to take a few sips.

Sitting down, she punched in her password and thought about Sam.

She was ever so grateful that he had been at home, and had subsequently come to her rescue. They had bonded, they had kissed, but romance had not blossomed.

Why was that, she wondered, as her login page came up.

Was it her? Was it him? Was it just the wrong time?

A knock on her office door brought her out of her reverie.

'Entrer.'

A woman entered her office, strode up to where she was sitting behind her desk, extended her hand, and said, 'Good morning Miss Pontiac' in English. 'My name is Petra Stevens, and I believe we have an enemy in common, namely a certain Steffie Baertjens, though that is, of course, not her real name.'

Sophie got to her feet, took the offered hand, slightly taken aback by this sudden intrusion. 'Hello. Yes, how ...' she began.

Petra interrupted, 'Her real name is Lucie Van Doorn, and she stole my identity, put me in hospital and stole my jewels, seven years ago in Cape Town.' The words rushed out.

Sophie released her grip on the woman's hand and walked around her desk.

She was recovering from the unexpected visitor, and, having digested what had been said, she spoke. 'Please, do have a seat. It seems we may have a lot to talk about. Cape Town did you say? Curious.'

Then, wheeling her desk chair around, she asked' Would you like some coffee or tea?'

Forty minutes later Sophie escorted Petra out of the building and they gave each other a brief hug before they parted.

Walking back to her office she mulled over all that Petra had told her, and her thoughts went back to Sam.

Two days after he had put her on the train back to Paris, he had called, had asked her how she was, and told her that he was going to take some time out. He would talk to the director shortly, and was going away for about six months, he said.

Whilst talking, her first thought was that he would go and see that woman from Boston, and felt a pang of jealousy as she sensed that he liked her.

But he said he was going to Canada.

Had their connection been too close, too personal, too soon?

She figured he just needed more time.

Or had she been too forceful?

She thanked him for being there and told him to take care and to stay in touch.

Back at her desk after Petra's visit, Sophie composed a message containing what she had just learned.

An interesting development.

What would Sam make of it?

After pressing 'send' on her computer, she said to herself in a whisper, 'So, where are you, Sam Price?'

New Brunswick, Canada

Tuesday 30th April

'Good morning, how may I help you?'

'Hi, I have an appointment with Mr Rozzini.'

'Your name, sir?'

'Price, Sam Price.'

The receptionist was a lady well into her sixties, well coiffured hair, well-spoken and, as she looked up at him over the rim of her glasses, her eyes clearly indicated she was well determined that no-one would pass without her say so.

She pressed a button on her telephone, spoke briefly and a reply came instantly on the speaker.

'Please be seated, Mr Rozzini will see you shortly,' she said, then dismissed him from her attention to focus on other matters.

Sam turned to sit down in the foyer area, but hadn't gone two steps when a man's voice called out to him, 'Mr Price? Please come this way.'

Sam turned to see the man, with a beaming smile on his face, standing a little way up the passage.

As Sam approached, the man extended his hand, 'Nico Rozzini' he said, his voice deep.

Sam took the hand and took note of the man who was four or maybe closer to five inches shorter than him. He was stockily built, wore an expensive dark suit and a pair of, most likely Italian, shoes, looking every inch a successful business man.

His hair was dark and combed back, he was clean shaven and his eyes a deep brown in colour.

'Pleased to meet you Mr Rozzini,' Sam replied, shaking the hand which had a firm grip.

'Call me Nico. Come in, come in,' and he led the way into his office.

The office was big and covered in a wall-to-wall thick carpet which was a shade of pale green and devoid of pattern.

The desk was a beautiful antique. It had a leather top set in oak wood.

There were several folders stacked on one side, a dark green telephone on the other and a small laptop in the middle.

The chair behind the desk was obviously leather and looked impressive.

There were two smaller armchairs on this side of the desk.

Three windows gave a view over the town that lay beyond.

On the opposite wall to where the desk stood, were three chairs surrounding a low coffee table.

Also in the spacious office stood an oak sideboard with an assortment of bottles and glasses on its top, a grey metal filing cabinet and two standard lamps.

What drew Sam's attention the most though, was what he had come here to see. On the wall behind the desk hung a painting.

It was big.

Sam estimated it would be around one and a half metres in length, by about a metre in height.

It was mounted in an ornate gilded frame, around two and a half inches in width.

The large painting was suspended by two wires.

It was alarmed, as a third, thinner wire, ran up from the middle of the back of it, up into the ceiling.

The scene was a seascape, a single vessel, a two-masted sailing ship, was struggling in high seas.

It was atmospheric, it was beautifully painted, it drew your attention from every angle of the room and pulled you into the very struggle the ship was facing.

You could easily imagine the roar of the wind and the crashing of the waves.

Look at it for a few moments and you could feel the anguish of the seamen aboard and sense the struggle they were facing.

'Well Mr Price, what do you think?'

'Please, call me Sam,' was the answer and without taking his eyes of the painting he asked, 'May I take a closer look?'

Nico Rozzini gestured him to be his guest, saying, 'Of course'

Sam walked behind the big desk, studied the painting carefully with the naked eye, then, taking a pencil torch from his pocket, looked at it in more detail for several moments.

'And there's something on the back,' Sam asked, continuing to study the work of art, 'you told me over the phone?'

'Yes.' He moved behind the desk and retrieved something from a top drawer. This he handed over to Sam. It was an A4 sized photograph.

'This was taken some time ago, at least ten years. Before I bought the company.'

Sam nodded his thanks as he took the photo and studied it for a bit, then said, 'So, when you bought this company, they left the painting behind?'

'I bought the business, lock stock and barrel. This was here, in this office.'

Sam came from behind the desk, took in the large painting for a few more moments, then turned to Mr Rozzini and gave him his full attention as he spoke, 'Well sir, this is a great painting. It's an oil on canvas. This photo shows the back clearly, so that's good. I will be taking a few pictures myself today to begin an initial search, but you have here a very nice work of art ...I believe it could be, by a Dutch artist, Jan Porcellis.'

Sam then continued, 'I see that is it titled "Ochtend Storm", which means morning storm. Looking at the colours of the sky and the light used, it suggests it is dawn, the break of day.

It is well executed, and a fantastic composition. The label on the back,' Sam said, whilst taking a closer look at the photograph he had been handed, 'tells me a few things, the title of the work, and it also says Rotterdam 1616, likely the date it was painted, the number 32 written on a separate label and then there is a scrawl of sorts, possibly added at a later date, showing the initials JP.'

Returning his attention to Mr Rozzini, Sam said, 'I can't see a signature on the painting itself, but this could be hidden, because the frame is not the original. Going by the style, this frame was put on around the mid-eighteenth century. The original would have been a plain, dark wood surround.'

Sam took a quick look around the office, then said, 'Looking at your ceiling, people have smoked in this room over many years. The painting needs a good clean. But it is a good piece, I will need to do quite some research, as to how it got here, who owned it before, how it got to be here in Canada, trail it back, as far as I can.'

Again looking at the painting, Sam continued, 'As it is though, it would fetch around ten to fifteen thousand dollars.'

'I was told it might be around that figure,' Rozzini replied. 'Are you saying it could be worth more? '

'Oh absolutely, it all depends on the provenance. The more I can show the painting's history, and if I can attribute this to it very likely being a Porcellis, the we are looking at substantially more, eighty to a hundred and twenty thousand dollars, maybe more,' Sam explained.

'Mamma Mia, goodness me, that much?' Rozzini exclaimed 'So, if you do this, this provenance, how much would that cost to do?'

Sam smiled at the man, 'I work solely on commission Mr Rozzini. The more it sells for, the more I get, so you see it is in my interest, as much as yours, to find out the relevant details. There's no cost to you.'

Twenty-five minutes later, a very upbeat Rozzini had organised coffee and had signed paperwork to state he would not sell the painting through any other auction or dealer.

Sam, having taken several photographs, said that he would be in touch soon, as at some point he wanted to have the gilded frame professionally taken off to check for a signature, and left the building.

Sam headed for the centre of the small town. The weather was good, a bright day with a cool breeze.

He crossed over the old stone bridge, the Petitcodiac River flowing beneath, and made his way to a nearby cafe.

Although having just had a cup of coffee, he fancied another, along with perhaps a slice of cake he thought, entering the cafe.

A few moments later he sat by the window, a hot coffee by his side and, what looked to be a rather tasty, big slice of fruit cake in front of him.

Stirring some sugar into his drink, Sam reflected on the morning, his first assignment on this side of the Atlantic.

Sipping the hot liquid he looked out the window and his mind went back to his apartment in Rotterdam, not that long ago ...

Many thoughts had been swirling around in his mind. A heart that was aching. A heart that was in somewhat of a quandary.

One woman, the American, Chrissie, and the time spent with her on the trail of her grandfather. The other woman, French, Sophie, and the trail of the missing Gauguin.

Two women.

He needed a break, A change of scenery. He just wasn't ready.

He had called Sophie, spoke to her for a while, and tried to explain his decision, had then also spoken to the director, saying he was taking a break for six months.

He spoke to Chrissie in Boston. Again thanked her for her generosity and spoke at length about his decision to go to Canada for a while.

Sam then contacted the Boston Auction House, Franck Huysen & Son, whom he had recently met, with regard to the miniature.

There was no longer a Franck Huysen, nor was there a son, but due to the fact it was a well-known and respected business, the name was kept.

He spoke to the directors, both of whom he met whilst last in Boston. They were both in their seventies, Walton and Stanhope.

Sam offered a proposition.

This was accepted.

As he put the phone down that afternoon, he visualised these two men and a smile crept on his face for they reminded him of the pair of old men on The Muppet Show, Waldorf and Statler.

Sam had then set about making all the arrangements.

A few days later, Sam Price, forty-seven years old, flew from Amsterdam to Halifax, Nova Scotia. A change of scenery. A change of place ...

The coffee was nice, so was the cake. Standing up he set his six-foot one frame into motion and left the cafe.

He passed by the old railway station, an imposing building, far too grand for the size of the town, built in the late 1880s. It had a magnificent facade and he half thought about taking a look around.

He was fond of old railway stuff, but, as he had to return here anyway, this visit would keep.

He walked past the police station towards a small car park on the opposite side of the road where he had parked his VW minibus.

Unlocking it he slipped behind the wheel then set about making some notes of his visit.

When he had learned of his appointment, Sam had done some preliminary research on the company and on the current owner, Mr Nico Rozzini.

He had purchased CP Holdings, a working mine, a little over ten years ago. It was in this small town called Harris, named after the man who had started the mine way back in the year 1819.

It had been a Joshua Parker, who, at the age of seventy-five, sold the mine to Nico Rozzini, after the mine had been in the Parker family for generations.

Sam always loved the research part of his job, and would later discover that it was a man called Charlie Parker the Third, who had originally set up CP Holdings in 1821.

Sam put his notepad down, then turned the key to bring the engine to life.

Though it was the body of an old classic VW, a 1968 model, the engine was much newer. The interior was posh with a couple of fine leather bucket seats in the front, the floor of the van carpeted in the back.

There was a small couch, a worktop with cupboards below, a fridge and a larger storage unit in the back covering the engine.

The wheels were twice the width of the originals and in the cab a new instrument panel contained a CD player, with USB access points and an up-to-date satnav.

He had purchased it shortly after his arrival in Canada when he saw it for sale on the forecourt of a garage close to where his apartment was. It had belonged to a guy who was much into climbing and hiking but through circumstances had to give it up.

Sam drove out of the small parking area, turned right, then drove up and out of town on the road that cut through the mountain range, heading for Moncton.

Taking in the beautiful scenery, Sam let his mind wander again to how it was that he got to be here, and how it was that he had chosen Canada.

He had always wanted to visit this country. He recalled reading a little history, that, particularly on the east coast, many folk had settled there from England, Scotland, Ireland, Scandinavia and mainland Europe over the past centuries.

It also occurred to him, that many would have taken, at least, their most valuable belongings with them.

There was art to be found, he was sure.

Finding an ideal apartment for rent on an online website, he made the arrangements and payments, and so ended up in Moncton.

The town was, Sam felt, geographically well-suited, with a major highway and a good train connection at hand.

The apartment was fully furnished and situated on the outskirts of town, adjacent to an industrial area and the location suited Sam fine.

Everything had fallen into place very quickly indeed. He had arrived, taking a taxi from Halifax airport all the way to his new address.

Seeing the van on the forecourt as he arrived, Sam had almost immediately walked over and had purchased the vehicle.

He then set about stocking the fridge and freezer, sorted out an internet connection, set up his music station, purchased several other items, including new bed linen and towels, and was ready for action, which was just as well, as he received a call from the Boston auction house asking if he would call on a Mr Rozzini of CP Holdings, regarding the value, and possible sale, of a painting.

Great, Sam thought, first potential client.

Sam drove through the gorge, then the road joined Highway 1 and it wasn't too much longer when he started to see the Moncton skyline in the distance.

He felt good.

It was good to have something to get his teeth into, researching a painting or piece of art was exciting for him.

Delving into the past, he researched when it had been painted, by whom, where it had been done, and then traced the trail of owners, throughout centuries in some cases.

Also there was intrigue: was the article stolen, or was it fake?

Though often times the research could be tedious and time consuming, he loved it.

He was closing in on his new home. A rumble in his stomach reminded him that it was lunchtime.

The apartment he had sourced via the internet and subsequently taken, was spacious.

The building was a trade outlet for anything bathroom or kitchen related, this business covered the whole of the ground floor.

The second level was split into two separate apartments. These had their own entrance at the front, a small lobby giving access to an elevator as well a set of stairs leading to the top floor.

Then, at the back of each apartment, another set of internal metal stairs led directly into their respective garages below.

All ideal.

Sam arrived at the back courtyard, clicked a button on a remote control and his garage door opened smoothly.

He turned the van around, then backed into his garage and killed the engine.

Going up the stairs with his notebook and camera, two things were on his mind. The first was, what was he going to make himself for lunch, the second, as he reached the top of the stairs and unlocked the door and entered the kitchen area of his apartment, was how the painting he saw earlier had come to be here, having started life over four hundred years ago.

THE PAST;

PERIOD I

THE YEAR 1762

In an old stone building in Haringvliet, Rotterdam, there was hammering going on.

A man was putting a crate together, banging in the last of the steel spikes.

The sound echoed all around, bouncing off the walls.

All else was quiet.

It was Sunday morning.

The old building lay adjacent to one of the many docks. Although several ships were berthed nearby, none were on this dock, but there was one due to arrive later in the morning.

Christoffer Rosenborg was done.

He put the hammer on the bench and took a look all around the crate he had assembled. It was only around thirty centimetres in width, but well over a metre in height and more than one and a half metres in length.

Satisfied that it was secure he walked back to the bench and gathered up some documents.

In the distance he heard church bells ringing.

Sliding the large door open just a little, he stepped out onto the wooden pier.

It was cold and there was a mist hanging over the water. He could barely make out the ship berthed in the next dock; the only thing visible were the two masts rising above the low-lying fog.

Another church bell began to chime, this one closer by and the sound carried eerily across the water.

It seemed he was the only one about.

Christoffer re-entered the building and slid the door closed. Two lanterns, one either side of the large door, were lit and provided a dim light throughout the shed.

He dragged the crate he had assembled across to where other goods were stacked. Three smaller cases, a large trunk and two leather bags.

These all belonged to him.

Born in 1727 in Copenhagen, he left home and journeyed to the Netherlands, where he studied at the Leiden University for three years.

Always having longed to travel, he secured work with the Dutch East India Company, also known as the VOC.

He spoke several languages, and despite being only twenty when he started, he secured a responsible role.

In fact he took on three roles. In the first, it would be his duty to conduct trade agreements with various groups in the Far East as well as establishing new suppliers and negotiating tariffs. For the second, he had the task and responsibility to ensure the correct loading and unloading of the ship and then thirdly, and this he took on himself as an extra interest, he would document the ship's journeys, the connections made, and the cargoes transported.

After thirteen years of service Christoffer parted with the company, wanting to do more freelance correspondence work, particularly travelling to places to document the state of play where there were skirmishes, unrest and war.

His language skills, he spoke five languages fluently, would help in meeting new peoples in different countries to expand his knowledge on customs, local rituals and generally how folk lived in various conditions.

Now he was embarking on another such journey, having previously only travelled to the Far East and South America, this time he was to cross the Atlantic and head for America and Canada.

It was time for a change of scenery, a change of place.

Through his connections he had secured passage later to-day. A Dutch coastal schooner would take him to Rouen, France.

There he would board a French galleon, bound for Boston, via Cadiz.

After he dragged the crate across the stone floor to where his other belongings were placed, he patted the wooden crate.

He was pleased, for inside was a purchase he had made only four days ago.

The auction had not been well attended and he secured the items at a great price.

He would be able to easily sell these in Boston, furthermore he had a trunk full of fine silk from Persia. Again, he would have no trouble at all in getting a good price for these.

This would provide funds that would enable him to continue to travel and explore.

From somewhere he heard the sound of a horn.

The church bells had stopped ringing.

Christoffer again slipped outside.

Coming in from the fog he saw a ship approaching.

From seemingly nowhere, several men had arrived, dock workers, ready to moor the ship and commence it's unloading.

The silence of earlier was broken.

The mist was lifting and the sun broke through the clouds.

FIFTEEN DAYS LATER

Charlie Parker was a large man. He was a jovial man.

He was always well-dressed, always had time for a chat, and almost always smoking a big cigar.

His vivid blue eyes were mostly sparkling joyously to accompany his broad grin.

But he was also a business man and had a finger in several pies: building projects, shipping and farming, and on some occasions those same blue eyes could have a piercing quality that showed intent and determination not to be denied.

The thirty-year-old had inherited his family's fortune ten years ago when both his parents had died from an illness that had rampaged through the city, taking over a hundred lives in just a few days.

But Boston recovered, and grew.

Charlie was in an exceptionally jovial as he puffed on his cigar.

He shot a brief glance out of one of the windows of his grand house that overlooked the harbour as he passed to fetch another drink for one of his many guests present.

The lavishly decorated front parlour was abuzz with the sound of voices, the clinking of glasses, and the sound from the man at the piano playing an assortment of popular tunes.

A blue haze of smoke swirled around the large room.

Two servants were also circulating among the guests, offering a selection of finger foods that were neatly presented on silver trays.

Charlie was exceptionally jovial, because, as he referred to her, his 'little woman', despite the fact that she was almost the same size as him, had just given birth to their first child, a son, Charlie Parker the second.

Had he stayed by the window a little longer, had he taken time to observe that late afternoon, he would have witnessed the docking of a large French three-masted galleon.

As a freelance correspondent, with the ability to speak, read and write in Danish, Dutch, French, Portuguese and English, the now thirty-five-year-old Christoffer had sold many news articles, established a lot of contacts, and was financially well rewarded for a job he loved doing.

He had contacted a French newspaper a week earlier, informing them of his intentions to check out the situation in Nova Scotia, in particular Halifax and Dartmouth because of the skirmished between the French and both the natives and the English and to enquire whether they were interested in securing his reports.

They were indeed most interested.

In view of this, he had asked for them to put him into contact with someone in Boston who could secure his easy entrance into America, and who could arrange for somewhere to live for about a week, in return for his reports which he would then send, via this same contact in Boston.

Knowing of his acumen and his detailed writings, they were very happy with this arrangement and told Christoffer they had just the man in Boston. This, of course he already knew, but didn't let on, astute operator that he was.

And so, a driver with a wagon, was waiting at dockside. His papers perused and stamped without fuss or bother and he was sent on his way. All his luggage, including the wooden crate, was carefully loaded on board the flatbed wagon.

Smooth and easy, the man in Boston had seen to that, also personally taking him to where he could lodge for a week or longer if needed.

Christoffer was well pleased.

He thanked the man, advised him to expect his reports every week from the moment he landed in Canada and said goodnight.

Eight days a week, the Beatles would sing in the 1960s, eight days it took for Christoffer to complete what he had set out to achieve whilst in Boston.

He found a buyer for all the silk he had brought with him, fine Persian silks that proved quite profitable.

After some investigation, and this he was good at, he found out just the right person to see with regard to what he had carefully packed in the crate he himself had built back in Rotterdam.

Standing in the doorway of the small house he had been taken to upon arrival, he awaited the man.

According to his research, this would be the man interested in buying what he had, moreover, a wealthy man to boot, one who could afford to pay the price he had in mind.

The man arrived, walked up to the doorway and jovially greeted him.

Christoffer showed Charlie Parker in and brought him to the front room of the house. There, the furniture pushed aside, in the middle of the room, stood the crate.

Aiming to make a show of its contents, Christoffer walked up to the crate which stood upright, then, with a flourish, pulled down the front panel to reveal the contents.

Both men were capable negotiators, both men were shrewd, the banter was friendly, the deal was made and both were satisfied.

Charlie Parker left the house, very pleased with his purchase.

Christoffer Rosenborg had arranged for passage to Halifax and would sail the next day, eight days after his arrival.

THE PRESENT;

MONCTON

WEDNESDAY 1ST MAY

The wooden boxcar stood alone and seemingly abandoned on rusty rails inside the old steel girded and tin roofed building.

The old man, Joe, had told him about the boxcar and that it was very old.

He wasn't wrong, it was indeed very old, most likely from the late 1800s.

It was thirty-six feet in length and the faint lettering could still be made out to read, Silver Line, on the left-hand side of the sliding door, and, Canadian Pacific Despatch, on the right.

Three lamps suspended from the crossbeams high overhead provided much needed light, as a cloudburst had almost turned day into night.

The heavy rainfall easily found the many holes in the old roof confirmed by the puddles created below them.

Sam walked over to the open large sliding door through which he had entered over half an hour ago.

He noticed some lighter patches appearing in the clouds overhead and figured the rain would ease up soon.

The Creedence Clearwater Revival classic song, 'Have you ever seen the rain' came to mind as he stood and watched for a while.

He was glad he had come.

The previous evening he had spent hours, looking at his laptop screen, scrolling and searching, typing and reading.

It was late evening when he had drawn up two timelines.

The first was a line that worked backwards, starting with a current date and the paintings current owner, Rozzini, then back to Joshua Parker, further back to Nathaniel and down the family tree, from Charlie Parker the fifth, back to Charlie Parker the fourth and to Charlie Parker the third, who had left Boston to set up the mine in Harris, and had set up the company, CP Holdings.

From there the timeline went back to Charlie Parker the second and finally to Charlie Parker, a wealthy and influential business man in Boston.

Sam's research had revealed that it had been this man who had originally purchased the painting. In fact, he had purchased three. Though he had not found any description of these paintings, nor, at this stage, who he had bought them from, it made sense in view of where the painting was today that the seascape in Rozzini's office must surely be one purchased in Boston in the year 1762.

The second timeline Sam had drawn up was much shorter with regard to information found.

Here Sam had started with the artist he felt had produced the painting, Jan Porcellis.

Starting with the date he found on the back of it, 1616, this worked well for him, for Jan commenced his art around 1612, was married in Rotterdam in 1605 and died in 1632, so it seemed likely that this was indeed the date the painting was done.

Sam also knew from his research, that some of this artist's works were not signed and that he regularly sold his work to support his lifestyle.

He travelled around a fair bit which meant many of his works could be anywhere. Not much help there.

Sam had then searched documents of art sales and auction, focusing on Rotterdam where the artist had lived most of the time.

This was time consuming and a strain on the eyes and every now and then Sam had to get up from his chair and arch the stiffness from his back.

He did find something to put into the timeline, assuming that the label on the back, as shown on the photograph that Mr Rozzini had given him, with the number 32 referred to a lot number, then using that in conjunction with the sales registers, he had found a likely candidate.

Lot number 32, seascape, storm, unknown artist, circa 1616.

The auction was held in Rotterdam in 1762, but he could not find a record of any buyers.

So, Sam now had a timeline running from 1616 through to 1762, which was still a gap of a hundred and forty-six years to fill.

And, how did the painting, bought in Rotterdam in 1762, get to Boston that same year. Who was it that had purchased it, and likely two others, and sold them to Charlie Parker?

Already late in the evening, he then noticed he had an e-mail from Sophie about an interesting development, a meeting with a woman who knew about Steffie Baertjens, who knew her real name, and knew about the connection with South Africa.

Sam wrote a brief reply, asking her to keep him informed and to be careful.

It had been after midnight when he had called it a day.

Waking up in the morning he decided, that, after breakfast, he would take some time out and wander over to the railway yard.

Though the city's railway station wasn't very large, with not a huge amount of passenger traffic, the shunting yard was big.

Sam took his camera and walked, for it wasn't far from where he lived. He found himself a spot on the embankment where he sat down and observed the goings on.

It had been around lunchtime when an old man approached him.

'Figure you might like something to eat,' the old timer said, sitting himself beside Sam and opening a parcel to reveal a selection of sausage, bread, cheese and biscuits.

'Wow, that looks good, thank you,' Sam said, then offering his hand' I'm Sam.'

The man, likely to be in his eighties, quite thin, wearing corduroy trousers and a rain jacket over a checked shirt, his hair grey and blue eyes set in a weathered face took his hand, 'Joe' he said, his grip firm.

It was nearly two hours later, when Sam slid open the large door to the old shed.

There were three pieces of rolling stock inside. On the right, an old tanker wagon, most likely from the 1960s, then, behind that stood an old flatbed railcar, this one a little older, built in the 1930s or 1940s Sam guessed.

But what interested him most, was the boxcar on the left side of the shed.

Walking up to and around it, Sam checked it out.

It was old, it was worn.

The stories it must be able to tell if it could talk. Well over a century old.

Sam took several pictures, then, with a little effort, managed to open the sliding cargo door and climbed inside.

He took more photographs.

What Sam noticed, and found most interesting, was a small brass plate. It was screwed above the sliding door, on the inside of the car.

Only about two inches in length and no more than an inch in height, it had the name 'SARA' engraved on it.

It was then when it suddenly became very dark in the shed.

The rain came down.

Sam went over to the bank of light switches and turned on the overhead lamps.

The rain thundered upon the tin roof; the sound almost deafening.

Standing in the doorway to the shed, Sam took in the moments.

To him it was always a great feeling, when you could hear the rain on the roof and you were sheltered and warm inside.

Standing there, leaning against the doorpost, watching the heavy rain come down from the sky creating a glistening railway yard, some of the rails gleaming like beacons in their drenched surroundings, Sam was glad he had come.

A moment to pause, to think.

The rain began to ease, the clouds began to break and it was becoming lighter again.

Then something caught his eye as he was about to re-enter the shed about sixty feet away, on the other side of the goods yard perimeter fence.

Here, he knew, was a small car park area that served the railway station.

Through the easing rain, he had picked up a movement.

It was a woman.

He could make out that she was blond, wore a long red trench coat of sorts, and was half running, half walking rapidly, towards a red sports car.

Sam watched as she reached the vehicle. Even from that distance, he could see that she was fumbling in her coat pocket for the keys.

Finding them, she unlocked the car door, opened it.

Then, like a blur, suddenly there appeared a dark van. It was either black or very dark blue.

The vehicle stopped right by where the woman was about to get into her car.

Sam just sensed that something was amiss and watched as the sliding door of the van opened and a man and a woman came bundling out.

They flanked the blond woman, grabbed her and dragged her into the van.

The man stayed inside the van, the woman, a brunette, then slid the door shut and quickly stepped into the red sports car.

The van took off, made a rapid turn and sped away from the car park.

The red car, after a small hesitation as Sam heard the engine surge, drove away following the van.

It had all happened in mere seconds.

But Sam, remembering, towards the end that he had his camera in his hand, quickly lifted it up and took several shots in succession.

What they would show, he didn't know, but what to do next, this was the problem.

He had left his apartment on foot. The goods yards weren't far away and the walk and fresh air, he felt, would do him good, especially after having spent many hours the previous evening looking at the laptop screen.

Apart from his camera, he had not taken anything else, not even his phone, purposefully leaving that behind as he wanted some quiet time to himself, so, he couldn't make a call.

To get to the station building and secure some help would take too long, it was a roundabout trek to reach it.

He didn't know where the police station was, so, by process of elimination, Sam decided to head home.

He turned off the shed's lights, closed the big door, then half ran and half walked, towards his apartment through the rain, which had eased quite a bit.

Karen Saunders. Thirty-nine, short cropped dark hair, brown eyes, around five-foot six in height.

She was the senior officer on duty.

A detective sergeant of the Royal Canadian Mounted Police.

She was informed, via the intercom on her desk, that there was a man, a foreigner, in the lobby, wanting to report a kidnapping.

She told reception to escort the man to her office, released the speaker button and looked at her desk.

There was a pile of folders on her left, and another pile on her right.

They were one officer down due to illness and another was away on maternity leave. Their other station, across town, had no-one to spare.

Underpaid and overworked she was thinking to herself as there was a knock on the door, which then opened as the desk sergeant led the man inside.

The foreigner.

Well, this ought to be good, she thought, then asked, 'A kidnapping? ...Mr?'

'Price, Sam Price. Yes, it sure looks that way.'

Detective Sergeant Saunders invited the man to sit. 'Go on,' she said, waiting, and also wondering what kind of accent this man had, possibly British, though she thought maybe Australian.

'Well, I was about sixty feet or so away, but through the rain I noticed this woman, a blonde woman, she was hurrying towards, I assume, her car. Then, as she reached it and opened the driver's door to get in, a van suddenly pulled up alongside, facing the opposite way. From where I was standing, I saw the side sliding door of the van open, two people got out, a man and a woman. They quickly grabbed this blond woman and dragged her back into the van.

'Then the woman from the van, a brunette, shut the door of the van, and got into the car. The van took off, turned around and exited the car park. This is the small car park by the railway station. Then the woman who had got into the car, a red car by the way, took off after it,' Sam explained, telling it a he remembered it.

The detective thought all this through for a moment, still wondering about his accent, but now also wondering if this man's imagination wasn't working overtime.

'You said, this all happened in the car park by the railway station' she asked, looking directly at him, into his eyes, which, she noted, were dark green.

Sam took off his glasses, wiped a few droplets of rain away, then set them back, saying, 'there is a small car parking area, by the perimeter of the goods yard, it's to the left of the main station building.'

'And this happened when?' she asked, breaking eye contact to write something down on the pad in front of her.

Sam looked at his watch.

From the shed he had jogged through the easing rain, making his way to his apartment. He had, upon arrival, looked up the address of the nearest police station, had then taken the back stairs down to the garage below, hopped into his van and made his way into town.

There was a space right outside the station.

'Twenty-three minutes ago' he answered.

'Really?' she said, again looking directly at him, 'and you didn't think to call 911?'

But before he could answer, the detective continued, 'Or perhaps you weren't sure what you saw, through the rain. Your glasses maybe fogged up? You were, what, sixty feet away, you said?'

Sam looked straight back at the detective, into her brown eyes. He sensed she had doubts about his story, even now detecting a little sarcasm in her voice.

Not breaking eye contact, he answered, 'I saw what I saw, and to answer your first question, I didn't have my phone with me. To clarify the situation, yes, I guess I was about that distance away, standing inside a shed in the goods yard.'

As she was processing this, Sam continued, 'I have only recently moved into this town. I didn't know where the police station was so I ran home, looked up the address, got into my van and came straight here. As you can see, I'm still wet from jogging in the rain. I saw what I saw, a woman being forcibly taken.'

Sam wondered what it was that made her suspicious. Was he too calm? Did she find the whole story unbelievable? Perhaps she thought that someone was pulling a prank of sorts on her. He steadily looked at her and waited.

One thing was for sure, he wasn't as fit as he felt he should be. His legs ached from the jogging and his heart was still beating a little too fast.

He also reminded himself to look into having his eyes lasered. Glasses did fog up at times in rainy conditions.

Detective Sergeant Saunders digested what he had said.

She, in turn, steadily looked back at him. What was it that niggled at her? What was it that made her suspicious?

He was calm, spoke very calmly and in coherent detail. His body language suggested that he was at ease, so why was she doubtful as to the truth of the story.

She looked down at her jotter pad, then up again at him, 'You say you were in the goods yard? And again before he could answer, 'So, you were trespassing, that is a restricted area ...'

'I was there checking out some old rolling stock, in one of the old sheds there, and, I had permission to be there,' Sam answered, then went on,' perhaps you could check to see if any of the surveillance cameras around the station have captured what I saw to check out my story.'

Ignoring his suggestion for the moment, the detective, still in two minds whether or not someone was setting her up, thinking of a couple of guys who might just try and play this kind of trick on her, said to the man opposite her, 'Who gave you permission? Did you slip the gatekeeper a few bills?'

Sam smiled.

He had wondered, in his mind, how he would relate what he had seen, and, what he figured the response might be. Would they instantly take his word, send a dozen patrol cars with flashing lights and sirens screaming? Not likely.

He was a little surprised, however, at the detective's lack of interest, Sam sighed audibly, then said, 'There was no-one at the gate, but I gained entry, and, I had the permission of Maureen Zimmerman.'

He watched her eyes, watched her face, waited for her response.

The response was clear.

Detective Sergeant Saunders felt herself colour, felt momentarily unable to speak and stared at the foreigner sitting across the desk from her.

Finally, she asked, 'Mrs Zimmerman, as in mayor Zimmerman?'

'Yes, I do believe she is the mayor,' Sam answered. Then, standing up, said, 'perhaps you'll look into what I've told you. The front desk has my details, I'll see myself out,'

and with that he turned and left the office, leaving a stunned detective sitting at her desk.

THE PAST;

PERIOD 2

THE YEAR 1821

Henry Hopkins mounted his horse, then, taking a small leather pouch from his saddlebag, said, 'For you', handing it down to the young Peruvian.

He then turned his horse towards the north and galloped away, not once looking back.

It was time to leave Peru. It was time to move on.

Two and a half years he had been there. A successful time and, for the most part, a quiet time.

But all that had changed in the past week.

They had been attacked by marauders, there had been six of them, on horseback.

Less than fifteen minutes later, they were all dead.

Henry had shot and killed three of them.

Sadly, they had lost one of their own.

It was time to move on, Henry reflected, as he spurred his horse on to catch up with his team.

He had arrived in South America, landing in Caracas, Venezuela in the year 1803, fresh from a ship that had brought him from England.

He hailed from the county of Cornwall where he had been a tin miner.

Stocky in build, he had long brown hair, a straggly beard and keen blue eyes.

Henry travelled on to Colombia, spent the next ten years there, bringing his expertise to work in a silver mine that lay between Cartagena and Bogota.

It was there he met fellow Cornish man, Richard Trevithick, also a mining man and a clever designer, having made huge advances in steam driven engines, including the design for a steam pump that could be used in mining.

Henry acquired two of these pumps, learned all about them and travelled on to Ecuador where he mined with great results thanks to the huge improvement in efficiency.

Henry stayed there for four years.

One evening, in a local bar, he got talking with some men. His Spanish, which was non-existent when he had landed on the shores of South America, was by now fluent and he found out about a mining opportunity in Peru. He even secured an old map of an existing mine.

Locking one of his pumps in storage near Quito, he took the second one, along with his team, and headed for north Peru.

Henry caught up with his team and together they rode on.

There were five men, two driving a one-horse wagon each, the other three on horseback.

They kept to the lower foothills of the Andes range and encountered no problems along the way.

Stopping briefly in the towns of Machala and Ambato, they finally reached Quito twenty-one days later.

Here Henry departed from the four men who had been with him for the past seven years. They expressed a desire to stay in Ecuador.

Four days later he had hired six young men, and after loading the pump and various other equipment, they set of for Colombia.

There were seven of them, three wagons, eleven horses, and Henry, keeping his trusty double-barrelled shotguns loaded and ready at all times.

Again they encountered no problems traversing practically the length of Colombia and arrived mid-afternoon in the port city, Cartagena, thirty-eight days later.

Henry Hopkins paid off his companions and, because of the contacts he had made in the city during the time he had worked in the region before, he had no problem in securing passage on a Spanish ship to take him and his equipment to Cadiz.

From there the former tin miner would seek passage to Canada as he had heard of the mining opportunities there, where it was still in its infancy.

Lucrative possibilities.

And so it was, that towards the end of the year 1821, Henry Hopkins, at the age of forty-six, landed in Halifax, Nova Scotia.

Pleased to once more be on solid ground after a fairly rough crossing over the Atlantic, he sniffed the air and was satisfied, wondering what challenges might lie ahead.

Hiring some men and two wagons, he set out for Sussex and from there up into the valley, to a small town named Harris. Here was a silver mine, started by a Mr Harris, who they named the settlement after, that Henry had heard about.

It was an interesting journey across such different terrain to what he had been used to in South America.

Henry's arrival in the town had not gone unnoticed by the town's people whose curiosity got the better of them. They asked who this man was, and what it was he had with him in those wagons. Very soon, Henry met a young entrepreneur.

A man just in his early twenties, who had, earlier in the year, purchased the mine and all the land around it, including the land upon which the small settlement had been built.

His name was Charlie Parker the Third, and he and Henry Hopkins made a deal.

THE PRESENT;

MONCTON

WEDNESDAY 1ST MAY

Sam stood by the large window in the lounge of his apartment.

The lights were off and he was staring into the darkness outside, though it wasn't totally dark as half a moon occasionally showed itself through the cloud cover.

Behind him on the left-hand side of the sizeable room, a door led to a small vestibule. From there, going anticlockwise was a door to a powder room, then the main entrance door to the apartment, which led to a foyer from where you could take either the stairs or a small elevator to the ground floor.

The third door off the vestibule led into a corridor that ran behind the length of the lounge.

Two doors from it led to the two large bedrooms, both with en suite facilities.

The corridor ended with a door leading to the spacious kitchen and dining area and through an archway back into the lounge.

Also from the kitchen area a door led to the metal staircase that led down to the garage below.

A roomy apartment.

Sam had returned from the police station, had showered, and then fixed himself some dinner.

It was whilst eating his meal and replaying the conversation in his mind that he had with detective Saunders, that he suddenly remembered his camera.

Dashing to his bedroom, he saw it where he had thrown it, on top of the bed.

He hadn't even considered the fact that he had taken some shots of the abduction when relating the story at the police station, but what, if anything, had he captured.

Turning the camera on, he focused on the small screen and was delighted. There were some images there.

He would see it better on his laptop so, quickly shoving in another mouthful of dinner, he set about firing up his laptop and retrieved the memory card from the camera.

Going back to the kitchen, he took one last mouthful of food, followed by a sip of water and went back to his desk in the lounge.

Inserting the memory card he pushed some keys on the keyboard. 'Right,' he said aloud to himself, 'let's see what we've got,' as the first pictured appeared.

Sam scrolled through the shots he had taken: photos of the goods yard, several of the two shunting locomotives doing their work, a couple of the old man, Joe, who had so kindly provided lunch. He was a former railwayman, and they had an interesting and lengthy conversation. He also turned out to be the father of the current mayor of Moncton, which in itself proved to be a helpful connection.

Then there were quite a few shots of the old rolling stock in the shed, a couple of atmospheric shots of the heavy rain, taken from the doorway of the old building, then, and yes, here they were. Four shots in all.

The first two showed very little, the rain still quite heavy at that time. The van and the car could be seen vaguely, but the figures were blurry.

The third shot was clear, much to Sam's relief, and the red sports car was clearly visible.

Sam noted that it was a classic car, a Triumph Stag, an English car.

There wouldn't be many of those around in these parts, he thought, then the fourth shot was the best of all. It showed the woman, the brunette, as she was about to get into the car. Her face clearly defined.

Also in this last shot, the van was sharper in focus. It was definitely dark blue. Moreover, there was a round sticker, about three inches in diameter, stuck just above the edge of the wrap around rear bumper on the side of the vehicle.

Sam sat back and smiled. He had no doubt that the detective would, at some point, contact him. These photos would surely assist her in the investigation.

After tidying up in the kitchen, Sam cleared the memory card after transferring the photos onto his laptop, with the exception of the two clear shots. Putting the card back into the camera, he then rummaged around, located a spare USB stick and transferred the two photos on to it.

Then he played some music through the good quality sound system he had purchased not long after his arrival as he liked to have music playing in the background most of the time. Sam paced the room for a bit.

He couldn't concentrate on his work at present, kept thinking back to what he had seen, kept replaying the scene in his mind, trying to recall if he had missed anything.

He turned the main lounge light off to better see the night life outside and stood by the window.

Being on the outskirts of town, it was relatively dark.

The rain had stopped some time ago now, but the road and the various courtyards in the industrial estate still gleamed from the damp in the light of the occasionally glimpsed moon and the few street lamps that were around.

In all the industrial units that he could see across the road, no light showed.

Checking the time, he noticed it was just past midnight.

Then, just as in the background Iron Butterfly's song, 'In-A-Gadda-Da-Vida' was entering the drum solo bit and Sam was thinking about turning in for the night, he noticed headlights in the far distance, to the left of his view, coming nearer.

Frowning, he tried to picture the local map in his mind. This had to be on the small road that led north, out of town alongside the Petitcodiac River.

He quickly reached for his camera, which he had placed on the coffee table, switched it on and, using the zoom, tried to capture the vehicle in the viewfinder.

He got it. But only for an instant as it disappeared behind the forest.

Sam realised he would not be able to see it again as it entered the built-up area of the outskirts of the city and beyond the range of his view from the window.

But in that instant, he had picked up, that this vehicle, was a dark van.

Again, using the zoom, he focused on the road the van had travelled on, in the direction it had come from.

The road wound its way, adjacent to the river, up into the hills.

Then Sam froze.

Slowly, he moved the camera back, to where he thought he had spotted something in the semi-darkness as the moon had once again appeared briefly.

There it was.

No doubt about it. There, in a sort of cutting to the side of the road, was the sports car, the red Triumph.

Sam moved into action. Racing to his bedroom, he pulled on a pair of sneakers, grabbed the keys to his van and to the apartment, put a jacket on, shoved his phone in a pocket and left via the back door down the steps and into his garage.

He quickly slipped in behind the wheel of his van, fired up the engine, used the clicker to open the garage door and accelerated away, using the clicker again to shut the door behind him.

Samuel had a good sense of direction, and going by a mental image he had of the local area, double checking this with the navigation system on the dashboard, he found the road that ran alongside the river and out of the city.

He encountered no traffic at all and the clock in the van showed it was a little before twelve-thirty.

Leaving the outskirts behind, he followed the winding road up into the hills, the river on his left.

With his headlights on full, he soon picked up the red car.

Sam slowed, turned off the road and into the cut away, and pulled up right behind the Triumph.

Leaving the lights on and the engine running, he unbuckled and jumped out.

The doors of the car were locked, and peering inside, Sam could see no-one.

Quickly scanning the area for a rock or something to break a window, in the hope of opening the trunk, his ears picked up a sound.

He stopped.

The new VW engine was purring quietly. It wasn't that that had drawn his attention.

He walked towards the road. He heard it again, a moaning sound.

The road was curved here, and quite high in elevation, and a crash barrier protected the bend. The sound, seemingly, came from the other side of the metal barrier.

Sam ran across the road, stubbed his toe on something, lost his balance and fell.

He landed on his right leg and right hand, slipped across the surface of the road, which was still damp from the rain and a little slippery, then crashed into the barrier with a thud.

A barrier that separated the road from the ravine and river quite some distance below.

Slightly dazed and in some pain, Sam got himself up.

He could now clearly hear the sound of the river; it's current no doubt increased due to the heavy rainfall earlier in the day.

Carefully he peered over the metal barrier.

Just then, the half-moon, which had been obscured for several moments, gave a helping hand.

There, about ten feet below him, was a ledge. It was some twelve feet in long, was no more than five foot at its widest, and tapered at both ends.

There she lay.

He could make out her blonde hair. She was lying on her side, wearing what looked like a heavy winter coat, a woollen scarf wrapped around her neck and what seemed to be a pair of hiking boots on her feet.

She moaned again. Sam saw her stir a little.

There was no time to lose. He needed rope. He had rope! In the van.

Sam scrambled to his feet, ran back across the road. There was no sign of any traffic. His leg, knee and hand ached.

Ignoring the pain he reached the van, got in, backed out of the cutting, then, because he needed the side door to be on the barrier side, turned the vehicle round, which needed a couple of goes on the narrow road, and reversed up the road, stopping where he had crashed against the metal rail.

Sam cut the engine, switched the headlight off, but left the parking lights on. He slipped from the driver's seat through the gap into the rear of the van.

He switched on an overhead light.

After rummaging around in one of the cupboards, he found the rope, then took his rain jacket off, slid the door of his van open and hopped out.

Tying the end of the rope to the post that supported the barrier he threw the rest of the length over the side.

His glasses had steamed up and so he decided to disperse with them, throwing them into the back of the van.

Taking hold of the rope, he stepped over the barrier and began to abseil down.

His footing slipped twice, but he managed to hang on to the rope. His hands, already burning with the strain his leg, knee ached, and his hand still throbbed.

His feet touched the ledge.

Sam looked down across the prone woman, she lay very still.

Taking a moment to catch his breath, and to formulate a plan, he stood on the ledge wishing he was twenty-seven, not forty-seven.

His breathing was laboured and he was sweating profusely. Carefully he bent down to her.

'Hey' he said, taking hold of her shoulder, 'hey, can you hear me?'

The scarf, he suddenly realised, was soaking wet, and so was the heavy winter coat.

Sam put two and two together.

She had been left here to die.

No doubt she was drugged. Then, when she regained some sort of consciousness, she could easily slip from the narrow ledge.

The heavy coat and scarf would ensure a certain death in the river below.

The scarf had to go and he began to loosen it. She moaned a little.

He successfully managed to free it, and flung it away, down into the gushing river below.

The coat had to be next.

With some effort, Sam got the woman into a sitting position. The moon, thankfully, was continuing to help out.

He brushed her hair, also wet, from her face. She looked ghostly white in the moonlight.

'Hey,' he said again, then slapped her gently on one cheek, 'come on girl, wake up.'

She moaned, her voice a little stronger by the sound of it. Then her eyes fluttered open.

'Well, hello there,' Sam said, his face close to hers, 'come on now, you have to help me here. Come on, okay'

She tried to focus on him. She was confused, but somehow understood or sensed that he was trying to help.

She nodded.

Sam heaved and struggled to get her to a standing position, all the while making sure his footing was secure and that he had a good hold on her.

His right leg began to protest, trembling.

He steadied it.

Focus! He screamed in his mind.

He began to unbutton the coat. She mumbled something unintelligible, then, as he had now undone the top button, she began to realise what he was doing, her hands began to fumble in an attempt to help, but she was too weak.

Then her head began to fall forward and he could feel her body begin to sag.

Mustering extra strength from somewhere, he held her, and managed to undo the remaining buttons of the coat. Then, by twisting and turning and heaving, he got the coat off.

It followed the scarf to the river below.

Taking a little breather, Sam steadied himself.

He then set about tying the end of the rope around her, across her back, under her arms and bosom, and knotting it securely on one side.

He was relieved to see that the rope was long enough and thanked the Lord that the previous owner had left his equipment to be sold with the van.

Sam had some slack left on the rope to work with when attempting to heave her up.

The action of tying the rope around her had revived her a little, her head lifted and she opened her eyes and looked at him.

She had blue eyes he noticed as the moonlight shone above them.

'Hi there,' he said. 'Welcome back. Now, listen, just stay right here, stand still, don't move, okay?'

She nodded.

Sam was pleased. He carefully climbed back to the top, thankful that she was starting to register what he was saying.

Once back on the road, he untied the rope from the post, took up the slack, then, looping it around the same post, he tied it onto himself, stepped over the barrier, grabbed the rope tightly and let himself go down.

His weight worked as a cantilever. As he went down, the woman came up.

It was working.

He pushed the pain away, ignoring it as much as possible, and slowly descended, wondering if he had ever sweated so much in his life.

It seemed like forever, but was probably only minutes before they were level with each other.

They hung there, side by side. Her face only inches from his.

She had passed out again and he had no strength to call out to her.

Struggling to breathe, Sam just hung there for a few moments, trying to replenish his lungs.

Then, slowly and carefully, all the while maintaining pressure on the rope, he climbed up a little way, grabbed hold of the rope a bit further up, climbed up a little more, each time heaving so as to keep her level with him.

A second heave, then a third and finally her shoulders were level with the top of the barrier.

Sam then managed to scramble up and over the metal barrier, without letting her slip at all, before reaching over, getting hold of her, and then pulling with all his might to flip her over and onto the road surface.

Once again Sam was struggling for breath and lay there for a moment, the half-moon still shining down in the clear sky.

Slowly his breathing improved, though his heart was thumping like a jack hammer.

Sam then forced himself upright, began to untie the rope from her body and, summoning all the strength he could muster, he gritted his teeth and slipped one arm under her shoulders, the other under her knees. Then he lifted her up, and got her into the back of the van, laying her on the carpeted floor.

Heaving a sigh of relief, he untied the rope from himself, unwound it from the post, gathered it together and threw it in the vehicle.

He stepped into the van himself, and slid the door shut.

Next he found a towel and a blanket in another cupboard, placed the towel under her head, positioned her in the recovery position, and proceeded to wrap the blanket around her as best he could.

He noticed his glasses, which he had thrown into the van earlier. He mainly needed these for long vision. Grabbing them, he put them back on.

She stirred again, moaned a little, then, her hand reached out and grabbed his shirt, which was soaked with sweat, and tried to pull him closer.

He looked at her, as she lay there, her face grey in the weak light of the van's interior lamp.

She tried to speak ...' Nnno---pp ...police,' she managed to stutter, 'nnno ... hos ...hos ...hospital.'

He understood, 'Okay' he managed to say, his breathing still laboured.

She released his shirt, lay her head down and mumbled something. It sounded like 'Thank you'.

Sam got up, slipped through the gap between the bucket seats and got behind the wheel.

He started the engine, flicked on the main headlights and took off.

In all that time there had been no traffic. Thankfully home wasn't far away.

He noticed the time on the dashboard clock.

One minute past one.

What had seemed like hours had all happened in just over thirty minutes.

Approaching the back of his apartment, Sam used the remote control and as he pulled into the rear courtyard the garage door opened.

Sam turned the vehicle around and reversed in.

Automatic sensors turned on the light.

He killed the engine, pressed the control for the garage door and got out.

He walked around the front of the van, then slid open the side door.

The woman was sitting up, looked at him and said, 'I'm going to be sick.'

And she was.

Sam rubbed her back gently with his left hand, then encircled his right arm around her and held her shoulder.

He waited until he felt her tension ease, then said, 'Come on, you need to get out of these wet clothes and into a warm shower. The thing is, we have twenty-six steps

to climb first.'

She turned her head to look at him and nodded.

He gave her a smile, then helped her up and out of the van, realising only then that she still wore those heavy hiking boots.

He felt they would be better left on now as they needed to climb a steel staircase.

She threw the blanket off, wrapped an arm around him and he put his arm around her, together they moved, and headed upstairs.

It was hard going. She was still very weak. He was exhausted and his body ached all over, but they reached the top of the first flight. Halfway.

'You're doing great,' he said, once again catching his breath and looking at her face, 'One more flight of steps.'

He noticed colour again coming into her face and her eyes seemed to focus better. Whatever the drug was that she'd been given, seemed to be slowly wearing off.

The second flight took less time and opening the door, Sam escorted her through the kitchen and into the second bedroom.

He realised that his music was still softly playing in the lounge.

'I'll put the shower on. Get it ready for you,' he said, leaving her sitting on the edge of the bed.

'There are plenty of towels and a bathrobe in there.' He came out again, then knelt down and proceeded to get her boots off.

She was slowly managing to unbutton her blouse and Sam noticed her fingers were steadier, she was regaining some strength.

A good sign.

The boots were off.

'Are you okay now? Can you manage?' he asked, trying not to stare as she took her blouse off.

She caught his eye, smiled, 'Go,' she said, her voice a hoarse whisper, seeing he was a little uncomfortable, 'I'll manage now, go.'

He leaned forward, kissed her gently on her forehead and left the room, and headed for his own room where he stripped.

Every muscle in his body was aching now. The pain that he had so long pushed back, began to register. Sam entered the bathroom, turned on the shower and noticed that his hand had been bleeding and that his leg was badly scratched.

The water would surely sting he thought, as he tested the water with his hand until it reached a good temperature.

Then, bracing himself, he stepped into the shower.

Under twenty minutes later he was dressed in fresh jeans and a t-shirt, making two mugs of hot chocolate.

The kitchen clock showed it to be two am.

He had turned his stereo off and had called out once, checking to make sure she was alright.

'Yes,' had been the simple reply, though 'No' would have been a more honest answer, she thought.

She had managed, with difficulty, to strip off and get herself into the shower.

The warm water had felt instantly soothing, but, then she was sick again and just sat herself on the floor of the shower cubicle.

Pulling her knees up and embracing them with her arms, she just sat and let the water run over her.

After a few moments the urge to be sick subsided and she began to relax, still being soothed by the warm water as it flowed over her.

Then she sobbed a little, her tears mingling with the water. Her chest felt sore.

Eventually she gathered the strength to get up, turned the shower off and stepped out.

As she carefully dried herself, still feeling somewhat disorientated, she noticed the rawness on her skin, particularly under her arms.

They were rope burns and she began to remember, though much was still unclear as she continued to dry herself. It was as if she was in a dream and everything was in slow motion.

She wondered about the man who had rescued her.

Who was he? How did he find her?

He was caring and gentle; she sensed that.

She felt comforted by his presence and she felt safe, she sensed that too.

Coming out of the en suite bathroom, she walked, still a little unsteady, to the bed, pulled back the covers and let herself fall forward.

Then, managing to pull the covers back over her, she fell asleep.

The kitchen, a spacious one, contained an oven, a hob and a microwave. These were all along the outside wall. Then there was a central island which had a worktop and sink with drawers and cupboard below.

Along the inner wall there was a large fridge freezer and another worktop above which was a row of cupboards.

Beyond the kitchen area, in the corner of the room, with windows on two sides stood a rectangular dining table with four chairs. A circular lamp hung from the ceiling above the table.

An archway, situated between the kitchen and dining area, led into the large lounge.

Sam poured out the drinks, then, as he hadn't heard any sounds coming from the guest bedroom for a while, went to investigate.

She was in bed.

Her blond hair, still damp from the shower, lay straggled across her face and on her pillow as she lay on her stomach.

She had obviously pulled back the duvet and collapsed into bed pulling the cover back over her, and had promptly fallen asleep.

Sam knelt by the side of the bed, gently pulled her hair away from her face and listened to her breathing.

It was regular and even.

Next he checked the bathroom, noticed she must have been sick again, poor woman.

Who was she?

Who had been responsible for this rather elaborate scene that had been staged to look like suicide.

Who was it, that wanted her dead?

These questions were running through his mind as he tidied and cleaned up the bathroom.

Once more checking that her breathing was regular and even, he left the room.

His body ached and was screaming for rest, but Sam forced himself to fetch some cleaning equipment and headed down into the garage to clean up the mess in the van.

He didn't want to face that smell in the morning.

Then, finally, he too went to bed, forgetting all about the mugs of hot chocolate that he had prepared.

He gingerly slipped under the sheets and was asleep in seconds.

THE PAST;

PERIOD 3

THE YEAR 1825

Henry Hopkins was struck.

He was flummoxed. Never before had he felt like this.

At a young age he had begun to work in the tin mines in his native Cornwall. He worked from early morning, as the sun was rising, to early evening, as the sun was setting.

Every day, except Sundays.

He went to church on Sundays.

Then, having heard wondrous stories about South America, he left home in search of adventure. He secured passage to Venezuela and duly arrived, albeit quite sunburned, in Caracas in the year 1803.

For the next seventeen years he worked in silver mines in Colombia, Ecuador and Peru.

He was now forty-nine years old and had been in Canada for just over three years.

But in all the places he had been, where he had faced danger, had to endure severe working conditions, had been injured, had been sick with fever and had been attacked by bandits.

In all those years, he had never felt like this.

He felt both weak and strong at the same time.

Felt both vulnerable and invincible.

Henry Hopkins was struck.

By love.

Charlie Parker the Third had been celebrating his twenty-fifth birthday.

It had been a grand affair in the old big house that he had purchased, along with the mine and much of the land around the small settlement.

He had purchased this from a man named Alfred Harris, who had originally started the mine and set up the community, and after whom the town had been named.

When young Charlie Parker the Third showed up, keen and wealthy, Alfred saw his chance to sell up and leave as he was keen to follow another dream, which was to prospect for gold.

That had been in 1821.

The party was fine, there was food and plenty of it. There was drink and plenty of that too.

There were fiddlers and there was dancing.

There were also Rebekah and Ruth. Mother and daughter.

They had not long ago arrived from Boston, having been recommended to come and stay with young Charlie by his grandfather, who was second cousin to Rebekah. They had relocated due to a family rift and tension.

Young Charlie had agreed to accommodate them as he was alone in the big house anyway, apart from three servants.

They had arrived, by horse and wagon, along with several trunks, cases, boxes and bags, only a day before the party.

It had been early evening, darkness having already fallen, and young Charlie had only briefly met the mother, Rebekah, at this time.

He had given instructions to the servants to settle them in as he had a number of tasks that he wanted completed.

The following day, he had been out, right up until minutes really, before the actual party began.

All was just dandy.

There were plenty of folk who attended.

The music was good and there was a great atmosphere in the grand front room of the big house.

Young Charlie and Henry had been standing together, both smoking a cigar, both smartly dressed. Chatting to each other.

Charlie had taken to Henry like a duck to water.

The man had a wealth of experience, knew all that there was to know about mining and, moreover, had brought along this amazing steam pump, which had increased the mine's output many times over.

They had just clicked, got on well with each other and so, not only did the mine flourish and grow, so did their friendship.

And so, there they stood together, talking.

In the far corner four men were providing the music, three on the fiddle, a fourth strumming a big bass.

Slightly to the right of where they were playing, a long wooden counter had been set up to serve as a bar, and two men, neatly dressed in white shirts and checked trousers, were serving the beverages.

Chatting together, their cigar smoke curled slowly upwards to then mingle with the blue hue of smoke from the many men who partook in the enjoyment of a cigar or pipe.

Several women were milling about, these mainly the wives of men Charlie had invited.

Then, a hush descended on the room.

The musicians were still playing, folk were still dancing, but there was definitely a change in the atmosphere.

Henry and Charlie stopped their conversation. They looked.

Two women were coming down the grand curved staircase, each in unison with the other as they took the steps down.

Both were stunningly dressed in colourful gowns.

Both were very attractive, their hair immaculate, their jewellery and their eyes sparkling.

Smiling as they came down the stairs, they knew at that point that most eyes were upon them.

The mother, Rebekah, made a beeline for Charlie, to introduce him to her daughter, Ruth.

In hindsight, Charlie wondered if he had managed to say anything intelligent at all, but recalls with amusement, that as he introduced his friend Henry to them, that he had equally been stumbling through his words.

Now, less than a week later, he and Henry stood in Charlie's office.

Both were looking out of the window onto the town below.

The settlement had already, in just three years, doubled in size.

How quickly things can change, Charlie thought, in so many ways.

He glanced over to his desk and to the large painting that hung on the wall behind it.

The seascape.

The old oil painting of a ship in a storm, the two-masted schooner being tossed about on rough seas.

Charlie could identify with the sailors on that ship.

He too knew the feeling of being tossed about, knew too the turbulence of life, it's ups and downs.

The painting, which he loved, might well have been lost had it not been for his grandfather who had originally purchased it.

Charlie the Third was the eldest son, but he was not the eldest child.

That was Charlene, born two years earlier, in 1798.

The early years were all fine and good.

But in his early teens, Charlie began to notice things. The first of these was that his father and grandfather were often at loggerheads. The second thing was that his mother and father were often arguing with each other, and the third thing was that his sister distanced herself from him and began to consider herself superior.

When Charlie had turned sixteen, he witnessed an argument that would change the course of his life.

His mother and sister were in a heated argument with his father.

Now, he wasn't very close to his father, nor his mother for that matter, but the gist of the topic was that as his sister, Charlene, was about to turn eighteen, she should receive a new allowance and be put in charge of running the family retail business, one of the many companies that the Parker family owned and operated.

His father did not have a flair for business.

The arguments young Charlie had often witnessed between his father and grandfather supported that fact.

Already decisions had been made that had proved costly.

Young Charlie had skills. He was an exceptional student and there was no doubt that his acumen would prove an asset in the family business, if there was a family business left with his father and sister in charge.

So he took the initiative, and went to his grandfather. The eighty-three-year-old was still the jovial man of old. Still smoked a cigar a day; still with those piercing eyes and that broad smile on his face.

All this despite the loss of his wife some years earlier, and despite the frustrating times he had with his son.

His only son.

Young Charlie and Charlie senior had a powwow.

They talked throughout the afternoon and well into the evening.

Already having had doubts about his son's ability to take care of the family business, and seeing his grandson grow and mature into a savvy young man, Charlie Parker senior had already drawn up several legal documents to ensure the continuance of what he and his father before him had built up.

So, when his grandson came to him that day to inform him of what he had overheard, it was time to further secure the future of the business.

Charlie watched his grandson as he stood by the window, looking out over the harbour.

He came over and stood beside him. Neither spoke now, all the talking had been done, the plans made, each now was lost with his own thoughts.

The moment made Charlie senior think back, way back, to this very room, this very house, and the time he had celebrated the birth of his son.

The old man sighed.

His normally sparkling blue eyes, tearing up.

He thought about the meeting he had with the man who had contacted him with regard to some paintings he had for sale.

He recalled the moment that the man had opened the crate and he saw the seascape for the very first time.

He had stared and admired it for some time.

Charlie glanced to a wall on the right; there it hung, the very picture.

He still loved it.

Originally, he had thought about giving it to his son at some point, possibly as a wedding gift, but knew by then that his son was not interested in it, and didn't like it, so it remained on the wall and there it still hung.

It wasn't the only painting he had seen that day when the front of that wooden crate had opened. The man had two more, also seascapes, most likely by the same artist. Each as breathtaking as the next.

Charlie had purchased all three of them.

But then his wife had a miscarriage a year later, and, as she was unable to have any more children, Charlie decided to sell the other two, keeping the one he had first seen that day.

He walked away from the window, over to the painting.

'I want you to have this also,' he said, indicating the seascape.

'Wow, really Grandfather?' young Charlie said, turning away from the window and coming over to his grandfather, 'I love this painting.'

'I know you do. That is why you are to have it.'

Charlie Parker the Third smiled as he thought back to that day with his grandfather, how all had changed from that moment.

He turned to his friend Henry, still standing by the window, still deep in thought.

Henry too, Charlie thought, must be feeling like the men on the ship in the storm.

The upheaval; the danger; the challenge.

Being tossed about.

For like himself, Henry too was to be married in less than a week from today.

He was to be married to the daughter, Ruth, such a beautiful and smart young woman.

There had been no doubts and no hesitations. This was the right woman for him and he considered himself a lucky guy.

And he, Henry, was to be married to the mother, Rebekah. There had been an immediate connection between them.

Married, both of them.

In less than a week.

He turned and they both continued to stare out the window.

THE PRESENT;

MONCTON

THURSDAY 2ND MAY

Detective Sergeant Karen Saunders sat behind her desk and was looking at the screen of her computer terminal.

'Shoot,' she said audibly to herself.

She pressed some keys, rewound the sequence, and watched again.

Yesterday, after the foreigner had left the office, leaving her speechless and a little annoyed with herself, she pulled herself together and started to make a few calls.

The first was to the railway station's security personnel.

Speaking at length, she was told that no suspicious occurrences had been reported, but that there was one camera that covered the adjacent car park area, and that they would find the recording she needed and get it to her.

The second call was to the front desk to ask for the full details that the foreigner had left them.

The third call was to her colleague in the station across town, and she asked if they had received any reports of an incident by the railway station, which they hadn't.

Neither in her call to the railway station, nor to her opposite number across town, did she mention the word kidnapping or abduction.

She was not convinced that this had been the case.

But now, as she watched the sequence from the camera at the station again, she began to wonder. In fact, more than wonder, for it was there, captured on film.

Despite the rain and the lens covered with many droplets, through the blur she saw a dark van race away out of the parking area, followed closely by a red car.

'Shoot,' she again said to herself.

At eleven minutes past nine in the morning, fireman Daniel Houseman, retrieved a dark green, good quality, heavy winter coat from the bank of the river.

The fire station, situated on the south side of the city, had its fire house, its command centre and a training ground backing on to the river, a little over five hundred yards from the city's southern-most bridge over the Petitcodiac River.

Daniel had been cleaning and inspecting one of its five fire engines when he noticed the coat.

Dragging it from the bank, he could see, that despite it being sodden, it was a good quality garment.

Taking a quick look around the embankment for anything else, he then took the coat and brought it inside the main garage that housed all the engines.

He checked through the pockets, finding just two items, a small bunch of keys and a membership card to a local fitness centre called 'ShapeShifters'.

The card was laminated and the name and address were clearly readable. Moreover the attached photo of the member was clear and undamaged.

Daniel got up, and with the keys and card in hand, headed for the office where he made a call.

Detective Saunders was just about to place a call, when the telephone rang.

'DS Saunders,' she said in answering the call.

She listened for several moments, said, 'Yes' a couple of times, 'thank you very much' once, and finished by saying, 'I'll be right over.'

She was putting on her raincoat and just about to leave the office when the phone rang again.

It was the front desk informing her that they had received a report of an abandoned car on the Eastern Canyon Road, just to the side of the road, a foreign red car.

'Damn,' she muttered to herself as she left her office.

Thirty-two minutes later she drove up close to where the red car was parked in a cutting off the main road. Leaving the police vehicle on the main road, she switched on the blue flashing lights and switched off the engine.

It was raining.

Picking up a clear plastic evidence bag from the passenger seat, she donned a pair of gloves and fished out the bunch of keys.

Selecting what was obviously the car key, for it had the word Triumph engraved on it, she took it from the bunch, put the rest back in the plastic bag and got out of the car.

Carefully she made her way to the vehicle, making sure she didn't disturb any fresh tyre tracks or footprints and walked around the Triumph sports car.

She tried the key, it turned, and with her gloved hand, she opened the driver's door.

After a little searching, she spotted the lever for the trunk and popped it.

DS Saunders walked around the back, saw that the trunk was empty, closed it and taking her gloves off went back to her police car. The rain was coming down heavier now.

Once inside she pulled out her phone and pressed a few numbers.

After making two brief calls she took another look at the membership card which was also in the evidence bag.

The card showed the name of the fitness centre, 'ShapeShifters', and had the address and phone number below the logo. The photo ID showed a woman with blond hair, and below that her name and address, 14 Woodend Road.

She was studying the photograph of the woman, when her phone rang. She answered and listened, said her thanks and ended the call.

Switching on her engine, the wipers cleaning the rain from the windscreen, she drove up the canyon road a little further, found a spot to more easily turn the vehicle and headed back to where she had parked earlier, the blue lights still flashing and waited, leaving the engine running. The wipers continued to clear the water as the rain was still heavy.

It wasn't long before her forensic team arrived.

Getting out, and in the pouring rain, she gave them instructions. She gave them the key to the vehicle and the bag with the ID card, and also, opening the trunk of her car, she pulled out the sodden coat and handed it to them.

She then instructed them to not only check the car and bring it in, but, when they were done here, to meet her at the home address that was on the card.

Taking the remaining keys that were on the bunch, she got back in the car and drove towards the city.

On her way to check out the home address, 14 Woodend Road, Detective Sergeant Karen Saunders gave thought as to how to approach the foreigner.

This Mr Price.

The security camera had indeed captured a dark van and a red car speeding away. It had also, despite the blurry condition of the tape, identified the driver of the red car as being a dark-haired woman, not a blond.

So, it seemed perfectly clear, that Mr Price had indeed, seen what he described.

'I saw what I saw,' he had said.

With her police light flashing, she reached the address in short time.

Keys in hand, she carefully approached the front door.

She had thought about securing some backup, but felt in no danger. She did though, notify control as to where she was.

Ringing the bell, she waited, listening.

Selecting what she thought might be the right key of the three remaining on the bunch, she inserted it into the lock.

It opened the door.

She drew her sidearm, then entered, calling out her presence.

With her foot she closed the door behind her and moved further into the house.

Checking every room, looking around and listening, she discovered that no-one was in the house.

Holstering her weapon she then made a more thorough search. Nothing seemed to be out of place or disturbed.

No sign of any struggle or break in.

Forensics might have more success she thought.

They arrived less than half an hour later and began their investigation.

DS Saunders left the house and her team there and headed for the fitness centre, in the hope someone there might be of help.

It was still raining.

THE PAST;

PERIOD 4

THE YEAR 1828

Charlene Parker was livid. Her mother was livid.

They both sat, bolt upright, around a large rectangular desk in the office of William P. Montrose, lawyer, situated in down town Boston.

THREE DAYS EARLIER

Six men, wearing long black coats and tall top hats, walked slowly, three on either side of the coffin they carried towards where a graveside had been prepared.

Behind followed a trail of men and woman, most also dressed in dark clothes.

Ahead of the pallbearers a robed priest set the solemn pace.

Charlie Parker had died.

He was a well-liked and well-respected man of influence in Boston.

The church service had been well attended, all the pews packed with many standing in the aisles or vestibule.

He had reached the age of ninety-six.

Two people were notably absent:

Charlie Parker's one and only son, Charlie Parker the Second, though for some this was not a total surprise as it was widely known that they had not seen eye to eye on many occasions.

What was more surprising, was the absence of Charlie's grandson, Charlie Parker the Third.

Where was he?

Several newspaper articles the following day would comment on these facts. One suggested that according to inside sources, young Charlie Parker the Third had left the family home seven years ago and had not returned, presumed to be living in South America.

But after the service at the graveside had been conducted, and a number of people had taken a handful of sand to throw over the coffin, or presented stems of flowers as a tribute, a man and a woman approached.

They came from the opposite direction to where the mourners were heading, being careful not to be noticed.

When all was clear, they came closer, the man with an arm around the woman's shoulder and the woman with her arm around the man's waist.

For some time they stood there, by the grave. The man visibly shaking as he sobbed.

Charlene Parker and her mother had been requested to attend the reading of the will in the offices of the law firm of William P. Montrose.

They duly arrived at the appointed time, both suitably dressed in solemn outfits, both with expressions of grief and sorrow on their faces.

But neither felt solemn or grief stricken in their hearts.

The opposite in fact was true.

They were inwardly excited in anticipation of what, they believed, would be coming to them.

Much was their shock and surprise then, after they had been seated along the rectangular oak table in comfortable armchairs, when two people were ushered into the room and placed on the opposite side of the table.

'Hello sis,' Charlie Parker the Third said. 'Hello mother, this is Ruth, my wife.'

Neither woman could find any words to say, to the amusement of Ruth who simply smiled at them both.

Before any conversation could begin William P. Montrose entered, with several folders and files, and sat at the head of the table, briefly acknowledging each person present.

'You will no doubt have questions,' he said, shuffling a few of the folders into some sort of sequence, 'but they will have to wait until I am finished. Am I clear on that?'

and here again he briefly looked at each of them, then continued, 'Good, good. Well then, let's begin'

Opening one of the folders, he said, looking at the two women on his right, 'Miss Charlene Parker, all of the jewellery and clothing items that you have obtained through the Parker Trading Company, over the past twelve years, are all yours to keep,' his voice a deep monotone.

Then, looking at the older woman, 'Mrs Priscilla Parker, the cottage, situated near Quincy on the coast, with all its chattels and goods, is yours outright.'

The mother and daughter briefly looked at each other, before once again turning their attention to Mr William P. Montrose, in full anticipation.

However, the lawyer now focused on Charlie and spoke directly to him as he opened another folder. 'Mr Charlie Parker the Third, there are of course a lot of details here, but in essence, the Parker Trading Company, Parker Shipping and Parker Farming, these, Mr Charlie Parker the Third, are all bequeathed to you'.

It was at this point, that the mouths of Charlene and her mother, Priscilla, dropped open. It was at this point, that both their faces turned the colour of beetroot.

And it was at this point they both became livid.

'No, no no ...' it was the thirty-year-old Charlene who first found her voice, 'that just can't be right, it should all come to us, through my father. I am the eldest. Daddy always said it would all come to me, I was the one who worked in the family business, not him, not Charlie!' she said, glancing at her brother across the table from her and practically spitting out his name.

'And the house, what about our house?' Priscilla demanded, now also having found her voice.

Charlie and his wife Ruth, sat and remained calm, saying nothing.

The lawyer, who always introduced himself as William P. Montrose, though no-one knew what the P stood for, cleared his throat.

'Miss Charlene, Mrs Parker,' he calmly said, in a tone that suggested they should listen carefully what he was about to say.

'Twelve years ago, in the year 1816, Mr Charlie Parker, senior, wrote up a new will. In it he completely disowns his son, your husband Mrs Parker, your father Miss Charlene.

'In the new will he bequeaths everything that I have mentioned to go to his grandson, Mr Charlie Parker here,' he indicated with his hand.

'In the year 1820' the lawyer continued, 'a large grant was made available to your son, Mrs Parker, your brother Miss Charlene, with which to set up a new venture, a new business.

'As your family lawyer, dealing with all manner of legal documents, purchases, taxes and so on, I can tell you, and in his will, it is clearly expressed for me to do so, that this venture was, and is, highly prosperous.

Mr Charlie Parker here, is undoubtedly a shrewd and capable business man.' William P. Montrose paused here for a moment to let that register.

'Whereas you, Miss Charlene,' he then continued, glancing at her before reading from the files 'and again, I am relating what your grandfather has written specifically, have contributed to a downturn in profit, a dissatisfied clientele-base and a tension-filled workplace due to your disregard for common courtesy.'

The lawyer looked again at the young woman, and although he had still spoken in his usual monotone voice, there was certainly a sparkle in his eyes as he had rather enjoyed reading out those instructions.

He himself had been at the funeral. He had a great liking for Charlie, had on occasions spent enjoyable moments in his company. As the family lawyer, and knowing the details he was about to share, it had lifted his spirits on the day of the funeral.

Charlene had gone from astonished, to livid, from beetroot red, to now an almost pale white complexion and looked quite subdued.

'With regard to your house, Mrs Parker, 'the lawyer continued in that same voice, 'this was in your husband's name, however, just over two years ago, he took out a loan against the house, a large loan with which he vanished, so, I am afraid to tell you, that unless that loan is repaid, the house belongs to the bank.'

Mrs Priscilla Parker now went almost as pale as her daughter. She was in shock, in disbelief. Tears appeared in her eyes and she sat, almost slumped, in the armchair.

For several moments, no one said a word.

Then it was Ruth, Charlie's wife, who spoke, looking directly across the table at her sister-in-law.

'Understand, Miss Charlene,' she began, her voice strong and direct, 'that as with immediate effect, you are dismissed from the company, and consider yourself fortunate,' she added, 'that we are not charging you with inappropriate use of company funds.'

Then, turning to the lawyer, all the while having held her husband's hand under the table, she said, 'Is that all for now Mr Montrose?'

'If you and your husband could come in tomorrow. A lot of paperwork to go through, documents to sign and so on, if that is convenient of course?'

'Of course Mr Montrose, about eleven?' she asked, to which he nodded.

After one more glance across the table, Ruth stood up and she and Charlie left the office. Other than the initial hello and introduction he had not spoken one word.

He was still grieving over the loss of his grandfather who he had loved so much.

'Take a moment,' William P. Montrose said to the mother and daughter. 'When you are ready, there are a couple of documents to sign.'

Then he collected all his files and folders and left the room.

THE PRESENT;

MONCTON

THURSDAY 2ND MAY EARLIER

He stirred and woke.

No doubt his body clock trying to remind him that he should have been up by now.

It was a little before eight o'clock, and Sam usually rose at around seven.

He lay there for a moment, his eyes registering that it was indeed morning, and the digital clock on the side table confirming it.

Mentally he calculated that he had only had about five hours of sleep.

He listened for a while, but there were no sounds to be heard in the apartment though he detected the sounds of cars and trucks moving about in the industrial estate in which he lived.

She, whoever she was, must still be asleep.

Had all that happened, really happened?

Flinging the sheets aside and getting up confirmed the answer.

His movement was laboured, he was sore, he was stiff, he was tired.

A nice shower would surely help, he thought, and headed into his bathroom.

Twenty minutes later he was dressed and making himself some breakfast, after having quietly checked on his guest.

She still lay on her stomach, the duvet had slipped to halfway down her back, he could see and hear her breathe.

Grabbing a slice of toast and a glass of juice, he went into the lounge, where, at the far end, he had set up his study.

A desk, a bookcase, a printer and other stationery equipment.

Sam switched on his laptop, then noticed two sheets of paper in the printer tray.

He had forgotten about these.

On the evening of his research, the day he had visited Nico Rozzini and had viewed the painting, his findings had concluded that it had been a Charlie Parker, who, in the year 1762 had purchased the painting, in fact, Sam had discovered, he had purchased three.

To find out a little more about this man, he had found some newspaper articles, both relating to his life and his funeral.

Sam had not read these through, but printed them out to look at later.

With all that had happened, he had forgotten about them.

Taking another bite of toast, he took the sheets from the tray and sat down behind his desk, also punching in his password on the keyboard.

One was an article written in the *Boston Commercial Gazette*. Charlie Parker was a wealthy and influential man in Boston, with businesses in farming, shipping and trading.

The article, written after his death in 1828, covered the man's life, his input into the economy, the number of people he employed and the trade he had brought to the city. It further wrote about the sad loss for all, and there was talk of a monument to be commissioned in his honour.

The second article, this in the *Boston Patriot & Daily Chronicle*, published a week after his death, was more in depth and also spoke of family rifts and tension, the fact that his son had not attended the funeral and, of interest to Sam, that the whole company would now be run by the grandson, Charlie Parker the Third.

Getting up to take a look at the timeline he had drawn up, which he had pinned to the wall next to the bookcase, to see where he fitted in, Sam could see that he was the great-great-grandfather of Joshua Parker who had sold the mine to Nico Rozzini in 2009.

There was something else exciting about this article, for it had a photograph of Charlie Parker, a very large and jovial looking man Sam thought, standing in a room in his house, but the exciting bit was that, in the photo, behind where the man was standing on the wall, was the seascape, the very painting he had viewed on Tuesday.

Furthermore, Sam noticed, as he peered closely at the photograph, the painting had its original frame.

'That must be very interesting' a soft voice said.

Sam looked up and turned around.

She stood in the archway between the lounge and kitchen area.

Wearing a white fluffy bathrobe, she had a towel in her hand as she was still drying her hair.

Her face shone, her eyes sparkled.

'Ah, yes, it is to do with my work ...how are you, you look a hundred times better than last night, or, really, I should say, early this morning,' he said, putting the article on his desk and coming towards her.

'I feel it,' she said, smiling. 'I don't suppose you have a hairdryer do you?' she asked.

He stopped in front of her and looked at her, studying her face, not quite sure how to proceed with the conversation, but answered, 'No, I haven't, er, can I get you some breakfast?'

'Breakfast sounds good,' she answered, smiling at him, 'I take it, you have all my clothes?'

He slipped past her into the kitchen, 'Yes, put them through the washing machine. I forgot, sorry, I'll stick them in the tumble dryer, be ready in no time,' he answered. 'What do you fancy, some toast, cereal, tea, coffee?' trying to keep the conversation casual, though he was desperate to know more about this woman, who she was, and why someone wanted her dead.

She felt that he was awkward, a little unsure and rather shy.

She walked up to him, not saying a word, then put her arms around his neck, hugged herself into him, 'You saved my life, thank you. Just, please, just hold me for a moment,' she whispered.

At the very same time as the fireman, Daniel Houseman, picked up the coat from the bank of the river on the south side of the city, Sam put his arms around the woman whose coat it was, held her firmly and said nothing.

Briefly he felt her body tremble, then it subsided and she relaxed.

A moment became several moments. Then she nuzzled into his neck, kissed him on the cheek and pulled herself free.

'Toast and tea will be fine,' she said, then continued to dry her hair.

The island in the middle of the kitchen not only served as a countertop and sink, but as a breakfast bar as well. There were two stools placed at one end.

Sam pulled one of them aside for her to sit on.

'How do you have your tea?' he asked.

'Not too strong and without milk or cream,' she answered, then looking at him, as he placed two slices of bread into the toaster, asked, 'so, my knight in shining armour, two things. First, who are you? And second, how did you find me? I have limited recollection as to what happened.'

Sam switched the kettle on, then turned and leant back against the counter.

Finally, he thought, normal chit chat was over. He guessed she must be as anxious to unravel the events as he was.

She stopped drying her hair, draped the towel around her neck and looked at him expectantly.

'Okay, well, here goes,' Sam answered, then blew out his cheeks and said, 'My name is Sam, Sam Price, as for my shining armour, I have to say, it got somewhat dented last night,' smiling at her. 'As to how I found you? Well, let be backtrack a little, then it will make more sense ...'

The toast popped up at this moment, Sam turned, put the two slices on a plate. The water in the kettle boiled as well and so he prepared her tea, all the while, relating the story ...

' ...it all began yesterday, at the railway station. It was raining hard. I was in the adjacent goods yard and I saw you, running in the rain, heading for that red Triumph. I guess that's yours?' he asked, placing the toast and tea in front of her.

'Thank you, yes, it's mine, go on ...'

'Do you want any butter or jam on your toast?' he asked her.

'No, this is fine, please, go on ...'

Sam leant back against the counter again and continued.
    'So, ...through the rain, I saw this van pull up alongside you. Next thing, this man and woman come bundling out, grab you, drag you into the van. Then this woman gets into your car, the van takes off, the woman in your car follows, and ... gone, the whole thing took just seconds really ...'

'You saw all this?' she asked, carefully taking a sip of tea. 'Then what did you do?' she asked, biting into her toast.

Sam smiled at her, then said, 'Mmm, I think at this point, we should go through the chain of events together, so, first of all, who are you?'

He studied her as she sat on the stool, piece of toast in her hand. The towel she had used to dry her hair still draped around her neck.

Her skin was smooth and had so much more colour than when he had first seen her on the ledge.

After chewing a mouthful of toast, she looked up at him. Her blue eyes clear and focused.

He held her gaze, looked from one pupil to the other and patiently waited.

IT WAS AT THIS TIME ACROSS TOWN

Detective Sergeant Saunders had arrived at the fire station.

She was handed the coat, the bunch of keys and the membership ID card.

Thanking the fireman for his diligence, she left.

The coat she placed in the trunk of her police car, the keys and ID she placed in a clear evidence bag, but not before taking a look at the photograph of the blond woman and reading her name.

'Alison Hudson,' she said aloud to herself as she got back in the car.

BACK IN SAM'S APARTMENT

'Okay, that's fair enough,' she finally answered. 'Well, my name is Alison Hudson, but please, call me Ally,' she said, then took another bite of toast.

'So' she continued after chewing, realising that she was much hungrier than she thought earlier. 'I had just arrived back from Halifax by train, had a few things on my mind, ran to the car, because of the rain. Then, before I could even react, I had been grabbed.'

A slight pause as she thought back, 'I remember the sudden panic I felt, a cloth of sorts was pressed up against my mouth, next I knew I was practically lifted and was put inside this vehicle. I was already beginning to get quite woozy, couldn't scream, tried, I think, to struggle, but it all happened so fast, then I felt something sting my neck, a needle I guess, and I blacked out.'

Taking the towel from around her neck, she put her head to one side, 'Can you see a mark?' she asked him.

Sam took a step forward, then leaned over and examined her neck, 'Yes, I see the mark. There's a little bruising too.'

'So,' she said, 'what did you do next?'

Sam straightened, took a step back to lean back once again against the kitchen countertop and said, 'Well, I didn't have my phone with me, couldn't call 911, I'm new in town, so, I jogged home to find out where the police station was and went there to report what I had seen.

The detective there, seemed, well, a little sceptical, perhaps thought I was making it all up, or maybe she thought one of her colleagues was having her on. Anyway, I left it for her to follow up and went home.'

Before Ally could respond, Sam continued, moving from the kitchen into the lounge, 'By the way, I took some pictures. I had my camera with me ...I forgot I had taken them. Didn't tell the detective, as I didn't remember till later, then took a look.' Picking up the camera, he switched it on, still talking whilst he brought up the two pictures on the viewfinder, 'I'll show you.'

But as Sam was about to head back into the kitchen, he glanced out the window and something caught his eye.

Sam stopped.

'They found your car,' he said turning to her. 'Come and see.'

What had caught Sam's attention was a blue flashing light in the distance, above the roofs of the factories in the industrial estate.

She approached from the kitchen and Sam pointed, 'See, see the flashing police light, there, that's where your car is.'

Standing close by him and looking to where he had pointed, Sam thought about the way she had embraced him, the way she had briefly cried, the way she had so gently kissed him.

'I see it,' she said, looking at him.

'Here, take a look through my camera, it has a big zoom lens,' handing it to her.

Taking the camera, she looked, refocused the lens and spotted the police car, then saw her own car. Even though the rain was quite heavy there was no mistaking that was her Triumph.

'I see a policewoman,' she said, handing the camera back to Sam.

Focusing on the scene, Sam saw her too, it was Detective Sergeant Saunders.

'This answers your second question,' Sam said, looking at her and seeing her knit her eyebrows together creating a frown, 'as to how I found you'.

Then continued, 'I just couldn't sleep, kept running the event through in my mind. Anyway, I was right here, by the window, I had the light off to better see outside. Something I do. Well, I noticed a set of headlights, on that road over there, heading into town. Curious, I took my camera, and looked. Saw it only briefly, but noticed it was a dark van, then I scanned the road and there it was. Saw your car, your red Triumph.'

'Wow, so it was pure chance?' she said, 'What did you do next?'

She looked at him. He returned her gaze, noticing again those lovely blue eyes and recalling when she had fluttered them open, on the ledge, a lifetime ago.

'What else do you recall?' he asked, ignoring her question for the moment. 'Did you regain consciousness at all?'

Ally looked out the window, then closed her eyes as she thought back.

Sam studied her. About five foot seven, slim, probably in her late thirties or early forties he estimated. Her blond hair almost dry, straggling to reach just below her shoulders.

She was devoid of any jewellery. He had noticed that when he had finally got her safely into the guest room and was preparing the shower.

No watch, no rings. Was she married? Had the abductors perhaps taken anything?

He watched her face as she tried to recall the events of the previous day. She was frowning, concentrating, then spoke, her voice, having been stronger earlier, again was just a little more than a whisper.

'I remember I was in my bedroom. I was lying on the bed. I know it was my room, but I just couldn't focus, and, I just couldn't move.' After a pause, briefly opening her eyes and giving him a glance, she continued, 'It was night time; it must have been because the light was on.

'I heard voices, a man's voice, I, yes, I think two men, and a woman's voice, I didn't recognise any of them.' Again there was a pause.

Sam could see that it wasn't easy for her. Putting the camera down on the nearby armchair, he stepped a little closer to her, and gently placed his hands on her shoulders. 'It's okay,' he said, comfortingly, 'just take your time.'

She placed her right hand on top of his hand that rested on her left shoulder, then spoke again, 'Oh gosh,' she said, looking up at him, 'my arm. They injected into my arm, the woman, she did.'

Ally released her hand from his, rolled up the sleeve of her bathrobe on her left arm and together they looked.

Another needle mark.

Sam gently took her hands in his, 'Go on,' he said.

She nodded and closed her eyes again. But after a moment she said, 'No, I don't recall anything else. The next thing I see, the next thing I remember, is you.'

She opened her eyes.

There were tears welling up.

He smiled at her, then, to lighten the mood, which he felt was the best thing to do, he said, 'Well, I had better tell you my shining armour story then.'

Ally looked up at him, firmly holding on to his hands and through her tears, she said to the man who had rescued her from certain death, 'Absolutely, you must,' and smiled.

THE PAST;

PERIOD 5

THE YEAR 1829

Ruth Parker had not wasted any time in relocating to Boston.

Everything had changed.

Four years earlier, due to a family feud, she and her mother had packed as much as they could onto a wagon and had, at the suggestion of Charlie Parker, travelled to Canada, to stay with Charlie's grandson.

Now she was back, and everything had changed.

Ruth was a well-educated and smart woman, with a business acumen and a competence that easily enabled her to mix and mingle with anyone from the top dignitaries and politicians to dock workers, farmers and shopkeepers.

Her husband, Charlie, was the entrepreneur, he was the dreamer, the visionary. He had the knack to outlay and picture a concept.

He could, as the saying goes, talk the hind leg off a donkey.

Ruth often smiled when she recalls the day she met him, at his twenty-fifth birthday party.

She and her mother had come down the stairs of that big house, knowing, and revelling in the fact, that practically all eyes were upon them.

Then they had walked over to him. She hadn't as yet, at that point, met Charlie.

Her mother had led the way and approached him.

He was standing with his best friend Henry.

Oh how lost for words he had been then, as was Henry, who was now her stepfather.

Yes, he had the ideas, but she was the one who was organised, who got things into motion, and who made it all work.

She placed both hands on her stomach. She was expecting their first baby.

Having dismissed Charlie's sister, Charlene, from the family business, that day in the lawyer's office, Ruth had set about repairing the damage that had been caused by 'that arrogant and selfish child' as she called her, even though she herself, at the age of twenty-seven, was four years younger.

She had spoken to every single employee of the trading company in person, then had spoken to them collectively in a meeting.

Furthermore she wrote an article for a local newspaper, outlining the new structure of the company, and had also contacted their many suppliers and redrafted new contracts with them.

She and Charlie moved into the big house on the harbour front, having paid the loan back to the bank.

The only drawback, the only sadness, was leaving her mother and Henry behind, in the town of Harris.

Charlie had gifted the big house there to them.

Standing in the large lounge, looking out over the harbour, Ruth was happy and contented.

Her family, the ones who had caused the rift and the fight that had forced her mother and her to leave, were no longer in a controlling position.

In fact, such was her and Charlie's influence and standing in Boston, several of her family members had quietly moved away.

Everything had changed.

Charlie entered the room.

It was a Sunday afternoon.

They had both gone to church in the morning.

He came up behind his wife and wrapped his arms around her, kissed her cheek and also looked out of the window onto the harbour. He asked, 'How is the mother of our child today?'

She placed a hand around his neck and kissed him, 'Just wonderful,' she replied, then, turning around within his arms, looked up at him and asked 'Well? Did you find out anything?'

Charlie, after the church service, and after dropping Ruth home, had gone to see a man with regard to a letter he had found among his grandfather's possessions.

'Oh, I did more than that,' he answered, smiling broadly, 'come and see.'

Taking Ruth by the hand, he led her from the room and into the adjacent room, the dining room, then all the way through it and around into the kitchen.

Charlie had, as quietly as he could, come into the house through a back door into the kitchen.

All was clear here as their servants had most of Sundays off and would likely be seen walking in the park.

There, leaning against a bank of cupboards, were two objects, both seemingly of the same size, but covered up by a green piece of material that seemed to Ruth to be old curtains.

'I found them,' he said, smiling at her, then with a flourish, pulled first one, then the other covering cloth away.

MEANWHILE 500 MILES TO THE NORTH

Rebekah sat on a cushioned cane chair, on the back porch of their house in Harris.

She too, like her daughter in Boston, was happy and content.

The sun was shining brightly on a lovely Sunday afternoon.

Earlier in the day, she and Henry had taken a buggy ride to the church that had been built at the edge of town.

Initially, as the first workers had arrived to earn their living from the mine, there had been only a few ramshackle buildings erected in the settlement, several of which had been places to drink liquor.

As the mine began to prosper and the settlement grew into a town, the buildings became better quality, and more dwellings were being erected.

Women came, families were created, and the town of Harris began to bloom.

It was then that a small church had been constructed.

Since then, and after Charlie and Henry had dramatically increased the output of the mine, further growth had developed, even more houses were built, several stores were set up, two blacksmiths, a grocery store, stables, three larger saloons, and a small hospital and a much larger church.

As a regular church goer from a very young age, this was important for Henry.

It was he who had placed a permanent preacher and his family in town and it was he who often read from scripture.

In the afternoon sun, Henry was working on a makeshift wooden platform upon which, stood a block of stone.

It stood about three feet high, around two feet wide and no more than four inches thick.

Henry had taken this block from the mine just over a year ago, as he'd had an idea, but had done nothing further with it until recently.

Recently his best friend young Charlie and Charlie's wife Ruth, who was now his stepdaughter, had left to reside in Boston.

Charlie had gifted them this house, the largest in town.

The very house where, upon the occasion of Charlie's twenty-fifth birthday, he had met Rebekah, now his wife.

First Henry had built a wooden platform in the back garden area of the house, close to the back porch. He then put together a wooden plinth, three foot square and two foot high. This he loaded with rocks and sand to give it stability.

He transported the block of stone and had it set upon the plinth.

Henry then began to carve into it, to sculpture it.

The rock was hard and consisted of a number of materials which gave it a shiny appearance, and it was most colourful as parts of it were quartz mixed with dioxide.

Regularly, as a way of relaxing, Henry would chisel away at it.

When he had first begun on the project and Rebekah watched him with interest as he worked, but could not see what he was going to create from this hunk of stone, she had said to him, 'What's the point, dear Henry?'

To which he, after a moment or two, had replied, 'Hopkins Point.'

'Then that is what you must call it' she had said, smiling at the man who, in such a short time, had made her feel like she had really never felt before.

Sitting comfortably on her cane chair, the sun pleasantly on her face, she watched him work, carefully chipping away at the stone with a small chisel and hammer.

The sound was pleasant.

She was very happy and content. The family feud was but a distant memory.

THE PRESENT;

MONCTON

THURSDAY 2ND MAY

Detective Sergeant Saunders walked up to the reception desk at the fitness centre.

She swept her left hand through her short-cropped hair, hoping to brush away the drops of rain that had fallen upon her in the short walk from her car.

'Hi,' she said, to the young, fit-looking, redhead who smiled at her.

Taking out her ID, she said, 'DS Saunders, I'm looking for some information on one of your clients, Alison Hudson?'

'Ally?' the redhead asked, her form-fitting outfit showing her physique, which must surely be a good advertisement for the centre, 'Ally, Miss Hudson, works here in administration, she's not here today.'

'She works here?' the detective asked.

'Yes, but she's been off since Tuesday. She was due back this morning, but hasn't showed up yet. She told me she was going to Halifax, family thing or something.'

'I'll need to speak to the manager, please,' the detective said, then answered her phone which had begun to ring.

The large clock on the wall behind the reception desk showed it to be two minutes past eleven …

The clock in the kitchen at Sam's apartment showed two minutes past eleven and the water in the kettle boiled, automatically switching the appliance off.

'Woah, did you say Rozzini?' Sam asked, stopping in his tracks and turning around to look at Ally who was seated in one of the armchairs in the lounge.

'Yeah, Julien Rozzini' she replied. 'Why?'

'Any relation to Nico Rozzini?' Sam asked, walking back towards her.

'Yeah …why?' she asked, frowning, seeing his puzzled expression.

Sam shook his head, 'No, it doesn't matter right now. Carry on, please. I'll …carry on, I can hear you,' and with that he headed back towards the kitchen.

Ally watched him go, then thought back to earlier, to his account of events …

… first he had related the sequence of events, upon hearing her moan on the ledge, with some humour and exaggerated feats of strength and stamina, which amused her greatly.

She was well aware, though, that it couldn't have been easy at all and that she would certainly have fallen to her death had it not been for his action, and that, despite his light-hearted version of the event, he had risked his life to bring her to safety.

He had then finished telling the story, saying that he had, after having showered, spent simply ages in preparing drinks and a sumptuous buffet for them to enjoy, only for her to have so rudely fallen asleep.

She shook her head and laughed at his humour, knowing full well that had not been the case.

He had then looked at her, and in a serious voice, with a look of concern on his face, said, 'Someone wants you dead Ally, why?'

'I know, and I will tell you why,' she answered, then sat herself on the arm of the two-seater couch in the lounge and prepared to tell her story.

She looked at him, then turned to look out the window as she thought it all through. How to begin? She noticed that it was raining.

Taking a deep breath, she began.

'A long time ago, I was in a relationship. It was good for a while, but, then I got pregnant. I was twenty-eight at the time. I had been in a relationship before, none felt ... right ... maybe this time ... maybe I just wanted a baby, anyway ...he didn't stay, he left, so ... There I was, I gave birth to a daughter ...

Theresa, my grandmother's name, I called her Terri ...' she paused here, got up from the arm of the chair, walked over to the window, looking out for a while, not saying anything.

Sam watched her, and waited.

'So, there I was,' she continued, turning around, again glancing at him, then she sat herself down in one of the armchairs, 'an unmarried mum. But I had some funds, I managed. I had a small apartment, but we made it work. She grew, started school, and all was going well really, then ...out of the blue, one day, he showed up, Julien Rozzini ...'

This was when Sam had interrupted.

She wondered how he knew the name, watched as she saw him in the kitchen preparing drinks.

At his suggestion, she carried on relating her story.

'Okay, so, yeah, he shows up, suddenly wants to be in her life, and in mine, would you believe. I mean, she is seven years old by now, and suddenly he wants to be her daddy?'

Ally got up from the chair, returned to the window and again stared outside for a few moments. It was still raining. She briefly wondered about her car. Was it still there? Did they tow it somewhere?

Then she refocused, and continued her story.

'So,' she said, turning around once again and looking at Sam as he brought in the drinks and a plate of biscuits on a tray, setting them down on the low table.

'I told him where to go, and not politely either ...then one day, not long after that visit ...' Ally paused, then taking another deep breath, sat herself down again, this time on the two-seater couch, and continued, 'I went to collect her from school, as usual, but was called into the headmistress's office, and there was someone from childcare ...I was accused of being an unfit mother! Terri was taken away from me, there and then ... I had to go to court.

'These were all trumped up charges. I hired a lawyer, but by the time I had proved the claims were false, Terri was gone, Julien was gone ...' Ally burst into tears.

Sam quickly sat down beside her, put his arm around her and held her, letting her cry.

He wondered how many times she had relived this event.

After some moments, Ally pulled herself together and went on.

'I went to court again. This time I proved, conclusively, that the whole thing had been a ploy to take Terri away from me by her biological father, by Julien.'

Ally, feeling comforted by Sam's arm still around her, looked across at him, tears in her eyes and continued the story.

'An immediate warrant for his arrest was made. The police searched and hunted for some time, but no trace was found.

I received compensation from the court, my lawyer saw to that, for false accusations, for taking the child away from me without substantiating the claims, and it was found that two people in childcare had taken a bribe. They were arrested and served time, though I would have liked to ...'

Ally paused, wiped her tears away with her finger and reached for her drink.

Sam asked, releasing his arm and also taking his coffee from the tray, 'So, when did all this happen?'

She looked at him, 'Ten years ago, in Portland, Oregon.'

Sam felt for her.

He couldn't begin to imagine how it must have been for her.

But, he thought, there must be a lot more to tell, for why else would anyone go to such lengths to, in fact, silence her.

Reaching for a biscuit and taking a sip of his drink, Sam was thinking that Detective Saunders would surely be calling on him soon, and what to do then?

Ally, for undoubtedly good reasons, hadn't wanted police involvement.

'Now, I know there's a lot more to tell,' he said, after some time of silence, his voice soft, 'but, I have a feeling that that detective is going to call, so, what's the play, what do you want to do next?'

Eating the biscuit he waited for her response.

She looked at him, sensed his concern, and could see that the man sat next to her, the man who had saved her life, was full of compassion.

Putting her cup down on the table, Ally said, 'I'll briefly tell you, what happened in the last week, where it has all gone wrong,' and she stood up, once again walking over to the window. 'Julien is the father. Why he suddenly wanted to get back into Terri's life, not that he had ever been in it, I don't know, but I do know, that his brother, well he is the one with the wealth, the connection and the influence ...'

Turning from the window, looking over to where Sam still sat on the couch, she said, 'It was he, I have no doubt, who orchestrated the whole false accusation thing, and his name is Nico, and you do know him, don't you?' she queried, waiting for a response.

'Not right now Ally, I will clarify in a moment. Please, go on ...' he answered.

'Okay, well then, just over three months ago, I found out where Julien is, through social media, a great place to find things out. Found him living in Halifax.

I knew I had to be careful, knew what he, and his brother, are capable of, so I looked around for work. Managed to get a position here, in Moncton, not too far away from Halifax, so I took it. Then I could investigate.

You see, I have, or rather, I had, a copy of the arrest warrant for Julien.'

Ally came back to sit next to Sam on the couch again, picked up her drink and went on, 'Then when I moved here, I discovered something else, quite by chance really. Working at the fitness centre, I found out that there was a member whose name is Rozzini.'

'Nice break,' Sam said. 'These things happen.'

'It was a woman,' Ally said, taking a quick sip of her coffee, 'Debra. Turns out she is the wife of Nico. Now, though the arrest warrant is only for Julien, the police in Portland do want to speak to Nico as a possible accessory. Now I had an address, whereas I hadn't got any closer to finding where Julien might live, here was a break, as you say, but it is also where I made a mistake.'

Taking another couple of sips, Ally put the cup down and said, 'I took a couple of days of this week. On Tuesday I drove to a small town called Harris ...'

'This is getting uncanny ...' Sam interrupted 'Sorry, explanation soon, carry on.'

Ally studied his face for a moment, then carried on, 'I drove out there, to Harris. It's not that far away. Initially I wanted to drive to the address I had, but on the way I had second thoughts about that, so, I drove into town. Then, whilst having some lunch and thinking through what my next move should be, thumbing through a local paper, I discovered, that Nico Rozzini is the owner of the mining company, CP Holdings.'

'This set me thinking again,' Ally said after a brief pause, 'I googled on my phone, and guess what I discovered?' looking at Sam and awaiting a response.

Returning her gaze, Sam frowned, thought for a moment, then answered, 'Julien is on the board of directors of this company?'

'You're just a little too smart' she said, giving him a mock scowl, 'close, but not quite, there is a CP Holdings Warehouse and Distribution Centre, in Halifax, and that, is run by Julien.'

'That's good work, a good result. So, where did you go wrong? You said you made a mistake?'

'Yeah, big one. The police station was right next door to where I was having some lunch. Stupidly, feeling very excited and very sure of myself, I went in.

Produced the copy of the warrant for the arrest of Julien, told them my story, then gave them Nico's address, and told them about Julien in Halifax.'

'The response was not what you hoped for, or expected?' Sam guessed.

'No, the guy I spoke to, took the warrant and went to see his boss, the chief I guess. Well, they both came out after a while, then this chief says to me that they will contact the police in Portland and take it from there, then asked for my details and sent me on my way, saying they would be in touch, but they had to go through the proper channels.'

'You didn't believe them?' Sam asked.

'I had a bad feeling. Didn't trust them. Felt relieved to be outside again, you know?'

'The next plan, was to go to Halifax?' Sam asked, prompting her to complete her story.

Ally sighed.

'Yes, I thought if I can find out exactly where Julien lives, then I would have something concrete. I had initially already planned to go to Halifax anyway to nosey around, but now I had more information. I did look for her name, for Terri's name, in the social media sites for that area, but no luck there.'

Sam watched her, finished his coffee and waited for her to go on.

'I found the warehouse, but I felt uncomfortable. All sorts of things began to go through my mind, the unhelpfulness of the police in Harris. The fact that, all those years ago in Portland, the Rozzini family had been influential. It stood to reason they might well be influential here too, and of course, in that small town of Harris.

It was very possible, that they had informed Nico of my presence.'

Ally paused, once again got up from the couch, and once again walked over to look outside, then said,' And now I'm sure, that's exactly what they did.'

Turning again, but staying by the window, Ally went on, 'So, I headed back home, decided I would contact the police in Oregon myself, but speak with the guy, the detective, who had been in charge way back then. Over the years I have kept in contact with him, though less and less as the years have passed.'

'I just don't know who to trust any more,' she said, coming away from the window and sitting herself down in one of the armchairs, 'that's why I asked you not to involve the police, or go to the hospital, thank you for that ...'

'I was worried for your health,' Sam said. 'You were soaked through, and I was sure you were drugged, but I could hear the importance in your words. Once I got you here though, and you were sick a couple of times, your breathing improved so when you fell asleep and your breathing was regular, I was relieved. Had it not been so, I would have had to call a doctor ...'

Ally briefly smiled and sat in silence for a while. Her eyes were still moist. Her complexion had paled a little. She looked tired.

Not surprising with everything she had been through.

Finally, it was Sam who spoke, 'You're right, the police in Harris must have informed the Rozzinis.'

Standing up and moving towards Ally, Sam said, 'They sure put a plan in action very quickly, obviously quite desperate for you to disappear. Still, such a rapid response may well have left clues for the police here to follow. DS Saunders is on the case.' Sam perched himself on the arm of the chair and took one of Ally's hands from her lap into his. 'They have your car. No doubt they will know about you, where you live, but will they find out what you were doing? I guess the bad guys will have surely searched your place.'

Ally placed her other hand on top of his and looked up at him.

Outside the rain lashed against the window panes.

'I was drugged and on my bed for several hours, so, yes, they will have searched my place, no doubt taken my laptop.'

The clock in Sam's kitchen showed ten minutes past twelve.

The clock on the wall of Detective Sergeant Saunders office ticked over to ten minutes past twelve as she entered, took her raincoat off and sat down behind her desk.

Switching on her terminal she read a few reports that had come in from forensics.

No prints on the membership ID card, on the winter coat they had found several blond hairs and a couple of brown hairs, but to get any DNA results from those would take time.

The house however, had given up a positive result.

They had found prints belonging to a Miss Karina West, a thirty-two-year-old, with priors for soliciting and drug possession.

It also stated in the report that she was a qualified nurse, showed an address in Halifax, and stated she was currently employed in a hospital in Dartmouth.

A photograph on the report showed a woman with short brown hair.

The same woman that had been driving the red car.

Detective Sergeant Saunders picked up the phone and dialled a number.

It was twenty minutes past twelve when Sam's phone rang.

THE PAST;

PERIOD 6

THE YEAR 1850

Sara Rebekah Parker was a very excited eighteen-year-old.

The five-hundred-mile journey had been the adventure of a lifetime.

Accompanied by a woman and five men, they had set out from Boston in a covered carriage, the two women inside, and two men on the drivers box guiding the two horses. Another two men drove an open wagon, containing an assortment of equipment, boxes, luggage and provisions.

The fifth man rode a horse and led a spare horse along on this journey, heading for the Canadian province of New Brunswick, specifically to the town of Harris.

This would be the first time she would meet her grandmother and her grandmother's husband, Henry, her father's good friend of whom she had heard many stories.

The trip was not a vacation.

Her father, still ever the visionary, had expanded the business in Boston, always with the support, guidance and strength of her mother. She was the person who sorted out the details, the day-to-day workings and running of the company dealing with not only the employees, but also the dealers and traders, and, importantly, those in government, the politicians and senators.

Though neither her father or mother had ever returned to Harris, since coming back to Boston some twenty years ago, they had regular correspondence every two or three months over the years.

Her father, wanting to keep her older brother in Boston, had suggested that she could take over the family business in Canada, learning from Henry, who by now, was in his mid-seventies. Whilst her mother had agreed the proposition, it had to be up to herself if she wanted to take on this challenge. He reminded her it might not be easy to leave her family and friends behind.

Sara had seriously considered the idea for a number of weeks, then had made up her mind that this would be a great adventure, though also a challenge that she felt she could face and tackle.

Of course it would also be great to finally meet her grandmother and Henry.

And so, late one summer morning, the entourage arrived in the small town to a dozen or more people awaiting them, including, of course, a beaming Rebekah and Henry.

Henry Hopkins was in his element. For the second time in his life he felt like a father.

He and Rebekah, though very happy and very much in love with each other, had not been able to have any children of their own.

Whilst of course Rebekah had a daughter, Ruth, Henry's stepdaughter, the bond had not been the same as he felt now, and as he had felt many years ago with another eighteen-year-old.

Henry mused over this as he walked proudly beside Sara, touring the various parts of the mine.

He thought back to when he was in Peru and had come across Zoltina, and had so immediately bonded with this young man. Henry had taught him many things and the young lad had been a sponge for all the information he gave.

And now, another eighteen-year-old, Sara, also with a thirst for knowledge, a hunger for learning and she hung on every word he spoke.

Henry had to agree that his friend Charlie, Sara's father, had been right.

She would indeed be the right one to take on the company. She was smart, assertive without being arrogant, and had tons of drive and ambition.

She had been taken down several of the shafts, had got stuck into the rock surface with an axe, had seen how ore was mined, how the pumps worked, had smiled and spoken to many of the men, had not worried about getting dirty, and had been an instant hit with the crew.

Now, already into the fourth day since her arrival, she sat in the plush office in a comfy armchair and was totally engrossed in reading the many reports and papers that Henry had given her.

Standing by the window that overlooked the town, Henry recalled the time he and Charlie had stood here together.

Twenty-five years ago that had been. A week before they were both due to get married.

He smiled at the recollection, then turned and watched young Sara for a while as she was totally absorbed in what she was reading.

Henry walked over to what was now his desk, behind which the large painting, the seascape, still hung. As Charlie's grandfather had gifted the painting to Charlie when he had set off from Boston, so Charlie gifted it to Henry before he and Ruth returned to their home city.

Sitting down behind his desk, he opened a top drawer, took out a book, flicked it open and, having dipped his pen into the ink, began to write.

These were his journals. He had decided some time ago that he wanted to record a selected series of adventures in his life.

Six years ago, is where he was up to in recording specific moments. It was six years ago when something happened that had almost cost him his life. Afterwards it was this that had prompted him to put down in words his experiences, his travels and the people who had made a marked difference in his life.

Six years ago, in the year 1844, there had been a severe flood in the town …

… It was the time between winter and spring. A time when some flowers and wildlife decided it was time to spring up and explore.

A time when other plants, trees and wildlife decided, not quite yet as there were still frosty mornings and snow on the hills.

It was neither winter nor spring.

The rain came.

The suddenness and the severity was unlike anything anyone had seen before, or since.

The heavens opened and the rain came down.

It quickly flooded the streams that fed the river that ran through the town.

The force of the water broke chunks of ice in the process, sweeping these down from the hills, along with a deluge of water, and all of it, heading towards the town.

It was also a time between night and day. A time when the dawn should have broken, but the sun and the light were unable to penetrate the darkness of the clouds for nearly half an hour.

It was neither night, nor day.

Then, as suddenly as the rain had started, it stopped.

The sun appeared, it was bright, and the dark clouds practically gone.

But then the sound came.

A rumbling sound, a gushing sound, a threatening sound.

Henry, always up early, had not long ago stepped inside his office on the first floor.

When the rain came down, he had stood by the window, watching with fascination the power of nature.

He was still standing by the window, when, for a moment, all went quiet, the rain had stopped, the sun had appeared.

Perhaps it had been the tremendous noise of the downpour that, when it stopped, made everything seem deadly quiet.

Then Henry saw something that made him anxious.

The water in the river.

Not only was it flowing very fast, but the water was rising, and rising quickly.

Then he heard the sound, the distant rumble.

Henry knew what was causing it.

Despite his age, he was sixty-nine at the time, he left his office, bounded down the stairs and reached the foyer.

Here, in a small room to the left of the reception counter, was the control panel for the mine's whistle.

This had been put in place many years ago, a blast on the whistle was a signal for the end of day shift but could also be used as an emergency signal, to alert the fire rescue and mine rescue team that there was a problem underground.

Currently there was no-one in the mine. The morning shift had not yet commenced.

Henry pushed the control button and blasted the air pressure controlled whistle a total of five times, five long whistles.

He heard the sound echoing through the town.

The roar from the hills was coming closer, fast.

The rumbling grew louder.

Henry left the room and saw some menfolk coming over the old stone bridge, coming for the early shift.

Bolting out of the foyer he yelled, as loud as he could, for the men to run quickly towards him, and as he ran further into the street, he waved frantically for others approaching the bridge to turn back.

Seeing Henry and picking up on the noise that was coming ever closer, they immediately understood and retreated, making sure no-one came closer to the bridge.

The group of men that had been closer ran into the foyer of the building.

Henry, returning also, gave them orders to find lengths of rope and to come back to the entrance of the building.

Henry ventured back out, looked to his left, towards the hills, and what he saw froze him to the spot.

Hurtling towards town and towards the bridge, was a towering wave of water, mixed with big chunks of ice and boulders and rocks and branches.

Fortunately, the other side of the bridge was higher ground, and thankfully the other men had understood Henry's frantic arm waving, the whistle and the roaring sound coming closer, and had stopped some distance from the bridge.

Henry could see that were he stood was not safe. He dashed back into the building, closing the heavy glass door behind him.

Four of his men had reappeared with lengths of rope.

Henry pointed to the staircase, shouted for them to follow him, and in the way he had earlier bounded down the stairs, he now strode up them, taking two steps at a time.

On reaching the first landing he turned, the four men with him also doing so.

The noise was deafening, a barrage of water and debris entered the town.

Through the windows of the foyer, they watched in horror as the torrent rushed by.

Big blocks of ice were being hurled upwards. It was as if the building was sinking below the water.

Then, with an explosion louder than a dynamite blast, the windows and the glass door of the foyer crashed into thousands of shards and pieces.

Henry and the men, just in time, bounded up towards the top of the staircase.

Water gushed in, the counter was reduced to splinters, two doors leading to other offices, a canteen and kitchen area stood no chance against the might of the water pressure and water flowed into the building.

From the top of the stairs, the five men watched in awe, as the whole foyer and entrance area became a seething sea of water and debris.

The rumble began to fade. The flow of water decreased.

Henry and the four men descended the stairs. Amazingly none had been injured by flying glass.

The water that had surged in through the foyer and into the building, had, inexplicably been sucked out again, leaving just a mass of glass, wood and rubble on the floor.

Henry reached the street first to take in the sight. The stone bridge, at one time completely submerged in the deluge, had withstood the onslaught and seemed perfectly fine.

The river, now looking to be only a little above its normal height, flowed rapidly underneath.

It was then that Henry spotted two people in trouble.

A man was in the river, on the far side near the bank. With one hand he held a child above the waterline. The other was wrapped around a sizeable tree trunk that had lodged there. There was no way he could move, nor was there any way he could hang on to either the tree trunk or the child forever.

Henry was about to move, but two miners pushed past him. One of them, as he was running across the bridge to reach the other side, was already looping one end of the rope around him. The second man, grasping what the first man had in mind, did likewise.

Henry ordered the remaining two men to go back inside the building and check on the situation there, telling them, they had this covered.

Henry then also crossed the bridge, looped the end of his length or rope around the far pillar of the bridge and walked along the slippery bank towards the other men.

The first man had, by now, reached the stricken man in the river, his colleague holding the rope attached to him, whilst he himself was now being held by Henry who, in turn, was secured to the bridge.

They grabbed the child first, handed over from man to man until Henry had him.

Others had come to assist and one of them took the young lad.

The man in the river was next to be pulled away from the strong current and to safety.

Cheers and applause rang out as they all made it safely onto solid ground.

There had been several injuries, but no fatalities.

The deluge had caused quite some damage to various parts of the town which took nearly four months to repair.

The town committee, of which Henry was a leading figure, agreed to spend some funds and put effort into works to score up parts of the river bank to the north of the town, much like the construction used to secure mine shafts.

It had been from that time on, that Henry had decided to journal his life's experiences and adventures.

Sitting at his desk and peering over to see young Sara still reading through the many documents and procedures he had laid out for her; he was glad to be doing these journals.

He would, when the time came, leave them to her.

THE PRESENT;

MONCTON

THURSDAY 2ND MAY

Sam answered his phone.

Making a face at Ally, he said, 'Oh hello Detective,' then listened for a bit before replying, 'well, thank you for telling me. At least I didn't imagine it all,' a pause, then, 'That's okay ...goodbye.'

Sam finished the call, looked over at Ally and said, 'As you will have gathered, that, was Detective Sergeant Saunders. First she informed me that there had indeed been, an incident, as she called it, and thanked me for bringing it to her attention. Then she apologised for doubting me.'

'That's it?' Ally asked.

'That's it, which is just fine. My feeling is to let the police sort it all out from their end, whilst we think of how to proceed from this end.'

'But, how do we proceed?' she asked, a frown appearing over her brow. 'I can't expect you to put yourself in any danger. That wouldn't be right at all.'

'Let me fill you in,' Sam replied, sitting himself down on the couch beside her, then taking hold of her hand in his. She clasped it firmly and affectionately.

'First of all, no-one knows your alive. The bad guys think you have by now well and truly fallen into the river and drowned. The police, may also believe you to be dead, so, that's in our favour.

Secondly, I have a way in which to, hopefully, obtain more information.'

Sam paused and noticed Ally's query in her eyes, the frown reappearing on her brow. 'As you earlier guessed, yes, I do know Nico Rozzini, though not very well at all. He is a client and I only met him for the first time on Tuesday.'

Taking a brief pause to give her a reassuring look, Sam explained, 'I am an art assessor. I work for an auction house in Boston. I go out and check on art pieces that clients want to put into auction. I look at the articles, then check on their provenance, and check their history, in order to price them right for the auction.

I take photos and prepare the illustration page for the catalogue, that is how I know Mr Rozzini.

He has a painting he wants to sell, and so I was in Harris, on Tuesday morning, viewing it.'

'Wow, that's some coincidence,' Ally said, looking at him, her hand still firmly in his grasp.

'Yes, though personally I think sometimes some coincidences are events meant to be.' Sam released her hand, got up and picked up the tray from the table. Taking it through to the kitchen, he said, 'Now I have to go back there, because I need to take the frame off, as it's not the original and there may well be a signature hiding underneath, who knows. Anyway, it's an opportunity for me to be there and hopefully snoop around a bit, ask a few questions.'

'You must be very careful, please,' Ally said, concern in her voice as she got up to follow Sam into the kitchen.

Sam placed the tray on the island, then turned and looked at her as she approached. 'Oh absolutely, seeing what they are prepared to do or are capable of, I'll be very careful indeed.'

Sam took a step towards her. She stopped in the archway between the kitchen and lounge. Sam gently took hold of her shoulders and looked into her eyes.

Though his heart was thumping like mad at this point, he spoke calmly, surprised that he could say anything at all as he, at that time, realised how attracted he was to her. 'Now, a few things that come to mind. One, you must stay here, certainly for now, out of sight. Your clothes will be dry by now, but I will get you some new clothes shortly. Second, you said you had a police report pertaining to the warrant for the arrest of Julien. You don't have another copy?'

'No, well yes, but it's on my laptop. I'm sure they either have it or have destroyed it'

Ally answered. She felt slightly weak at the knees as he looked into her eyes as he was holding her so reassuringly.

'Very true. Still, now that the police here are investigating, they will do a complete check on you. They'll no doubt discover why you are here, they'll connect the dots, hopefully. In the meantime, so this is the third thing, I suggest we should focus on the whereabouts of your daughter. What do you say?'

Ally said nothing for the moment and drew herself closer into him. Nestling her head against his neck, they embraced.

Feeling safe and secure in his arm, Ally thought about the past weeks.

When she had found clues to the whereabouts of Julien, she had been optimistic and buoyant. Finding Nico's address had boosted her optimism.

But the events of yesterday were still swirling around in her head. Though she felt protected and comforted in his arms, she couldn't help think how different it could have been. She accepted that she would have surely died, had it not been for this man who now held her and was so willing to help her. She certainly didn't want any harm to come to Sam.

Pulling her head away from his neck and looking into his eyes, she said' I just can't sit here though. I have to do something.'

Sam released her, smiled, planted a quick kiss on her forehead and said, 'And you will, but first, it's past my lunchtime.' He headed into the lounge where he inserted a USB drive into his stereo system and came back towards the kitchen.

Ally was still under the archway.

The sound of 'America' emanated from the speakers as the song 'A horse with no name' began to play.

MEANWHILE IN ANOTHER PART OF THE CITY;

DS Saunders looked at her watch and realised why she was hungry. It was past her lunchtime.

She grabbed her raincoat and headed out the door.

She would stop and get some lunch on the way.

Now that forensics had finished, she was going back to the house where Miss Alison Hudson resided.

It was pretty clear that she had been abducted, or worse, possibly killed, but, to what end.

According to the information she had found at the fitness centre, Miss Hudson had been employed there for a little under three months, and was well liked and very efficient in her work. She had previously worked as an administrator for a travel company in Vancouver.

DS Saunders had also found out that the car, the red Triumph sports car, had been purchased in Dartmouth around three months ago.

A warrant for the arrest of Karina West was in place and she hoped to hear back soon from her counterpart in Halifax.

She collected lunch from her favourite deli with coffee to go and was soon at the address, which, according to a text she had received moments ago, had been leased to Miss Hudson, three months ago.

'So, who are you, Alison Hudson?' DS Saunders said aloud to herself, whilst sitting in her car and having her lunch. 'More importantly, where are you?'

Taking another bite of her pastrami filled baguette and following that up with a sip of her latte, she continued conversing to herself.

'Or, even more importantly, are you still alive?' She often found herself thinking out loud in her work.

'Why was your car on the canyon road, and why was your winter coat in the river?'

Taking another bite, she thought for a few moments, before continuing the conversation with herself.

'And why did you take a train to Halifax?'

She made a mental note to check CCTV footage at Halifax station to see whether or not Alison had met with anyone.

Then, drinking the last of her latte, she got out of her car and walked up to the house.

The forensic report had stated that the prints belonging to Miss Karina West were found on the closet door in the master bedroom and on the light switch in the kitchen.

The master bedroom was where she would start, she thought to herself, closing the front door behind her.

It would have been helpful to have some more bodies on the investigation, but staffing levels were low at present.

Her captain had promised her more assistance should she find more concrete evidence of either abduction or murder.

'In the meantime Karen,' she said to herself, 'just get on with it.'

THE PAST;

PERIOD 7

THE YEAR 1866

Thirty-four-year-old Sara Parker was crying.

Her heart was heavy.

To lose one family member was hard, to lose two in as many days, was unbearable.

Her father, Charlie, was on one side of her, her mother, Ruth, on the other.

They held each other and were the last people remaining at the graveside.

Henry had taken ill, Rebekah had cared for him for two days, then had fallen ill herself.

She had been the first to go, slipping away in her sleep. Henry had been unaware, had a fever, kept slipping in and out of consciousness and passed away the day after his wife.

Having been told by the doctor that the prospect for Henry didn't look good, after all he was ninety-one years old, she had sent word to Boston.

Two days ago, in the early evening, they had both arrived.

It was a tearful reunion, for not only did they share a loss, but Sara had not seen her parents since leaving Boston sixteen years ago.

Now the three of them stood in silence.

Both Sara and her mother Ruth had tears rolling down their cheeks.

Charlie drawn and solemn.

The double funeral had been a big affair. Practically the whole town had come out to pay their respects. Both were enormously well-liked, loved and respected.

'Now we mourn,' Charlie said after some time, 'but this evening we will celebrate the lives of Henry and Rebekah. We will remember them with fondness and thankfulness.'

Then the three of them turned around and together walked along the path, heading back into town.

The party, the wake, would be held in the big house where Henry had met Rebekah and where Charlie had met Ruth.

The house would now pass on to Sara, along with the mining company which she, with the help and guidance from Henry, had learned to run very successfully.

There had been some doubts early on about a woman to run a business, a woman to make decisions, a woman to be the boss over many men.

But Henry, a towering figure, figuratively speaking for he stood no more than five foot six, was hugely respected and admired.

Every day the men would see Henry with Sara, teaching, instructing, showing.

Almost every day for well over five years she was instructed in every aspect of the mine. She went into the tunnels, actively took part in the physical work, trained in explosives, trained in the working and maintenance of the pumps, and trained in harnessing the horses to the wagons.

She had many times, taken a wagon load of shale and ore down the road where, close to the coast and about eleven miles from the town, stood a factory with special grinding and sifting equipment and also smelting furnaces where the silver was extracted from the ore and quartz from the shale.

From there, the finished product would be transported, with good security, to Halifax for sale both nationally and internationally.

Sara had also on several occasions driven this route and knew the full workings of the sales and administration offices there.

Every conceivable aspect of what the company was involved with, she had observed and executed.

The doubts anyone had about this young lady being able to work this business, to run this company, had completely evaporated within the first year.

As she stood on the third step of the staircase leading up from the foyer, on the first working day back, for work had stopped totally on the day of the funeral, out of respect to Henry and so that any and all would be able to pay their respects, it was her they admired and applauded as she spoke to them, as she encouraged them and rejuvenated them.

It was a gift she surely inherited from her mother.

A week after the funeral and three days after her mother and father had set off on their return journey to Boston, Sara left the house after a light breakfast, walked along the top bank of the river, crossed the stone bridge and, instead of going across the road into the entrance to the company building, a totally restructured entrance and foyer area after the flood of 1844, now with a small paved square along the frontage, she turned left and headed down the road, towards the stables.

There was a small stable block at the smelting plant, but the main stables were here in Harris.

It was a large barn, capable of stalling thirty horses, the feed, the harnesses and other tack, and lay adjacent the river and with plenty of grazing fields nearby.

Several other buildings had been erected here. There was a smithy, an essential element, a carpentry shop, a storage facility, and a small cottage, for there were always at least four men on duty. There were also two silos connected to the mine, which would fill up with ore and shale to be shovelled onto wagons destined for the smelting plant.

Sara loved horses, and would come here often, but more so in recent days.

With a determination in her step, she headed straight for the main stable block.

It was time.

She wasn't getting any younger.

She wanted babies.

It was time.

Carl was tall, he was blond, he was handsome, and had the most gorgeous blue eyes.

He was softly spoken; he was kind.

He was also extremely shy.

She knew he would be about. He was always around at this time of the morning.

He was one of several men who looked after the horses well-being, including the feeding, the grooming, the harnessing and the hitching to wagon, and checking their health and their hooves.

She entered the large barn through an open door.

There he was, brushing down a large mare.

He heard her approach and smiled.

Sara noticed he was the only one here. Often, at this time of the morning, he was the only one here.

She smiled at him, and walked right up to him. She gave the mare a quick look, gently rubbed the horses nose, then, she turned to Carl, put both arms around his neck, drew herself up to him, and kissed him.

Henry's sculpture stood in a far corner on the back porch of the big house.

He had finished it many years ago, had chiselled a square plinth for it out of a hard white stone and had secured the sculpture on to it.

The two-foot-high piece of rock had a mainly light grey sheen to it, but here and there quartz showed through in colours ranging from a translucent orange through to shades of yellow, and even a light green streak could be seen.

Henry had polished it, smoothed the edges and had roughly carved the title of this work on one side of the plinth, which was about three foot square and six inched deep.

The title had come about after his wife, who had, at the beginning of his work on the piece, asked, 'Henry, what's the point?'

After some thought, he had smiled at her, and had said, 'Hopkins point', and so it was and so it had been carved into the base.

Under Sara's supervision, four men lifted the piece and placed it on a hand cart. Together the group walked to the main building where Sara had chosen a spot, on the paved square by the entrance, for it to be securely placed.

'Well Henry,' she whispered to herself, when all was in place, 'here it is, and here it stands.'

It had a strange sort of oblong shape and about two thirds of the way up, and no more than two inches from the left-hand side, Henry had drilled a small hole into which he had inserted a small emerald.

Sara had noticed early on that often the rays of the sun would catch that pale green precious stone and it would sparkle and gleam.

What it was meant to represent, she did not know, perhaps only Henry knew, Maybe he had written about it in one of his journals.

Journals that he had already passed on to her several months back, perhaps having an inkling that his health was failing.

She hadn't, as yet, started to read them, but promised herself to begin to do so soon.

Almost every day when she came to work, before entering the building, she would put her hand out and touch the sculpture.

'Good morning Henry', she would often say in her mind.

THE PRESENT;

THE TOWN OF HARRIS

FRIDAY 3RD MAY

Sam stood next to the sculpture. He had arrived a few minutes ago.

Late yesterday he had found a picture framing shop in Harris itself, spoke to the owner, realised he knew his onions and asked him to meet him outside the entrance of CP Holdings.

It was a clear day. The sun was shining through scattered white clouds and the temperature was mild.

Whilst waiting he studied the rock sculpture and couldn't get his head around the fact that the shape looked familiar to him.

The embedded emerald caught the sunlight and winked at him.

Looking at it more closely and feeling the smoothness of the rock, he was sure the precious stone had been purposefully placed in that position.

Interesting, he thought, though little could Sam have imagined that the very man who had created that sculpture, had once been the owner of the beautifully painted miniature that he, along with Samantha and with the help of Chrissie, had been searching for.

'Mr Price?'

A man, in his sixties, Sam figured, approached him.

'Mr Nugent, I take it?' Sam responded, offering his hand.

Moments later they both entered the foyer area and walked up to the reception desk. From there they were instructed to go up to the first floor where they entered another reception area.

Sam had been here before, a mere three days ago.

The same receptionist was there, again, well coiffured, smartly dressed, looking every bit as efficient as the other day and recognised Sam.

'Good morning Mr Price,' she said, 'Mr Rozzini is unavailable today, he asked me to inform you that the painting has been taken from the wall and is placed on the conference room table. That's the third door on the left, please, go ahead.'

Sam thanked her, Mr Nugent nodded at her and they both headed for the third door on the left.

This is good, Sam thought. With the boss being away, surely it's an opportunity to snoop around a bit.

He opened the door to the conference room.

Sam took off the satchel he carried across his shoulder and placed it on a chair. The large painting lay on the table, a soft beige coloured blanket underneath, a white bed sheet covering over the top.

Sam peeled the sheet away and both men looked at the picture.

'Very dirty,' Mr Nugent said, studying it in detail.

'Very,' Sam agreed. 'Let's turn it over, then you can dismantle the frame'

This was the first time he had the opportunity to see the back for himself.

While Mr Nugent set about taking the ornate frame from the picture, Sam, using his trusty pencil torch, examined the back.

There were no other markings, other than those he had seen on the photograph he was given.

Hopefully, the large frame removed; more might be revealed.

Using an array of tools he had brought along, Mr Nugent worked on the frame.

He worked his way carefully around it, making sure he didn't miss any of the many staples.

Sam, having spotted the security camera, placed in the top far left corner of the rectangular boardroom, immediately upon entering the room, moved about, watching the man at work whilst, surreptitiously, looking around the room.

The painting lay on a boardroom table, made of oak, which was a good ten feet long. In preparation for them coming, ten carver chairs were all lined up along the wall beneath the windows, well out of the way.

Quite considerate, Sam thought and thought that it had probably been the efficient receptionist who had been in control of that.

Two large lamps were suspended from the ceiling above the table, a further two lamps stood on either side of an oak sideboard placed on the inner wall, opposite the windows.

The two smaller walls were adorned with several framed prints, all photographs of the mine, the tunnels, the smelting plant, the horses and wagons, the miners, the previous owners, and several shots of the town itself, all taken over the many years of the mine's existence.

These fascinated Sam and he spent some time in closely looking at each one, there were forty-eight in all.

He then had a thought about the possible usefulness of these historic photos and grabbing his camera from his satchel, took several shots of both walls.

Mr Nugent informed Sam that he was ready.

Together they carefully wriggled the frame loose and took it off.

The difference in colour where the frame had been, was noticeable.

Sam, again using the pencil torch, checked all around the border on the back of the painting.

Mr Nugent carefully place the frame pieces on the carpeted floor, then, using some string he had brought, began to secure them together.

Sam's heart skipped a beat.

He stood still.

The light of the torch focusing on one area, Sam peering closely.

What he had found, written, faintly, along part of the backing, on what would be the bottom left had side of the painting, was exciting.

Sam moved away to grab his camera, then came back and took pictures.

Then, having checked the back thoroughly, he asked Mr Nugent to help him turn the painting over.

Whereas on the back the colour difference had been noticeable, on the painting itself, the difference was staggering.

Both men looked in awe, as the border of the oil painting looked as if it was painted a few days ago.

The sheen, the gloss, the vibrancy, the colour of the sea at the bottom, the colour of the sky at the top.

It was so obvious how great the painting would look, once it had been cleaned properly.

But however closely Sam looked, again with the light from the torch, he could find no signature anywhere.

He sighed with disappointment.

Sam thanked Mr Nugent and escorted him to the reception area carrying the frame pieces he would keep as part payment for his assistance. There were of no value to Sam as they did not belong with the picture.

Saying goodbye, Sam then asked the receptionist to come and take a look.

She smiled at him. It softened her face. He had no doubt that the lady was efficient and stern, but saw a softer side for just a moment.

Sam showed her the painting, showed the difference where the frame had been and told her the whole painting would look like that when cleaned.

He then told her he would get some gear from his van, that he would carefully wrap the picture and take it to the Maritime Museum of the Atlantic, in Halifax, who have agreed to clean it professionally.

This he had also agreed with Mr Rozzini.

'Yes, I can see what a difference it would make. Mr Rozzini told me it could be worth around a hundred thousand dollars? Is that right?' She asked him, turning to head back to her reception desk.

He walked along with her, and replied, 'Indeed, it could fetch that at auction, maybe even a little more.'

Giving her a nod and saying he would be back soon, Sam headed for the stairs.

Crossing over the old stone bridge towards where he had parked the van, Sam was excited about what he had found on the painting, but he was also a little disappointed. Firstly, he had not found a signature, but secondly, and more importantly, the security in the building was top notch. It would not be easy to snoop around unobserved, if at all.

The previous day, being careful not to shop too much in one store, Sam had purchased a variety of clothing, undergarments, shoes and accessories from five different outlets. Furthermore he had bought an assortment of toiletries, cosmetics and other related items as well as a small suitcase, a pair of pyjamas and a hairdryer.

Two final items he purchased were a new phone and a new laptop for her.

Bringing them all back he had faced a barrage of, 'You shouldn't have; this is too much; I'll pay you back,' all the while with a smile of delight on her face.

He had also contacted the Maritime Museum in Halifax. He had come across them before in some research he had done several years ago, and he made a deal with them.

Then he spoke to Mr Rozzini, trying hard to push away any feelings he had about the man, keeping it professional, telling him of his plans of which he approved wholeheartedly.

Heading back across the stone bridge, carrying a large tote bag, he once again passed by the sculpture and reminded himself to some pictures of it before he left.

Sam then re-entered the building and went back upstairs.

Sam quickly tried the handle of the second door on the left along the passageway, as if by mistake, knowing it to be Rozzini's office. It was locked.

In a way he was glad. It would have been suspicious to spend any time in there, besides, though he hadn't noticed it when he was here earlier in the week, he felt sure that there would be a security camera in there also.

Moving along he then entered the conference room and set about carefully wrapping the painting in order to transport it safely.

Thirty-five minutes later he thanked the receptionist, wished her a good day and holding the wrapped painting in one hand, the satchel across his shoulder and the tote bag in the other hand, Sam left the premises.

He hadn't forgotten about the sculpture. He set the painting and tote bag down, carefully leaning it against the foyer window, fished out his camera, took several shots and continued on his way.

A little later he placed the large painting on the floor of his van, thinking back to the moment he had placed Ally's limp body there, not all that long ago.

He slipped behind the wheel and dialled the numbers to call the new phone.

'Hello?'

'Hey, it's me, how is your morning going? Sam asked.

'Good to hear your voice. I was worried you might do something, well, something that might get you into trouble. Are you okay?'

'Fine, though I'm sorry, but I was unable to snoop around, too much security, and, as you told me this morning, very sternly, from what I recall, was not to take any risks.'

'So, you actually listened to me?' she replied, laughter in her voice.

'Of course, now, listen, I did have an idea earlier, CP Holdings is a public company, therefore, there must be, somewhere, a list of their holdings, their properties and so on ...'

'Of course!' Ally interrupted, 'I should have thought of that! You mean, we can find out where Julien lives? Checking property owned in Halifax, was that your idea?'

'Absolutely, never know what it might throw up. If you can have a crack at that. I'm done here, so, on my way back home.'

'I'll get right on it. Drive safe,' she said and finished the call.

Sam turned the key and the engine kicked into life.
Briefly the words of his late wife came to mind once again, 'Go and find someone to love'.
Words she had spoken softly to him before slipping away.
Well, Sam was thinking, turning out of the parking area and pointing the vehicle in the direction of home, it wasn't likely going to be Sophie, a spark that had started, really didn't burst into flames.
Was it possibly to be Chrissie, he surely was fond of her.
What about Ally? He wondered, it felt as if he might be developing feelings for her.
Pushing the thoughts away for the moment, Sam concentrated on driving.
Earlier, just as he had turned out of the car park, had he glanced across the road over to the police station, he would have seen Detective Sergeant Saunders get out of her car.

DS Karen Saunders was angry and annoyed.
She turned into the car park for the police station, noticed that the slot for the chief was vacant and inwardly smiled as she pulled into it.
Police Chief F. Brown, it stated on the blue and white sign.
It seemed as if he might not be in.

She felt angry because in her research into the life of Miss Alison Hudson, she had discovered that the woman had faced severe injustice.

It was an injustice that had occurred some ten years ago, but one that had left her being robbed of her daughter.

She had read through everything pertaining to the court case, had been disgusted at the behaviour of two people from child welfare, and had been left wondering about the quickness of the court ruling that had originally deemed Miss Hudson an unfit mother and the severe lack of follow up procedure in order to bring a seven-year-old girl back to her mother.

She felt annoyed at herself for her reluctance to take the foreigner's story seriously from the very beginning.

Had she done so, might things have been different, she wondered.

She didn't know, but knew it was unwise to beat herself up about it, instead, her resolve to get to the truth of the matter was greatly intensified.

DS Saunders showed her credentials to the desk sergeant who eyed her up and down and reached for the phone into which he spoke briefly.

Shortly thereafter an officer entered the reception area. He was in his forties, thickset with a mop of brown hair.

His bushy eyebrows almost connected in the middle and his light blue eyes had a watery appearance.

His uniform shirt didn't fit very well, two buttons around his stomach area were straining under pressure and threatened to pop loose at any time.

He wore no tie, and the top button was undone revealing an off-white t-shirt underneath.

He was smoking a cigarette, which is against regulations, and the scowl on his face suggested very plainly he had no pleasure in seeing her.

'What d'ya want ma'am,' he asked, chewing gum.

DS Saunders was now even more pleased. She was going to enjoy the next few minutes.

'Can we go somewhere private?' she asked.

'Sure, this way,' was his answer and turned.

He ambled along a short corridor, entered an office and sat heavily into the chair behind the desk.

Detective Sergeant Karen Saunders, having now secretly turned on a tape recorder, couldn't believe how rude this man was.

'Well?' he asked.

She pulled out a sheet of paper from her briefcase. Upon it was a blown-up photograph of Miss Alison Hudson.

'I believe this woman came into this station on Tuesday.' She placed the paper on the desk in front of him, remaining standing and watching his reaction.

He glanced down, picked up the paper, then handed it back to the woman, 'Didn't deal with that,' he said. His eyes suggested that that was the end of the matter.

'Very well' DS Saunders said, internally very pleased for he had confirmed what she had believed to be the case, Alison Hudson had been here.

'Please advise your chief that internal affairs will be calling on you. This woman had legitimate documents and court orders. She was sent away from here and no follow up was done on the matter,' she said, placing the paper back in her briefcase.

She then turned and headed for the door, where she turned around and said, 'Also, inform the chief, that this woman has now gone missing, and that this office will be held accountable, and possibly charged with accessory to murder'

After opening the door and stepping through, she turned once more. The officer's face had turned almost purple. She said, 'Have a nice day.'

Smiling at the desk sergeant on the way out, she was glad to be outside.

Not just to get away from that officer, who was a sorry example for the force, but also from the smoke he kept exhaling in her direction.

She got back into her car, half wondered whether or not to stay in the chief's parking slot, but decided against it. Instead, she drove out and crossed the road to a public car park and there parked her vehicle in a place from where she could clearly observe the coming and going into the police station.

Glancing over to the passenger seat, she saw the camera, it was ready, and underneath lay a folder, which she slid free and opened.

Her research on Chief F. Brown.

Already many things pointed to a serious crime.

The abduction at the railway station, the finding of the abandoned car, the winter coat in the river. These were suspicious.

Finding the fingerprints of a known criminal in the house, finding few or no fingerprints where there should have been, also suspicious.

As for motive, she had that as well.

Researching the background of Miss Alison Hudson had most certainly provided that.

DS Saunders had delved back in time, and discovered the injustice of what had occurred, what had happened to Miss Hudson in Portland Oregon.

She had traced the fact, that four years after the event of her daughter being taken, without any trace of her whereabouts, Miss Hudson had moved to Vancouver.

Perhaps a lead had taken her there, that was not known, what the detective had found out, was the reason for coming to the East Coast.

The Rozzinis.

The name on the arrest warrant was for a Julien Rozzini, though, reading through the reports, the police back in Oregon had suspected the involvement of Julien's brother, Nico.

Detective Sergeant Saunders had made a note to herself to make contact with the detective on the case back then, had discovered that he had since retired, but could well be helpful in her enquiries.

Further leads had come to light. In the car, the red Triumph, a receipt had been found on the floor, a receipt from a cafe in Harris for last Tuesday, and, at the house, they found a train ticket, a return fare to Halifax on the Wednesday.

Putting all these things together, DS Saunders surmised that Miss Hudson had found a trail, leading to Halifax, and leading to Harris.

She also guessed that it might have been likely she had called into the police station.

The rude officer had surely confirmed that she had indeed been there, and this acknowledgement she had recorded on tape.

Having read what had happened in Portland ten years ago, and from what she had found out about Nico Rozzini, owner and operator of CP Holdings, she suspected he might wield some influence in this small town, hence she'd taken her tape recorder for evidence and protection.

Shortly before her arrival she had received a call from her forensic team to inform her a scarf had been found, along the same bank where the coat had been found, and that hairs found on the scarf matched hairs found on the coat and in both the car and house.

Hair belonging to Miss Alison Hudson.

With that knowledge she had gone into the police station.

She wanted to stir the pot, see what she could shake loose.

She also had with her copies of the original arrest warrant, something she wanted to bring into play later.

Sadly, it now seemed very likely that Miss Hudson had been thrown into the river.

She was nearly through reading again the report she had formatted on the chief, when she heard squealing tyres and saw a police car turn off the road and slot into the chief's parking space.

Grabbing her camera, she focused the lens and started shooting.

THE PAST;

PERIOD 8

THE YEAR 1889

Men in smart jackets and trousers, men in suits, all of them wearing caps or hats. Even some bowlers and top hats were to be seen.

Women dressed in their finery, wearing jewellery, carrying fine handbags, some had parasols at the ready, for it was a glorious day.

Children, running around, dressed as if for Sunday school, excited.

Almost the whole town had come out.

Work had begun on building the railway station four years ago.

Work had begun on laying the tracks four years ago.

Labourers had been drafted in from near and far. A large lodging camp had been set up about four miles from the town.

Equipment and tools were brought in from Montreal.

Henry Charles Parker had started it all.

He was a visionary, much like his grandfather, but he also had the drive, the stamina and the leadership, to carry out the plans he had.

He stood there, a tall figure, like his father, very blond hair, just like his father's.

Wearing a fine suit, checking the time on his fob watch.

Twenty-two years old.

He had started the project, his vision, his dream, four years ago, with the total support of his parents, Sara and Carl, who stood proudly just behind him.

Sara, still a striking woman at the age of fifty-seven, dressed in her finest outfit, had her arm around Carl.

She looked across at him and smiled. Often she would think back to that day, when she had boldly stepped into the barn, walked up to him and kissed him.

Two young girls were chatting and giggling close by. Their fourteen-year-old twins. Rebekah and Charlotte.

When they had wed, Carl took on the Parker name, something he was very happy to do as he had lost his parents when he was a small boy.

He had been raised in an orphanage until he was thirteen when he had run away.

After nearly two years of roaming around, he found himself in the stables belonging to the mine.

One of the hands working there, arrived, saw him and saw his natural ability with horses as Carl had entered a stall and was rubbing the hind leg of a big horse having seen that it was bothering the animal.

The company took him on as a stable boy and Carl never looked back.

On marrying Sara, whom he loved more than he could ever say, he was happy to take on her name. It meant family to him, parents, grandparents, siblings.

Family.

They named their firstborn, a son, Henry Charles in honour of Henry who had meant so much to Sara, who had taught her wisely, and who had been such a loving person, a father really, to her, ever since arriving here, and also after Charlie, her father, who had seen her potential, and who had entrusted her with the responsibility and challenges of running the company.

She had been just eighteen when she arrived in Harris.

Her son, at eighteen, began to work on his vision.

Today, was a day of celebration, for her, for him, for the town.

Henry Charles had organised the labourers, and set about building the camp, building the station and constructing the depot.

He was everywhere, checking and encouraging the workers, and ensuring the equipment was ordered and being delivered.

Together with three men who had come from Montreal and who had experience in laying track, they set about designing the route.

The first line, was going to be a direct connection between the mine and the smelting plant, near the coast and near a small settlement named Sackville.

The second line would then run from there into Halifax.

Finally a third line would be running alongside the first and second, but going from the town itself, connecting the two towns.

Harris to Halifax.

The first spur, from the mine's new storage building, set adjacent to the old barn where the horses were stabled, took two years to complete, and included three side spurs providing passing places.

The second section, running from the smelting plant into the harbour depot at Halifax, took less than a year.

Towards the end of the third year after the project began, Henry Charles took delivery of a locomotive and eight ore wagons.

This was a 4-4-0 configuration, 'American' style locomotive, built by the Canadian Pacific Railway company.

After some teething problems and a track slip, the first haul of shale and ore was transported by locomotive in the third month of the fourth year.

The impressive station building in town was completed at around the same time, as was the third and final section of track.

Hundreds of people were milling around on the station's two platforms.

On a warm day in July, they were full of expectation as the first locomotive to come into the station was due to arrive.

Two blasts on a steam whistle in the distance drew a loud cheer.

Then the sound of the train was to be heard, with people leaning to see up the track.

Another loud cheer went up as the train came into view, the same make and model as the first one Henry Charles purchased.

It chugged noisily and slowly into the station. It was an impressive sight, a moment in history. An event that would not be forgotten.

The massive locomotive pulled two passenger carriages and two boxcars along the platform and duly came to a stop three inches from the buffers.

Henry Charles made his way back towards the front of the platform, folks cheering him, and clapping him on the shoulders as he passed.

The passenger cars were most luxurious, padded seats, fold-up tables and wall-mounted lights.

Henry took delight in showing his mother and father all the features as he walked them through the first carriage.

He then drew their attention to a small brass plate above the rear door that led to a small balcony from which one could also enter or exit the carriage.

He explained that there was one such plate on each end of the wagon.

His mother read out the name 'Henry H' she said, her voice no more than a whisper. Henry Charles noted his mother's emotion.

'The other passenger car has the name 'Rebekah', he said proudly, then invited them to follow him.

He exited the carriage, gave a signal to someone at the front that it was now okay for the public to come and inspect, then took his parents to the first boxcar.

In white lettering, the words 'Silver Lines' were boldly painted on one side of the sliding door, and 'Canadian Despatch' on the other.

Sliding the door open he invited them to take a look inside.

Then stepping in himself, and showed them the little plate above the door.

They both looked.

'SARA'

'And of course, the other one has your name father' he said beaming.

'I am so proud of you,' his mother said, embracing him.

Carl, not one for speaking a lot, nodded, and grabbing his son's shoulder squeezed it in thanks.

They stepped out of the boxcar.

Many folks were milling around the platforms and looking through the carriages.

There was a great atmosphere all around.

A couple of men with photographic equipment were getting many shots.

The headlines in the local paper the following day would read, 'Steam comes to Harris'.

THE PRESENT;

PARIS

SATURDAY 4ᵗʰ MAY

Sophie Pontiac and Petra Stevens sat side by side and perused the many sheets of paper on the table before them.

'So' Petra explained, 'this is my evidence trail.'

'Seven years?' Sophie asked, turning to look at Petra.

'Not quite,' was the answer, and Petra elaborated, 'the first six months, well, to be honest, my head was all over the place.

I got divorced.

There was a lot of paperwork to sort, house and furniture to either sell or divide.

My ex stayed in the States, he married again about three months later. Anyway, as I told you, I had a great settlement from the insurance company as the jewellery and clothing I had was well covered, this, plus half the sale of the house, and then the money from furniture I sold. I was financially in a good way.'

Of course then there was the task of moving, finding a new place to live, thinking about whether to go back to work, so, the time just passed by really.

In the meantime the police were just getting nowhere, no clues whatsoever.'

Petra paused for a moment. Sophie watched her just stare into space for a bit, waiting for her to continue.

She had suggested they come here today, Saturday morning being relatively quiet as many of the surrounding offices were closed.

'Also, at the time,' Petra said, coming out of her reverie, 'I had to totally rethink who I was. I put myself out there and asked for the truth from some of the people I knew back then.

The truth was painful to hear.'

Turning to Sophie, she continued, 'These things, like being attacked and robbed, make you think, don't you agree?' She picked up her glass of white wine and took a sip.

Sophie silently agreed. These things do make you think.

She thought back to when she had been in a dangerous place, when a young man had come at her with a knife …

Petra spoke again, 'So, about six or seven months after the attack, I came home one day after work, I had a new job by then, clerical work in a telephone company, and I took my coat off and stopped by the hall mirror.

For some reason, it seemed like it was the first time I had really taken a look at myself.

I stood there, for some time, then made a promise to myself to search for and find this woman who had attacked me, who had stolen my identity, my jewels, particularly my diamond necklace set which my grandmother had given me.

'At that point, I felt I really had to change.

Away went the arrogant and selfish attitude.

I became calmer, easier to talk to, more patient, listened to others.

I cut down severely on my drinking, and, slowly but surely, began to get a new perspective on my life.'

Petra took another sip of wine, then said, 'I just had to spend whatever time I could, in resolving this case, in finding clues, sniffing out a trail.

I needed this because I felt that I wouldn't be able to fully move on until I found her.'

Sophie nodded in understanding, also sipping her wine.

'I obtained, I had a right to them, my case files and everything the police had accumulated up until then, which wasn't a great deal,' Petra said, leaning forward and pointing to a sheet of paper on the far left. 'That's it there.'

Then, pointing to the sheets above it, she said, 'I took it up from that point. I spoke with the people from the bank where she worked and I was even allowed, though accompanied by a detective, to go to the apartment where Lucie van Doorn had lived.

This was paid for on an annual basis, so it had been kept just as she had left it when she went to work that day.'

Taking three sheets of paper, she handed them to Sophie to read, then said,' I spent over four hours in the place, going through her stuff, her clothes, her books and photo albums to get an idea what kind of person she was.'

Sophie took the sheets.

Petra fell silent again, gave a sigh as Sophie began to read and thought back to that day.

Placing the empty glass on the table, Sophie was soon engrossed.

Earlier they had met outside the cafe, as per Sophie's suggestion, then had entered and settled themselves on a comfortable two-seater couch.

After ordering drinks, Petra had then fished out reams of paper from her satchel and had placed these is some order on the low table in front of them, all the while again running through the events of that day, seven years ago.

Whilst Sophie was reading, Petra caught the attention of a waiter and ordered more drinks.

Although it was approaching lunchtime, it was still reasonably quiet in the cafe.

Sophie put the first sheets back on the table, then picked up the next few in the sequence Petra had laid out and again took to reading as the waiter brought their drinks.

'This one starts nearly two years later,' Sophie observed, turning to look at Petra.

'Yes, I had many scribbles and thoughts, but nothing definite, nothing of any relevance until that time. My first concrete clue really. I got really excited about that one. That's when I decided to stop work and pick up the trail.'

Sophie studied the woman for a moment, picking up her glass to take a sip of wine.

She had already heard the story of the attack at the airport, which Petra had briefly told her about when she first met her. The police report, including a report from the hospital, was far more detailed and Sophie realised the severity of what had occurred.

The woman who had attacked her was now known as Steffie Baertjens, so how did Petra find out? Putting her glass down, she continued to read.

Petra sat back in the couch, glass in hand, and thought back to when she had found that clue ...

People share all kinds of things on social media, from what they had for breakfast to the discomfort of an ingrown toenail. From the beauty of a rainbow to the severity of a hailstorm.

Funny things, sad things, all kinds of things.

A video clip that someone had posted was a small assortment of near misses in traffic situations.

Petra suddenly froze, nearly dropping the pot of yoghurt she was eating.

She replayed the clip, then paused at the point where she had spotted something.

The film clip showed how a youngster on a bicycle very narrowly escaped being hit by a minibus, but it wasn't that that drew her attention.

A woman was walking along the pavement. Petra recognised the dress.

She was wearing her dress!

Moreover, as she studied the frame closely, this woman was wearing her shoes as well.

The side on view didn't reveal the woman's face clearly, but Petra just knew, without a doubt, this was the woman who had attacked her.

Her hair was now blond, but it was her, of that she was sure.

She noted the name of a store that was in the clip, which the woman was passing, and after some research found that the video clip was taken in Seville, Spain.

The following day she resigned from work, and organised her travel arrangements as there was no time to lose. The clip on social media, she worked out, was less than a month old.

Three days after seeing it, she arrived in Seville ...

The cafe was getting busier. Three young ladies looked somewhat put out, seeing two women and a table full of papers in what was probably 'their' seat in the cafe.

Neither Petra nor Sophie noticed.

'Oh my goodness' Sophie whispered audibly at one point, then turning to look at Petra, 'That's just awful!'

Then asked, 'You really think this is what happened?'

Petra knew where Sophie was up to in reading through her notes. She took her mind back to that day. A very sunny and hot day ...

She had been in Seville for nearly a week.

Searching through newspapers, just walking around town, checking telephone directories and, having decided to rent an apartment for a month, continuing to scroll through the internet, searching social media.

Then, one evening watching the television, the news was on.

Not understanding Spanish very well at all, she still caught the gist of what had happened.

A Belgian tourist coach had slipped off the road and over-turned. Many were hurt and three people had died.

On the news coverage, she watched the scene, then caught her breath, for she saw a glimpse of a woman.

It was the same woman she had seen in the clip.

Not only that, but she was once again wearing an outfit that she recognised. One of hers!

It was too late to go out now; nothing to do but wait until morning.

The crash happened just a few miles from Cadiz. The injured were taken to hospital there.

Petra set off early the following morning.

She caught the earliest high-speed train and arrived there in under two hours, right in the heart of the town.

Four and a half hours later she stood on the pier looking out to sea.

Deep in thought.

She was somewhat frustrated, but, with at least an idea form-ing as to how to proceed from here.

As her Spanish wasn't great, in fact less than useless, she decided that she needed to rely on her charm and wit, and so promptly marched into the central police station.

With the documents in her hand and a story in her head, she had talked her way into seeing a senior detective, fortunately for her, a man, and he was soon captivated by her charm.

He proved to be very helpful indeed.

They hadn't discovered until quite some time after the ac-cident, when forensics had finished processing the scene, that travel documents, including passports, had gone missing. They then combed through some video footage, and found the cul-prit, a woman. A blond woman.

Here Petra was able to be of great assistance by providing the detective with more photographs and further details of the woman, including her real name, Lucie Van Doorn.

Sadly an ongoing search had still not turned up the where-abouts of this woman and Petra, having thanked the detective and left the police station, found herself at the dockside looking out to sea and reflecting on what her next move was going to be. She had been so close.

Little could she have known that over two hundred and fifty years ago, in the year 1762, a certain Christoffer Rosenburg sailed from that very place, heading for Boston, and that her quest would, at some point in the future, connect with that event.

Nor could she have imagined, that less than two hours ago, a private yacht had set sail and among the passengers was a blond woman.

The yacht was bound for Monaco …

Petra ordered lunch for them both, leaving Sophie totally engrossed in reading the reports and the evidence timeline she had created over the years.

She felt good, felt relieved in a way. All these years, she had focused so much on finding that woman, and her determination was such that all else was seemingly meaningless.

But as the lunch was duly delivered and she gently prodded Sophie's shoulder for her attention, she realised she had a friend, an ally in her quest.

Sophie was surprised to suddenly see the food, smiled a thank you. 'So sorry, I was just so wrapped up into what you have written and found.'

'Carry on,' Petra responded, 'but don't forget to eat something.'

She selected a baguette from the platter and thought back. Was it really already seven years ago? Was it really nearly five years ago that she went to Seville? Went to Cadiz?

Shortly after her arrival at the seaport, on the high-speed train from Seville, she had gone straight to the police station. She was able to clarify why she had come, what she had seen and who the woman was that was at the scene of the bus accident.

Showing them a report she had of the initial attack and robbery, in Cape Town, showing them photographs of Lucie Van Doorn, telling them what she had uncovered, they had responded well.

Looking through footage captured on film and cameras, they had also spotted the woman at the scene.

Further enquiries were swiftly made, seven people were in hospital, three had died and twelve others had minor injuries.

Petra had been allowed to accompany the police, as they spoke to the coach driver and passengers. It was discovered, as bags and luggage was checked, that five passports were missing. All belonging to females.

Afterwards Petra remembers walking down to the harbour. Needing some fresh air, needing to work out her disappointment. So close!

She had five names. Would her assailant be trying to use any of these?

Sophie took a break from reading, grabbed something from the platter and gave Petra a smile.

She wondered why Petra had not written down these five names despite knowing them. Sophie figured none of them can have been the name of Steffie Baertjens, so how did Petra find that out? And how did the fake Gauguin fit in?

So many directions, so many twists and turns.

Taking as sip of wine, Sophie thought back to the time when she had also done a lot of reading, perusing through the journals of Sam's great-grandfather, the ambassador.

THE PAST;

PERIOD 9

THE YEAR 1903

Jan Smettens was a diplomatic courier working for the British Embassy in Cape Town.

Jan Smettens was also a thief, a conman and a smuggler.

He had bided his time, done his research and, when the time had been right, he made his move.

First, with false documents and references, he secured a post with the British embassy.

A courier vacancy that had come up; he knew that it had.

Part one of his plan, was completed.

As a courier he had access to the embassy, made contact with the current ambassador and, when it came to delivering important papers, either within the city or within the country or, and this was key, overseas, he had special privileges, such as easier routes through customs or security and access to places not available to the public.

The second part of his plan would reveal itself to him in due course, as he became familiar with the routine and layout of both the embassy and the ambassador's residence.

The third part of his plan, he knew was a matter of time. Patience was needed, and Jan Smettens was a very patient man.

Ambassador Samuel Wilfred Price was born in London in 1870.

Schooled in Eton, he joined the diplomatic corps when he was twenty-three.

Samuel was destined for great things. At the age of 28 he was appointed as ambassador and posted to Copenhagen, Denmark.

Here he met and was taught French by Mette Sophie Gad, wife of the French painter Gauguin.

As an art lover and coming from a wealthy background, he already had several pieces of fine art, including paintings and sculptures.

It was later that same year,1898, that he purchased the 'Woman on the shore' from Mette. Gauguin had posted this and several others from Tahiti where he was painting at the time.

In 1901 Samuel was appointed to Cape Town.

Little did he know or could even imagine, as he diligently recorded events and activities, as well as documenting, with photographs, his purchases and sales of art, in his journals that one day, his great-grandson would be investigating the trail of the Gauguin he had purchased in Copenhagen. Nor indeed could he have considered that the very same painting would be involved in a serious crime.

In the year 1904 Samuel was appointed ambassador in Paris.

THE PRESENT;

HALIFAX

SATURDAY 4TH MAY

Donald McGrath greeted Sam with much joviality. The sixty-two-year-old was the current curator of the Maritime Museum in Halifax.

'Welcome, welcome,' he enthusiastically said, whilst pumping Sam's hand vigorously. 'After your call I contacted a counterpart of mine in Amsterdam. He speaks very highly of you, Mr Price, very highly.'

'Well, that's great, and please, just call me Sam, and it's me who is thankful to you. Having this painting cleaned so quickly by your people, is just wonderful.'

'Not at all, not at all. Please, follow me. I look forward to seeing it. It's possibly a Porcellis, you said?'

Sam picked up the wrapped piece of art, then followed the man along a wide corridor, into an elevator and down to the basement of the building.

'You can see for yourself. I'd like your opinion. This is a fine museum, right on the waterfront here. I believe there are quite a lot of art and artefacts associated to the Titanic here?'

'Oh indeed,' Donald said, turning his head to look at Sam, 'and quite a collection besides; a good account of the maritime history of Nova Scotia.'

'I have only recently moved to Canada. I'll surely be checking it all out,' Sam replied.

'Excellent, excellent,' he said. 'This way please.' He led the way through another two narrower corridors and then into a large room. Sam identified this straight away as a preservation room where the art would be cleaned, or restored, or both.

Moments later Sam had unwrapped the painting and laid it on a large square table.

Another man had entered, wearing a white laboratory coat and was simply introduced as Al.

They all studied the painting for a few moments.

'Wonderful, wonderful,' Donald said. 'Goodness me, it is very dirty isn't it.'

'Nearly two hundred years of hanging in a room where people smoked,' Sam answered.

After several more moments Donald turned to Sam, 'Any chance we might acquire it?' he asked.

'I'm not sure at this stage Donald. I am still investigating and it is not up to me, but the Boston Auction House I work for, they may be interested in a private sale, but let me finish my research. I will, of course, relate your interest to my boss.'

'Thank you, thank you,' Donald replied. 'My, my, I have never seen a Porcellis before, not in real life. Photographs of course. This does remind me of his style. Do you think it's by him?'

'Too early to tell,' Sam answered. 'Once it's cleaned it will make determination easier, but, as I said, still some research to do, which, Donald, is why I can't stay today, but again, I do appreciate your assistance'.

'Not at all, not at all, let me walk you out. We'll get on this today. I will contact you when it's done.'

Fifteen minutes later Sam left the museum, and walked to the other end of the boardwalk where he had left Ally in a cafe.

MEANWHILE 01.15PM HALIFAX AIRPORT

Karina West sat at the departure gate awaiting the boarding of her flight to Miami.

Sunshades pushed up onto her forehead, she sat, relaxed, playing a game on her phone.

She was chewing gum, she had no idea she was being watched.

She had earlier cleared security, browsed a little among the cosmetic counters, then sat on a stool by the bar and consumed a glass of white wine. Karina had then strolled to the departure gate for her flight.

A first-class ticket and a four-star hotel waiting for her. Sunshine and pool.

What could be better and what could possibly go wrong.

Everything had run smoothly. Though the planning had been in haste, the execution of it was faultless.

She stopped chewing for a moment, and looked up from her game to check the board.

Her flight should be boarding any minute now.

She could have availed herself of the first-class lounge, but, noticing a large group of businessmen entering, she decided to forego that option so as not to draw attention to herself.

When suddenly two men sat down, one on either side of her, and she looked from one to the other, the colour drained from her face.

BACK AT THE HARBOUR CAFE

'How did it go?' Ally asked.

'Great. They should have it cleaned in about four or five days. They'll give me a ring,'
    Sam replied, sitting down. 'How about you, get any further with the search?' looking at her open laptop.

'No, the property search didn't help, at least, not in the way we hoped,' she answered, given him a quizzical look.

Sam gave his order to the waitress who appeared at his side, then turning back to Ally, 'But you found something?'

'Perhaps, just an oddity. Let me explain CP Holdings is a big concern. Lots of property in Harris, then there's the big smelting plant near Sackville, also the warehouse depot, right here on the harbour front.
    'The private house, the address I found where Debra, Mrs Rozzini, lives, is listed, as well as seven other residences.
    But, there's no private dwelling in Halifax at all, so, disappointment there, but look, I found a property listed, purchased in 2012, in a very small town called Buchans, in Newfoundland.
    Bit odd don't you think?'

Sam looked at where she pointed on the screen.

'All their property is around this region. Why would there be a house listed as part of the CP Holdings properties, in Newfoundland?' she queried.

'A summer house maybe?' Sam suggested.

His lunch arrived, along with the mandatory coffee.

'Yes, maybe. I tried to google it, but, no, luck, can't seem to find it, so, yes, maybe a business retreat or something.'

'I've been thinking ...' Sam began, after chewing a mouthful of toasted cheese sandwich.

'Dangerous,' Ally interjected, grinning cheekily.

Already she felt such a close rapport with this man; a man she had only known for a few days. Although she would never forget that he had saved her life, putting that aside she felt a connection, a closeness.

He smiled back at her, 'I think we should talk to Detective Sergeant Saunders. I know that she now believes that what I told her I had seen, did indeed occur. Not only did she tell me, but we saw that she found your car.'
    'Therefore, they know your name, would have checked your house, your work, so, I believe, considering the circumstances, that the detective will have delved deeper into who you are and why someone would want to abduct or harm you. After all, finding your car up the canyon road, she may well consider that you were thrown into the river. Anyway, I do believe we should talk to her now, don't you?'

Ally took in what he said.

She herself had thought things through as well and come to the same conclusion.
    She had put herself in danger by going it alone. Sam was right, it was time to speak to this detective.

MONCTON
1.40PM

Her phone rang.

She answered, listened for a while, then said, 'Can you sit on her for a bit, no contacts, no calls?'

Listening some more, then, 'Thanks, I'll call you.'

Seconds later her phone rang again.

BACK IN HALIFAX

Walking along the boardwalk, Sam gave his phone to Ally.

He had wanted to ring Detective Sergeant Saunders and was about to, but Ally had said it would be better if she talked to her.

She took the phone from him, looked at the number on the screen and pressed the numbers.

'DS Saunders,' a voice said.

'Hi, Detective, I'm Alison Hudson. I would like to talk with you.'

There was a brief pause at the other end, then 'Are you alright Miss Hudson?'

'I am safe and I am with Sam,' Ally replied.

'Sam? As in the foreigner? Mr Price?' came the question.

'Yes, I am safe, thanks to him. Do you ...do you know about me? What happened in the past, why I am here?' she asked.

'I do,' DS Saunders answered. 'I am glad to hear that you are alive. I do know your history and the injustice you have faced, yes. I'd like to talk with you, face to face. Whereabouts are you?'

Sam, who had been listening, gestured he would like a word.

Ally nodded and handed the phone over to him.

'Hi' Sam said, 'not that I don't trust you, but just being careful, do you know the Cockahoop Basketball Club?'

'I do. I know where it is' was the reply.

'Can we meet there? Say, in about an hour and a half?' he asked.

'Agreed,' DS Saunders replied and broke the connection.

Sam put his phone away, put his arm around Ally's waist and together they walked back to his van.

Ten minutes later they were on the road, heading for home, heading for Moncton.

DS Karen Saunders was relieved.

The woman was alive.

She was puzzled however, for how did she meet up with the foreigner?

Sitting back in her chair she thought for a few moments.

Then she picked up her phone, made a call to her colleague in Halifax and asked for a favour.

THE PAST;

PERIOD 10

THE YEAR 1924

A dynasty, generations of acumen and toil, years of bartering, trade, acquisitions and deals, hours and hours of sweat and tears.

All that had been built up, through tears and tantrums, through good times and bad, all now hanging in the balance.

All now resting on the turn of a card.

Nathaniel Parker, twenty-six years of age.

Earlier in the evening he had been dressed smartly, finest quality trousers, shiny brown leather shoes.

A white shirt with a frilled cuff had looked pristine beneath his waistcoat, which had a soft paisley pattern woven into a grey cloth. A matching jacket, made from pure wool finished the ensemble.

Now, some hours later, the jacket was on the back of his chair, the waistcoat was undone as were the top two buttons of his shirt, a black bow tie, earlier present and smartly tied in place, was nowhere to be seen.

The room, one of several that led from the large main hall, was dimly lit, except for a good set of lights that shone upon the table.

There was a hue of bluish smoke that permeated throughout.

Seven men sat around the only large oval table in this room.

There were some occasional chairs; some occasional tables. Men and women sat about on these.

A row of barstools, all occupied, stretched along the front of the mahogany counter behind which were two barmen, though at this moment, neither barman moved.

At this moment there was a hush around the room. At this moment all eyes were upon young Nathaniel, though most had no idea who he was, other than 'another American'.

Nathaniel's three times great-grandfather, was Charlie Parker.

His own father, Charlie Parker the fifth, had not been an entrepreneur of the quality of previous generations, such as Charlie Parker the Third had been, for it had been the latter that had grown the family business immensely, together with his wife Ruth.

They had been blessed with two children, a son, Charlie Parker the fourth, and a daughter, Sara Rebekah Parker, whom had taken on the business in Canada, with great success, thanks to her ability and her mentor, Henry Hopkins.

Eventually Charlie the fourth, Nathaniel's grandfather, had taken on the family business in Boston. He had maintained it well, had married well, but been a more laid-back figure than his astute father.

They had only one child, a son, and Charlie the fifth came into the world.

As he grew, he grew away from the family. He was wild, selfish and arrogant.

He had little interest in the family business. He had little interest in working at all.

His main focus was womanising and gambling.

The apple, in this case Nathaniel, had not fallen far from the tree.

Nathaniel was perspiring, but the day before he had been buoyant and had received great pleasure from wandering around the casino, playing a game here and there, flirting with waitresses, female dealers and women in general.

Monaco. The Monte Carlo Casino.

A high-class establishment on the Mediterranean coast. A drawcard for the rich and elite from around the world.

It opened in 1863 and was where you would find the celebrities of the day, be it well known politicians, tycoons or royalty.

Well-to-do debutantes and an assortment of arrogant playboys also frequented the tables here.

The day had started well for young Nathaniel. He had come away the day before well up in winnings and had left the premises with a woman on each arm.

Today was different. Having started well, he had been drawn to a high-stake card game. Over several hours his luck had swung like a pendulum, but in the last thirty minutes, it had all been downhill.

Now, he sat, sweat on his brow, sweat droplets appearing on his temples.

He had lost heavily already, but had continued, hoping his luck would change.

It hadn't.

The turn of a card. Did his opponent have the better hand? The other five had dropped out, leaving just two of them.

The hush broke into a murmur, the onlookers whispering to one another.

The barmen stopped polishing the glasses.

Young Nathaniel had lost.

Lost everything.

The moment passed. People began moving, and the others around the card table made conversation and ordered drinks. The winner of the massive hand tried not to show the great delight he felt.

A young man appeared at the shoulder of Nathaniel, who sat very still, half slumped, stunned and with no energy whatever.

Percivald Quinton.

He had been quietly watching the proceedings from the barstool for some time.

The day before he had noticed the young man, had watched as he gambled, as he drank, as he flirted.

He had made some discreet enquiries and had found out a little about Nathaniel Parker.

Now, seeing him totally devastated, broken. His shirt clinging to him as he sat there perspiring and dazed. His face almost the same shade as his shirt.

Now it was time to act, to intervene, to help out.

Percivald Quinton had finished his drink then walked over to the table.

Now he stood beside the seated man.

Leaning forward, he placed a hand on Nathaniel's shoulder and whispered into his ear.

Nathaniel took in what was whispered.

Then looked up at the stranger beside him and nodded.

Still keeping his hand on Nathaniel's shoulder, he straightened and smiled.

Percivald Quinton from New York.

THE PRESENT;

NEW YORK

SATURDAY AFTERNOON 4ᵀᴴ MAY

'So, you and Sam, anything going on?' Tammy asked Chrissie as she opened the letter she had just been given.

Walking over to the big panorama window that overlooked Central Park, Chrissie turned to look over her shoulder, gave Tammy a quizzical stare and asked, 'What do you mean?'

But Tammy just smiled and concentrated on reading the contents of the letter.

Chrissie stood by the large window and looked out. It was a beautiful day and many people were out and about. She noticed a lot of, what she surmised would be, office or retail workers grabbing an afternoon break in the vast park that stretched below her.

She pondered on the question Tammy had posed.

Anything going on between her and Sam?

Their time together in Genoa had been comfortable and amicable. He had been the perfect gentleman, had helped her solve her grandfather's disappearance.

Had comforted her.

They had dinner that evening, though mainly in silence, reflecting on what they had learned that day. The company was warm and felt good.

She had briefly wondered about a possible romance with him that evening as they ate at the hotel.

But though he had been attentive and charming, she couldn't get a reading on how he felt.

Goodnight had been a kiss on the cheek.

The following day she flew back to Boston, via Paris and he back to Amsterdam.

'He's not long been widowed,' Chrissie said, without turning around. Then, sensing that Tammy had read the letter, she turned and asked, 'Is it about your grandmother?'

'Didn't he tell you?' Tammy asked, joining Chrissie by the window.

Sam had rung Chrissie nearly a fortnight ago. They had spoken briefly, amicably. He had then told her of his plans to go to Nova Scotia, that he would keep in touch, and that he had gathered some more information for Tammy. He had sent a letter to her, if she could get that to Tammy as he didn't have her address.

She said she would.

'The name, or confirmation of a name, of who possibly might be your grandfather, he said.'

'The details are all here; the fact that they travelled to the States together, shared a cabin on the boat, that information we didn't have before.

That sure points to the fact, that he must be my grandfather, but why did she make no mention of his name; I mean, none whatsoever, that is so strange.'

'It is, but even though something possibly happened that your grandmother just didn't want to share, by all accounts, what she did write in that letter to you, she did meet and fall in love with this guy,' Chrissie said.

'True. The fact that they shared a cabin on the boat surely does clinch it for me, which brings me back to you and Sam. His wife passed, what, four years ago? Come on Chrissie, maybe you just need to make the first move,' Tammy said, and teased, 'after all, there is a sparkle in your eyes when you speak of him'.

Chrissie threw her a mock scowl. Then smiled and said, 'He's not ready. Maybe someday. Maybe I will make a move. Maybe I'll go and see him in Canada. So, how is your love life?'

Tammy smiled, glanced out of the window then turned her gaze back to Chrissie and said, 'Come on, I've got to go to work. Come with me and then later, well, I have an idea … and thanks for coming to deliver this letter in person. You will stay a few days won't you? And you have to thank Sam for this information on my behalf,' then smiling, left the room to get ready for work.

Chrissie smiled as well. Not much later both women walked down the wide corridor that led to the front door of Tammy's luxurious apartment.

On the right-hand wall, two large painting hung side by side. Both seascapes.

Neither of them glanced at them as they walked by.

Whilst Tammy and Chrissie rode the elevator down from the twenty-eighth floor, Detective Sergeant Karen Saunders drove her police car to the Cockahoop Basketball Club.

THE PAST;

PERIOD II

THE YEAR 1938

Zeta Bell sat on one of the many benches dotted around Boston common.

It was sunny, but a cool breeze blew in from the sea. It was early fall and evidence of the coming colder weather was visible from the many leaves that had already fallen.

Zeta sat quite still. Contemplative. Trying hard to keep her emotions in check.

The thirty-six-year-old had just visited her husband in a nearby hospital.

He was in private care being treated for a form of cancer.

Whilst the prognosis was positive, the cost was inhibitive.

Jonathan Bell, a former athletic coach for the Canadian Olympic Team, had at first refused to accept treatment as the cost was so high, but Zeta had told him around. They had been unable to have any children, all they had was each other as both sides of the family were too far away.

His family, just one brother left, was in Vancouver; her family were way down in San Francisco, California.

So Zeta had made the arrangements. They had sold several of their belongings to fund the trip and treatment. They had been given a fair-sized sum of money that friends had very kindly raised.

She now sat in the park.

In her lap lay her prized possession, a wonderfully painted miniature that had once belonged to her great-great-grandfather.

Jonathan would definitely not be pleased with what she was about to do, but do it she must. Weighing the worth of the item against the worth of the man she so dearly loved, this was how it should be.

She had already spoken to the auction house here in Boston, a reputable firm, called Franck Huysen & Son.

Taking a deep breath, she got up from the bench and made her way there.

They were much taken with the item, and spent considerable time looking at and discussing it.

Zeta wandered around the showroom whilst waiting.

She stopped by a cardboard box containing books. Her husband loved to read. As he would be needing to rest for some time, some fresh books might help him through the boredom of that for he was not a man who liked to sit still too much.

Flicking through the various titles, she came across what looked like journals, three of them, with smooth black covers.

When she opened one of them, she couldn't believe what she was reading.

For several moments, everything stopped. Time stood still, the world around her ceased to exist and it was through several coughs and an 'Excuse me madam,' from one of the auctioneers, that she was drawn back into the living world.

'Sorry, sorry,' she said, quite flustered, then composed herself and listened to what the man had to say.

The value of the item she had brought in was way more than she had imagined and, after agreeing to a fixed reserve, she signed some papers and then asked about the journals she had found.

The man checked the cardboard box, then went away, returning after about seven minutes.

'This box came in, along with some furniture and a pair of valuable paintings, in fact these ones here,' the man said pointing to the wall behind them. 'The contents of this box have very little value, so if those journals are of interest to you, they are yours to have.'

Zeta thanked the man profusely as he wrapped them in some brown paper and handed them to her. Before she left, Zeta took another look at the two paintings. Both were scenes of ships at sea and looked to be wonderfully painted.

Zeta left nodding a goodbye to the man. The auction would be held in four days' time.

On a rather more blustery and autumnal day Zeta arrived for the auction.

Her husband's treatment was going well. A three-hour operation the day before yesterday had been successful.

He was recovering well and should be able to go home in about four of five days' time.

Walking from the hospital, through the Common en route to the auction house, Zeta was thankful.

Upon arrival she walked around the rectangular room with its dark beams and high ceiling. The room was buzzing with people today.

The shutters were closed on the three large windows and three rows of four overhead lamps shone brightly upon the many things on display on tables, in glass cases and on the polished wooden floor.

Zeta looked at the faces of the many who had come, of whom around half were women, and pondered who it might be that would possibly buy the item she had placed up for sale.

She had already spotted it, made a mental note of the lot number and, now and then, checked to see if anyone was interested.

Zeta also made a note of the lot number for the two large paintings, the two seascapes, that she knew had been together with the journals she was given.

The auction was about to begin and the folk moved into an adjacent room where five rows of benches, placed in three sections, faced a wooden rostrum.

The lot for the two paintings came up early on. There was quite a bit of interest with several people raising their number until only two remained.

The auctioneer, with a clear and booming voice that Zeta felt could surely be heard three blocks from here, looked from one to the other as he called out the price.

Then one of them threw in a substantially higher bid. The other dropped away.

Zeta took note of the number on the paddle of the man who had purchased it and who had turned around to smile at someone in the back of the room.

Some twenty minutes later it was her item that came up for sale.

Zeta sat more upright, and was more alert, hoping and praying it would sell well.

Would it reach the reserve? Would it exceed it?

Again there were several bidders to begin with, but they easily fell away to leave just two, and then one.

Zeta was thrilled. First of all, she took down the number of the man who had purchased the item, then she focused on him.

He was small man, had a mop of grey hair, wore horn-rimmed glasses.

His jacket was tweed, with leather patches on the elbows, and he wore corduroy trousers.

Zeta was sat only four people away from him and got a good look at the man who certainly seemed pleased with his purchase.

As for herself, she was very pleased indeed, for it had sold well over the reserve price.

This would now pay comfortably for the rest of the hospital bill and her accommodation whilst here in Boston.

THE PRESENT;

MONCTON

SATURDAY 4TH MAY 3.20PM

DS Saunders drove her police car onto the courtyard in front of the old building and parked it alongside a metallic blue VW van.

The building, which looked like a barn, had seen better days.

The wooden exterior was weather-beaten and could sure use a lick of paint.

There were no windows at all to be seen and a large double set of doors marked the entrance.

A worn metal sign, tacked onto one of those doors, read 'Cockahoop Basketball Club'

There was a bell. She pushed it.

A bell rang somewhere in the interior. Then, she heard shuffling footsteps and the door opened.

A tall lanky man, wearing a pair of glasses that were perched upon the end of his nose, smiled a greeting.

He had almost white hair, what was left of it, his blue eyes were keen and his smile was infectious.

Detective Sergeant Saunders took an instant liking to this man, who must be well into his eighties.

'Well, to see such a beauty stand before my very eyes, does me good,' he said, then extended his bony hand, 'Erik Erasmussen, at your service.'

Smiling, she took his hand which had a firm grip, 'DS Saunders,' she replied, 'here to see Mr Price?'

'Come in. He and the lady are expecting you,' he answered and, after letting her in, closed the door and led the way.

The interior was in much better shape, the foyer area was tidy and quite freshly painted and, as she walked into the main hall, the auditorium, she was surprised by the quality of the basketball court. The seating arena, the overhead lamps, even a modern looking scoreboard adorned one of the walls.

The old man stepped aside and she could see the foreigner and a blonde woman sitting in the front row of seats on the far side of the court.

The old man shuffled away and disappeared from sight.

'I hope you understand why I didn't come forward sooner,' Ally said, getting up from the bench and starting across the court towards the detective.

'I'm Alison Hudson, though please, call me Ally, and,' turning her head briefly to look at Sam, 'and don't blame him either. I insisted on no police involvement. I think you know why.' She extended her hand.

DS Saunders took the offered hand. 'I do know why. I am glad you are safe. As for, Mr Price ...' looking around Alison towards Sam on the bench, 'I am not sure how he got further involved in this ...'

Sam made to get off the bench, but Ally turned, gestured for him to stay put, and said, 'Please, let me do the talking Sam, okay?' Turning back to the detective, she said, 'Please, come and sit with us,' and went back to sit with Sam.

DS Saunders followed and sat on the edge of a bench across the aisle from them.

'Sam said we needed to talk with you,' Ally began, sitting sideways on the bench, facing the detective, having now also taken hold of Sam's hand which she held tightly.

'He said you could be trusted, and figured that you would have done your research into my past. Our telephone conversation earlier confirmed that, so, let me first explain my side of the story, okay? '

'Please,' the detective said, taking a quick deep breath. She already felt for this woman, having read all she had been through. Now, sitting face to face with her, she couldn't help but admire her even more.

'It all began when I found Julien Rozzini on social media coverage of some sort of party at the Halifax yacht club. This was a breakthrough, so, naturally, I was excited, but I knew I also needed to be cautious, and to be sure,' Ally said. Then taking a breath, continued,' I needed to find out more. I was living and working in Vancouver at the time. I looked for a job, had no luck in Halifax, but there was an opening for a full-time administrator, here, in Moncton.

'I applied for the job and got it. Then moved here, rented a house, and so was all set to spend time searching in Halifax for the whereabouts of Julien, but, more importantly, in the hope of finding my daughter.' Ally paused again, and looked at Sam, still holding his hand tightly. 'Then I caught another break. Where I work, at the fitness centre, I came across a member, whose name was Rozzini, a Debra Rozzini. Turns out she is the wife of Nico, Julien's older brother, who is not a very nice person either.

'Anyway, I was elated. I had an address, so, taking a couple of days off, I thought I would first drive to Harris to check out the address I had.

However, when I arrived in the town, I had some lunch first, in a local cafe next to the police station.

There was a local newspaper on the seat next to me, I perused it and discovered that there is a large company in town, a mining company called CP Holdings, and, this was owned by Nico Rozzini.'

Ally paused and looked at Sam again, and then looked back at the detective who was following her every word.

'On my phone I googled the company and found out that this company had a distribution centre, in Halifax, and, who was the managing director of that centre? None other than Julien!'

'Really?' DS Saunders interjected, 'Sorry, carry on.'

'I was feeling pretty good then. Feeling confident I had him at last, so, I marched straight to the police station next door. I showed them a copy of the original arrest warrant for Julien, told them where to find him, and, that Nico was also wanted for questioning, and thought ...well, it doesn't matter what I thought, it was, just, well, I got a bad feeling in there. They practically threw me out, saying they would be in touch, but had to go through "Proper channels".'

Ally paused again, Sam's free hand was gently rubbing her shoulder and she felt comforted by his presence.

DS Saunders waited patiently; there was more to come.

'I felt low. Having been so upbeat, I felt deflated. Headed back home, nothing more I dared to do there in Harris. So, having given myself a talking to that evening, the following day I set off for Halifax. I was going to find that warehouse.

'Which I did, I took a few shots with my phone, but I was too scared to just go in.

'My next move was to reach out to the detective in Oregon, the one on the original case, though he is retired, I felt I needed to tell him what I had found out, so, headed back home, by train.

'Then, as you know, all hell broke loose. It was raining, I was tired, I was disappointed, and I just wanted to get home. I ran to my car, and then, bang, it all happened so fast, I had no chance to react.

I was grabbed, drugged, then taken to my house.

Later, when I was coming around, I was lying on my bed, then I was drugged some more. An injection into my arm, ...' she rolled up her sleeve and showed the mark, which was still clearly visible.

Taking hold of Sam's hand again, she went on, 'I don't remember at all what happened next, not until Sam pulled me up. They had taken me to this, what I believe is called Canyon Road. Now either they threw me off the edge of the road, or, they somehow lowered me down. I just don't know, but think it was the latter. I ended up on this narrow ledge, about eight feet or so below the road.

'I know I was in pain, I was feeling cold and wet, and feeling sick.

I also remember that I just couldn't move, which was just as well because if it hadn't been for Sam I would have, at some point, fallen off this ledge down to the river below, and that would have been the end for sure.'

Ally paused, looking down at the floor, she had paled a little in recalling the events of that day.

The detective broke into her thoughts, 'Did you at any time see them, your attackers? How many were there?'

Ally looked up at the detective. 'I can't remember seeing any of them. There were three of them, though. Two men, I heard their voices, can't be sure of course, but they sounded young, then a woman. She was the one who injected me. She sounded older, also I think, she was in charge.'

'Okay, well done. That all fits together, so far,' DS Saunders said, then deliberately looking at Sam, asked, 'It still doesn't explain, how you became involved.'

'It was the car,' Sam answered. 'What I didn't tell you at the station, for no other reason than that I forgot, was I managed to snap a few photos, four in all as it turned out, when I was in the goods yard ... with permission.' Sam added, giving the detective a brief smile.

'I didn't think about it until later that day, checked them out. Two shots were too blurred with the heavy rain at that point, but the other two were clearer. A shot of the side of the van, definitely dark blue, and it had a sticker near the back, I'll show you in a minute, then a clear shot of the car. I recognised it as a Triumph Stag. Not too many of those around anywhere, let alone in these parts, and on the shot you can clearly see the face of the brunette who got into it.' Sam pulled the camera from his jacket pocket, handed it to Ally, who handed it to the detective.

'Press the green button on top, then the green circle on the back' Sam advised.

Having cleared all his photos from the camera, leaving just these two, the detective brought up one, then the other, looking at them carefully, then said, 'These are good, but ...'

'I know, we should have come to you with these, my fault, I insisted, no police.' Ally said, in anticipation of what the detective was about to say.

'I understand that, but I was going to say ...'

'I still haven't explained how I found Ally ...' Sam interrupted.

'Exactly, please do' DS Saunders said.

'I couldn't sleep. Kept thinking about what I'd seen, over and over. By the time I'd remembered about the photos it was already late, and I felt it would keep till morning. anyway, I was pacing my lounge.'

'By the way, I live just across the road from here. We are, as you know of course, at the edge of the city's north side. Now, it was around midnight. I didn't have the main light on, so I could see quite clearly outside. I noticed a pair of headlights coming down the Canyon Road, heading into town.

Out of curiosity, I grabbed my camera, located the vehicle, zoomed in, just before it disappeared from view.

It was a dark van, so, perhaps I had a feeling or instinct. Through the lens of the camera, I searched along the road, then saw it, the red Triumph.'

Sam released Ally's hand, got up from the bench, stepped onto the court and faced the two women.

'I just knew I had to do something. No point in calling the police, it was after midnight for one, and, who would take me seriously, no offence ...' Sam said, looking directly at the detective.

'I deserve that. Go on,' the detective said, meeting his eyes and beginning to warm to this foreigner.

'Got in my van, drove up Canyon Road, found the car and pulled up behind it.

There was no-one in the car, thought about smashing a window to open the boot, sorry, the trunk you call it, but then I heard a moaning sound.

That's when I found her, lying on this narrow ledge.

Managed to climb down, had some rope in the van, and got her up and out of there.

She was semiconscious most of the time, but did speak to me, imploring me not to take her to a hospital, or contact the police.

So, I took her home ...' Sam explained.

'He makes it sound easy. Let me assure it, it wasn't. I know that I am alive because of what he did, and he risked his life, to get me of that ledge,' Ally said, looking at the detective, then turning to Sam, 'Come, sit down. Let the detective tell us what she has found out, I'm sure she has been busy.'

Sam pulled a USB stick from his jeans pocket, walked up to the detective and said, 'I'll swap you. The photos are on here, so I'll have my camera please.'

'Sure, of course,' she answered, 'thank you' then to Ally, 'Well, I have been busy, but it's my job. Truthfully, I should have been involved much earlier. I apologise for that, specially to you Miss Hudson.'

'Once I had confirmation that an incident had indeed occurred, I had CCTV footage from the station sent to me, and your car was found, from that point on, I have focused on nothing else.'

'We are short staffed at present,' the detective sergeant went on, 'but that's no excuse. Anyway, everything sort of happened at once.

First, your car was spotted, then a green winter coat was found on the river bank. This had your membership card for the fitness centre in it. I'm guessing they put that in your coat when they dressed you. This then all tied up with the ownership of the car and your address.'

DS Saunders paused here, then, like Sam had earlier done, stepped from the bench and onto the court, where she looked at both in turn. 'I delved into your past, Miss Hudson; discovered the terrible injustice that was done to you. I am so sorry, I can't even begin to think what you went through, or are going through still.

'I found the Rozzini connection in Harris, went there, and popped into the police station, as I guessed that you might have gone there; not a very nice reception. It confirmed to me, that you had indeed been there.'

Again a little pause, before she continued, 'This was yesterday, I lit a rocket in there. The chief was out and I was just about to go back in when he arrived, but I decided against it. Felt it better to leave it to internal affairs ...

'With the information you have now given me, I can get a court order for Rozzini's financials. They, I'm sure, will reveal a few things.

'Also earlier today, we picked up the woman, got her prints from your house. She has a criminal record, hence we tracked her so quickly.

She is a qualified nurse, so yes, it was surely her that drugged you.

I have no doubt that she was hired to do a job. She is being transported to here; can't wait to question her.'

'I don't suppose you've located Julien?' Ally asked, 'or my daughter?'

'Sorry, no. Now, I need to get back to the station. I'll get my team to follow up on the van.

'It's best you stay out of sight for now.

'I promise I will call you with an update this evening,' DS Saunders said, looking at her watch.

It was nearly four o'clock.

The detective looked at them both then, with a look that meant business, she said, 'You will stay put, understood?'

'Absolutely,' Sam answered, getting up from the bench, 'but before you go, Ally found something that may be of interest.'

Ally got up as well, then reached into her handbag which she had placed on the row of benches above where she and Sam had been sitting, and pulled out a sheet of paper.

'I printed this out,' she said, handing it to the detective. 'It's a list of properties owned by CP Holdings. There's one that, we feel, stands out, it's in Buchan, Newfoundland.'

DS Saunders took the sheet, glanced down the list, spotted the one Alison had mentioned and looked up at them, standing side by side before her.

'Interesting. I will follow this up, thank you, Miss Hudson, Mr Price,' she answered, nodding to them both, then, turning on her heel, she walked across the court to the foyer.

Moments later Sam and Ally heard the front door close and a car starting up.

Sam turned to Ally, 'Now, you will stay put, won't you, Miss Hudson?' he said jokingly.

'For now, Mr Price, for now' she answered, then linked her arm around his and together they walked across the court.

THE PAST;

PERIOD 12

THE YEAR 1940
SAN FRANCISCO.

The Japanese were threatening. There was chaos in Europe.

A package arrived by post.

Carlos Huanca picked up the parcel, seeing it's from his daughter Zeta in Halifax.

It will have to wait, he says to himself, puts the parcel down on the table in the hallway and leaves the house.

His wife, Maryanne, is with their other daughter, Zefora, who is just about to give birth to her third child.

Their son, Zoltina the 3rd, is deployed. He is a pilot and flies one of the four sea planes that are part of the armament of the cruiser, the USS San Francisco.

'It all seems to be happening at once,' Carlos thought, ramming his cap on his head as he walks down the road towards the hospital only a few blocks away.

His wife, busy with their daughter Zefora and her children as their son in-law, Michael, is also deployed.

He himself working long hours to keep the business going.

The war coming as he was about to retire.

He was tired and his knees ached every day.

It was a Monday, it was November, and it was threatening rain.

After walking the first block, Carlos began to feel a little better, the stiffness in his knees eased up and the fresh breeze coming from the Pacific was soothing.

He let his mind wander a moment, thinking that he and the family had been here in California for over sixteen years already.

Eldest daughter Zeta had been the first to move, leaving Acapulco to come here to San Francisco in 1922.

Such was her report on the city, as she was studying and working in a hospital, the very hospital he was now heading for, that he and his American born wife decided to leave Mexico and come to America.

A move he never regretted.

Fortunately they had built up quite some wealth during their time in Acapulco, had managed to sell their business and properties, and so were able to secure a house and a small business not long after arriving here 1n 1924.

Carlos reached the end of the second block, turned left and up the path to the hospital entrance. He wondered if he was a grandfather for the third time yet.

MEANWHILE SOMEWHERE
ON THE PACIFIC OCEAN

In the cockpit of his Curtiss Seagull, Zoltina the 3rd, better known as 'Z', checked the various instruments on the panel.

The plane sat upon the launching rails of the New Orleans Class Cruiser, named the USS San Francisco, which was en route to Pearl Harbour for maintenance.

He gave the thumbs up and a steam powered blast shot the plane forward and into the sky.

The Japanese were a threat and his mission was to scout the ocean for any possible sightings of the enemy.

He swung the plane to port, then levelled out, climbed to a higher altitude and, when he was satisfied that everything was running smoothly, concentrated on scanning the ocean below.

Z was happy to do his duty for his country, proud to do so, but would rather have been working alongside his father in the business that, had the war not intervened, would be his by now, and his father happily retired.

Not long after the family had arrived from Acapulco, his father had set about creating a new business. First he had secured berthing rights at the Embarcadero, at Pier One, right on the harbour front.

Then, secondly, he sourced his first boat, a fair-sized vessel which he refitted and repainted.

He named her 'Zeta' after Z's older sister.

Soon the Zeta was plying to and from Sausalito, carrying both passengers and freight.

Over the vast Pacific Ocean the engine of his plane was humming along nicely.

The weather was a little overcast, but it was calm as Zoltina made a slow starboard turn.

In the distance he could make out the mountains on the islands that made up Hawaii.

The sea below was void of shipping.

Young Zoltina was fifteen when the 'Zeta' was launched.

He remembers the occasion with fondness as it was the last time the whole family were together.

His sister had been offered a position in a hospital in Seattle and was shortly to move there.

Just before he turned twenty, his father bought a second boat, refitted it, repainted it and this one he named after Z's other older sister, Zefora.

Eight months later, on a Sunday afternoon, she was launched.

Zoltina made a slow full turn and dropped in altitude by several hundred feet, then again, focused on the sea below.

He spotted a ship, in the distance, and as he got closer, saw that it was a cruiser. It was one of their own, also heading for Pearl Harbour.

He dropped more altitude, then waggled his wings in a friendly hello as he flew over the ship.

He then turned to port once more, climbed back to his original altitude and began to make his way back to his ship.

The family business, 'Huanca Bay Transport' was doing very well, but it was another eight years before the third, and final, boat was purchased, fulfilling his father's wish to have one named after each of their children.

Then the war was on the doorstep and Zoltina enlisted.

His father and team worked on the new acquisition for a considerable time, first of all it was a much larger boat, and secondly, it was in bad repair.

Zoltina made a final turn to starboard, then started a slow descent, radioing ahead that he was coming in to land.

The sea was relatively calm, but as was the way the cruiser would, at the right time, make a hard turn to either starboard or port, thus creating a calming wake, which made it easier for the seaplane to land.

Then it was a matter of taxiing closer to the ship and come onto the 'shed', a cargo netting, from where the crane could hook the plane and lift it back on board.

No sign of the enemy, that was good.

But little did he know, that it would be another six years, before he would launch the third boat, emblazoned with his name, Zoltina 3rd, on the bow and stern.

This third and final ship in their little fleet, would solely be used for harbour cruises, viewing both bridges and Alcatraz, a growing tourist attracting.

BACK ON DRY LAND

Carlos was a grandfather for the third time, and for the third time had a granddaughter.

Mother and baby doing fine.

Back at the house, the housekeeper had taken the parcel from the hallway table and placed it on the desk in the study.

Carlos would never open it.

THE PRESENT;

SAM'S APARTMENT

SATURDAY EVENING 4ᵀᴴ MAY

Ally stood in the archway between the lounge and kitchen-diner area and watched.

Sam was oblivious to her presence, concentrating totally on dinner preparations.

The aroma from the various things he had on the cooker, pervaded throughout the kitchen. Whatever it was he was concocting, it sure did smell good.

The clock in the kitchen showed it to be a little after five o'clock.

He had told her dinner would be around half past five and had asked her if she had an aversion to eating meat, or if she had any allergies.

After replying that she hadn't and didn't, he got busy, with music playing softly in the background, and he hadn't said a word since.

She smiled at the thought of their recent conversation with the detective and how protective she had been of him, defending, or certainly deflecting, any possible accusation the detective might throw at him.

At one point she recalls even feeling a pang of jealousy when the officer had spoken to him and she had sensed an attraction.

She smiled even more as she felt that, even if she had, he certainly wasn't aware of it.

How her life had changed so quickly in such a short time, from a near death experience, to, yes, she dared to think it, falling in love.

She shook the thought from her mind. Her daughter came first. Was she now at the point when she'd discover where they had taken her?

If only the phone would ring. If only that detective would call with some answers.

She wished she had some time with this woman, the one who had abducted her, drugged her, the one would had left her for dead.

She would get some answers!

Sam was still totally unaware that she had been standing there for some time, when the doorbell rang.

'I'll get it,' Ally said.

As soon as she had, Sam called out, 'No, be careful!'

Sam took the other door from the kitchen, walked down the hallway towards the front door and met Ally as she had come through the lounge.

Sam shot a quick look through the spy glass.

'It's the police' he whispered loudly, 'quick hide!' and opened the door.

'Amusing,' DS Saunders said, 'may I come in?'

Sam smiled and Ally smiled, 'Of course, please.' Sam said.

'Actually, dinner is almost ready. Would you like to join us?' Sam asked, gesturing for her to follow Ally into the lounge.

'Mmm, it does smell good, 'DS Saunders answered, sniffing the air, 'another time perhaps. I still have a lot to do tonight, but wanted to give you an update personally.'

'Let me turn a few things down in the kitchen first, 'Sam said, heading in that direction.

Ally invited the detective to sit, looking at her face and trying to decide if the news she had was good or bad.

Sam returned and sat next to Ally in the two-seater.

DS Saunders looked at them both and began, 'Okay, first of all, I haven't got a court order for the financials yet, but, I will get that on Monday. I'm sure it will have something to reveal. The woman, I'm happy to report, sang like the proverbial canary, so, let me tell you the scenario.'

Opening a folder she had with her in order not to miss out any details, she continued, 'The woman is Karina West. She has a criminal record for soliciting and for drug possession, which is why she was in the system and why we were able to identify the prints we found at the house so quickly.

'She is a registered nurse, so is not only able to administer any drugs, but, working at a hospital in Halifax, she also had the means to obtain them.'

Pausing briefly, she looked from one to the other, noticing she had their full attention, and went on, 'She was approached by a guy named Phil Madison. She knew this man as she used to work for him. He runs a nightclub and escort service.

He gave her an envelope with specific instructions on what to do, where to be and to be careful to follow the instructions to the letter.

'The rendezvous point was Amherst. It's where coaches stop and there is a big filling station there. She was picked up by two young men. She didn't know them, nor ever knew their names, but did pick up that they were from Harris.'

Another pause, then, 'Although these guys knew what to do, also having some instructions, they were to obey her at all times as she held the overall plans.

She did say that she had to improvise a little, as neither of these men knew how to drive a stick-shift car.'

Smiling, Sam said, 'I wondered about that.'

'Indeed,' DS Saunders said, also smiling, 'we had to find someone from our forensic team who could drive the thing.'

'So,' the detective continued, 'all went according to plan, and, yes, they lowered you onto that ledge, which means that someone who worked out all these details knew it to be there.

All of this was to make it seem like suicide, at some point you would stir and fall from the ledge into the river.

I asked her why not throw you in straight away, and the answer given, was to give them time to establish an alibi.'

'It was at this point in my interrogation, that I decide to inform her that you had not fallen off the ledge, and that you were very much alive.

She seemed relieved at this news, but also was now anxious as she hadn't been successful in her task.

As I said, her best option was to co-operate, this she did, from that point even more so.'

'She was scared of this Phil Madison, I guess,' Sam queried.

'I impressed upon her that she would be safer in our care, yes. So, what happened next was that, because the two guys couldn't drive the car, she drove it up the Canyon Road so she was there when you were lowered down, which was not in the original plan. This in turn meant the house wasn't cleaned properly.

'She asked how we found her so quickly, and it was due to that very fact. At that point she cursed the world and every one in it.'

'So, this Phil, did you say, Madison, he was behind it all? No, he was instructed, wasn't he?' Ally asked.

'Without a doubt. This is not what he gets himself involved in, not normally, so someone either offered him a great incentive, or, had some power over him.'

Then the detective, quickly looking through her notes not wanting to miss anything, said, again looking at them both, 'Soon as we had his name, my colleagues in Halifax were on it. We hadn't allowed her to make any calls at all, with the exception of a lawyer if she had one, but, anyway, she declined.'

A brief pause, 'So, we have Phil Madison in custody and I'm heading over there myself right now,' DS Saunders said, and got up from the chair. 'Sorry I haven't got anything else at present, but, making progress.'

Sam also stood up, 'Thanks for stopping by and telling us in person, and if you have any news later this evening, please call.'

Ally, also stood up, 'Thank you.'

DS Saunders nodded at them both and headed for the door. Then, as Sam opened the door for her, she said, 'Enjoy dinner, it sure does smell good,' and turned and headed for the elevator.

Sam closed the door and went back into the lounge. Ally stood by the window.

He came up behind her, wrapped his arms around her, put his head on her shoulder, kissed her neck and said, 'We are making progress. We will find her.'

Her left arm reached up and she placed her hand behind his head on his neck, then turned her face, kissed him on the cheek and said, her voice only just above a whisper, 'I know.'

It was during dinner, which was Sam's take on a Nasi Goreng, an Indonesian dish, when Ally exclaimed, 'Oh my goodness, I've just thought of something.'

Taking another mouthful of food, she left the table and dashed into the lounge, where she opened up her laptop which she had earlier placed on the coffee table.

Whilst it was loading, she dashed back to the table, 'So sorry Sam, the food is delicious by the way, I just have to check this out,' then, taking another mouthful, dashed back into the lounge and sat on the two-seater.

'No problem, you go girl,' Sam said, taking a sip of coke, then followed her out to the lounge and watched as she was busy typing and scrolling.

Seeing that she was totally absorbed, he went back to the dining table, had some more of his meal and another sip of drink.

Then, standing in the archway, he watched her, unaware she had been doing the very same, earlier.

'Okay, got it!' then looked up, saw where he was and caught his eye, 'Don't just stand there, come over here!'

Sam dutifully came over and sat next to her, looked at the screen and waited for her to explain.

'Do you remember me telling you about how I found Julien?' She turned to look at him.

'Yes, through social media, some party at a yacht club in Halifax, I seem to recall,' Sam answered.

Locking her eyes with his, she said, 'I'm glad you were paying attention, yes, a party at the yacht club. Just now I wondered who else was at this party, perhaps I thought, this Phil Madison guy that the detective mentioned was there too, and look!'

Sam looked at a page with a number of photographs, people dressed in posh frocks and natty suits, and, reading the names below each picture, lo and behold, there was Julien Rozzini.

Beside him was a tall redhead with a dress that struggled to contain her figure, and, on the other side of this redhead, Mr Phil Madison, with another woman in a form-hugging dress beside him.

'Wow' Sam said, having leant forward to better see the pictures.

'I hope you meant wow, there he is, Mr Phil Madison,' Ally said, teasing him.

'Of course, but look what it says about these two gentlemen. Did you see that when you first found these pictures? It reads, "Company directors, Julien Rozzini and Phil Madison with their wives Sandra and Bella".'

'Oh my gosh, no, I didn't notice that before. Strange, I guess this must be a different article than the one I saw covering the same event.'

'This is a great find though Ally, it means there is definitely a connection between Madison and Rozzini, well done you.'

'We could post this to the detective, we should, don't you think?' she asked.

Sam grabbed his phone, checked for the information, then answered, 'Yes, she called me. I have her number, but I don't know how to ...'

'Here, let me, 'Ally offered, taking the phone from Sam. She looked at the number and dialled it.

'DS Saunders.'

'Hi, it's me, I have found a photo online that you should see. Can I send it to you?'

Sam watched Ally as she deftly moved her fingers over the keyboard, then on his phone, and after a few seconds he heard the detective's voice say, 'Got it,' then after a pause, 'Excellent, well done. Thank you, I'll be in touch.' The phone went dead.

Ally handed the phone back to Sam, then sat back on the couch and exhaled audibly.

Sam got up, stopped in the archway, turned and said, 'I'll clear the table, then perhaps we can have a go at digging into those names, Phil Madison, and the two wives. Somewhere someone might have revealed something useful, what do you think?'

Alison stood up, walked up to Sam, took hold of his face with both hands, then gently and softly kissed him on the lips.

'You clear the table, I'll do the dishes, then yes, good idea. We'll see what we can unearth. Thank you by the way, for dinner, it was delicious even though I didn't quite eat it all.'

She released his face and moved past him into the kitchen.

Sam turned and, feeling rather wonderful, set about clearing the dining table.

Her lips still so fresh in his mind he could taste the sensation. Without saying a word he brought the dishes to the kitchen. The words of his late wife suddenly springing to mind once more. 'Go and find someone to love.'

Forty-two minutes later, three things happened almost simultaneously.

Sam called out, 'I think I might have something here ...' He was sitting at his desk in the lounge.

'Really? So have I' Ally called from where she had re-stationed herself at the dining table.

Then Sam's phone rang.

'Sam Price,' he answered it.

'Evening detective. Yes of course you may,' Sam replied, holding the phone for Ally as she came out of the dining room. 'DS Saunders would like to speak to you.'

Alison took the phone from Sam, pressed the speaker button and said, 'Ally here.'

They both listened as the detective spoke, at the end of which Ally said, 'Thank you very much detective. Hope to hear from you soon.'
The call ended.

'Well, that's a dead end for a while, 'she said, handing the phone back to Sam.

'Indeed, Phil Madison lawyered up immediately, Julien has disappeared and no luck in locating Julien's wife,' Sam summed up.

'And she can't go to Harris at this stage, not until she has back up from internal affairs, but she will go through the financial statements of CP Holdings and of Nico Rozzini on Monday,' Ally added.

'In the meantime though, you had something?'

'I did. I have, I think, but you were first,' she reminded him.

'Okay, so it's age before beauty,' Sam said, smiling. 'Fair enough. Well, I found out about this guy, Phil Madison. He used to own a nightclub in San Francisco, then an incident occurred about four years ago, a dancer was attacked. She was raped and later died in hospital. Apparently it all pointed to Phil as the main suspect, but not a great deal of evidence, then, one day, he disappeared. Gone.'

'Interesting,' Ally said, 'actually, very interesting. Well, I researched Julien's wife, Sandra, discovered her name before she married, Pentegrass, quite an unusual name, so, I hoped, relatively easy to track.

'I wondered if Julien had known her in Portland, and, low and behold, I believe he must have, because that was her hometown.

I lost track of her for a few years, but found her again, this time in 2005, and, guess where?' Ally asked.

'San Francisco? Sam guessed after a moment or two.

'San Francisco,' Alison confirmed.

THE PAST;

PERIOD 13

SAN FRANCISCO
NOVEMBER 1946

Six-year-old Emily Nicholson held on tight to the bars of the railing as she watched the scene on the pier.

She was excited. She wore a brand-new frock. It was yellow and rose. White socks slipped into a pair of blue shoes. A bow in her hair.

Emily was excited, because it was her birthday.

Earlier she had been told that they were all going to see Uncle Zee's new boat.

It was also the boat's birthday she was told, as it would be launched today for its first public voyage.

She didn't quite understand what all that meant, but was happy when told they would go onboard and sail around the harbour. Also, that there would be party food and balloons and all sorts.

Chin just managing to rest on the handrail, she watched the proceeding on the pier, wide-eyed. There were indeed balloons, lots of them. There was also a group of six men playing tuba and other instruments.

There were lots and lots of people, waving and cheering.

Two men were on top of a small van with cameras.

Just a moment ago, she heard the noise of the engine starting, then there was a blast on the ship's horn.

Earlier her uncle Zee had shown her where he would drive the boat and told her, when the tooter goes, they would be on their way.

The engine growled a little louder as the boat left the dock-side and Emily dared to stop clutching the bar with one hand and began to wave back.

In the wheelhouse Zoltina the 3rd swung the big wheel and pointed the bow towards the magnificent Golden Gate Bridge, that lay in the distance.

On the port side he could see his young niece waving excitedly.

A little further along from her were her two sisters, also waving, and their mum and dad, his sister Zefora and her husband Michael.

Also on the left-hand side, they passed by the moored vessels that made up the Huanca Bay Transport Company, the Zefora and the Zeta.

Zoltina was not the only one in the wheelhouse. Not long after he had sounded the ship's horn, a woman had entered.

She now stood slightly behind him. She didn't speak, but gently, in a comforting way, put her hand on his back, rubbing it up and down several times, before resting her hand on his right shoulder.

She knew that this would be a difficult day.

A joyous day, yes, the launch of the boat in the fleet that bore his name. Joyous because it marked the culmination of many years of work to refit and ready this boat. It was slightly bigger than the other two in the fleet and would be used, starting properly tomorrow, with the harbour tours, four of them each day, including an evening dinner and cruise.

A happy day also as it marked the birth of his third niece, Emily, who was so excitedly still waving at the people on the shore.

But sad as well.

For on this day, six years ago, not long after his father had visited his third grandchild in the hospital, Carlos, on the way to the harbour, had suddenly collapsed.

Knowing he wasn't feeling at all well, Carlos sat himself down on a chair outside a cafe, a mere spitting distance from where the boats were moored.

There he had simply closed his eyes and died.

His heart stopped, was more or less the medical report.

Zoltina was deployed, was in Hawaii at the time.

She held his shoulder, watched him at work, watched him steer and navigate towards the bridge on this lovely day.

The harbour was calm, the sun shone and there were numerous fluffy clouds dotted in the blue sky.

On both sides of the wheelhouse she could see the family and invited guests on this inaugural cruise wandering around the decks.

Zoltina briefly released his hand from the helm, placed it upon hers that rested on his shoulder, then resumed steering with both hands.

Millie smiled briefly as she recalled the first time she met him.

It was at the hospital where she was a nurse.

It had taken him four days to get there. After having briefly spent time with his mother and sister, he had come to the hospital.

He was exhausted.

Zoltina was taken to see his father's body. After a little while he left that room and wandered around the hospital for a bit. Finding a small lounge he had sat down, staring into nothingness.

It was almost midnight.

It was then when she had first seen him.

Sensing his pain, seeing he was so very tired, she sat down, next to him. After some moments, she took his hand, which was resting on his knee, and held it in hers.

She didn't speak.

More time passed. Apart from them, no-one was in the lounge. It was quiet.

Then he turned to her; tears were rolling down his cheeks.

She drew him close to her, placed his head on her shoulder, then held him until his body stopped shaking.

Zoltina, as he navigated towards the bridge, was also thinking back, drawn to that time when he had come home to his distraught mother, his tearful sister.

Feeling his wife's hand on his shoulder took him back to that night.

What a comfort she had been. Not long after he recovered, had regained control of his emotions, had better control of his breathing, he had looked up at her.

He had been about to try and speak, but a buzz on her pager summoned her to an emergency situation.

It had been three days before he had been able to find her.

There was so much he wanted to say to her, to thank her and to show his appreciation of what it had meant to him, but when he found her, and she walked up to him, a big smile on her, in his opinion, most beautiful face, he hadn't been able to utter a word.

Once again she took control of the situation, walked right up to him, gave him a hug, then had whispered into his ear.

'You know my name. When you're ready, find me, and ask me out,' she had said, then giving him another big smile had left him standing there.

Zoltina swung the boat slightly to port.

They were nearly under the magnificent bridge.

On the deck and in the lounge area there was a hubbub of chatter and laughter.

The family milling around along with many invited guests, some dignitaries including the mayor.

Many friends.

He had been happy to see his mother smile.

A day of mixed emotions.

Though his sister Zefora was there, with her husband Michael and their three daughters, Zeta had been unable to come.

Having nursed her husband back to health, it was now her who was laid up in bed with a severe back problem.

Zoltina swung the helm to starboard as they sailed beneath the bridge.

The Golden Gate Bridge is a suspension bridge that spans the Golden Gate, which is a one mile straight that connects San Francisco Bay with the Pacific Ocean.

The bridge, a great feat of engineering and not just a landmark but a recognisable structure around the world, was opened on the 27 May 1937.

The folk on deck looked up as they sailed beneath it.

In the large lounge area a small band was playing, food was being served and of course, there was cake.

Emily's eyes shone with delight as she walked past the table and chatted to a couple of friends that she had been able to invite today.

Another, bigger party would be held at home later in the afternoon.

Once having gone beneath the bridge, Zoltina swung the boat around to commence their journey back, which would take them around Alcatraz.

Millie kissed him on the cheek and said she had better do some mingling and asked if he wanted anything to eat.

He said he was fine, but Millie smiled and would bring something up to him later.

As she left the wheelhouse she thought back to the day he had finally actually spoken to her.

It had been three days later.

He had been to his father's funeral and was about to be deployed again.

This time he had been forthright and confident, had found her, had walked up to her and had looked into her eyes.

He told her not to go anywhere, that he would be back once the war was over and that he would then take her to be his wife.

He didn't ask, didn't propose, just stated his intention.

But he wasn't arrogant, or domineering.

She had met his gaze, heard his words and could hear and see that he was very much in love with her.

And that was all she needed to know.

You know where to find me, she had said, then had stepped forward and ever so lightly kissed him on the lips.

Zoltina glanced over his shoulder as his wife left the wheel-house, then returned to concentrate on his navigation, smiling.

He was a lucky guy.

The weather remained good, the bay was calm as he steered his boat around Alcatraz, heading back to the pier.

HALFWAY AROUND THE WORLD, IN PARIS;

Whilst Zoltina was a smiling and happy man taking his boat out on its maiden voyage, nine hours later, Rosemary Quinton entered her hotel room.

Once safely there, she threw herself on the bed, broke down and cried.

Only moments earlier, a man, dressed in a blue workman's over-all, had come out of that room, having exchanged a painting that hung on the wall for another one.

Walking down the 'Staff only' staircase of the old hotel that was situated opposite the Grand Opera House, in central Paris, he went right down to the basement, not meeting anyone at all en route.

Disposing of the exchanged painting, a brown coloured and rather dowdy view of an old cathedral, in the refuse container, he then proceeded to strip out of the pair of overalls, wrapping these up in a bundle.

Tucking them under his arm, he left the basement area, climbed a short set of steps up to street level, opened the door and walked away.

Jan Smettens smiled briefly, never looked back and headed for the railway station.

He was sixty-seven. The game was up, he had been betrayed.

And despite years of excellent planning and execution, despite the many profitable jobs he had organised and undertaken, he now had nothing to show for it.

He was on the run, with very little funds at the ready.

Walking along, he thought back to his biggest coup, the best job, the best robbery, the most detailed and worked out plan he had ever conceived and achieved.

He had everything in place, all the elements ready to come together ...

CAPE TOWN, 1903

The ambassador's residence needed to be fumigated. Pest control.

A vicious variety of woodworm as nasty and dangerous as termites. Rooms had to be sealed and controlled.

It was part two of his plan.

The first had been to obtain the position of courier and build up trust.

The third part of his plan could commence.

The heist ...

Jan Smettens arrived at the station, purchased a ticket for Marseille and boarded the train fourteen minutes later.

... the heist was well executed.

The papers were full of the story the following day.

A diamond robbery of a magnitude not seen before.

The third part of his plan, completed.

Next was to hide the stolen diamonds.

Part four of his plan.

He had already chosen how, not only to hide the stones, but how to get them out of the country as well.

The ambassador, whom he had befriended, Samuel Price, had a collection of very nice paintings. Jan knew that, from time to time, he would sell one or two in order to then purchase and admire some new ones.

One of the paintings he had was a Gauguin, 'Woman on the shore' painted in 1898.

The ambassador had a frame put on this as, he had explained, he had bought it frameless from Gauguin's wife, in Copenhagen.

It was a wide and ornate frame.

Ideal.

Whilst the room was in lock down for fumigation, with dust sheets covering all the furnishings, the paintings in those rooms were removed.

This was in the year 1903.

All he had to do then, was to wait.

In 1904 the ambassador was appointed to Paris.

He moved, along with all his possessions, including all his paintings of which one held all the diamonds within its frame.

The local crew, including the fake pest control people, were all paid off handsomely.

Only two others were involved in the actual robbery and knew of the diamonds and the plan, his nephew and niece, brother and sister.

And so, the three of them travelled to Paris.

Four years later, in 1908, the painting came up for auction and Jan purchased it.

Then it all went wrong.

Back in the hotel room in Paris, Rosemary sat on the bed, the ivory miniature in her hand.

On the wall in front of her hung a painting. She looked at it for a while, never considering the fact that the painting on the wall and the ivory she held in her hand would form a connection some seventy-three years later.

Jan Smettens reached Marseille and looked for a way out, for the law was after him and he did not want to go to prison.

THE PRESENT;

MONDAY 6ᵀᴴ MAY

Sandra Rozzini, formerly Pentegrass, sat back in her window seat and blew out her cheeks.

Looking out the window as the plane banked over San Francisco Bay, she noticed the little island that contained Alcatraz.

So far, so good. A few hours away from Hawaii and, hopefully, safety.

She did not want to go to prison.

She had sensed something had either happened, or was about to.

Julien had been on edge, had been on several intense conversations on the phone with his friend Phil and with his brother Nico.

All was not well.

She was worried. She was angry with herself. She was scared. It was time to run.

She called her friend Bella, Phil's wife, and not mentioning her feelings, she informed her she was off to Portland, to see an ailing relative.

Bella was not in a chatty mood, perhaps she too had a sense of foreboding.

She made very little attempt in conversation and made an excuse to ring off.

Something was definitely amiss.

Sandra got her things together, made sure she had her credit cards with her and her passport, and got a taxi to the airport.

Julien had left the house earlier and had not told her where he was going, or when he would be back. He had a leather hold-all with him.

She entered the airport terminal and briefly wondered if Julien was also on the run.

Taking the first available flight out, she flew to Montreal.

From there she purchased a flight to San Francisco.

After her arrival there, she arranged a package to be delivered by courier and then bought a ticket to Hawaii.

As the plane ascended to its cruising height she let herself relax a little.

Whilst she had been worried, whilst she had been angry with herself, mainly for letting revenge get her into the position she now found herself in, mostly, she had a feeling of guilt.

A couple of months ago, reflecting on her life, Sandra had written a letter, a long letter, though perhaps more a statement.

In it she detailed what had happened some ten years earlier.

It was a confession.

Shortly after take-off, as the plane had banked over the Bay and she had spotted Alcatraz, she had shuddered.

She most definitely did not want to go to prison.

Whilst in San Francisco airport terminal, she arranged the bulky letter to be delivered.

Just prior to her flight.

A flight, hopefully, to freedom.

As Sandra's flight reached cruising height over the Pacific Ocean, a courier arrived at the gates of a private school.

SAM'S APARTMENT

'Percivald Quinton ... I know that name ...' Sam said aloud to himself, 'and that auction date, it's the same ...'

'Another interesting read?' Ally asked, coming from the kitchen to see Sam standing by his desk and reading an e-mail on his laptop.

Sam turned around.

He took in what he saw before him.

Ally, blond, attractive.

He could, in that moment, feel his heart beat in his chest.

He smiled at her.

'Ah, yes, it's an e-mail from the auction house in Boston. I sent them the details of the painting in Nico's office, together with some photos. They just got back to me with some interesting information.

'They recall, and by "they" I mean the two old guys who now run the auction house, Walton and Stanhope. Funny really, when I first met them I had to stop myself breaking into a grin for they reminded me so much of the two old men that sit on the balcony in The Muppet Show.

'Anyway, they recall selling two very similar paintings, two seascapes, way back in 1938.'

'Moreover,' Sam turned back to read the message on his laptop, 'they sold them both, to a Mr Percivald Quinton.' He looked over his shoulder as Ally had now moved to his side.

'And.' he went on, looking at the screen again, 'they were sold, by a Beatrice Parker, another name that rings a bell, look, I'll show you the timeline I've constructed with regards to the painting, building up the provenance of it …'

He felt her face close to his as she bent forward to see the screen. He pressed a few buttons. Scrolled with the mouse and brought up a new image.

'See,' he said, ever so quickly turning his head and placing a kiss on her cheek, 'I traced this back to the original owner of the mine in Harris and, in particular, of course, to the painting.

Now, Rozzini bought the mine from a Joshua Parker. Tracking back through the family, I came to Charlie Parker the third, who set up the mine and the company, hence the name CP Holdings.'

Ally, at this point, turned her head and kissed him on the cheek.

'And ...' Sam went on, 'he came from Boston' refocusing on the screen and the story he was telling, trying hard to ignore the lovely sensation on his cheek where she had gently kissed him and the very closeness of her presence.

'Tracing the family line back even further, I got on to the grandfather, Charlie Parker, the first, see?' Sam asked, pointing on the screen.

Again Sam turned his head, a move she anticipated, she moved her head also and their lips touched.

Ever so briefly.

Sam cleared his throat and continued, 'It was this man, an influential man in Boston, who had purchased the painting, this was back in 1762.'

'As a matter of fact' Sam continued, his lips tingling, 'I found out he had purchased three, all of them seascapes, and, I am thinking, very likely all of them by the same artist. I mentioned this information to the guys; this obviously stirred a recollection, and so this e-mail from them.'

'And,' Sam went on, though inwardly he really wanted to just turn and kiss her again, but managed to re-concentrate on the screen, 'they gave me a year, 1938, and the name Beatrice Parker. See, here is where she fits in; she was the wife of Nathaniel Parker and they had a son, Joshua.

He is the one who sold the company to Rozzini.'

Ally briefly noticed where he was pointing on the screen, then leaned closer and gently bit his earlobe.

'So,' Sam managed to say, then again quickly turned to face her, looked into those lovely blue eyes, and said, not taking his eyes off her, 'getting back to this Percivald Quinton, the man who bought the paintings, the other two, well, he is the father of a Rosemary Quinton, and she, is the grandmother of someone who was involved in a previous case I was working on ... what a small world ...' His voice trailing off as he leaned closer to her.

They kissed.

Then several things happened at the same time.

In the town of Harris, a team of five from internal affairs walked into the police station.

Also in Harris, in the office of Nico Rozzini an event occurred. There was a shot.

And, the doorbell rang at Sam's apartment.

THE PAST;

PERIOD 14

THE YEAR 2014
PART 1

She stood leaning on the aft rail of the yacht, drink in one hand, and cigarette in the other.

Cadiz was disappearing in the distance.

Had she had a pair of binoculars at hand and focused the lenses on the dockside they had recently left, she would have seen the figure of a woman.

A woman who looked much like her. A woman whom she had so brutally attacked a little over two years ago, and whose identity she had taken.

Maybe she had a sense of the other woman's presence nearby. Maybe she had a sense that her past might be catching up with her.

She shuddered ever so briefly.

Then, as she watched the wake of the yacht, she thought about the past ...

Lucie van Doorn had quickly dropped the stolen identity.

The passport and travel documents she had in the name of Petra Leyland.

There had been a moment of tension, when she had landed at Heathrow Airport, London, and was about to go through customs and passport control.

Had her victim regained consciousness earlier that she had planned for; had she been able to relate what had happened; had the police figured it out; would she be arrested in a few moments.

But there were no problems.

She did realise and had already researched her route, that she needed to get to mainland Europe as soon as possible.

Her destination was the Netherlands.

Though having lived in Cape Town for most of her life, she had maintained her knowledge of the Dutch language and spoke it reasonably well.

Two big suitcases, a cabin bag and a handbag. She was loaded with luggage.

But however inconvenient, she was determined to keep it all.

Taking a taxi, she first headed for St. Pancras Station.

Here she purchased a first-class ticket to Brussels with funds she had found in abundance in the handbag of her victim.

Twenty-five minutes later she was on board the train and as it rolled out of the station, she checked the time and wondered if the real Petra Leyland had been able to tell the police what had happened to her.

In Brussels she transferred on to another train, heading for Amsterdam, but en route, she changed her plan. She got off at Antwerp Station.

Here she stored all her luggage, all except the handbag, in the left luggage area.

She then discarded all the stolen documents, including the airline tickets, which she had placed in an envelope, in a nearby rubbish receptacle.

She stopped on the steps by the station, took a deep breath and sighed with relief.

She hadn't realised how much tension she had really felt, but was now relieved.

She took in a breath of air, and felt safe. Good and safe, and with a resolute step headed into town.

As she walked along she rehearsed a new name in her head. For some reason, she chose Steffie as going to be her first name. In her mind formulating sentences, like 'Hi, I'm Steffie', 'hello my name is Steffie' and so on.

Taking a turn and entering a road leading away from the shopping street, she came upon a row of apartment buildings.

She stopped, looked around and walked towards the lobby of the second building. Here she read the names on the letterboxes. Sixteen in all.

One name stood out for her. Reading it a couple of times, she decided it was for her.

Opening her handbag, she took out a pen and notebook, then scribbled down the name and the house number.

She made sure she knew the name of the street before walking back into the centre of the city.

As she was walking along, she again began to rehearse in her mind, 'Hi, my name is Steffie, Steffie Baertjens ...'

Lucie flung the remainder of her cigarette into the sea, drank down her wine and turned to head inside.

She was looking forward to getting to Monaco.

Who knows what doors might open for her.

The owner of the small yacht was not on board. The boat had been laid up in Cadiz whilst having a new kitchen fitted. A skeleton crew now sailed her to Monaco, where the owner would board and travel on to the Greek islands with his new wife. His fourth she was told.

She was on board courtesy of Eduardo.

Eduardo was a navigational equipment expert and she had met him in Paris.

He lived in Seville and she had quickly hooked up with him and moved in.

Three months ago.

But it was time for a change, time to move on.

She saw Eduardo at the bar, just finishing a drink. He slipped from the bar stool, saw her, smiled and excused himself.

He said now that the yacht was in full power he had to do some maintenance and equipment tests.

She smiled back, headed for the stool he had just vacated and helped herself to a drink from an open bottle of wine.

The massive twin engines throbbed powerfully as the yacht picked up speed.

Eduardo was alright, she thought to herself, but, it still was time for a change.

The identity which she was currently using, wouldn't do for much longer.

Sipping her wine, she let her mind wander back to the past once again ...

Back to that first day in Antwerp.

Having decided on a new name, she now needed to find a way to get some documents made.

She walked into the suburbs of the city to locate what she would deem a second-rate hotel of sorts. One where money spoke and no questions were asked.

She found such a place.

Telling a story of having had a fire in her house and needing somewhere to stay quickly, for probably about a week, she gave her new name and the address she had decided upon, and flashed the cash.

Having got the key to her room and briefly checking it out, she then headed back to the station, picked up her luggage and took a taxi to her new lodgings.

Despite her efforts, visiting bars, asking discretely, flirting and chancing entering some unsavoury looking places, she had no luck in securing any false papers or contacts to obtain them.

She sold some of the jewellery to top up her cash flow, went from a brunette to a blond and was at the point of travelling to Amsterdam the following morning when, during the evening, there was a disturbance at the small hotel where she was staying.

An opportunity presented itself to the forty-five-year-old.

So on the spur of the moment she went into action.

Outside, below on the street, two men were fighting while a woman stood close by.

This woman she had seen before.

This woman, occupied the room next to hers.

Moreover, she was blond, didn't look too much different from her, though likely at least five years younger.

She swiftly left her room, went to the one next door and without hesitation put her shoulder to the door and crashed it open.

A quick look out of the window saw the fight was still going on, but sirens were heading this way.

Quickly she searched the room and found what she hoped she would find.

A passport.

Leaving the room she closed the door and was pleased to see that, at first glance, it didn't appear to look broken.

Entering her own room she was in time to see the police arrive in the street below.

The fight had been broken up. An ambulance was coming up the road and the woman, together with one of the men, were put into a police car.

Brilliant.

She booked a taxi for early the following morning and packed up her belongings.

Discarding one of the two big cases she decided to take just one, plus of course the easy to roll cabin bag and the handbag.

The handbag that, when she had eventually taken a good look into it, once on board her flight to London, had been treasure for it contained a fair amount of cash, both in sterling and in euros.

Heading for the Antwerp train station early the following morning, she was relieved to be on her way. She had not slept very well at all. The woman from next door might arrive back at any moment and would no doubt cause a ruckus.

She made sure to inform the driver that she was excited as she was on her way to Amsterdam. Once inside the station however, she bought a ticket for Paris ...

On board the yacht night was falling.

The powerful engines drove the ship onwards and she and Eduardo ate in the newly fitted kitchen.

There were four men on board and three women, including herself.

The skipper, in the employ of the yacht's owner, and his wife. Then there were two deckhands, taken on just for the journey to Monaco, Eduardo, who was also employed by the owner, and the third woman was one of the chefs and was in the employ of the owner who had made his millions through a chain of betting shops. It had been her job to oversee the installation of the new kitchen equipment.

They ate more or less in silence. No sign of any of the others. He smiled at her.

She sighed a little, smiled back.

Definitely time for a change, she thought to herself.

She excused herself to have another cigarette and found herself back at the stern.

The wake a frothy track in the dark sea barely lit by a sliver of a moon ...

Again she recalls feeling quite relieved as the train pulled out of the station.

After ten days in the Belgian city of Antwerp, it was on to Paris.

The passport she had stolen from the room next door was not new, already seven years old, but valid.

It was an American passport. Wendy Romano Mann. Thirty-six. Some nine years younger.

But other than a strict custom control, who would take a close look at it, she thought, and felt it would do nicely.

Upon arrival in the capital of France, she looked through a variety of brochures on the station concourse and chose a good class hotel in the Opera area of central Paris.

A taxi took her there.

This time, speaking English, with, what she hoped was some sort of American accent, she asked for a room, told them a story of a theft of her credit cards, produced cash and her passport and was readily accepted as being Wendy Romano Mann, from Boston.

They took a copy of the passport and handed the document back to her, then organised a bellhop to take her luggage to the room.

Ten minutes later she sat on the edge of the bed and began wondering about her next move.

She flung herself backwards on the bed and lay staring up at the ceiling for a while, thinking she quite liked this exciting rogue lifestyle.

Sitting up again, she took a look round this room, and studied the painting that was on one of the walls, opposite to where she sat.

What she couldn't possibly know, was who it had been that was in this very room.

The furnishings were different.

The bathroom en suite was renewed and the curtains, blinds, carpet and bed were modernised.

But it was the same room where some 68 years earlier, Rosemary Quinton had broken down in tears, and where she also had sat, and looked at the very same painting ...

Again flicked her cigarette into the sea and went back inside.

The wind had become stronger and cooler.

It was soon time for bed.

Tomorrow she would be in Monaco.

THE PRESENT;

PARIS

A LITTLE BEFORE MIDNIGHT MONDAY 6TH MAY

Sophie sat up in her bed, laptop open. The clock by her bedside illuminated the time as being a minute to midnight.

Her guest, Petra, had turned in for the night about forty minutes ago.

Typing away, Sophie was writing down her recollections of the past couple of days.

She paused as she took a sip of her hot, though by now more tepid, chocolate and thought back to when Petra and her had left the cafe last Saturday afternoon ...

'So she went to Monaco?' Sophie asked, as they were walking towards her office at the Paris Fine Arts Auction House, 'but you still haven't said anywhere in your notes how you came to find out that she was called Steffie Baertjens,' Sophie wanted to know. 'And what about those five passports she had stolen? You write that you had the names, but haven't said what they are.'

Petra smiled across at her as they walked on, 'Still to come. Be patient Sophie. The frustrating thing is that it wasn't until the following day, in the afternoon, that the police officer from Cadiz contacted me to say they had found footage of her boarding a yacht that was bound for Monaco, that the boat had already docked there and the local French police were not going to board her, but discretely check her out.

My Spanish officer sounded rather irritated by that. Anyway, had I known the previous day, I would have been able to get there in time.'

After a small pause and working their way through a group of young girls, Petra continued, 'So, no, I had no idea of her name at that time, not the one you know her by, and no, she didn't use any of the stolen passports, or their names.'

They reached her work and Sophie unlocked the door. It was her day off, but they had decided that they had taken up enough time in the cafe and a bit of fresh air would do them good, so they suggested to walk a while and continue in Sophie's office.

Whilst the French woman was preparing the coffee, Petra sat herself down in the very chair she had sat in when she first met Sophie.

She thought herself fortunate to have a new friend, a new confidante, someone to share her story with.

Sophie came in with two cups of coffee and sat herself down.

On a small table between them, Petra had laid down the remaining pages of her investigation.

Sophie once again took up the reading.

Petra sat in silence and in thought as she carefully sipped her drink ...

... having received the news about the yacht heading for Monaco, Petra was in a quandary.

The yacht had moored. The woman, no doubt, ashore.

By the time she could get there, what were the chances of finding her?

She was on the trail.

She had to keep going.

The following day she went to Monaco.

'Aah, so that's how you found out her name,' Sophie said, looking up from the notes, 'you found the yacht'.

'Yes and no,' Petra answered, smiling over the rim of her coffee cup, then put the drink down and explained.

'Well, my Spanish policeman gave me the name of the yacht. He also knew who owned it, but didn't divulge the name and he was not on board at the time.

Also, as I mentioned earlier, the French police were going to keep an eye out for this woman. They had been sent photos and clips of her, but they were not going to board the yacht.'

'So,' Petra said, deciding she needed to stand up and walk to the window of Sophie's office, there she turned, 'I went there, to Monaco, to the harbour and found the boat.

It was in a secluded and gated marina, but I just joined a group who were just entering and wasn't stopped.'

'You're a brazen hussy,' Sophie said jokingly, a little in awe of her new friend's drive and commitment.

Petra smiled back, stayed with her back to the window and went on to say, 'I walked along the jetties to reach the boat, then called out and a man appeared.

'I had a large photo in my hand, which I showed him, and said, "Looking for this woman, I believe she's on board?"

He came down from the yacht to meet me, looked at the photo, but he already knew her, that much I could see on his face …

He looked at me, didn't ask who I was or anything, or why I was looking for her, he then told me the story.

How they met, that they had lived together for the past three months in Seville.

He acknowledged that he is sure she used him.

Shortly after arrival, he told me, he had a meeting in town. When he got back, she was gone. Not only that, but it was discovered she had stolen a small painting from the master bedroom.'

'Gosh, she is such a bad person,' Sophie interjected, 'to put it mildly.'

'Absolutely' Petra agreed, then went on, 'so, this guy, his name was Eduardo, told me he knew her as Wendy, Wendy Romano Mann, and that she was from Boston.'

'Did you inform the police? Did they inform the police?' Sophie asked.

'Eduardo told me the yacht's owner was due in town the following day. The skipper had spoken to him and was told not to inform the police. Also that he would speak to him, to Eduardo, most likely to fire him.'

'Poor guy. But what did you do?' Sophie asked, taking a sip of her coffee, looking up at Petra who was still standing by the window, then before Petra had replied, 'And this still doesn't tell me how you found out about her name being Steffie, here she was, what Wendy somebody or other.'

'Yes, indeed, Eduardo knew her as Wendy Romano Mann. No, still to come Sophie. As for what I did next, well, it was obvious she was on the run. Stealing the painting sure confirmed that. I felt going to the police wasn't the answer as they had been reluctant to check out the yacht, so, frustratingly, I went back to where I had left my luggage in a hotel lobby and then had my room made ready. I needed to think about my next move, having now come so close, twice!'

'I'm sorry,' Sophie said. 'I can imagine how you must have felt, still, you must have gotten further, lot's more here to read,' taking hold of several sheets of paper she, as yet, hadn't read through.

'Before you do, 'Petra said, coming away from the window, sitting down again and placing her empty cup on the table, then looking directly at Sophie, said, 'You told me about your connection with our 'Steffie', the Gauguin that you had which she tried to sell and turned out to be a fake. Do you have any idea as to who might be the person who faked it? Did you research that?'

'Funny you should ask that, I mean, at this point,' Sophie answered, getting up from her chair and walking around to behind her desk.

Opening a drawer, she retrieved a folder, opened it up as she was returning to her chair, then said, 'No concrete proof, but according to some, let's say experts, they suggest the fake might have been painted by an Italian chap, name of Roberto Solari.'

THE PAST;

PERIOD 14

THE YEAR 2014
PART 2

Roberto Solari settled himself in the first-class carriage.

He had spent a few days in Monaco with his ailing sister and was glad to be on his way home again.

Eighty-five years of age. He had arthritis in his fingers and knees. No longer could he easily hold a brush. Added to that, he had the onset of Parkinson's.

At times he would wonder, giving his right hand a massage with his left, why it had only affected this hand, his painting hand.

A woman came bundling in, with a mustard-coloured suitcase and a large handbag which she plonked down on the seat opposite as she sat down.

Roberto noticed her hair was wet. Caught in the sudden but short downpour which his knee had earlier predicted would be imminent.

Rubbing his knee, he studied her briefly as she was settling herself in.

Her somewhat bedraggled hair was shortish and blond. He noticed her clothes were of good quality, as was the handbag and suitcase.

She wore a nice watch but there was no jewellery on her fingers.

He figured her to be around forty years of age, though these days, he thought smilingly to himself, it was sometimes strange how some girls of twenty could look like they were in their mid-thirties and how some in their late forties, seemingly appeared to be less than thirty.

But his painter's eye was still sharp. He noticed details. Her hands, the skin under her chin, these all revealed telltale signs that this woman would be in her early forties.

She turned and noticed him looking at her. He smiled and nodded a greeting.

She smiled back.

A whistle sounded and almost immediately the train rolled away leaving Monaco and heading for Paris.

The woman turned her suitcase around, opened it and was fumbling around for a bit in search of something.

Roberto saw something that caught his eye. He saw a small painting.

Twenty by thirty centimetre. Oil on canvas, slim frame.

He knew this painting.

Knew the artist.

'That's a nice painting,' he said to her, speaking French.

She turned to look across the aisle at the old man. Frowning, she then picked up what he had said, turned to look at the painting, then turned back to him.

'Aah, oui,' she said.

Realising she was not French, he spoke in English.

'You have a nice painting; I know the artist ...' he said.

Never miss an opportunity. It had become her motto ...

Look for something or someone, to take her to the next chapter of her life ...

She realised she was on the run. Had to stay on the run until she could get some solid anchorage and safety somewhere.

Using the false passport had enabled her to check into the hotel as Wendy Romano Mann. A very nice hotel.

Coming down the stairs to visit the bar and restaurant that first evening, she took a look around, then sat herself at the bar, ordered a drink and waited.

What opportunity would present itself, she wondered, sipping her white wine.

She longed for a cigarette, but quashed the urge.

'Eduardo,' he said his name was, and in broken English he explained he was in Paris on business, lived in Seville, and would she join him for dinner?

The following day she had travelled with him to his home in Spain.

She felt good, no questions asked, no need to give proof of identity.

He had accepted that she was who she said she was.

All was well.

But she became bored.

THREE MONTHS LATER.

He had returned from a business trip to Athens and had secured a new job.

That of equipment maintenance for not only a small yacht, but also for a mansion in Greece and another near Toulon, southern France.

Several days later he had taken the train down to Cadiz and later that day had invited her to come down and they would sail to Monaco.

She sensed an opportunity; saw an opening to another adventure.

Not long ago, when she had purchased a new suitcase, a lovely mustard colour, she was already planning for the next opportunity. The piece of luggage was a good size, yet lighter and more manoeuvrable.

The chance for a change came sooner than she expected.

She packed her things into her new case. This she strapped onto the Vespa she had been given by Eduardo. He had said for her to catch the train as had he, but she chose not to.

She wanted to feel free, to feel the wind in her face, and, she didn't care about the scooter as she would not be coming back.

Once she was in Monaco, she would find a way to disappear.

Her time with Eduardo was alright, but she longed for more and was almost constantly aware that she shouldn't get complacent.

For one, the crime she had committed in Cape Town was such that she would still be sought, and possibly caught, even if two years had passed.

Secondly, stealing the passport from the woman in the room next to hers in Paris might also have repercussions.

Staying with Eduardo just wasn't safe enough.

Two days before she travelled to Cadiz, he had rung with the invitation. She had worked frantically the following morning, clearing all her belongings.

Placing what she wanted to discard in the old luggage, she dragged these down to a nearby church for distribution.

They were most appreciative.

Closing the door of the apartment and leaving the keys behind, she started the scooter, put a pair of sunshades on and set of.

Bye-bye, Seville.

It was about half an hour from Cadiz when an unexpected opportunity presented itself.

It hadn't happened that long before.

A coach had left the road and crashed down an embankment.

She stopped. An idea formed in her head.

Parking a little further up the road, she got off and went down the embankment where she mingled with and comforted some of the passengers for a few moments. As yet she could hear no sirens heading their way.

She then climbed into the overturned coach, took a quick look around and then spotted what she was looking for, the satchel that tour guides usually carried, which would hold travel permits, documents, reservations and, passports.

Rummaging in the bag, she found a handful, quickly scanned through them and stuck five of them under her blouse just as she heard sirens coming closer.

Leaving the bus she again mingled and spoke to the wounded passenger.

She then slipped away from the crowd, back up the embankment. Some cars had stopped and several people were coming down as the ambulance arrived. She could hear more sirens coming nearer.

She then started the scooter, and left. Not realising that one of the wounded passengers was filming all the time ...

Once they were moored in the marina in Monaco, she watched Eduardo leave the yacht and walk along the jetty, heading into town as he was to have a meeting with the team that represented the owner.

There was now only one person left on board. A deckhand.

She had already made use of the lack of people to snoop around on the journey.

Make use of opportunities, she reminded herself.

So, when the coast was clear and Eduardo was out of sight, she moved into action.

Her case was ready, she was ready, just a few things to get.

Sneaking quietly into the master cabin, she retrieved a few trinkets that she found in a drawer and took a small painting from the wall.

These she placed in her case, then, waving goodbye to the deckhand she wheeled her case down the jetty and into town.

It was threatening to rain ...

'You do?' she asked him, taking the picture out of her case. She then crossed the aisle over to where he sat and handed it to him.

'Is it good?' she asked, 'I got it from a friend, but I'm not sure if I like it.'

He studied the painting briefly, then looked up at her.

'You are going to Paris?' he asked.

She noticed his eyes, light brown in colour, were bright. It was almost as if he was probing her mind.

She had an instant liking for this old chap.

'Are you travelling to Paris?' she asked, not answering his question just yet.

'Going home. I live there,' he replied, handing the picture back to her, 'I have visited my sister.'

Then, as she returned to her side of the carriage and placed the painting back into her case, he asked, 'You want to sell it?'

The train had picked up speed once it was free from the suburbs and another shower was coming down, the rain streaking across the windows.

Again she sidestepped his question, closed the case and placed it on the floor, then, turning to him, she again walked across the aisle, sat opposite him and giving him all her attention, she asked, 'Do you have a room, in your house I mean, I'm looking for somewhere to stay, just for a little while, perhaps, well, perhaps I could exchange the painting for rent?'

He mulled this over for only a moment, before saying, 'How long would you want to stay?'

She smiled at him, was pleased with herself.

As the train sped through the countryside of southern France she had taken another opportunity.

A safe place to stay, a safe haven, at least for a little while.

Though she knew she was aiming to take advantage of him, she did sense that this man, though elderly, was no mug.

In fact, she thought he was rather shrewd, and, going by his smile as he awaited an answer, she was sure, that he was, certainly at one time, quite the ladies' man.

'A week?, ten days maybe?' she carefully suggested.

THE PRESENT;

PARIS

A LITTLE AFTER MIDNIGHT MONDAY 6TH MAY

Sophie finished her chocolate drink and then continued typing away on her laptop, Petra had gone to bed and she wanted to record all that she visualised had happened, all that she had been told, recalling the many notes she had been reading earlier ...

Sophie put the sheet of paper down on the table, sighed and rubbed her eyes, she had done a lot of reading.

'So,' she asked Petra, standing up to stretch her back a little, 'do you think she made a mistake? I mean about giving that name?'

'Maybe,' Petra answered, 'she was pretty confident, and let's face it, here we are, some four years later, and though close, I haven't caught her yet.'

After a few moments of silence, Petra continued, 'So, perhaps a mistake, but, thanks eventually to more helpful French police, CCTV caught her boarding the train to Paris, however, this wasn't until I had arrived in Monaco and had then informed them of what I knew about Lucie van Doorn, that they investigated.

'She purchased a first-class ticket to Paris, and used the name Steffie Baertjens. That was the first time I knew of that name, and, we know, it is also the name you know her by, when she tried to sell the fake Gauguin, and when in Amsterdam.'

'Come on,' Sophie said. 'We'll pick up your luggage from your hotel. I'm actually off work until Tuesday, so, you're staying with me, and between us, we will find her.'

Petra got up, once again feeling comforted in having found a new friend, asked 'Are you sure?'

But the look that Sophie gave her was clear that any argument was futile.

Then, as they both left the office, Petra agreed, 'Yes, we will find her'.

Sophie finished typing.

She was back at work tomorrow, so she had better get some sleep.

Despite their effort, they were unable to dig out any further information.

Closing the laptop, she put it away, them whispering to herself as she got back into bed and turned the light out, 'We will find her.'

Whilst across the Atlantic in Moncton
Monday 6ᵗʰ May

'We have found her,' a buoyant DS Saunders said as she entered Sam's apartment.

Ally came from the lounge and practically flung herself at the detective.

'Oh thank you, thank you' she said, embracing the policewoman.

DS Saunders, almost struggling for breath, managed to untangle herself from Alison Hudson, who then flung herself at Sam, sobbing.

'Actually,' the detective continued, 'she found us. That is, she contacted the police department in San Francisco, who, in turn, contacted me. Let me explain.'

Sam invited the detective into the lounge and, still holding on to Ally, followed her.

Once seated, and with Ally having more or less composed herself, the detective spoke and explained how the headmistress of a girls' boarding school had contacted the police as one of her pupils had received a letter in which it was revealed, that the pupil in question, a Theresa Pentegrass, was in fact the daughter of an Alison Hudson.'

Sam, his arm around Ally who still had tears on her cheeks. Both of them were focused fully on the detective.

'So, it turns out the letter was written by Sandra Rozzini, formerly Pentegrass, who, confessing to the whole scheme, named the main culprits as her husband Julien together with Julien's brother Nico.

'The girl, sorry Miss Hudson, your daughter, was also in the letter informed that, you, her mother, was still alive as she had been informed when she was taken from you, over ten years ago, that you had died and that they, being this Sandra and Julien, had adopted her.

'The police duly came to the school and then, with information contained in the letter, contacted me.'

'Is she, is she alright?' Ally asked, 'and Sandra, where is she? And Julien?'

'Your daughter is alright. She's at the school, being counselled, a lot to take in for a young lady, a lot to take in for anyone,' the detective answered, looking directly at Ally.

'As for the woman, Sandra, the letter was sent by courier from San Francisco airport. The police have since learned that she took a flight to Hawaii, but had already landed by the time they had all this information.

The police there are searching,' the detective's voice was soft and compassionate.

'As for Julien,' she went on, 'he also disappeared, but, thanks to that address you found, Miss Hudson, the one in Newfoundland, he has been located and arrested, shortly to be transported to Halifax.'

Ally turned to Sam, 'I'll have to go and see her.'

'Absolutely, I'll organise travel for you in a moment,' Sam said, planting a kiss on her forehead, then turned to the detective and asked, 'and, what of Nico Rozzini, and the two guys who abducted Ally? ... And the crooked police chief?'

HARRIS

Chief Brown had seemingly lost the will to live.

His ruddy face had been almost beetroot red in the beginning, but now he sat ever so still, handcuffed to a chair in one of the offices.

The colour had totally drained from his face.

He looked vacantly at the floor, perhaps hoping a hole might appear into which he could crawl.

In another office, the deputy was similarly cuffed and equally silent and in thought.

Beads of sweat were forming on his forehead.

In an office in the mining company, Nico Rozzini had taken a step to end that same feeling that the chief had, the loss of the will to live.

He had followed up on that feeling.

Seeing nowhere else to go, nothing else to be done, he took a pistol from a drawer in his desk.

A single shot rang throughout the building.

The wall behind him, where not long ago the large seascape had hung, was splattered with blood.

The secretary, having rushed over after hearing the shot, had shaken her head, had tutted and had returned to her desk to ring the police and ambulance.

THE PAST;

PERIOD 15

THE YEAR 2015

Steffie was annoyed with herself.

Ending the call she cursed her own stupidity.

She had become too confident, had let her guard down.

It was now a year ago that she had met Roberto and moved into his house.

An opportunity she had immediately sensed was possible the moment she met him on the train.

What a time it had been, for he was quite the character.

Currently he was in the south of France. His arthritis was getting worse, his Parkinson's had now affected his whole right arm and he was tired.

He was with his sister, still ailing, but still alive.

The warmth of the Mediterranean sun was pleasant and better for health.

She put the receiver down. It had been the Paris Fine Arts Auction House that had called, a Miss Sophie Pontiac.

There was seemingly a problem with the Gauguin she had placed up for auction.

She had told the woman she would be happy to talk it through and hopefully provide further information, could she come around tomorrow, trying her best to keep her voice as calm as possible, though inwardly, a little worried.

Though her French had improved considerably whilst with Roberto here in Paris, she still preferred to converse in English most of the time, having taken a liking to the accent she had developed being the American from Boston, being Wendy Romano Mann.

Tomorrow!

Steffie would, by then, no longer be here.

Damn! She cursed herself again.

It was all going so well.

She had the run of the house in an outer suburb of Paris.

Enjoyed going to the local shops with Roberto and seeing, practically hearing, other women tutting and men eye her up and down.

In time she grew to trust him. In time she opened up to him.

The painting that he had seen on the train, the very painting that had been the start of the opportunity she had taken, was sold.

He told her what he sold it for and she had gasped, not realising it's worth.

Stay as long as you like, he had told her.

Eventually she had told him how she had obtained that painting. Stolen it. She told him of her past, of many of the things she had done.

Many, not all.

He had listened. He had not judged.

Not only that, but he began to reveal more about himself.

When she at one point showed him the five stolen passports, he said, in return for these, would obtain good documents for her.

Finally, nearly three years after having arrived in Antwerp and choosing a new name for herself, she now had a passport in that name.

She was now Steffie Baertjens.

Many stories he regaled to her, either when sitting in the small back garden, or comfortably in the lounge by the hearth.

One of these stories really grabbed her attention.

The diamond story.

It had been on a sunny afternoon. Already she had been with Roberto for over six months. She was safe.

She helped around with the household chores and was ever thankful that she had come.

She and the old man got on well. His health though, was failing.

So on this sunny afternoon, in the back garden, the sun warming his arthritic hands and knees, he told her a story.

Her French was improving, but his English was very good, and he told her this story in that language.

'When I was seventeen, I met a man called Jan Smettens,' he said, 'it was 1946.'

On the copper and glass garden table in front of them, Roberto had placed what looked like a scrapbook of sorts.

This he leaned forward for and picked up, opened it and retrieved a photograph.

He showed Steffie.

It was a black and white photo, it showed a tall man, wearing a fedora hat, and a very young Roberto, taken outside the Monte Carlo Casino.

'I was a street artist, in the main, hunting for rich ladies or men whose portraits I could paint for them. This man, Jan, liked my work and gave me a commission.'

Roberto took another photo from the scrapbook and showed it to her.

'This looks familiar,' she said, studying the faded sepia photograph. 'Yes,' she confirmed, looking at Roberto, 'I saw this painting, or probably a copy of it, or certainly a lot like this, in a hotel room, here, in Paris.'

He frowned, looked at her briefly, took the photo back, frowned for a moment longer, then went on to explain the story.

'This painting, was the commission. To copy it. It is a Gauguin.

But the true story about the painting came out later.

I took it with me, I had some digs not far outside the town centre at that time.

Worked on it for three weeks.

He was amazed and excited, then told me the story of the diamonds.'

'Diamonds?' Steffie asked, her ears pricking up. 'Do tell.'

'Well, it's some tale, so I will need another glass of wine,' he asked.

Fetching some more wine, Steffie then sat and relaxed in the warm afternoon sun and listened to the tale.

'The painting, the Gauguin, had been owned by an ambassador, English chap.

Now this was in Cape Town, your hometown so you told me. Well, my man, Jan, had a plan. You see, he was a burglar, and he planned to steal some diamonds.

This, he and his team, successfully did. Now somewhere in there,' Roberto said, referring to the scrapbook on the table, 'is a newspaper article about this robbery. Now, this was a long time ago, in 1903, it was the biggest of its kind at the time.'

Roberto paused for a bit, took some wine, rubbed his hand which was giving him some trouble, then continued.

'Now Jan managed to get hold of this painting, which, as you can see in that picture, has no frame. But, it did have. It had a wide and ornate frame, according to Jan, and he hid the stolen diamonds inside that frame.'

'Clever idea,' Steffie observed.

'Indeed, especially for the fact that this painting belonged to the ambassador. You see the chap, this British ambassador, was appointed to Paris in 1908.

Now, this is more than four years later. Of course all his possessions go with him. Jan understood, or had found out somehow, that the ambassador occasionally would sell a painting in order to purchase a new one, and this he did, though if he hadn't I figure Jan would have found a way to get to it. Anyway, the painting was sold at auction and Jan bought it.'

Again Roberto took a little break, drank some more wine and carried on with the story.

'Jan told me he felt very upbeat, for time had passed and the diamonds would be a lot easier to sell by now. So, he purchased the painting. I just remembered, it was titled, 'Woman on the shore'.

Steffie listened intently. This story intrigued her. She also couldn't help wonder about the painting she had seen in the hotel room. Could it be the same painting? She felt Roberto had hesitated a little, when she mentioned it.

Roberto continued, taking hold of his right arm to stop it from shaking. 'Now, I mentioned he had been working with a team. This team was in fact his nephew and niece. Now, they hadn't been as patient as Jan, but he persuaded them to hang on. In the meantime they continued with doing the odd burglary here and there, mainly in the south of France.'

Roberto sat a bit more upright in his chair and looking directly at Steffie, said, 'This is the interesting bit.'

'The painting was purchased, they went back to Jan's place. He was at the time living in Paris, to make sure he kept his eye on the ambassador's painting.

They dismantled the big frame, and to their shock and horror, the diamonds were not there!'

'Wow!' Steffie exclaimed, 'What happened?'

'Jan told me he was totally dumbfounded. He said his niece and nephew were instantly suspicious, accused him of double crossing them and walked out. He said he never spoke to them again.'

'Do you think perhaps they took the diamonds?' Steffie asked. 'What did he think?' sitting on the edge of her seat, fascinated by this development in the story.

'No, he himself had placed the diamonds in the frame. This whole thing troubled him. He had no answer.

510

In fact he was so worried that he'd been found out, he immediately moved. To stay in Paris was not an option.

He gathered a few things together and drove south, taking of course, the painting with him. This at least, on its own, was still a valuable item.'

Roberto sat back in his chair, the wine was soothing, the warmth of the sun was soothing, and relating the story had brought back memories of days gone by, also soothing.

'Jan went to Marseille,' Roberto again spoke. 'There he lived and stayed for the next thirty-eight years, until he met me in 1946, in Monte Carlo.'

'I painted the Gauguin, which he still had. He hadn't dared sell it, and so began my new career, to fake the masters. I've done a few.

Not so much for the money, really, but for the challenge.'

'And the diamonds?' Steffie asked.

'Don't know, he told me this story, whilst I was painting the copy.

He took both paintings, paid me well, said he would reframe them.

During the three weeks that I was making the copy, I saw him every day as he checked on progress.

Afterwards I never heard from him or saw him again.'

Some more time passed. The afternoon sun was heading towards the horizon.

The birds were happily singing and a light breeze rustled the leaves of the trees in the garden.

After some time, it was Roberto who spoke, 'You say you saw this painting, in a hotel room? Are you sure?'

Steffie took the photo from the table, had another look at it, then answered, 'Yes, I'm sure it was this painting.'

No more was said.

He was with his thoughts, she with hers.

The story captured her imagination. She wanted to find out more and so started to search out more on this intriguing story.

One evening, when Roberto had already gone to bed, she took out his scrapbook from a drawer in the dresser where he kept it.

She started to thumb through it.

Opening her laptop, she made notes of all the details she could find amongst the various scraps of paper, starting with the newspaper article that reported the theft of the diamonds.

She then searched for whatever other information she could gather. It had been close to midnight, when she spotted another newspaper article.

A very recent one.

A guest, staying at the very hotel in Paris where she had stayed, in the very room in fact, informed the management that he thought the painting, the Gauguin, looked to be genuine.

The hotel duly followed up on the man's advice, who was an auctioneer from Amsterdam, and so, subsequently, the painting would be placed up for auction.

Steffie blew out her cheeks. Already having found out a lot of information, she was now keen to have this painting.

The auction was to be held in two days' time.

Steffie thought about the whole story. If this Jan character, had been the only one to place the diamonds in the frame then, she concluded, somehow the owner of the Gauguin must have found out.

'So, Mr Ambassador,' she said aloud to herself, 'did you find the diamonds. Did you figure something out, put two and two together, and if so, Ambassador Samuel Price, where are they now?'

THE PRESENT;

NEW YORK

11.35AM TUESDAY 7TH MAY

'Oooh,' Chrissie called out, 'an e-mail from Sam', in answer to a ping on her recently purchased tablet.

'My, my, Chrissie,' Tammy said, smiling, 'you are so flushed with excitement!'

Chrissie briefly looked up from her tablet, scowled at her friend, then resumed reading for a moment. 'Gosh, who would have thought that. Quite a coincidence. Well I never.'

They were both sat in, what Tammy referred to as the relaxing room, at the back of her restaurant.

The same restaurant she once worked at as a waitress, but now owned.

All the lunchtime preparation was done. Soon they would be open for lunch.

They were alone in the room.

'Come on, stop it. Tell me, what is he saying. Does he want to marry you?'

'You stop it,' Chrissie replied. 'No, he is asking about a couple of paintings, large ones, featuring sailing ships; he refers to them as seascapes. He says here that your great-grandfather, Percivald, purchased them at an auction in Boston, and, get this, it was the very same auction where my grandfather bought the miniature!'

'You mean ...' Tammy asked, interrupting.

513

'Yes, the very one your grandmother, well, you know, how incredible is that?'

'These paintings,' Chrissie said looking across to Tammy, 'I'm sure are the ones hanging in your hallway. I've seen them, I haven't really looked at them, but I've seen them.'

'They were there when I inherited the apartment,' Tammy answered. I thought they were rather nice. They are in the hallway as you say, so, what's the connection? What is Sam working on?'

'There is a third, painting I mean. When Sam was researching into that one, he discovered about the two that were purchased by Percivald. All three of them were originally bought in Boston, way back in 1762, by a Charlie Parker.'

'Are they by a known artist?' Tammy asked. 'I have looked at them, saw no signature, but, as they looked fine in the hallway, I left them there when I redecorated the place.'

'So how crazy is that,' Tammy said after a pause. 'It's possible then that your grandfather, met my great-grandfather. Anyway, they were in the same room, same auction that's unreal.'

'Sam is asking,' Chrissie said, reading on her tablet, 'if I could ask you if you know about these paintings, or have record of this purchase, and, if you know, by chance, what connection he, Percivald, had with a Beatrice Parker.'

'I'll have a rummage. In truth I know very little about Percivald. It would be interesting to find out more. I do know, reading through Grandmother's letter that he wasn't perhaps the greatest father. Says he just gave her money and told her to go and do whatever.'

'What shall I tell Sam?' Chrissie asked.

'Tell him,' Tammy said, looking directly and intently at her friend, 'that I have the paintings, that he should come and see them for himself, and that he should take you out to dinner.' Tammy gave Chrissie a big smile, then got up to get herself and her staff ready for the lunchtime service.

MONCTON
12.10PM, TUESDAY 7TH MAY

Sam sat on the old flatbed railcar. Beside him on several paper plates were a selection of cheeses, sausage and bread.

A couple of cans of beer were also present, though Sam drank very little in the way of alcohol, only the occasional wine or lager. This was a thank you lunch.

He had contacted the old man, Joe, to meet him here. in the old goods shed.

To the right stood the old boxcar.

Joe was perusing a series of pictures that Sam had brought along.

'There she is,' Sam pointed out at one point, 'see that woman? Well, her name is Sara Parker, beside her there, is her husband Carl, and on the other side here that's their son, Henry Charles.'

Joe studied the picture. Sam explained further, 'He is the one who brought the railroad to Harris, constructed the line from the mine to the smelting plant at Sackville and then onto Halifax.

Also, the boxcars you see in the picture, one of them is the very one that's here.

It has her name Sara, above the door on the inside.'

Joe nodded whilst eating, totally absorbed in the pictures.

Like the last time he was here, it again was raining.

Sam munched on a sandwich as he thought about the events that had unfolded since ...

Mr Nico Rozzini was dead.

Shot himself in the very office Sam had been in to look at a painting, a week ago.

Looking through the partially open sliding door of the goods shed, through the light rain he could see the railway station.

Through the rain he had witnessed an abduction.

A week ago.

Very early this morning he had taken Ally to the airport in Halifax, driving, for the most part in silence, in his van.

He had hugged her and kissed her.

She had tearfully hugged and kissed him back.

To see her daughter, to be reunited with her daughter after ten years, was the most important thing right now.

To be with her, to give one hundred percent, to re-establish the mother and daughter bond.

This was most important.

He had been adamant.

A relationship that was surely possible just would not be right, not at this time.

Though it fairly broke his heart, he was insistent. She had to go alone.

He arranged all the travel and Detective Sergeant Saunders was organising for someone to meet her at the airport in San Francisco and take her to the boarding school.

Ally had, through tears and sobbing, agreed that it was the for the best.

So, in almost silence, he drove to Halifax.

Neither spoke much at the airport either.

After she checked in, she held him, they hugged and kissed.

Sam watched until he saw her no more, then turned and, with a heavy heart, headed back to his van.

The words of his late wife, once again resonated within him.

'Go and find someone to love,' she had said, in that warm, caring and loving voice.

Tears were in his eyes as he drove out of the car park and headed for home.

Later he focused on work, to take his mind of Ally. He also had the idea of speaking to Joe, and invited him to lunch at the goods yard, which he readily accepted.

Sam broke from his thoughts and looked at the old man sitting next to him, sifting through the many pictures Sam had brought along. He had printed these out from the series of photographs he had taken in the boardroom that day when they were taking the frame of the painting.

A pictorial history.

The old man was totally engrossed.

Sam selected another bread roll, stuffed some salami and Brie into it, took a sip of his beer, then took a bite …

Then there was an e-mail back from Chrissie.

After coming back from the airport, Sam had concentrated on his research into the painting. Discovering about the auction was an incredible coincidence. He wanted to know if more information might be found with regard to the other two paintings

Not long before he prepared all the lunch and set out for the goods yard, he had sent Chrissie an e-mail to see if she could ask Tammy about it.

Then, just as he was about to leave his apartment, he had an e-mail back from Chrissie.

Chrissie.

There had been a time, when they were together in Genoa, that he had wondered. Had even thought briefly about a potential relationship.

He had chickened out, backed off.

Why had he done that?

She was lovely.

He read the e-mail with interest. Turns out Chrissie was in New York staying with Tammy. Turns out the two painting are hanging in her apartment and Tammy would try and find any relevant information about her great-grandfather.

Also Chrissie had asked him to come over to New York so they could have dinner and share notes.

Sam ate and thought about his options.

Thought about what he should do next.

He still had a commission to finish. The oil seascape, currently being cleaned at the Maritime Museum in Halifax.

Who would it belong to now? He wondered.

Going to New York might indeed fill in the painting's provenance, as at one time the three paintings had been together.

Then, to make choosing a direction even more difficult, there was Sophie.

He knew she was still trying to find the real Gauguin, the one once having belonged to his great-grandfather, the ambassador. Sam thought about the journals that he, the ambassador, had written. They had found some good information in them before. He had not read through them properly, was there more to find?

Was there something he had missed?

Joe asked him a question, breaking through his thoughts.

'So, what happens to this painting now?' he asked, holding a picture that Sam had taken of the seascape on his first visit to the mine.

'Good question Joe. I have to wait until things settle. A lot of investigations are going on.

It might be the wife, it might be the brother who inherits, I don't know.'

Sam's mind wandered again as he took another bite.

He was relaxed, just sitting here on the old flatbed railcar. The rain was still coming down lightly and forming little puddles on the floor below the holes in the old tin roof.

But, what to do? He thought to himself.

Was he in love with Ally? He felt he possibly was.

Did he like Chrissie? Yes, very much so.

And Sophie was nice.

'And this one?' Joe asked, showing him another picture.

Sam looked at it. It was the one of the sculpture, outside the entrance to the mining company.

'Aah, yes, Hopkins point,' Sam replied, taking hold of the printed image. 'Found out a little about a man, called Henry Hopkins, well liked and loved in Harris, quite the figure. Haven't quite figured how he fits in with the Parker family yet.

The sculpture was interesting. Something about it that reminded me of something, but can't think what. Anyway, the little emerald you see here,' Sam said, showing the place on the picture, 'I'm sure it isn't placed randomly, but I figure it must refer to the title of the sculpture, on the base here, see, Hopkins Point.'

Joe took the print back, looked at it some more, then continued looking through the others that Sam had brought along.

Arching his back a little, Sam then jumped from the flatbed and walked over to the shed's sliding door.

He watched the rain still coming down, though unlike last time when it was deafeningly thundering upon the tin roof, there was no noise, a gentle and soft rain.

Again he thought about what his next move should be.

What about these three women. It was all very well falling in love. That part seemed to be quite easy, but was it real love. Was it more than a longing?

What's more, would they, or could they, love him?

Ally. Beautiful. He was sure he had strong feelings for her, maybe even in love, but what about her feelings for him?

He had saved her life. Would that prove difficult in a relationship?

Chrissie, also a lovely and attractive woman. He had helped her find out about her grandfather. She was grateful for that. Could that affect any deep relationship?

And there was Sophie, the feisty French woman. He had come to her rescue after the knife attack. Would that be an even balance in a relationship?

A ding on his phone sounded. He took it from the pocket of his jeans and looked at the screen.

It showed there was a message, an e-mail, from Sophie.

PARIS 4.45PM TUESDAY 7ᵀᴴ MAY

Sophie put her phone down, having just sent the e-mail to Sam.

She had been at work today, but as it was quiet, left at four o'clock wanting to get back to her apartment and compile a report for Sam.

Saturday had been good. Reading through all the evidence that Petra had gathered over the years was fascinating.

She had decided to bring Petra to her place so that the both of them could spent a concentrated effort on following the direction that Petra had found so far.

Sunday had been relaxing, they had bonded well and had spent hours in scrolling and searching, unfortunately, without any further success.

Monday morning as Sophie was preparing some breakfast for both of them, Petra came into the small kitchen and stood in the doorway.

It was a moment or two before Sophie realised she stood there, then when she did, knew that something was wrong.

Petra was crying.

'Sorry Sophie,' she managed to say, 'I have to go, I just have to go …' and left to head back to her guest room.

Obviously something awful had happened. Sophie turned off the cooker and went after her.

She stood in the doorway and watched as Sophie was packing her suitcase.

'Can I help? What's wrong? What's happened?' she asked.

Petra stopped for a moment, walked over to Sophie, hugged her tightly, then took hold of her face, looked into her eyes and spoke, 'I'll leave all the notes, you must carry on, you must …' then turned around to carry on packing and explained, 'a friend has just sent me an e-mail, a friend from a long time ago. It seems my ex-husband's second marriage broke down some months ago, but she informs me, he is seriously ill …'

'I'm so sorry …' Sophie whispered.

'I was not a good wife to him, in fact rather horrible. I have to go to him. I need to go to him … this quest, this venture of finding Steffie, this revenge really, has taken too much of my life I realise. Sorry, but I need to see him, to be with him, … I hope you understand …'

'Oh absolutely,' Sophie had replied, 'What can I do to help?'

Sophie had then sourced a flight and connections whilst Petra finished packing and taken her to Orly Airport.

'Please keep in touch?' Petra had asked.

'Of course.'

They hugged and Petra was gone.

Determined to set aside the disappointment, Sophie had, upon her return to her apartment, spread a number of sheets on the dining table, then drawn up a timeline. This she had learned from Sam.

On it she wrote what was known. The facts and the dates and the places.

Then, once having established all that, she grabbed bits to eat and wine to drink as she went along. She spent the next two hours on her laptop and discovered something rather odd.

In her previous research she had come to a conclusion that after Jan Smettens had purchased the painting in 1908 it had since stayed in the family.

It had eventually been sold in a house clearance belonging to a Miss Steenwoude, an elderly woman who had never married and was, according to initial research, a full cousin of Jan Smettens.

She had then assumed that it had been this painting that Steffie had purchased in an auction in Amsterdam, from which she had found the address.

The very address she had managed to escape from that evening and Sam had come to her rescue.

This, however, she now discovered, was not the case.

The painting Steffie bought was the one which had been found hanging in an hotel room in Paris, discovered by a guest who thought it was a genuine Gauguin.

Further research had deemed it the real thing, but Sophie knew that this wasn't so.

So, then re visiting her research, she discovered that the painting having belonged to this Miss Steenwoude, also called 'Woman on the shore', was not the one she originally thought it was. This one was also put up for auction, remarkably at more or less the same time, but in Groningen, not Amsterdam.

Later that Monday evening, pacing up and down on bare feet, the night dark and overcast, Sophie was trying to make sense of it all in her mind.

She had written these new details on her timeline.

She had been unable to find out who, if any, had purchased this second painting, the one she now believed to be the one once owned by Sam's great-grandfather, ambassador Price.

She would e-mail Sam the next day, after work.

He had contacts; he might find out who purchased it. He surely would be interested.

Sophie started to prepare her dinner and wondered where Sam was. She also remembered the information they had found about Steffie that she had travelled to Florence, why?

ROME, ITALY 5.15PM

She walked up the path, getting her keys out to unlock the door when she felt that there was someone behind her.

Turning she was stunned to see two men there. Two Italian policemen.

And judging by the look on their faces, she knew the game was up.

No way out. Even if there was, she found that her feet had stopped.

They felt like leaden blocks, and she couldn't move.

Then another person appeared.

Stepped between the two.

A face she knew. A man she knew.

Eduardo.

Once again she had become complacent. Once again she had been confident, self-assured and in control of everything.

She should have learned, should have taken heed, should have been always careful.

That time, nearly four years ago now, when the woman from the auction house in Paris, Miss Sophie Pontiac, had telephoned her with regard to the Gauguin and the need for further documentation as to how she had come by it had taken her by surprise.

After all, it had been sold as a known Gauguin when she had purchased it in Amsterdam.

She should have listened to Roberto who, at the time, and after viewing the painting and recognising it as the copy he had made way back in 1946, had told her, hang on to it for a few years, then sell it on.

But she had been disappointed, had believed this to be the real article, the genuine Gauguin, for she had bought it with only one purpose in mind.

She felt it would hold a clue as to the whereabouts of the diamonds.

To discover it was the fake that Roberto had painted was a blow.

It wasn't long after that day that Roberto took himself off to stay with his sister on the Mediterranean coast as his health was worsening.

The phone call from the French woman, had thrown her into a panic. She had not conceived that there would be any problem selling it.

She decided that day, to leave the house in the Parisian suburb and travel back to Amsterdam to the place she had stayed before whilst in the city for the auction. One of Roberto's many contacts. She had also, cleverly, she thought, given that as her own address.

That had, in the end, been a mistake, for it was how Miss Pontiac, nearly four years later, who had found her.

Again, in a panic, she had told the young man, also living in that house, to deal with her.

Another mistake, for the French woman had managed to escape.

So once again, she found herself on the run.

Timing was of the essence.

Rapidly packing her case, she scrolled online and bought a ticket for the first flight to anywhere in mainland Europe, then ordering a taxi heading for Schiphol Airport.

Unbeknown to her, a man named Samuel Price came to the French woman's aid, just as she was checking in for her flight. A flight to Florence, Italy.

During her time in Paris, when Roberto had provided her with false documentation, she had set up a bank account, having thus far only been able to make any transactions in cash.

It was now an opportunity to establish a credit line.

With this now available, she had not only been able to purchase the Gauguin, but now also, once again on the run, had been able to quickly secure travel and accommodation.

She felt she could breathe at last as the plane taxied along the runway and lifted up into the evening sky.

Her self-assurance fully returned, when she had cleared customs and was in a taxi heading for the railway station.

Less than ninety minutes later she seated herself in first class.

The train pulled out, leaving Florence behind and heading south, destination Rome.

Roberto had contacts throughout Europe. He had a list of names which she had obtained a couple of years ago now. It had proved helpful in the Dutch capital, it gave a couple of options in Rome, Roberto's hometown.

That blasted French woman, Steffie thought, not for the first time, why had she, after all that time, decided to search for her?

She must lie low for a while. She promised herself, she swore, she would not get complacent again.

She would be on guard, careful, at all times.

She obviously hadn't been.

Eduardo looked directly into her eyes.

Defiantly she looked straight back. But only for a moment, then broke eye contact and looked at the path beneath her feet.

How? She wondered, had he found her?

She looked up.

He had gone.

She finally got her feet to move and walked up to the waiting policemen.

It had been seven years since she left Cape Town.

The Italian police contacted the Dutch police who, in turn, notified the French police, and they contacted the Spanish police.

Still a South African resident and a wanted criminal, it was to there she was going to be transported.

Seven years after the crime she had committed there, she was charged and sentenced.

Steffie Baertjens was no longer.

Lucie van Doorn was found guilty and imprisoned.

Long before all that, in fact the morning after the Italian police had taken her into custody, the French police informed Sophie.

She in turn sent off an e-mail to Petra in America, and was about to send another message to Sam, when her phone rang.

HALIFAX

WEDNESDAY MORNING 8ᵀᴴ MAY

Sam sat comfortably in the first-class lounge at the airport in Halifax.

He had arrived early, checked in, then had sat himself down, laptop open in front of him, a coffee and two croissants nearby.

He had been busy. This was a good thing, fixing his attention and mind on something other than what he was feeling in his heart.

The e-mail he received from Sophie, whilst standing in the doorway of the goods shed, watching the soft rain, had kick started his reaction. Things to be done!

'Sorry Joe,' he apologised, 'have to go'

Sam then tidied up the lunch things, left all the prints with Joe saying he would get them back at some point, shook the old man's hand and left the goods yard.

Upon his return to his apartment, he first contacted Donald McGrath, curator of the Maritime Museum in Halifax.

They had finished cleaning the painting, which was now ready for collection, and Sam informed him, though not in detail, as to what had occurred, to hang on to the painting for a few days, and also that he hadn't forgotten to see if the museum might acquire it.

Donald had, in his enthusiastic way, told Sam it had been a pleasure and thanked him several times.

Sam then arranged flights to New York, taking Chrissie up on her offer to have dinner and share notes. He was also looking forward to meeting Tammy, whom he had not met before.

He then set about doing research, in response to Sophie's e-mail.

Just over three hours later, in the early evening, Sam sat back and looked at the formulated information he had gathered.

It confirmed what Sophie had discovered.

There had been indeed two paintings, two 'Woman on the shore' works by Gauguin, being auctioned at practically the same time, in almost opposite sides of the country.

The one in Amsterdam, purchased by Miss Steffie Baertjens and subsequently ending up in the auction room in Paris where he had first seen it and queried it, proved, after further investigations, to be a forgery.

Then, there was one in the northern city of Groningen, catalogued as a copy, but it seemed now to very likely be the genuine article.

Sam found out the relevant details about this auction as she had asked him to.

Too late to call now, he would ring her in the morning.

Sam checked the board. Still plenty of time before boarding would begin.

He drank some of his coffee and then ate the first croissant.

Sam smiled as he thought back to his phone call to Sophie earlier this morning.

She had been very excited, and before he could give her the information he had found, she told him about the capture of Steffie Baertjens in Rome.

Sophie had then gone on to tell all about Petra and her going back to be with her ex-husband in America.

Having listened patiently, and with interest, Sam sensed she had stopped to take a breath, and told her of his findings.

He gave her the name of the man, a young student, who had bought the painting in 2015 and gave her the name of the university where had had been studying at the time, as they would likely be able to give her his address.

Sophie said she would follow this up immediately.

Sam finished his breakfast, shut down and packed his laptop, and got ready to board his flight to Boston. From there he had a connecting flight to New York.

NEW YORK
WEDNESDAY AFTERNOON 8ᵗᴴ MAY

Christina Small, better known to her friends as Chrissie, felt surprisingly nervous.

She checked the board again.

His flight was on time and due to land in fifteen minutes.

Though her friend, Tammy, often teased her about her feelings for Sam, Tammy was not wrong. She did have feelings for him.

Nothing had developed before, but perhaps he hadn't been ready then. How would they get on now. Could a spark that she felt was there, ignite at last?

He had responded quickly to her invitation to come to New York.

Would he have feelings for her? Had he met someone else?

She was forty-seven. Though she'd had several short-term relationships over the years, nothing that really blossomed into a loving and long-term relationship.

Sam was kind. He was caring and he was a gentleman.

She checked the board again and to her surprise the time had just gone quickly because it showed that the flight had landed.

Just breathe and act normal, she told herself. If something was to happen, let him make the first move.

Changing her focus in her mind, she wondered about the project he was working on that connected a painting he was commissioned to sell to the two paintings in Tammy's hallway.

She and Tammy had taken a good look at them, even took them off the wall to see the back, but found no name, no identification, nothing at all.

What was he working on? He sounded keen to come and share notes, and he had accepted her offer to have dinner.

Was that a sign? Was that hope she could build on?

She blew out her cheeks. Why was she so nervous. Come on girl, get a grip, pull yourself together, she admonished herself.

Sam spotted her. Saw her smile. Quickened his pace, then with his free arm, the other holding onto his suitcase, he hugged her, then kissed her on the cheek.

'Good to see you Chrissie,' he said, smiling.

'You too' she answered back, kissing his cheek.

'Come on, Tammy is dying to meet you.'

The view from her large living room overlooking Central Park was breathtaking. Taking in this vast panorama, Sam stood there. He had been introduced to Tammy, shown to his guest room, the apartment had a total of five bedrooms, been given a quick tour, and now drank in the view.

He asked' 'So, this was Rosemary's?'

'Yes, can you believe it? It took me some time to grasp it all,' the petite blonde replied.

Her hair was cut short, she had very clear blue eyes and was now an astute business woman and qualified chef.

Chrissie, in the cab from the airport, had told Sam all about her.

'You saw the paintings? As we came in? Chrissie and I did take a look at them, but found no labels, no signature, nothing.'

Sam pulled himself away from the window, entered the hallway where they hung side by side.

Looking at the size and length of the hallway, he said to Tammy, 'You know, this third one should really be here as well, three in a row would look truly great.'

'Is it for sale?' she asked.

'Not yet. Things to be sorted out,' Sam answered, studying the large paintings on the wall, then turned to look at Tammy, and said,' but I will see what I can do because, they actually do belong together. The one I am investigating, is titled, "Ochtend storm", meaning, morning storm, looking at these two, this one on the left here, is in the evening also depicting stormy weather, the other one is clearly in the day, and the weather is calm, I see them as a set, morning, day and night. May I take them down?'

Sam first took one, then the other and carried them over to the dining table where Tammy had placed a lightweight blanket for protection.

The girls were right, there were no labels and this Sam discovered, was because the backing on these painting had been replaced.

With Tammy's permission and a little box of tools she produced for him, he carefully unscrewed the frames, noting that these weren't the originals ones either.

With his trusty pencil torch, he examined the bottom left-hand corner on both paintings.

Suddenly something else made sense.

On the painting which belonged to Nico Rozzini, he had, with the help of Mr Nugent, taken the frame off to discover on the back, very faintly, written in pencil in the bottom left-hand corner, a notation.

He thought at first that it had read, the number 13, followed by, what he found so exciting that day, the name. A name he knew, that of Christoffer Rosenborg.

What he realised now, is that it wasn't the number 13, but 1-3, for these two paintings lying face down on the dining table were number 2-3 and 3-3, both also followed by the name Christoffer Rosenborg.

As the ladies were close at hand, practically one on each shoulder, watching him work with interest, he explained.

'Christoffer Rosenborg is a name that you will have heard me talk about Chrissie,' to which she nodded. 'He is the chap who must have purchased these at auction, in Rotterdam in the year 1762, and later that same year, sold them to a Charlie Parker in Boston.'

'Are they by the same artist you think?' Chrissie asked.

'These two don't have the labels that the other one had. The original backing on these have been removed, but the pencil notations confirm that they belong together, and are therefore also painted by the same artist, by Jan Porcellis.'

'I don't want to sell these' Tammy said, as Sam was putting the frames back onto them, 'but I would like to find out about buying the other one. Also, I don't know why my great-grandfather was keen to buy them that day, incredibly at the same auction where Chrissie's grandfather was, and I have no knowledge as to who this Beatrice Parker was, sorry.'

'That's okay' Sam answered, 'but I will do my best to get you the third painting.

Sam hung the paintings back in the hallway.
    'So, Mr Price, as you are taking Chrissie to dinner this evening, you can tell her all about what you are working on. I get the feeling it's intriguing'

Sam, in the process of hanging the second painting, failed to notice the dig that Chrissie, blushing a little, gave Tammy, who was broadly smiling, with her elbow.

'I have an idea that you know a great restaurant?' Sam said, turning and looking directly at Tammy, who was still smiling, 'Of course, best in town, and, it's on me.'

The now thirty-six-year-old Tammy had worked hard over the past few years. The restaurant she had once worked in as a waitress was now hers. She had taken a management course as well as taking French cooking classes.
    The establishment, originally opened by a French couple in the mid-eighties, featuring mainly seafood dishes from the south of France, was now a touch better in class.
    Tammy, with her love of Paris, had, after discovering that it was only just surviving, made radical changes, giving the place a facelift, and, with a change of direction, chose the French capital as her source for inspiration.
    She changed the name and registered it as 'La Petit Tresor', the small treasure.

The décor was Parisian art deco, the colours were a mixture of vibrant and muted shades. The menu was small, enabling her to really do all courses very well.

Tammy changed the menu every month, with the exception of the favourites, and, judging by the attendance, business was good as the restaurant was full.

Chrissie told Sam how hard Tammy had worked and studied, how this place had been favourably mentioned in various magazines, and that Tammy had won an award as well.

They sat in a far corner.

The window by their side overlooked the sidewalk and road that ran parallel with Central Park.

Sam studied the menu, quickly saw what he wanted, and looked across the table at Chrissie.

Whereas Ally was altogether stunning, Chrissie was attractive.

He liked her face. It was a kind and loving face.

He recalled when he had first met her, in Boston.

Remembering her excitement as she had found something in her grandfather's diary that day, in her house. How he had watched her, as she, with her bare feet and toes that were curling and uncurling on the carpet, had been so focused on her laptop.

With a slight sigh he also remembered how he had felt that day.

Yet, a few days later, when they had been in Genoa, he had purposefully remained at a distance.

Too afraid to let his emotions show?

Now, here he was, with her. Dinner.

The atmosphere was good, music from the twenties and thirties playing softly in the background.

After showering and changing for the evening, he and Chrissie had casually walked from the apartment to the restaurant.

Tammy had left quite some time earlier to make sure everything was ready for the evening service.

A waitress came and they ordered.

Earlier, when he was again taking in the view from the vast window on the 28th floor of Tammy's apartment, he heard Chrissie approaching.

He turned around and smiled. Chrissie was wearing a pale green dress, reaching to just below the knees, stockinged feet into a pair of dark green shoes and she had on a matching open cardigan. Her blond hair was curled and swept back on one side.

'Wow, you look lovely,' he said. 'I feel a bit under dressed now' smiling and looking down at what he himself was wearing. Black denim trouser, a patterned shirt, a plain soft leather jacket and shoes of the same beige colour.

'You'll pass in a crowd,' she said, smiling and then, 'well, let's go, shall we?'

Sam helped her on with her jacket and they left the apartment.

It was Tammy herself who brought them their starters, not missing an opportunity to wink and smile at Chrissie. Sam noticed it.

Just before tucking in, Sam picked up his glass. They had chosen a red wine, Chrissie picking up on what Sam was about to do, picked up her glass. They chinked together and Sam said, 'Here's to adventures in art,' and smiled.

Conversation was casual, infrequent, but the pauses in between as they enjoyed their starters, was comfortable.

At one point their eyes met. Her light green eyes seemingly questioning him.

He smiled and could understand her look.

He was questioning himself.

It was time, to share what had happened, so much, and all in a week and a day.

'I've been working on this commission,' he began, as they awaited their main course, 'the third painting.'

Chrissie was all attention, she felt as though something had happened, something romantic she feared.

'Well, something unexpected happened,' Sam said, taking a sip of red wine and looking into her eyes,' I witnessed an abduction.'

At this point her eyes widened. She was about to react, but Sam pressed on.

'It's a long story, but I was able to help, In the right place at the right time and all that. Her name is Alison, prefers to be called Ally.'

At which point Chrissie felt her tummy churn slightly. He had met another woman, he was in love with someone else, she thought, but tried to remain calm, She didn't say anything for fear her voice would give away her emotion, and continued to listen.

Sam went on to explain about the daughter that had been taken from this woman

and how she was now, after ten years, reunited with her.

He told her about the owner of the painting and that he shot and killed himself and related the story of the corrupt police officers and other culprits in this matter.

'Thing is this, Chrissie,' he said, taking another sip of wine and still looking directly into her eyes, 'time has passed since Sonja died. But I am still, somewhat floundering, unsure of my feelings. I meet a woman, think, well, you know, I have feelings and so on, but then I question those feelings, afraid of them perhaps, or not wanting any disappointment, or questioning whether I'm actually good enough, or ready enough.'

Sam paused to take another sip from the glass he held in his hand, and still holding Chrissie's gaze, continued, 'There is this bakery in the street below my apartment in Rotterdam, a favourite shop. I go in and there is this lovely glass cabinet, with a wonderful selection of cakes. Mocha, strawberry, almond, with cream or without, a selection of biscuits, and I just love biscuits.

Anyway, the thing is, I can't just order everything and eat them all. I choose one, well, maybe two, then, the following day or the day after, I might choose a different one, or two.'

Sam put the glass down, took hold of Chrissie's hand that was resting on the table, then looking once again into her eyes, he said, 'The thing is, I can't just look at a beautiful woman, and say, oh yes, I'll have that one today, then meet another woman and say, oh, I'll have this one today. Love is precious, love is special, love is not just for today, love is far more than just being attracted to someone,'

Sam held on to Chrissie's hand and as she didn't speak and was totally focused on him, Sam sighed inwardly, but knew he wanted to tell Chrissie the story.

'On the day that she died, that morning, she whispered to me, holding my hand, just as I am holding your hand now, and she said to me, "Go and find someone to love." Those words are with me, almost every day, and I have never told that to anyone before.'

Sam paused. His eyes were tearing up.

Chrissie gripped his hand tightly for a moment. Her heart was thumping in her chest. Her tummy was now in quite some turmoil and her throat felt dry.

With her free hand, she reached for her glass, took a sip, then, looking into his eyes, managed to ask, 'And, have you found someone to love?'

Sam smiled at her.

He could feel the tears in his eyes, but it didn't bother him.

Have I found someone to love? He asked himself. He had thought so, but being with Chrissie, and opening up to her, felt very nice, very natural, secure.

'Well, this is it, Chrissie, I'm not the type of guy who will ...just ...'

'I know you're a kind and caring, a gentleman' Chrissie interrupted, then heard herself ask, 'so, this Ally?'

'She is catching up, not having seen her daughter for ten years. It hasn't been easy. It is important for her to establish that true mother and daughter bond. I could see that, I insisted on it',

Tammy again appeared at their table and served them their main meal. She couldn't help notice the tears in Sam's eyes and that they had been, until her arrival, holding hands.

She looked at Chrissie. The said, her voice barely above a whisper, 'I hope you enjoy.'

They both said, thank you, in unison.

For a while, Chrissie didn't speak, starting on her meal she thought things through in her mind. He had insisted she go and be with her daughter, did that mean, she wanted to be with him, or he with her?

'Mmm, this is really nice, 'Sam said, after a while 'So, when are you going back to Boston?'

Chrissie looked up at him, then answered, 'Day after tomorrow. You're going back tomorrow aren't you?'

'Yes, I have to follow up on a few things with regard this painting, also still have some research to do about how Tammy's great-grandfather fits in with the Parker family, in particular Beatrice Parker.'

They ate some more in silence. Chrissie was aware that the conversation was back to, normal, but was still thinking about how he had opened up to her and told her something he had never shared.

EPILOGUE;

SAM'S APARTMENT, MONCTON

WEDNESDAY EVENING 15ᵀᴴ MAY

It had been a warm day. He had driven to Harris, had, with the permission of DS Saunders, visited Debra Rozzini, Nico's widow.

He stood by the countertop in the kitchen, waiting for the water to boil in order the make the last coffee for the day.

Already a week ago, he thought as the kettle automatically clicked off. A week ago he had enjoyed dinner with Chrissie.

Pouring water into the mug, he reflected on that evening, when he had opened up to her, had told her the words his late wife had spoken to him.

Taking the drink to the lounge, Sam sat himself on the couch and looked at the two folders that he had placed on the coffee table.

He put the mug down onto a coaster.

'Right' he said aloud to himself, 'time for a debriefing.' then smiled at his own silliness.

He slid the first folder, on the front cover of which he had written a heading, 'Gauguin/Porcellis' towards him.

Opening it, he took out the sheets within, and, not being able to sit still just now, he took a careful sip of the coffee, then got up and walked around the lounge.

With many things on his mind, he spoke to himself, 'One thing at a time Sam, one thing at a time,' then began to read his findings.

Sophie had successfully tracked down the purchaser of the Gauguin, the one that was auctioned off in Groningen.

She had informed Sam that he was still a student at the university and not only liked the painting, but had dreams of one day going to Tahiti where this work had been painted.

She had told the student those dreams could soon be true as the painting was very likely a genuine Gauguin.

Sophie offered to sell it in Paris on his behalf to which he agreed.

Once back in Paris it was soon confirmed that it was indeed a genuine work by the artist, the real, 'Woman on the shore'.

Sophie furthermore had some additional information. On the back of this painting she had found a label. A small label, with neat, what Sophie described as a woman's, handwriting. A name. Victoria Thompson.

Sophie suggested that he might check through his great-grandfather's journals to see if the ambassador knew this woman.

Lastly, in this long e-mail that she had sent him, she wished him well, told him she missed him and asked when would she see him again.

He had written back, told her he would look into the name, but that he most likely would not be back until August or September. Then wished her well and said that he missed her too.

Sam bent down to take another few sips of his drink, then read the next heading, the painter Porcellis.

His research had discovered that there had been a total of three painting that had been purchased at auction in Rotterdam in the year 1762 by Christoffer Rosenborg, who then sold them, later that same year, to Charlie Parker in Boston.

Two of them, he had found out, thanks to the good memory of the two old men, the current proprietors of Franck Huysen & Son auction house in Boston, were sold to a Percivald Quinton.

These now hung side by side in the apartment in New York that Tammy had inherited from her grandmother, Rosemary, daughter of Percivald.

With Nico Rozzini having shot himself and brother Julien facing a lengthy time in prison, the mine and all the properties of CP Holdings now belonged to Nico's wife who he had visited earlier today.

She had no idea of the existence of Theresa, daughter of her brother-in-law, nor had ever heard of Alison Hudson, until the police had informed her of this.

In fact it had been DS Saunders who had explained the situation and had told of Sam's involvement.

She had been friendly and kind when he called. He felt for her, a mother with two teenage children who would have to come to terms with what had happened, as he left.

He was also most grateful for her, for she had insisted that he keep the painting.

Upon his arrival home, Sam had contacted the curator of the Maritime Museum in Halifax, the jovial Donald McGrath, apologizing, but explaining about the other two paintings in New York, and that this one should go there.

Sam suggested that it was very possible, to at some point, have all three of them for an exhibition.

He told Donald he would send a photo of the other two to him, and if possible could he get a frame put on that would match the other two?

This had been received heartily, and when Sam said he would come and collect the painting, Donald had offered to frame it, properly secure it and have it shipped to the address in New York.

Sam agreed and told him the museum would receive a healthy donation in the near future.

Finishing his drink, Sam put the first folder down and picked up the second.

This one he had titled; 'Ally/Chrissie/Sophie.

He briefly wondered why he had written them in that order, then opened up the folder.

The top of the single sheet of paper he had written; 'Affairs of the heart'

Sam smiled.

As almost always, he had music playing in the background. Though usually he was partial to a biscuit or three, he had eaten less these past weeks.

Was he thinking of his figure? His fitness? Or was he aiming to impress?

Alison Hudson. Ally.

Tall, blond and very attractive.

He had spoken to her earlier in the week.

She and her daughter, Theresa, who preferred to be called Terri, were slowly bonding.

They had decided to go to Hawaii together and were in fact about to leave for the airport. Some time away from it all would help them bond, she had said. She also said she missed him.

He said to have a great time, an important time, and that he missed her too.

Sam's ears pricked up as through the speakers the Eagles came on, and quite coincidently, it was the song, 'Take it easy'.

He stopped pacing and listened to the words, the words that had come to mind that day shortly before he left Rotterdam to travel to Canada.

Sam walked up to the stereo unit and turned up the volume.

Words that spoke of the songwriter having seven women on his mind, came through the speakers.

Then, it had been three, his late wife Sonja, Sophie and Chrissie.

Smiling, he thought, he now had four, adding Ally.

'I'm catching up,' he whispered, still smiling.

Sam sat on the couch, sheet of paper still in his hand and looked at it.

In his mind he, once again, could hear those words, 'Go and find someone to love.'

On the sheet he had just written, the three names
Sophie? Chrissie? Ally?

BOOK 3

ONE OPTION

PROLOGUE;

NEW YORK

PRESENT DAY – SATURDAY 18TH MAY

A handbag. A shiny black leather handbag. A single strap. A clasp running along the length of the top. A style from the mid-sixties. A designer bag of its day.

She knew this bag.

Tammy woke, sat upright and reached over to turn her bedside lamp on.

Just after 4am.

Why of all days should she wake early today. She didn't need to be at work until a little before lunch today.

She flung herself back down.

A dream. She had a dream.

All she could remember, was the handbag. The black leather handbag.

She knew this bag, it had belonged to her grandmother.

After a few moments she knew she wouldn't be able to get back to sleep and got up.

Ten minutes later, having showered and dressed, she was in the kitchen fixing herself a glass of orange juice and making some toast.

The black handbag.

Tammy headed into the wide corridor. When she had first arrived here, still full of awe at the size of her inheritance, she had taken in all the fittings, the décor, the furniture, the paintings on the wall and the numerous pieces of china or glass that were distributed around the vast apartment, but had not discovered a secret cupboard until some months later when she began to redecorate.

She reached the panel, pressed it inwards, heard the click, then released her hand.

A panel in the wall popped open.

Reaching around with her hand, Tammy found the light switch and put on the light, recalling the first time she had done so, wondering what this secret cupboard might hold.

She had been disappointed. Four old suitcases, a few clothes and shoes, a pair of curtains, and old chair and a broken standard lamp.

But there had also been a handbag, an old black leather handbag.

Entering the space, she found the bag, retrieved it from a shelf, then came out, switching off the light and pressing the panel shut.

Tammy paused for a moment as she looked at the paintings on the wall opposite.

Three large seascapes.

They looked wonderful together. The third painting had arrived yesterday, from the Maritime Museum in Halifax, accompanied by a letter, and all arranged by Sam.

She had the buildings maintenance man hang it for her.

All now in correct sequence too, a morning, day and evening scene.

Maybe that is why she had dreamed, Tammy wondered as she made her way to the kitchen with the handbag as the two she originally owned had been purchased by her great-grandfather, Percivald.

She placed the bag on the countertop, took a sip of her juice and then, once again, opened the bag.

Initially she had made a cursory search in the bag when she had found it, but there had been nothing inside.

More carefully now, she felt inside the bag and her heart skipped a beat when she realised that there was something there.

Discovering a zip that ran along the inside top, practically camouflaged, she unzipped it and reached inside.

An envelope. She pulled it out.

It was addressed to Rosemary, had an address on it Tammy didn't recognise, presumably where her grandmother had lived prior to this apartment.

Looking closely at the stamp and franking, she noted it was dated 1946.

Tammy retrieved the letter from the envelope.

A brief, handwritten note, which read;

'Rose,

Chap you came back with from Belgium, Bastiaan Bouten, had him checked out.

The bounder is married, dealt with him, sent him packing back to his homeland.'

Then at the bottom it was signed with just initials. 'P.Q.'

Percivald Quinton.

Tammy blew out her cheeks. She had learned from her grandmother's letters how her great-grandfather had not been the best of fathers to her grandmother. Not mean or bullying or anything like that, but just that he had been never there. He gave her money to do as she pleased but was rarely home.

This letter she had found reflected that. It was without affection, without love. It was business-like and cold.

At least this was the answer as to why her grandmother hadn't named the man she had, way back then, fallen in love with.

The man, whom Sam had researched and found to be a Bastiaan Bouten, very likely her grandfather, and who had shared her cabin on the ship that journey.

So, Tammy silently said to herself, rereading the short note, he was sent packing back to Belgium.

This was an interesting find. This was something she needed to tell Chrissie.

For if he went back, if he was forced back, if indeed he was a married man, well, he may have tried to retrieve …

Glancing at the clock on the wall in her kitchen, Tammy realised it would be far too early to ring.

She munched on her toast, drank some more juice and read the short note once more.

Dealt with him. What did that mean?

Chrissie needed to know; this was an important development.

He went back to Belgium, presumably back to Antwerp where her grandmother had met him.

All that time ago, seventy-four years ago!

THE PRESENT;

LOGAN INTERNATIONAL AIRPORT

BOSTON
SATURDAY 18TH MAY

Chrissie Small sat in the first-class lounge and was a little anxious.

Spring rain had unleashed upon Boston accompanied by a fierce wind from the east and the visibility was fairly low.

She wasn't anxious about that; flights were still going out on schedule.

Sipping her coffee as she waited for her flight to board, she brought to mind the call she had received earlier, from Tammy ...

'I found a letter ...' Chrissie heard after she had sleepily answered the phone with a questioning 'Hello?'

'Sorry, what?' then sitting upright in bed, realising and registering the voice being that of Tammy, 'Letter?'

After listening for a moment, trying to take in what her friend was saying, she said she would shower, fully wake up and call her back.

Then, spotting the bedside clock, realised it had just gone 6am!

Whilst showering she thought about her friend, thought about what she had found, thought about how they had met and thought about Sam.

Wearing just a bathrobe, her blond hair tied back into a ponytail, she fixed herself some breakfast, juice, tea and toast.

Outside, she noticed, it was raining lightly.

Feeling that she was now properly awake, she ate her breakfast, got dressed and called Tammy back ...

She saw her flight was ready for boarding.

After having spoken to Tammy, more alert, she had then pondered whether or not to ring Sam, or send him an e-mail.

Chrissie got up and joined the queue to board her flight to Halifax. She was anxious.

Settling herself down, it wasn't long before she drifted away in her thoughts ...

Ten days ago she had dinner with Sam in New York. She recalled how her heart had ached as he told her the story of another woman, a woman he had helped. A woman who, she could sense and see, he was fond of.

But her heart had quickened it's beat, when he told her she had gone to be with her long-lost daughter.

Her heart had quickened even more and her stomach tightened when he had taken hold of her hand.

He had then, tearfully, shared what his late wife had said to him, moments before she had passed away. Something he hadn't shared with anyone before ...

The doors closed on the plane and the crew began their ritual safety checks and procedures.

The aircraft started to move towards the runway. The wind assisted rain had eased a little.

Looking out her window, Chrissie smiled as she remembered. She had bravely asked the question, after he had shared his wife last words, had he found someone to love?

He had smiled, but not answered.

Though she had wanted to initiate a move, she was still sensing his loss, not just of his wife, but of the woman he had insisted should go alone to bond with her daughter.

Pushing further for an answer might well not be the reply she was looking for.

The dinner had resumed to a normality, a comfortable atmosphere. She enjoyed his company. They had walked back to Tammy's apartment, had shared a last coffee for the evening and as he had a very early flight the following day, he retired for the night. He had briefly kissed her goodnight, on her lips.

The following morning he was amicable, there was no tension between them and again he kissed her on the lips before leaving.

The engines roared into power and the plane began its run for take-off.

Chrissie sighed. Her stomach was tense. She was worried.

As the wheels released their hold on the ground and the plane soared into a rainy sky, she looked out the window and brought her mind back to earlier …

After Tammy had revealed to her what she had found, Chrissie felt it was best to e-mail Sam. Though she wanted to hear his voice, she was a little reluctant to talk to him, afraid her voice either might break or that she might say something for which the time was not right.

Going about her day it wasn't until lunchtime when she first became a little concerned that he had not replied.

Pacing her living room for a bit, she decided to call.

That's when she became more concerned, became anxious. He didn't answer.

Something was wrong. Something had happened, she was sure of it.

The case he had been working on involved some desperate criminals.

What had happened?

Where was Sam?

As the plane flew over the bay and swung to the north, Chrissie thought back to the very first time she saw him.

On her doorstep. In search of a piece of art.

One that her grandfather had purchased.

THE PAST;

PERIOD I

PART I
THE YEAR 1938

Professor Edward Small, known better as Eddie, wandered around the auction room. A rectangular room, dark wooden beams, high ceilings, three windows on one wall high up, which had been shuttered closed.

Overhead lights, three rows of four large domed lamps brought bright light upon the many things on display.

There were several long benches, tables and glass counters placed on the well-polished wooden floor set up in sections so as to be more easily accessed and viewed by the fairly large crowd of people.

An estimated one hundred and twenty.

The fifty-five-year-old professor had been drawn here for one thing only. The advertised miniature, possibly, as stated, by the classical artist of miniatures, Giulio.

He had already spotted it, displayed in one of five glass cabinets, and taken a look.

It looked good. There was no doubt he wanted it.

The small card beside it stated an estimated date of circa 1600, which the professor knew would be in the right region for it to be by Giulio who had died in 1578. He also knew that ivory was very hard to precisely date.

Wandering around some more he checked out a few more items.

The auction would begin soon and when that time came, everyone moved to an adjacent room where rows of benches were set up facing a rostrum.

He took his seat. His registration card at the ready.

Also on the card had been the name of the seller, a Mrs Zeta Bell, from Halifax, Nova Scotia. He wondered how she had acquired it and what she could tell about it.

Four days earlier Zeta Bell had arrived at the auction house.

A reputable firm, she had been told, called Franck Huysen & Son.

Her husband, Jonathan, was in hospital undergoing treatment for cancer.

Already they had sold several of their belongings, for the medical costs were inhibitive. They had also received funds from friends and family for which they were grateful.

Zeta had taken her husband to Boston for specialist treatment. The prognosis was good.

But with some funds still to raise she had made up her mind to sell a very dear possession.

Her husband didn't know, would probably not be pleased, but sell it she must.

They had no children, only each other.

The painted miniature she had been given by her father, just had to be sold.

Whilst the piece was being looked at, Zeta came across a box of odds and ends, and rummaging through, she spotted some, what looked to be, journals.

Three of them.

Picking out one, she flicked though and gasped as she began to read.

So much was she focused on what she was reading, the auctioneer had to cough several times in order to get her attention.

The value of her item was much higher than she expected and after signing some papers, she asked about the journals.

As they were deemed of little value, she was given them.

On the day of the auction she arrived in a buoyant mood as the operation the day before had been deemed successful and her husband would fully recover.

Finding a seat she wondered who might buy her miniature.

She had never before been to an auction. It was rather exciting.

The auctioneer had a booming voice that Zeta felt could be heard three blocks away!

The lot number came up. Zeta watched.

Hoping and praying that it would reach the reserve price.

There were several bidders and the price went up and up, then some dropped away and only two bidders remained.

Then only one.

Sold!

Zeta was thrilled.

She took note of the number of the man who had purchased the item, then studied him as he was seated only four people away from her.

He was a small man, had a mop of grey hair, and wore horn-rimmed glasses. He wore a tweed jacket and corduroy trousers.

She was thankful as the price had gone well over the reserve.

It would now comfortably cover the remaining medical and accommodation costs whilst here in Boston.

Professor Small was thrilled.

Exiting the auction house with his purchase, he walked towards the Bay, passed by Faneuil Hall and not much later was sat in his favourite eatery with a bowl of lobster bisque and a chunk of brown bread.

He looked at the item he had purchased. Studied it back and front. Indeed no signature to be found on this beautifully painted miniature.

The scene was that of the building of the Tower of Babel.

The details were exquisite.

He was sure he held a piece of art made by the classic master of miniatures, Giulio Clovio.

Admiring it that day, he would not have even remotely considered that eight years later he would travel to Europe with it and not be heard from again.

THE PRESENT;

NOVA SCOTIA

SATURDAY 18TH MAY

Chrissie had booked a rental at the airport and drove towards Moncton.

She realised, only after she had been mid-air for a while that she did not have Sam's address.

But she knew someone who would surely know.

She recalled Sam's story about the abduction, thinking that he probably left out many details, but recalls him mentioning the name of the police detective.

Saunders.

So using her tablet she punched up the details of Moncton, New Brunswick, and saw on the map on her screen that there were two police stations.

Thinking back he had spoken of the railway station, and the goods yard.

This was helpful. She noted the police station nearest to that location and took note of the address.

Upon arrival she had once more tried to call, but it rang a couple of times before cutting out.

She was getting more and more anxious.

Where was he?

Entering the town she followed the satellite navigation system in the rental car and it wasn't long before she was parked right outside the police station.

Walking into the reception lobby a little before 4 o'clock, she asked the man behind the counter, 'Hi, I'm looking for an officer Saunders?'

Detective Sergeant Karen Saunders, of the Royal Canadian Mounted Police, walked in at that moment and heard her name.

'I'm DS Saunders,' she said, walking across the lobby.

'Hello,' Chrissie answered, turning and then said, 'I'm Chrissie Small, I am a friend of Sam, Sam Price, I believe you know him, he mentioned you.

The thing is, he's not answering my e-mails, his phone keeps cutting out, and I'm worried that something has happened to him ...'

Thirty-nine-year-old Karen focused her brown eyes on the woman before her, saw the genuine concern and said, 'Come with me. Have you checked out his place?'

'Eh no, I felt it best to just come straight here.'

'Okay, come with me. Your concern worries me, let's check it out.'

Chrissie followed the detective and got into the police car which was parked just in front of her own rental.

'So,' the detective asked, as she put her flashing lights on and took off rapidly, 'you are a relative, friend?'

Chrissie had only just clicked her seat belt in place when the police car sped away.

'A friend, good friend, he helped me find my grandfather.

'Sam is good at helping people it seems,' the detective said, throwing Chrissie a sideways glance before taking several bends and turns rather quickly. The flashing lights helped clear the road. She did not however use the sirens.

'He told me about this woman whose daughter had been taken from her?'

'Miss Alison Hudson,' the detective answered, 'some bad people involved, which is why I too am worried that something might have happened to him ...'

With squealing tyres they arrived.

Chrissie trying hard to keep pace with the detective as she entered a lobby, then not bothering with the lift, took a door to the stairs and bounded up.

Chrissie arrived as she pounded on the door several times, but then deftly, with some tool she had at the ready, opened the door.

'Stay behind me,' she said, then taking her gun out, entered.

'Stay right here,' Chrissie was told.

Detective Sergeant Saunders, knowing the apartment's layout, moved quickly and almost silently, going down a hallway and coming back into the foyer area through a different door which startled Chrissie.

'No-one home, come on, we will check it out carefully,' the detective said, 'along the corridor here are two bedrooms, try not to touch anything but see if you spot anything unusual, I am going down via the back stairs to the garage, see if his van is there or not.'

And with that she turned and left Chrissie to it.

The detective was also worried. This didn't help her own feelings. Carefully Chrissie opened the door to the first room, everything looked tidy.

She was just about to leave, what she surmised was the guest bedroom, when she almost bumped into the detective.

'His van is there, very worrying' she said, gasping slightly for breath as she had run quickly up the metal staircase that connected the apartment to the garage below.

'Nothing seems out of place here,' Chrissie answered.

They both entered the next room. The master bedroom.

A quick look around found nothing unusual.

Chrissie walked out of the bedroom and into the kitchen-diner area and from there through an archway into the lounge.

Then, sniffing the air, she said, 'I smell smoke, cigarette smoke. Sam doesn't smoke.'

'No, you're right, he doesn't. I don't think he would allow anyone to smoke in here. It also means something else,' the detective said, sniffing the air and joining the other woman in the living room.

Chrissie turned to the detective. 'He was here, not that long ago,' Chrissie said.

'I tried to ring him this morning, e-mailed him, this morning, not like him not to reply, I guess he must have been here, certainly yesterday.'

Detective Sergeant Saunders nodded, then pushed some buttons on her phone.

Whilst she was talking rapidly on her phone, Chrissie called Tammy in New York.

'I'm here, and Sam's definitely missing. I'll keep you informed, I'm with the police at the moment.'

Listening for a bit, she then said, 'Will do,' and ended the call.

'A friend, Miss Small?' the detective asked.

'Close friend, in New York,' Chrissie answered, 'and please, call me Chrissie.'

'Karen,' the detective said, extending her hand.

Chrissie took it and as they shook hands, Karen's phone rang.

'Okay, yes, hang on, 'the detective quickly took a pen and notebook from the top pocket of her jacket, wrote down a number then said, 'Get hold of forensics, get a couple of bodies here, as in straight away, okay?'

'Are you from New York?' Karen asked, finishing one call and making another.

'I flew in from Boston,' Chrissie answered.

'Miss Hudson? it's Detective Sergeant Saunders.'

Chrissie took another walk around the apartment. She was worried.

    The detective was worried.

    Where was Sam?

    The whole place looked very tidy, too tidy?

    She entered the kitchen area, being careful not to touch anything.

'Miss Small?' Karen called out, coming through the archway.

    'Got hold of Miss Hudson. She's the woman who Sam helped, well rescued really, she is flying here tomorrow. She was staying here for a while, will have a better idea if anything is missing, she did say that there is ...' and the detective walked over to one of the kitchen benches, straight to the large jar with the word 'flour' on it, took the lid off and peered inside, 'a spare set of keys in the flour jar' and with that, reached her hand inside and pulled the bunch of keys from it.

'So, this Miss Hudson,' Chrissie asked, following the detective into the kitchen.

    'What is she like?'

Karen turned and faced Chrissie, 'A stunningly attractive, tall, leggy blonde, worse luck,' she answered, smiling, 'but she is also a very nice woman, and had gone through a rough patch ...'

'Sam mentioned her. I think he had feelings for her,' Chrissie answered, 'but he told me he had insisted she needed to be with her daughter?'

'Yes, her daughter was taken from her, illegally, ten years ago ...'

The doorbell rang.

'Stay here,' the detective said, then taking her gun from its holster, made her way to the door.

She came back followed by two women, both carrying small cases.

'Let's go. We'll go back to the station. Leave them to it. Once they are done, you can come back here. I have no doubt that Sam would be okay with that.'

'That's sounds good, thank you,' Chrissie answered, preparing to leave the apartment with the detective, who, at the last moment, threw the bunch of keys to one of her forensic colleagues.

Getting back into the police car Chrissie noticed it had begun to rain lightly.

Though still worried about Sam, she felt comforted to be in the presence of this detective, who certainly seemed very determined to solve the mystery.

She thought back, more relaxed now as Karen drove at a sensible speed, to the call from Tammy about the letter she had found which had prompted her to call Sam in the first place. The letter from Tammy's great-grandfather, Percivald Quinton.

THE PAST;

PERIOD 1
PART 2

BOSTON
THE YEAR 1938

Beatrice Parker held the hand of her four-year-old son, Joshua, and watched the proceedings from the back of the auction room.

The young lad watched with interest, though a little apprehensively as the man at the front, standing there with a sort of hammer in his hand, had such a loud voice.

He winced every time the hammer came down with a bang, along with a very loud 'Sold'.

Beatrice had four lots in the auction. Three pieces of fine furniture, sold separately, and one lot of two large paintings.

It was going well. The pieces of furniture featured early on and sold well.

But it was particularly the paintings that she was looking forward to appearing.

The lot came. Two large oil paintings.

They were shown. Both featuring scenes of ships at sea.

The bidding commenced and was running along nicely.

Beatrice smiled, when all of a sudden, a bid was shouted out, a sudden and big increase. There were no challenges. Sold.

The man who had stood up to make this bid, turned and smiled.

Beatrice smiled back.

He said he would see her right. He had.

His name was Percivald Quinton and way back in the year 1924 he had come to the financial rescue of her then husband. Nathaniel.

Fourteen years ago.

Nathaniel had been a handsome, debonair and funny man. He had swept her off her feet. She was happy.

His family was sound, a prosperous and influential family.

Upon his marriage, Charlie Parker the fourth, his grandfather, had deemed the young man now to be settled and capable of running the business in Boston.

Nathaniel's father was not on the scene.

A womaniser, gambler and often drunk, he had moved down south, Chicago was thought to be the place to where he escaped.

However the move to hand everything over to Nathaniel proved costly.

Less than six months into their marriage and running the family business, a quite large concern, with in the main retail and shipping businesses, Nathaniel wanted to have a taste of Europe. He had heard tales of fabulous women, wonderful theatres and top-class casinos.

As a top business man, he felt he ought to experience this, in order to pick up some ideas on improving the company ventures.

This was his excuse. When he arrived in Monte Carlo, the temptation was too much. It was a case of the son not falling very far from the apple tree.

He gambled and lost.

Lost it all.

But someone had been watching, observing and waiting.

And at the right moment, walked over and stood beside Nathaniel, who at that time sat slumped, totally defeated, and desperate.

Percivald Quinton bent down and spoke softly. Introducing himself and outlining a plan.

That was fourteen years ago.

Twenty-six-year-old Nathaniel returned home like a dog with its tail between his legs.

The deal Percivald had made was simple.

Nathaniel would work the business. Carry on as if nothing had changed.

But Percivald had drawn up documents and became a silent partner.

Seventy percent of all profits, would come to him.

Seventy percent!

Nathaniel bucked up. The devastation of the loss had sparked a fire.

He had seen the light, though he kept the whole affair a secret.

His hard work paid off.

The company even grew under his leadership.

But Nathaniel knew that the more he made a profit, the more Percivald would get.

Many years later, not long after their first child was born. Nathaniel decided he could no longer keep the secret.

He wrote a long letter to his wife, revealing all, and left the house. It was assumed he had gone to Chicago. He was not heard from again.

Beatrice was left, literally, holding the baby.

Charlie Parker the fourth had passed by now. She had the company on her shoulders and a baby at her breast.

Beatrice contacted Percivald Quinton.

Now four years on, things were about to change again.

The Parker company in Boston was to be sold.

The house and other assets. All to be sold.

Beatrice had contacted the family in Harris, Canada, and they had been more than willing to have them come up there.

Eventually it would be her son, Joshua, who would inherit the mining company there, which he would sell, at the age of seventy-five, to Nico Rozzini

Percivald had told Beatrice he would see her right financially.

Though he owned the company, he said he would sell some furniture and the two paintings on her behalf.

He had already decided to have the paintings for himself, but buying them through the auction was a better paper and tax trail for him. He stood up and made a sizeable offer for them.

Turning and smiling at Mrs Beatrice Parker he sat down and felt good.

Beatrice would head north for Canada five days later.

She would never see or hear from Percivald Quinton again.

THE PRESENT;

SAN FRANCISCO

SATURDAY 18TH MAY

Alison Hudson stood transfixed in her kitchen.

She had half wondered whether or not to inform her daughter of this new development, but decided against it.

She had only the previous day returned from her holiday with her daughter and had taken her daughter back to the boarding school. It was important for her to get back into a routine, and studying was important.

They had bonded well, taking in the fact that her daughter had been told she was dead and had lived with that assumption for ten years.

Their reunion had been tentative and tearful.

Alison, Ally as she preferred to be addressed, had taken her daughter for a trip to Hawaii. To get away from it all, to reflect.

To relive and share as much as she could of the past ten years.

They had not talked much at all when they were first re-united. The days following had still been tentative and Ally decided that a holiday would be a sensible move and so had made the arrangements.

They had not spoken much at all during their flight.

But the beach-side apartment was comfortable and the sound of the sea comforting.

That first evening, they sat down and through tears and many moments of silence Ally had spoken to her daughter. The ice was broken.

In those moments of silence, she just looked at the young lady before her, now eighteen, only seven when they had taken her.

566

She had been totally focused on what Terri was saying to her. Trying to drink in every moment of her life that she had missed out on.

Several times they had just cried and hugged each other, both seeing the hurt and pain in each other. Ally told of a truly positive clue, when she had located the whereabouts of her father Julien, in Halifax.

Told of her move from Vancouver to Moncton, her job at the fitness centre.

Then of her trip to Harris and the subsequent events.

Told her of Sam. How he had rescued her. Helped her.

How she had fallen in love with him.

They talked, cried and hugged until well after midnight, with the ranch slider door leading to a large porch area left open to hear the sound of the waves as they crashed onto the beach less than thirty yards away.

Terri had asked who this Sandra Pentegrass was, the woman who had written the letter of confession which she then had sent by courier to the school.

Ally, having by now remembered, recalls a girl of that name in the class below her at her school in Portland.

She had married Julien and, as she confessed, was part of the plan to have Terri taken away, part of the plan to resettle her in San Francisco, to change her name and invent the story of her real mother's death.

'But why?' Terri had asked at one point.

Ally had merely shaken her head. She couldn't, and still didn't, understand. Was it just revenge? She then wondered why it was she had chosen Hawaii as a destination for her and her daughter to bond and get to know each other.

She knew from the police that Sandra had taken a flight to Hawaii.

Did she hope to spot her, to find her, confront her.

Was she out for revenge herself?

Maybe.

Their time together, their holiday, was over.

They had walked, and shopped, they had talked and cried. They had shared and bonded.

Standing in her kitchen, all these things going through her mind, a tear rolled down her cheek.

She was alive, because of Sam.

Now he was gone, disappeared. She felt sure that someone was taking revenge.

Coming out of her reverie she wiped the tear away.

She had found the right flight connections and booked them.

An early flight to Toronto, then another to Halifax.

She picked up her phone and punched in the number for Detective Sergeant Saunders.

THE PAST;

PERIOD 2

HALIFAX, NOVA SCOTIA
THE YEAR 1940

Wrapping up the parcel securely, Zeta thought back, back to that day she had sat for a while quietly, on one of the benches in Boston common. Her husband was in hospital, getting ready for surgery. She had already, prior to them leaving Halifax for Boston, decided that there was just no other way, she had to sell the item.

Sell the dear little miniature that her father had given her just before she left San Francisco.

Listening to the story he told her about it, how it had come into her family, all that time ago.

She began to write the address on the parcel, ready for posting.

She remembers so very well the last time she had taken a good look at it, the feel of it, and the story behind it.

The miniature, the scene of the building of the tower of Babel, was so beautifully painted on ivory.

It was given to her ancestor, given to Zoltina Huanca, in Peru, in the year 1821.

She then walked to the auction house. She had called them, they expected her.

She had handed over the item.

Then, whilst waiting had come across a cardboard box.

Rifling through the contents she noticed three books, thinking of her husband who would be bedridden for some time, she picked up one of these books. Could be something interesting for him to read.

What she discovered, took her breath away. It left her in somewhat of a daze and it took several coughs of the auctioneer man to bring her out of that daze.

What she had seen upon opening one of those journals, were the words, handwritten, 'The life and times of Henry Hopkins'
Henry Hopkins
The very same Henry Hopkins who had been in Peru.

The very same Henry Hopkins who had given her, goodness knows how many times great-grandfather, the very painted ivory miniature she had been given and was about to sell.

Telling her husband she wouldn't be long, just up to the post office, she took the parcel and left the house.

Still reminiscing about the huge coincidence of finding those three journals, on that day, in that place, it was as if she was getting something in return for parting with the ivory painting.

Not much later Zeta Bell posted the package to her father, Carlos, in San Francisco.

Though she had originally thought it might be of interest to her husband as he was convalescing, he had a number of other books he preferred to read first and in the end they remained on the bookshelf.

Zeta was sure her father would be most interested and perhaps should have sent them much sooner.

CALIFORNIA

5 DAYS LATER IN SAN FRANCISCO

Carlos Huanca picks up the parcel, sees that it is from his daughter Zeta.

He feels the weight and thinks it is most likely a few books she has found in some market or other.

She knew he liked to read and his study was well stocked with shelves of literature.

He puts the parcel down again in the hall table and leaves the house.

His wife Maryanne is with their other daughter, Zefora, who was just about to give birth to her third child.

Carlos wearily made his way up the street. His knees ached and he was tired.

His son Zoltina the third, was deployed. War was coming.

It was Monday, it was November and it was threatening to rain.

He reached the end of the second block, his knees easing up a little as he turned and headed up the path to the hospital. Carlos was a grandfather for the third time and for the third time had a granddaughter.

Mother and baby doing fine.

Back at the house the housekeeper took the parcel from the hall table and placed it on the desk in the study.

Carlos would never open it.

THE PRESENT;

SAM'S APARTMENT

SUNDAY 19ᵀᴴ MAY

Chrissie stood in the top floor lobby area awaiting the elevator which was on its way up.

A ping announced its arrival and the door slid open.

Wheeling a suitcase, a handbag slung over her shoulder, Alison Hudson came out, and stopped before a woman she had heard of but never seen.

Chrissie smiled a welcome, not really sure what to say to the woman, who, as Detective Sergeant Saunders had described, was indeed very attractive.

'You must be Chrissie.'

Releasing her hold on the suitcase as the elevator door closed behind her, Ally embraced the other woman.

'And you must be Alison,' Chrissie said, hugging the woman back.

Chrissie released the hold, and led the way into the apartment.

'I am in the guest room ...'

'That's very considerate, though ...' Ally answered, walking through the corridor towards the master bedroom and entering 'we actually never ...' then turning and facing Chrissie, ' ... you?'

'No.'

Chrissie spoke again, 'I'll get some coffee ready, or tea? I guess the detective has filled you in on what we know so far?'

Ally followed Chrissie out to the kitchen. 'Yes Karen filled me in, she wants me to check over the place, see if anything is missing.

The forensic team discovered that the front door and light switches in the hallway had been wiped clean, also they found no laptop nor Sam's camera, His van is still in the garage below.

Someone has taken him, forced him to go, but who and why?'

'Coffee, or tea. What about something to eat? You have been travelling all day, I can fix you something.'

'Thank you, I'll have a coffee, but first, I'm going to have a quick shower, and a change of clothes. Give me ten minutes or so,' Ally responded and headed back to the bedroom.

Chrissie put water in the kettle, started to prepare drinks, and thinking about something to eat, she suddenly felt hungry and realised she hadn't eaten since breakfast and it was now nearly three thirty in the afternoon.

She thought back to the previous day, going back with the detective to the police station ...

Not long after entering her office and inviting Chrissie to sit, her phone rang.

'Ah, Miss Hudson ... Sorry Ally ... Yes, wait, let me get this down ... Okay, go.'

She wrote the details on a notepad, then, after the call she showed it to Chrissie.

A flight from San Francisco to Toronto, then connecting to a flight to Halifax. The expected arrival time.

'I'll make a few calls,' Chrissie said, looking at the details. 'I'll arrange for a helicopter to fly her from Halifax to here.'

'You can do that?'

'I can do that,' Chrissie answered and began punching some numbers on her phone ...

The water boiled and the kettle switched off.

Getting mugs and coffee from the cupboard, Chrissie was about to prepare the drinks when Ally suddenly appeared, just a towel around her, her hair wet and bedraggled, her face flushed.

'Come quickly, you need to see this!' she said and headed back. Chrissie followed.

Ally stood by the door of the en suite, 'Look,' she said gesturing for her to come into the bathroom.

Chrissie slipped past Ally and looked to where she was pointing.

There, on the steam covered large mirror, at the top left-hand corner, two words had appeared.

Open-mouthed she stared.

'Find Sophie'.

For several seconds, neither woman moved.

'Do you know who Sophie is?' Ally asked.

Chrissie, coming out of the bathroom, said, 'That has to refer to Sophie in Paris, she is the manager of the Paris Fine Arts Auction House, Sam worked for them, before coming over to Canada.'

'I'll take a picture before the mirror clears,' Ally said, reaching for her handbag.

'Good idea, this means ...' Chrissie began.

Ally had her phone, took a couple of pictures and, understanding what Chrissie was thinking, said, 'this means that Sam was in here, was aware of what was going on, couldn't do much, but left a clue.'

'Exactly, perhaps you could …' Chrissie began

'Look around for any other clues? I'll just get dressed. By the way, there is a hair-dryer in your room, may I?'

'Of course … I'll get those drinks, and something to eat for both of us, whilst we consider what this might mean …' Chrissie said, heading back into the kitchen.

Ally appeared in the kitchen several minutes later.

Her long blond hair was dry, and she was dressed in jeans and a short-sleeved top she said, 'By the way, thank you, for arranging the helicopter. That was a nice surprise.'

'No problem, seemed the best way to get you here. Fancy a sandwich?'

'Yes, feeling hungry actually …what has happened to Sam?' Ally said, then rushing forward towards Chrissie, the two women again embraced.

Pulling herself free after a moment, Ally looked at Chrissie, 'Sorry.' She wiped away a few tears, 'When I heard about Sam, heard about you, flying all the way from Boston, well, I was jealous. Sam spoke of you. I can see, you too have feelings for him, and though, well, you are my rival, you are also a comforting presence.'

Chrissie looked at the woman before her.

About two inches taller, and so attractive. She too had felt a pang of jealousy, but she too could see Ally's genuine concern and feelings for Sam.

She too was asking herself the question, what has happened to Sam?

'You have a good look around. I'll fix us some lunch' Chrissie said.

Ally nodded, then set about to search the place. She spoke as she was walking around the apartment.

'The forensic team found that the front door and light switch-es around the hallway were void of any prints, suggesting they had been wiped clean. That was evidence that something wasn't right. Also they found no laptop, nor Sam's camera, again, strong evidence, there should also have been ...'

'Ally, come in here!' Chrissie interrupted.
Ally who was in the living room at the time, came rushing in.
'Look,' Chrissie said, showing her a plastic tub of margarine that she had just taken from the fridge, the lid was in her oth-er hand.

Ally looked.
Inside the tub was a mouse.
Pulling it from the tub, Ally said, 'It's Sam's computer mouse! He was not very good on his laptop without it.'

'He writes a clue on the mirror, he hides his mouse in the fridge, he knew that something was about to happen!' Chrissie figured.

'Yes, and if he hid the mouse, then ...'

'He'd have hidden his laptop ...' Chrissie finished, Placing the margarine tub on the counter, she looked around, then opened the oven door.
There, on the bottom shelf, was a large roasting tray, and in it, wrapped in tin foil was something, covered by a grill-ing rack.

At a quick glance it would not look suspicious.
Chrissie pulled the tray out, then Ally took out the item in tin foil and unwrapped it.
'Sam's laptop' she said, her voice more like a loud whisper.

'This means that the other ...you see Chrissie, Sam bought a lap-top for me, but I left it behind, it's not here, so ...'

Chrissie thought about this find for a few moments, then turned to Ally, 'This is how I figure it ...' Walking into the living room, she spoke her thoughts, 'Sam knew that something was about to happen. He must have had a little time, so he hid the laptop, hid his mouse, and left the other laptop, your laptop, out, because whoever was coming would know that there should be one, which means they knew who he was ...'

'We need to keep looking,' Ally interrupted Chrissie's thoughts. 'You're right, he knew that something was about to happen. He had little time, couldn't hide his camera as it would be expected to be here, but if he had a notion, then, might he have been able to ...' Ally walked over to the large window overlooking the industrial estate, recalling how Sam had that evening seen something that had then subsequently prompted an action that led to him saving her life.

It had been late afternoon when the detective had rung her. Told her of the woman who had flown from Boston and that they were now in Sam's apartment, that he was missing and that someone had been here recently, likely the evening before, because they could smell the cigarette smoke.

Had Sam seen something from the window?

'What are you thinking?' Chrissie asked.

Ally turned, 'I'm thinking that Sam may well have spotted something from the window. It was evening, it was dark and, I know that he would often just have this room in darkness and look outside.

I think he saw something, or someone that spurred him into action, hiding the laptop, the mouse, and ...possibly, he might have taken photos. Couldn't hide the camera, as you said that had to be here, but ...'

'Taken out the memory card?' Chrissie finished.

Outside it was getting darker and again it was raining lightly. April showers seemed to have rolled into May.

Chrissie and Ally sat side by side on the sofa.

On the low table in front of them was Sam's laptop, the, by now, cleaned mouse, and an SD memory card.

Ally had found it in the bathroom cabinet, neatly placed under a wrapped bar of soap.

She had also found the power lead for the computer and, in between having something to eat and drinking coffee, had filled Chrissie in not only on all that had happened with regard to her abduction, but also on the findings of Detective Sergeant Saunders.

'So,' Chrissie wanted to know, 'the only people unaccounted for from your ordeal are a woman named Sandra, who wrote her confession, which she had couriered to your daughter and then flew out to Hawaii, not been seen since, and another woman, called Bella, who was the wife of a guy called Phil Madison who is in prison in San Francisco.'

'That's right, and neither seem likely candidates. For one, Sandra has certainly not returned to mainland USA, and Bella, well, again, not likely.'

Ally had fired up the laptop, knew and punched in Sam's password, which was, she explained to Chrissie, his late wife's name and their date of marriage, and waited for the screen to come on.

Taking the memory card, she inserted it.

What would they find? What had Sam taken a picture of?

Who had he taken a picture of, and what did it have to do with Sophie?

Due to the time difference, Chrissie had been unable to contact her as yet. The only number she could find was that of the Paris Fine Arts Auction House and it was the middle of the night in Paris.

Clicking a few times with the mouse, the photos emerged.

Two pictures. Both taken from the lounge window showing the scene across the road.

The first photo was of a large van, red in colour, and two men standing, talking to each other it seemed, by the side of it.

The second photo showed that a car had arrived and a woman was getting out.

'Sam must have had a feeling,' Chrissie whispered.

'Yes, he must have sensed something, knew these men perhaps? More likely the woman.'

They both stared at the second picture.

The woman was a brunette, probably in her forties.

Who was she?

In unison they both sat back, then looked at each other.

'We need to get these to the detective,' Chrissie said.

'Absolutely, I have her number. I'll ring her. We can e-mail these photos through, also the words on the mirror.'

'Agreed,' Chrissie said. 'Tell her that I will contact Sophie tomorrow morning'

'Okay, so, tell me, who is this Sophie in Paris?' Ally asked

THE PAST;

PERIOD 3
PART I

PARIS
THE YEAR 1946

Once safely in her room, she threw herself on the bed, broke down and cried.

Rosemary Quinton had started her European sojourn in Rome, the eternal city.

It had always been her intention to finish in Paris, the city of romance.

Never would she have imagined her trip to turn out as it did.

It was an eye-opener for her to see the damage of war. Mixed reactions to her walking around the streets of Rome. Suspicion, anger, thankfulness. Whilst she had visited the sights she had wanted to see, she never felt completely comfortable.

Also her funds were quickly running low. It was far more expensive than she imagined.

It was good to finally get away. Leaving Rome and heading for Genoa.

Then things went from bad to worse as she sought a way to obtain more funds.

Her father had given her a sizeable sum, but food and lodgings had severely depleted those funds, and her father was goodness knew where and unreachable.

With great fear and a troubled mind she had left Genoa behind, also leaving behind a man who had died in her presence.

She was mightily relieved when she wasn't stopped upon arrival in Paris.

But now, finally feeling a sense of safety, all the emotions came to the fore.

She sobbed and sobbed.

Finally pulling herself together, she freshened up and sat on the edge of the bed for some moments.

She studied the painting, she assumed a print, that was on the wall above the wooden chest of drawers that together with the bed and a dressing table made up all the furniture that was in the room.

Rosemary walked around the city over the next three days.

But despite the music that permeated through the air from the many bars and cafes, despite the joy and laughter she encountered, the smiles of the people, despite the invitations she received to come and join a party here or there, despite the beauty of the fabulous buildings all around, and despite the smile she placed on her own face, she was unhappy.

Sad and feeling lost, guilty and alone.

So it was that she left Paris. Booked a train to Antwerp.

Flying was too risky. She wanted to go home. Going by ship would be the best option.

Sailing from Antwerp to New York was her aim.

She picked a hotel near the docks. Then upon investigating the immediate area and looking for a place to purchase a ticket, she physically bumped into a young man.

He was apologetic in Flemish. She was apologetic in English.

He asked if he could be of help as she seemed to be looking for something.

She told him she was looking to get a passage to New York.

He knew where to go.

Romance blossomed.

THE PRESENT;

PARIS

MONDAY 20TH MAY

Sophie had only just entered her office, taken her coat off and was hanging it on the hook of the coat rack, when the phone rang.

'Is this Sophie?' a female voice asked, then followed on, without a confirmed answer, 'My name is Christina Small, I am a friend of Sam ...'

Sophie's mind was whirring. What had happened? Something had happened, she could feel it in the pit of her stomach.
   'I am Sophie, has something happened to Sam?'

'I am calling from Canada from Sam's apartment. He has disappeared; we think he was taken by someone ...'

For several moments Sophie was silent. Something was stirring in her mind.
   'Sophie?'

'Sorry, yes, Chrissie, I know who you are, Sam went to Boston, met you there, then you and he went to Genoa. I know, Sam told me about it, to do with your grandfather I believe ... but why are you calling me? Sam is not here.'

Chrissie listened to the French woman speak, her English was very good, Sam had spoken of her, she briefly wondered, did she perhaps hear a tone of anxiousness in her voice ... 'Are you okay Sophie? I mean, you are not in trouble?'

'No, do you think I might be?'

'Not sure. We found a message written on the mirror in the bathroom. It just said, "Find Sophie". Do you know something that might explain Sam's disappearance?'

Sophie suddenly remembered what it was that was nagging at her.

'Goodness me!' she exclaimed. 'Our office here was broken into, four days ago, but as far as we can tell nothing was stolen. We think someone was looking for information.

We informed the police. We have security footage of a woman.'

'Brunette, in her forties?' Chrissie interjected.

'Oui,' Sophie answered.

'Do you know her?' Chrissie asked next.

'No, but if you have seen this woman over there, then it must be Sam's address that she was looking for, but I do not know her, or why she would know we have his address.'

'We originally thought his disappearance might have to do with how he helped a woman called Alison Hudson, did Sam ever mention her?'

'Oui, but only that he was helping her to find her daughter?'

'Yes, but if you are connected, we may have to look at another reason. The words that Sam wrote on the mirror, "Find Sophie", suggest that perhaps he thinks you might be in danger, or that you might be able to help.'

'I will check again with the police. I must help to find him, okay?'

'Yes, of course. I'll give you my number, call me if you have anything, okay?'

'Yes, thank you,' Sophie said.

The connection was broken and Sophie flicked through numbers on her own phone, then pressed some buttons.

It was whilst she was waiting for a connection that she realised it must be the middle of the night in Canada.

Her stomach was churning. She had sensed the tension in Chrissie's voice.

Whatever was going on, she would do all she could to help.

A man's voice came on the line.

Sophie spoke rapidly and with urgency, explaining why she was calling him.

THE PAST;

PERIOD 3
PART 2

SAN FRANCISCO
THE YEAR 1946

Millie Huanca sat in a cosy chair in the big study. It was late at night. The only light came from the tall standard lamp by her side. On a small table to the other side of the armchair a cup of hot chocolate was cooling down.

Her husband, Zoltina, after the exciting and emotional day, was already fast asleep.

Millie turned over another page of the journal she was reading.

Strangely, she had only found it two days ago.

Taking a careful sip of the drink, Millie thought back over the past couple of days ...

Preparations were in full swing.

Zoltina was working all the hours he could. In two days' time, they would launch the boat.

The third in the fleet of Huanca Bay Transport.

The other two were named after his sisters, Zeta and Zefora.

On Saturday he would steer the Zoltina the third out into the Bay.

Not only that, but on Saturday it would be little Emily's sixth birthday, third daughter of sister Zefora.

Sadly it would also be the sixth anniversary of the passing of Carlos, Zoltina's father who had, shortly after visiting his new born granddaughter, been walking towards the pier, when he felt unwell, sat down in a cafe, and simply closed his eyes and died.

It was going to be an emotional day.

Whilst her husband was busy at the pier making sure the vessel was fully prepared and ready to take on board a select group of passengers, family, friends and the mayor himself for the launch, Millie, with the help from mother-in-law Maryanne and two servants, prepared the house.

A big house overlooking the bay, which Carlos, when he and Maryanne moved from Acapulco, had purchased.

It was also when, doing a bit of a tidy-up in the study, Carlos had loved his study, that she stumbled across a parcel.

The study was lined with three large bookcases containing a great selection of mainly historical books. None of his three children were avid readers and were seldom found in the study.

When Carlos had died, it was Zoltina who inherited the house, though with the intention that Maryanne would live there also, until death.

Millie recalled when, shortly after marrying Zoltina and coming to the house, she had found the study fascinating. She, unlike her husband, loved to read.

Though she had been here many times, that morning, she opened one of the bottom drawers of the large leather-topped oak desk.

A parcel was there. Still wrapped.

Discovering it was from her sister in-law, Zeta, whom she had never met, and seeing that it had been posted five days before his death, Millie worked out that Carlos could well have received it that day.

In all the turmoil of that day, someone had just put the parcel away.

Opening it, she discovered three journals.

Taking another sip of her hot chocolate, Millie continued reading.

The pages had revealed the story of a precious item.

An oil painted miniature on ivory. The writer of these journals described the time and moment when he first seen it, and it was when he was writing about the times and adventures in

South America, eventually coming to Peru, that Millie realised why it had been that Zeta had sent these to Carlos.

Placing her empty cup on the table, Millie shifted slightly in the chair, and a piece of paper partially showed itself, two pages on.

Millie, excited by this find, took it out, opened it and read its contents.

'Hi Dad, this is the part where the ivory miniature comes into the possession of our family, read all about it!

Love, Zeta.'

Millie read on and discovered how Henry Hopkins, having originally purchased the item in Caracas in 1803 had given it to a young Zoltina, her husband's two times great-grandfather in Peru, in 1821.

Millie was about to put the journal away for the night and head up to bed when another slip of paper appeared.

Slipping it free from the pages, she opened and read it.

'Hi Dad, I am sorry, but I had to sell the miniature to pay for hospital costs for Jonathan. I know who bought it at an auction in Boston.

A man named Edward Small.'

THE PRESENT;

SAM'S APARTMENT

MONDAY 20ᵀᴴ MAY

It was late afternoon

'So Sam helped you find out what happened to your grandfather?' Ally asked, preparing something in the kitchen.

'He was a professor,' Chrissie answered, coming from the lounge and standing in the archway, watching as Ally prepared lunch. 'Professor Edward Small, lecturer in science at MIT, in Boston.'

'He bought an ivory miniature, in 1938. Now Sam was on the trail of this piece of art. This led him to my door last month, gosh, only last month, it seems like I've known Sam for ages ...anyway.

'Granddad had taken the ivory to see a man in Rome, Italy, but he never got there, went missing.

'When my dad died, and left me the house, I found some clues and decided to go and look for him, find out what had happened. This was back in '97. Went to Rome; found out he had never reached there; came home disappointed.

'Then Sam knocks at the door. Next thing we are both searching in Genoa. Anyway, we found out he had died there.'

'And,' Ally wanted to know, 'did you find the ivory?'

'No, not then, but Sam and I did find a clue. Someone else had been looking to find my grandfather. We had a name, Tamara Wilson, from New York.

I found her, spoke with her, she is one of my best friends now, lovely young woman.

It turns out that it was her grandmother who had been with my grandfather when he died.'

'Wow, quite a story, but still no miniature?'

'No, but in, well a sort of diary really, that Tammy's grandmother wrote, we found clues and Sam worked out where it might be.

'However, this might now not be the case, because the reason I tried to ring Sam, and discovered he was missing, was to inform him of a letter Tammy found.

It seems that there is a possibility that it may no longer be where they thought it was.'

'Sounds intriguing,' Ally said, looking up and catching Chrissie's eyes.

Strangely, the two had bonded as they shared a common concern.

Ally turned back to what she was doing on the gas hob, stirring a few things.

She had earlier suggested to Chrissie that she would make the dinner for them both. It would give her something to do, as there really wasn't anything else they could do.

Chrissie also turned, and headed back into the lounge.

It had been nearly three o'clock in the morning when she had made contact with Sophie in Paris, as they were five hours behind Western Europe's time-zone.

She hadn't slept much since. Sitting herself down on the couch, she let her mind wander.

In the kitchen Ally too was reliving the day in her mind …

It was her phone that awakened her. She reached for it and said a sleepy 'Hello?'

It had been detective Saunders.

Sitting up in bed Ally took note of what she was told.

Ending the call she remained sitting upright for a few moments.

In Sam's bed.

Though they had cuddled and kissed, neither had taken it further.

Right now she longed for him, wanted to be with him, hold him. Why hadn't she slept with him? Would he have wanted to?

He had told her a couple of times, she recalled, that to find her daughter and to bring those who had tried to kill her to justice, was the priority.

She had agreed that it would be best, no distractions.

She remembers the tearful farewell at the airport. Had seen his emotions.

But he had clearly let her go.

Released her to be with her daughter.

Again she had agreed that it was the right thing to do. Again she had, as the plane took off from Halifax, felt such a thankfulness for him.

His kindness in laying aside his own feelings for her.

Feeling her eyes welling up, Ally threw the cover aside and headed for the shower.

Whilst dressing she wondered about Chrissie.

She could see and sense her feelings for him. There had only been the odd moment or two when she had felt a degree of jealousy.

She had felt quite a relief, learning that Chrissie, like herself, had not slept with him.

Walking into the kitchen, Ally realised Chrissie was already up and about and a wonderful smell hit her nostrils.

'Morning,' Chrissie said, smiling, 'breakfast?'

'Smells great, thank you,' Ally replied. 'Karen rang earlier, woke me up actually, they traced the number of the van, it's a rental from downtown Halifax. They are chasing the information given including bank details. The name was under Roberts, ring any bells?'

'No,' Chrissie answered, gesturing for Ally to sit down by the table which she had prepared. There were juices, coffee, toast and coming out of the sauté pan, an omelette, which she cut in two, sliding the halves onto plates.

'And the car? I know we couldn't see a plate number in the photo.'

'Nothing on the car, nor the woman, or even the two young men,' Ally answered, sitting down and pouring coffee into a mug.

Chrissie joined her at the table.

'I got hold of Sophie,' Chrissie said, pouring coffee too. 'She's alright. As I was talking to her and explaining why I was calling, she was quiet for a moment. Then she remembered that, four days ago, their offices had been broken into, nothing was taken, apparently, but things had been disturbed. They checked security footage. It had been a woman, no doubt looking for an address for Sam. She described the woman. Fits with the one in the photo.'

'Oh my goodness, and she didn't recognise this woman?'

'No, but she is going to, probably already has by now, send an e-mail, so, in a moment, could you check Sam's laptop. If the pictures are there, we can forward them to the detective'

'Mmm, this omelette is yummy, I'll get the laptop ...' Ally said, then taking another mouthful left the table to return seconds later ...

Ally's thoughts returned to the moment.
    She was making sure she had the cooking under control and was almost ready to serve up when a phone rang.
    It was Chrissie's.

Walking from the living room into the kitchen, Chrissie was listening.

Then turning and walking back into the lounge, she said, 'Hang on a minute Sophie, let me get some paper ...'

Several moments later Chrissie returned to the kitchen.

Ally turned off the gas, wiped her hands on the apron she had found and was wearing, and looked at Chrissie expectantly.

'That was Sophie. She had a visitor, a man she knew and contacted after I spoke with her. He is from Interpol.

He is going to investigate. Sophie gave me his number and asks if we could get that to Detective Sergeant Saunders.

'So, we'll do that in a moment. Let's eat first. You've been working away there for quite some time. It's smells really good and I'm hungry'

Ally nodded in agreement.

THE PAST;

PERIOD 4
SAN FRANCISCO

THE YEAR 1962
PART 1: EMILY

Emily Nicholson stood leaning on the railing. She fondly recalled the time she had stood on the same spot, sixteen years ago. She had barely been able to look over the top of the wooden railing as she waved to all the people on the pier. It had been her sixth birthday and the maiden voyage of the harbour cruise ferry, named Zoltina the third, after her uncle Z.

That was then. She now stood five foot eight. Wind was tugging at her long auburn hair as the ferry, on a harbour cruise, turned slightly to starboard.

Ahead the Golden Gate Bridge was looming nearer.

The wind was chilly. It was November.

Across her shoulder two straps were attached to her favourite items. One connected to a small transistor radio.

She would regularly be tuned into KEWB and listen to Casey Kasem.

Emily loved the music of the day.

The second strap was attached to a camera. The Canonflex 35 mm SLR camera was a gift from her aunt and uncle.

Camera in hand Emily took several shots as the boat left the pier and headed out into the Bay.

She also turned around and took one up towards the wheelhouse where her uncle was piloting the vessel.

He waved at her. She waved back.

Earlier, when she had been there prior to departure, her radio had been on and the Four Seasons came on with, 'Big Girls Don't Cry'.

She liked the song, and listened to the words as her uncle was making sure all was ready for getting his boat on the way with another load of passengers.

They would enjoy the cruise and a light lunch.

The words struck a chord today.

Would she be crying later, she wondered.

Emily turned and watched the San Francisco skyline as the boat headed towards the bridge.

The ferry, one of three that made up the Huanca Bay Transport company's fleet, was the only one used for cruises, both day and night. The other two were strictly for ferry crossings.

Twenty-two-year-old Emily let the wind play with her hair as she thought back, reflecting on her life thus far, for she was about to embark on an adventure.

The youngest of three, she had two older sisters, Zoe, two years older and Katrina, four years older.

She learned that the day of her birth was also the day her grandfather, her mother's father, had died.

Her father was often away. She wasn't close to her mother, or her sisters, but at an early age took a liking to uncle Z and his wife Millie.

In her early teems she would often, after school, drop in to see her aunty and spent many hours in the study, a fabulous room with shelves and shelves of books.

Emily liked to read.

When she was twelve, her father left. Her sisters became even closer to their mother and Emily often felt the odd one out.

She focused on school, focused on learning, and began to get an idea as to what she wanted to do and achieve.

She grew tall and fit, played basketball, and took up running.

Uncle Z told Emily about her other aunty, Zeta, who was a very good runner and even went to the Olympic Games.

Emily was impressed. She had heard about her aunty and uncle who lived in Halifax but had never seen them.

Though the wind was chilly, Emily felt it was refreshing and took a few more photos as the boat sailed beneath the famous Golden Gate Bridge.

Taking a deep breath, listening to the sound of the boat slicing through the waters, the sound of chatter and laughter from the passengers that were, in the main, indoors now and enjoying their lunch, Emily wondered what might lie ahead.

She closed her eyes briefly, then once again thought back …

When she was just fourteen, the situation at home became worse.

Her sisters, sixteen and eighteen now, were close to her mother.

When during some horseplay in the lounge, the sisters broke a vase, they blamed their younger sister.

Her mum believed their fabricated story and she was punished.

Emily had begun to realise that her mother was not as she used to be. Though never close, she had been closer to her father, she noticed a difference. Her mother had begun to drink more alcohol.

When her mother that day, after listening to her sisters' false accusations, lashed out, she lost her temper and struck Emily several times.

Emily had said nothing, had not argued or even tried to state her innocence.

She left the house that evening, having packed a few things, including school books, she walked to her aunt and uncle's house.

Auntie Millie saw immediately that something was very wrong and took Emily into the study.

She heard and saw what her sister-in-law had done.

Early the following morning Zoltina went over to his sister's house.

He confronted her, confronted his nieces, who, having been quite shocked as to how their mother had reacted the previous afternoon, cried and confessed.

For Emily everything changed, for the better.

She stayed with her uncle and aunt who applied for, and were granted, legal guardianship ...

The boat turned a little to port before straightening and then slowly made its way around Alcatraz.

The wind, now playing with her hair from the other side was pleasing.

The song she heard earlier, in the wheelhouse, came to mind again, 'Big girls don't cry'. She hadn't, when at a young age she had been hit, but would she now?

She was about to leave all this behind, at least for a while.

Emily took a few more photos as they rounded the island to head back to the pier.

The camera was a gift at her graduation.

Learning had come quite easy. She loved to read, and loved to study. Though tall, fit and attractive, with many a young lad trying to impress her, Emily wasn't interested.

She would often spend time with her aunt in the study, a quiet place, then head in to her room after dinner for an evening of listening to the radio.

She had graduated with honours with a master's in geology.

Uncle Z and Auntie Millie were there, and were so proud. Unable to have any children of their own, they were more like her parents. She truly felt like a daughter.

She loved them both, yes, she thought, leaving for a while, she would surely cry.

Just over a year ago, one afternoon with Millie in the study, her aunty told her about Zoltina's father, Carlos, who had been the one to stock this room with all the books, taking many years to do so.

She also told a little of the family Huanca, their history and then produced three journals.

'These are journals written by a Henry Hopkins. He came from England, and went to South America, and when he came to Peru, he was the man who was so instrumental in the education of a young lad, called Zoltina.

I won't tell you anymore. Read about it, in these journals. As you are studying geology, you'll find them very valuable, I'm sure.'

It didn't take long for Emily to be totally engrossed. And reading these journals also gave her a direction, a challenge.

The boat docked, uncle Z bringing it smoothly alongside the pier.

She smiled at the departing customers as she made her way to the wheelhouse.

It was time.

Time to say goodbye.

Three hours later she was at the airport. Boarding had begun.

She was excited to experience flying.

The Douglas DC 8 stood on the tarmac. Emily, camera at the ready, took two shots, before climbing up the stairs to enter the plane that would take her to Lima, Peru.

The plane was not full.

Sitting by the window Emily had a free seat next to her. She placed her camera carry case on it, opened it and took the camera out again.

She had also purchased an extra eight rolls of film and a couple of lenses.

Looking out the window she saw the propeller gathering momentum and heard the sound of the engines revving up.

Her suitcase was in the hold and a carry bag was in the locker above her.

The only other piece of luggage she had brought was a handbag, inside which was her transistor radio. What kind of music would she hear in Peru she wondered, as the engines roared to full life and she felt movement as the chocks were taken away.

A stewardess came down the aisle, checking that all the seat belts were securely fastened.

The plane began to taxi towards the runway.

Henry Hopkins' journals had been a great source of information. His knowledge of mining was immense, his travels were exciting, and reading his life story inspired her to head for Peru, to the very place where he had taken a young man under his wings.

A young man that was her three times great-grandfather.

Uncle Z and Auntie Millie had encouraged her to follow her dream, but at the same time had pointed out the challenges and dangers she might encounter.

The plane turned and stopped for a moment. It was on the runway.

Then the engine throttled to full power. The propellers spinning.

Emily was pushed back in her seat and the Douglas DC 8 gathered speed along the runway.

Then the ground lost its hold on the wheels and the plane ascended into the blue November sky.

Emily suddenly realised she had been holding her breath. Exhaling first she then breathed in through her nose. Her ears were blocked as the plane climbed higher.

Just over five thousand kilometres later the plane landed with a gentle bump.

Emily was impressed with the skill of the pilot to land so softly.

A little later, handbag and camera case in hand, she left the plane.

Though early evening, it was still warm.

The terminal was a hive of activity. Emily was easily the tallest woman there.

She had learned a little bit of Spanish and gave it a go when taking a taxi to the hotel she had booked by telephone.

The 1960 Ford Galaxy droves smoothly through narrow and cobbled streets towards her hotel on the waterfront.

Her attempts at the language were met with smiles and nods and were responded to in broken English.

The people were friendly and accommodating.

Her room, with a view over the ocean was small, but clean and comfortable.

After dinner which was, she was told, chicken and spices and vegetables, and very tasty, she headed for her room and got into bed.

A long and exciting day.

Tomorrow would be another long day as she would set out, by bus, for Trujillo.

Once in bed she fell asleep almost straight away.

Rising early, Emily washed, dressed, and taking her camera took several shots of the hotel, the seafront and surroundings, before having breakfast and getting a taxi to take her to 'estacion de autobuses'.

The temperature was already climbing and the bus terminal was busy, milling with men, women and children, not to mention chickens, goats and pigs.

The bus was another Ford, the same that many schools in America use for the transportation of children to and from school.

Emily secured a spot by the window, her suitcase was loaded at the back and, though the station was very busy and numerous buses were around, her bus was thankfully not full.

They left the terminal seven minutes behind schedule.

The journey was breathtaking.

Emily drank in the scenery, listened to the other passengers in the bus chattering away, and the sound of the engine as the bus rode over the Pan-American highway, heading north.

A little over a hundred and fifty kilometres later the bus drove into the city of Huacho.

A sizeable city, founded back in 1571 and situated some 200 feet above sea-level, where Emily was able to stretch her legs, take a comfort break and have something to eat, before boarding for the next stage.

Camera at hand and ready to capture more scenes.

The second major stop was a town called Chimbote, again a chance for a stretch of the legs and a bite to eat.

Once back on the bus, now only one hundred and thirty kilometres from her destination, Emily loaded her third roll of film into her camera.

Next stop, Trujillo.

THE PRESENT;

PARIS

TUESDAY 21ST MAY

Sophie left the office of director Emmanuel Sauvonne.

Yesterday she had informed him of the mysterious disappearance of Sam Price, told him of the message on the mirror and that she was going to help find out what had happened.

He had totally supported her and told her if there was anything she needed, she need but ask.

Later that day a contact, who she had met not long ago, from Interpol, arrived and she gave him the information that Chrissie had sent, along with the report of their recent break-in and the image of the woman, who very likely, was the same that had turned up in Canada.

A report she had also forwarded to Chrissie, via Sam's e-mail.

Informing the director of the weeks' schedule and that she had left her assistant in charge she walked back to her office.

Once seated behind her desk, Sophie searched for a number, then dialled it and waited.

'Find Sophie' were the words Sam had written on the mirror.

She had read and reread all the notes that Chrissie had sent her.

Why the message on the mirror?

'Ah, yes, hello, 'she said, speaking in English. 'Martijn? This is Sophie Pontiac ...'

Finishing the call, she then booked a train fare online.

Then she made a second call, ordering a taxi.

After running through the order of business for the next few days with her assistant, Sophie put on her coat, grabbed her briefcase and handbag, and left the office.

The taxi arrived just as she left the building.

'Find Sophie'. Why those words, she again pondered, getting into the taxi and giving the driver instructions.

Was she in danger? Did she know something that was important? A connection with Sam's disappearance?

She checked her watch as she exited the cab and entered her apartment to collect her luggage. The taxi waited.

Less than five minutes later she reappeared and continued her journey.

Thirty-five minutes later, she made herself comfortable in the first-class section of the high-speed train, destination Rotterdam.

MEANWHILE IN AMERSFOORT;

Martijn Vogel placed the telephone back in its cradle and continued to write on a pad. Martijn was the lead detective of the burglary section of the Amersfoort Police Department.

Alongside his colleague, Froukje Boersma, they investigated break-in crimes in a sizeable region surrounding the city in the centre of the Netherlands.

He'd just finished writing some notes and taking a sip of his coffee when his colleague entered.

'Sam Price has gone missing,' he said, looking up at her.

'Missing?'

'Yes, Sophie, the lady from Paris, just called, and explained the situation as far as she knew it. She's on her way to Rotterdam. I'm going to meet her, check out Sam's flat.'

'She called you?' Froukje asked, sitting herself down behind the desk opposite him.

Smiling as she fired up her laptop.

'Maybe she likes me?' he answered, getting up to put on his coat.

Checking through the window he noticed it was a clear sky. It looked like it was going to be a nice day.

'Maybe you like her?' she said. 'You did spend some time together not that long ago.'

'It was all work,' he replied, 'as it will be now,' then smiled and left the office.

'I hope Sam is alright,' she called out after him.

'So do I,' he called back, 'so do I.'

As Sophie's train rolled smoothly alongside the platform at Rotterdam Central Station, and Martijn was turning of the main highway and heading for Sam's flat, Chrissie had showered and dressed and was making toast whilst opening her laptop when Ally appeared in the kitchen.

'Hi,' she said sleepily.

Chrissie gave her a smile, then typed in her password. The toast popped.

'Want some toast?' she asked Ally who was opening the fridge.

'No thanks, not yet. Just have some juice for now.'

'Goodness!' Chrissie said, looking at her screen, 'Detective Karen has been busy, she has some info here.'

Ally, juice bottle in hand, walked over and stood beside Chrissie. They both read the e-mail, then they looked at each other, 'Boston?' Ally asked.

The e-mail stated that the rental van had been returned to where it had been hired from in Halifax. It had been under a company name that was still being researched.

Another bit of information that had been found was that a man and a woman, matching the description of Mr Sam Price and the unknown woman in the photograph, had boarded a train bound for Boston, the same evening Sam had taken those photos and had left that message on the mirror.

Friday evening, the day before Chrissie had arrived.

'Boston, that's where you live isn't it?'

'Yes, the police in Boston are looking into footage, to see if they actually arrived there,' Chrissie answered, rereading the e-mail from detective Saunders.

'Also,' according to this e-mail, 'they are checking border control to ascertain who entered the states from Canada that evening.'

'Why Boston?' Ally asked, drinking her juice.

'The only thing I can think of,' Chrissie answered, 'what with Sophie's name on the mirror, is the auction house connection, the one Sam works for.'

'True,' Ally said. 'It's what took him to Harris. It's how he knew Rozzini. Good thinking Chrissie, so, do we tell Karen?'

Chrissie took a bite of her toast, thought about the situation for a few moments, then, finishing a mouthful, she said, 'Yes, we will tell the detective. Let's also wait to see if there is any confirmation that they indeed got to Boston, then, I feel, we should follow that trail, go to Boston too. It really is our only option.'

Ally's phone in her bathrobe pocket, buzzed.

'Hi,' she answered, 'Chrissie and I have just finished reading your e-mail ...'

'Okay, ... so, they did go to Boston?'
  'Hang on Karen, let me pass you on to Chrissie, she has an idea ...'

Chrissie took the phone, explained her thoughts, listened for a few moments, then told the detective that she and Ally would follow the trail and could she e-mail this extra information to her.
  'Better get ready. I'll arrange flights. We are already nearly three days behind them, but at least we have a trail of sorts,' Chrissie said, handing the phone back.

Ally took her phone, then looked at Chrissie, 'I ...' she began, I need to pay ...'

Chrissie cut her short, took a gentle hold of Ally's shoulders and said, 'I'm quite a wealthy woman, thanks to Sam, so, don't even go there, but we need each other, we need to be a team. It's not just me or not just you, it's us, okay?'

Ally nodded, then hugged Chrissie briefly, before turning to get ready.

Chrissie returned to her laptop, saw that the detective had already sent the new information, and began searching for flights to Boston.

MEANWHILE IN ROTTERDAM

At just before 2pm Martijn was the first to arrive at the flat in the Schiebroek suburb of Rotterdam.

On the phone Sophie had told him that whilst Sam was away a cleaning lady would come in once a week, but she didn't know which day that would be.

She had also told him that she had a key, one Sam had given her when she had stayed here. Sophie arrived a few minutes later. Key in hand.

She had, prior to going back to Paris, been trying to pry the key from her key-ring to give back to Sam, but he had said, 'Hang on to it, you never know, might come in handy one day.'

She had thought about that very conversation on the train earlier.

Was it a premonition?

'Thank you so much for coming' Sophie said, walking along the passageway towards the door where Martijn was waiting.

'My pleasure,' he answered, smiling. 'Any further news?'

Sophie shook her head then unlocked the door and opened it.

Martijn grabbed her shoulder gently, and held her back to go inside first.

They entered and Sophie closed the door.

The detective moved quietly and quickly through the two bedroomed flat.

'Nothing seems disturbed, no sign of any break-in.'

'What do you make of the message Sam left on the mirror?' she asked, placing her handbag on the coffee table and heading for the guest bedroom.

'Find Sophie?' he replied, 'I've been thinking about that, and all that has occurred over there that you informed me about. The fact that Sam took a couple of photographs, suggest he was suspicious. Perhaps had a feeling, but the message on the mirror that suggests to me that he didn't know what it was all about, until they, whoever they are, were in his apartment.

Therefore, it could be that you are in danger, and to find you in order to protect you, or that you know something that is of value, something that will help in locating Sam.'

Sophie came out of the guest-room, armed with three big books.

'Exactly, my thoughts too. I don't seem to be in danger, so, I have been thinking what I might know, or how I might help Sam.

These books, they are journals, compiled by Sam's great-grandfather, the ambassador, Samuel Price'

Sophie placed them next to her handbag, then sat down.

'I asked you here in case this place had been burgled. After all, they, whoever they are, broke into the offices at the auction house. Anyway, you are a busy man, so thank you for coming. I am going to look through these. I believe the answer can be found in these journals'

Martijn looked down at the French woman on the sofa with a smile. He liked her, 'I might as well help you,' he said, 'seeing as I am here. What is it we are looking for?'

Grabbing the top journal, Martijn sat himself in the single armchair and looked at her expectantly.

'Thank you,' she said, smiling at him. Then feeling herself colour a little, she took hold of the second journal and opened it. 'These are full of the details of his work as an ambassador, but also detailed descriptions and photos of the art that he purchased over the years.'

'Now, we had been investigating a Gauguin, though that has been resolved. I can't help but think there might be a connection. I remember when I located the genuine Gauguin that I found the name, Victoria Thompson, written neatly, on the back of it, and a date, 1903.'

Sophie looked up again and across to the detective, 'so, mister friendly detective, could you see if you can find any reference, to that name? I am going to study the various pieces of art that the ambassador purchased. Might be a clue there.'

607

'Okay that's fine ...' Martijn began, but was interrupted, 'Goodness, I am so sorry,' she said, putting the journal down, 'first I'll make you a coffee, I know you and Sam are always in need of one.'

He smiled at her as she got up and headed towards the kitchen.

Taking a notebook and pen from his pocket, he wrote down the name and date Sophie had mentioned.

Victoria Thompson.

Who was she he wondered.

THE PAST;

THE YEAR 1962
PART 2; JOSHUA

The nearby clock tower chimed the hour. It was 6pm.

Still over twenty degrees Celsius, it had been a warm day.

Joshua was studying the board at the bus station.

His Spanish was practically non-existent, but surely he could work out a bus timetable.

Close by a bus pulled in. Joshua stood up straight as he had been bending down to view the low noticeboard. At over six foot he stood out from the crowd.

Passengers disembarked from the recently arrived bus.

Then Joshua was struck.

A woman appeared.

She was tall; she was gorgeous; she was a vision to behold.

He stood quite still and watched as she waited for someone to pass her the suitcase from the hold of the bus.

She then turned and headed straight for him.

Joshua found that he just couldn't move. He watched her approach. Noticed she had blue eyes, noticed her long hair, dark blonde in colour.

She saw him. Met his gaze and smiled.

Then walked on by.

Getting some control of his body back, Joshua turned and looked at her as she headed into town.

Judging by her confident stride, he figured she knew where she was headed.

From where he stood, he could see, in the distance, the entrance to the hotel where he was staying. It was one of the best in town, and closest to the bus terminal.

He wondered who she was, where she had come from and what she was doing here, in northern Peru.

She did indeed stop at the hotel entrance, and entered.

Joshua, forgetting about sorting out a timetable for the following day, made his way to the hotel determined to find out who she was.

Increasing his speed he half ran half walked up the road and entered the lobby.

She was at the front desk, checking in.

He sat himself in one of the comfy armchairs that were placed around a round low table just to the left on the main entrance.

He watched her, and heard her, she spoke in English, but with the odd word of what he assumed Spanish, thrown in. This obviously to the delight of the man who was checking her in.

He smiled a lot.

This could also be, of course, Joshua mused that she was strikingly attractive.

Letting out a sigh his mind began to wander, taking his thoughts back, to why it was he was here ...

'Perhaps you'd like to have dinner with me this evening?'

Joshua started. He hadn't seen her coming. He quickly struggled to get to his feet, realising that he was blushing and was struggling to actually say anything at all.

'Okay then, I'll meet you here, say, in about forty minutes? I'll let you sort out a reservation.'

She turned and headed for the elevators, trundling her suitcase behind her, a camera case and her handbag across her shoulder and the room key in her hand.

Joshua realised then that his mouth was half open, The second time in the last twenty minutes.

He blew out a sigh, let himself drop down into the chair. Who was she?

Checking his watch, Joshua got up again, organised a reservation in the dining room and headed for his room on the second floor.

Taking the stairs, he thought back on his life, recalling that day in Boston, listening to the auctioneer and holding his mother's hand tightly ...

Beatrice and her four-year-old son Joshua left Boston and travelled to Harris, in Canada.

She had no family left, there was nothing for her here. She had been totally in love, wholly swept of her feet by Nathaniel. Had been so happy with him.

Reading his letter of confession, realising he was gone, was a blow.

But news of Nathaniel, news of how he had lost the family business had reached the ears of the family in Canada.

Beatrice received a letter, inviting her and her son to come and live with them.

A letter written by Henry Charles.

She gratefully accepted, and was truly and warmly welcomed.

She quickly caught up with all the family connections.

Her ex-husband's grandfather, Charlie Parker the fourth, was the brother of Sara who married Carl, keeping the Parker family name.

They had a son, Henry Charles and twin girls, Rebekah and Charlotte.

Sara died in 1919 and Carl within a year in 1920.

Henry Charles, named after Henry Hopkins and Charlie Parker the third, married Clara and they had a son, Albert, who was born in 1898.

It had been Albert, by now a forty-year-old who had not married, who had received Beatrice and her son upon arrival.

Joshua was later told, on a few occasions that it had been love at first sight, and so they married and he became his stepfather.

This resonated in his thoughts as he prepared for dinner. Looking into the mirror, the twenty-eight-year-old Joshua smiled, feeling as though he was in love.

Love at first sight?

Hoping that he would find his voice, he waited in the lobby for her to come down.

Who was she? Why had she come here?

He sighed as she came out of one of the elevators.

'So, what brings you here, to Peru, to Trujillo?' Emily asked.

She had spotted him immediately upon leaving the elevator and had walked over to him, smiling.

After a somewhat formal introduction, he extending his hand and merely saying 'Joshua,' and she, taking his offered hand had responded with 'Emily'. They had walked towards the restaurant area, and it wasn't until seated that Emily spoke, deciding she had to get the conversation going.

'Ahh, yes, well, I have an interest in mining ...' a waiter appeared at their table and they both ordered drinks, 'and what about you?' he continued, picking up the menu card to study it.

Emily also looked at the menu, then having made up her mind as to what to order, she said 'That's very interesting, mining. Well that's sort of also why I am here, though my first goal is to find a cemetery here in Trujillo. An ancestor of mine is buried there.'

The drinks arrived and they both ordered.

'Your ancestors came from Peru?' he asked, taking a sip of his drink and beginning to feel more relaxed.

'Yes, I have recently been reading some journals that have come into our possession, very interesting, written by an Englishman, Henry Hopkins ...'

'Henry Hopkins?' Joshua interjected, 'that's unbelievable. Henry Hopkins, the mining expert? Well I never.'

'You know this guy, I mean, obviously, you know of him, how?' Emily queried, her eyes wide open, looking across the table directly into the eyes of the man she had only just met.

She noted that they were dark blue in colour.

Joshua was momentarily transfixed by her gaze. He too noted the colour of her eyes which were a light green.

'Aah, yes, well, I live in Harris. That's in Canada, not far from Halifax. Henry Hopkins arrived there, in, well, can't recall the exact date, early 1800s, around 1820 I think. Anyway, he and one of my ancestors, Charlie Parker the third, made a deal. They operated a silver mine, very successfully too. I am to inherit this company, so, wanted to learn more about mining and about a particular mine, here in Peru, in fact, about ten miles or so from here.'

'Wow!' Emily said. 'That's just such a coincidence. My ancestor, the one who is buried here, is the father of Zoltina my descendant who travelled to Mexico, and who worked alongside Henry Hopkins. '

THE PRESENT;

NEW YORK

TUESDAY 21ST MAY

'I can't just do nothing; I have to do something ...' Tammy said, over the phone.

Chrissie on the other end replied, 'Okay, well, seeing as you speak French and like Paris, would you like to go there, meet up with Sophie, help her over there whilst Ally and I follow the trail here.'

'Okay, sounds like a plan. Send me an e-mail with her details. So, you're heading for Boston, sounds like you're getting on with your rival!'

'Tammy, stop it. She is lovely, and yes, she may be my rival but not right now. Anyway, Sam knows how I feel about him; no doubt he also knows how Ally feels about him. We'll cross that bridge when we get there. I'll send you the info on Sophie, and, thank you. We still have no idea what is going on or why he, seemingly willingly, has gone along.'

'Okay, I'll make arrangements,' Tammy replied, then in closing, she said, 'You take care now, and keep me informed, as I will you.'

Tammy smiled as she hung up. She loved teasing her friend, but was also very fond of her, and the bond they had so quickly made with each other was strong and comforting. She would do all she could to help Chrissie find out what had happened to Sam.

After several calls to organise good cover and staff for her restaurant, and after sending an e-mail to Sophie, Tammy started to pack her cases and ensure she had all her travel documents ready to fly to Paris.

She recalled the first time she had flown to Paris, fifteen years ago. She was living in her Hoboken flat then. She recalled her excitement and smiled at the memory from so long ago.

As Tammy descended by elevator to the ground floor, across the Atlantic and five hours ahead in time, in Rotterdam, Martijn Vogel found something.

Sophie had made herself at home, and prepared some snacks for both of them. She'd asked the detective twice if he was sure he could spend time on this to which his answer the first time was, 'absolutely', and the second time it was a mere look.

Sophie had smiled and continued to peruse the journal, the second one; Martijn was still reading through the one he had picked up.

'I have something here,' he said, looking across to where Sophie sat.

'I saw the name, Victoria, so I read a little further on. Thankfully the ambassador's handwriting is tidy. There is a section here where he mentions his assistant, Victoria, that she is taking care of a situation.

A pest problem was discovered at the embassy, some type of woodworm. He writes that three rooms of his residence are being cleared and in need of fumigation by pest control.

As he is away on diplomatic business in Johannesburg he notes that there is a man, a recently hired courier, named Mr Smettens, who will assist in the moving of furniture and paintings in order for the pest control people to be able to do their work.'

'Smettens?' Sophie queried, 'I'm sure that's Jan Smettens, I came across his name in the search for the provenance of the Gauguin.

He purchased the Gauguin in Paris in 1908. I also knew he had been in Cape Town, but didn't realise he actually knew the ambassador. That's a great find, though not sure if it is connected with Sam's disappearance. What date is that?'

'This was, let me see, in 1903,' Martijn answered. 'It doesn't mention this Victoria's last name, but she must be the one you're looking for?'

'Absolutely, I'm sure. You say 1903? and three rooms had to be fumigated?'

'Yes, furniture and paintings to be moved from those rooms. In case of fumes or dust, I assume,' Martijn replied. 'What are you thinking?'

For a few moments, Sophie said nothing, then, raising her right forefinger in a gesture for Martijn to hold on a moment, she flicked through the journal she was looking at. Checking the dates, she turned over page after page, then stopped.

'Your journal commences in 1903, right?' she asked, looking up at him, to which he nodded.

Sophie said no more and for the next few minutes; was totally absorbed.

'When I was researching into the Gauguin,' Sophie said at last, looking up at the detective, 'I could never work out when it was that a switch was made. You see, the painting was copied. A very good copy, had many people, including me, fooled. I'm thinking, with this Jan Smettens working for the Embassy and him purchasing the painting years later in Paris, I wonder if it was exchanged at this time, when the pictures were removed whilst the rooms were fumigated.

'I found photo's that the ambassador took of the paintings, he kept a good record, and it shows it hanging on the wall in, what I believe must be one of the rooms that was cleared. This must be the time it was changed, I think, though,' Sophie surmised, 'why would he buy a fake many years later, if it indeed was changed?'

Martijn tried to follow where she was going with this, then remembered something, his detective brain shifting into top gear.

'Wait,' he said. Then looking in the journal he read for a moment, then said 'Listen, the ambassador wrote just a few lines, a few days earlier. Obviously a top story of the day, but there had been a jewellery robbery in the city. Apparently a big one with the police placing extra people at airport and ports. Now, this is speculation, but what if that robbery and the fumigation of the ambassador's residence, were connected?'

Once more Sophie raised her finger, then putting her journal aside, reached for her laptop, typed away for bit, found what she was looking for and began to read.

Martijn watched her.

He had been attracted to her last month, when helping her after she had been attacked and was taken to safety by Sam, bringing her to this very apartment.

He smiled, studied her as she was totally focused on what she was reading.

She was rather attractive. Slim, brunette, brown eyes, in her late thirties. No rings on her fingers, and, as far as he knew, not in a relationship.

She looked up, caught his eyes, noticed he blushed a little and smiled at him.

'I think you are right. I can see why you are a detective. Just been reading about the robbery. Only diamonds were stolen, and quite a few. To date still the largest theft and no-one ever caught. '

'So, how do you suppose, the two events might be connected?' she asked, after a pause.

'Well, 'Martijn answered, 'you said you found the name, Victoria, on the back of this painting, the genuine one, yes?'

'Oui'

'So, why would she put her name on it. Is it possible that she was involved, somehow, and could the diamonds have been hidden, in, say the frame of that painting?'

'Oui, for sure. Now that does make sense. The paintings belonged to the ambassador, they would go with him when he was appointed to another post. His next one was Paris, and I know that Smettens went to Paris because he bought the painting.

I wonder, this Victoria, must also have gone to Paris. She wrote 1903 on the back, can you go further, see if you find any more mentions of her?'

'Sure ' he answered.

'Wait, of course!' Sophie exclaimed, 'The frame was different. When I found the real Gauguin, the frame was different, as was the frame of the fake, so, after Jan Smettens purchased it, the frame was changed, so that's it! It must be. The diamonds must have been inserted into it!'

Martijn looked at her. She had a puzzled expression; obviously something didn't quite fit in with that theory.

The sun shone brightly in the afternoon sky Martijn noticed as he got up and called

his colleague in Amersfoort.

He had rung her earlier, and had asked if there were any major incidents, to which she had replied that there weren't any.

She then asked him how he was getting on, with the French woman, teasingly.

'Some sort of a breakthrough, maybe,' he told her, 'you sure you are okay?'

'I'm fine. Everything's under control, carry on, with the search I mean,' again with that teasing tone in her voice.

He smiled, didn't quite know what to say, so said, 'Goodbye Froukje.'

'Are you sure you can spend all this time on this?' Sophie asked.

'We are on to something here, Sophie, we must follow it through.'

'I'm not sure that we are. I also know that a criminal, the woman behind me being attacked, and who was involved in the fake painting, Steffie Baertjens, although her real name is Lucie van Doorn, currently in prison in Cape Town, was desperate to buy the Gauguin in Amsterdam in 2015.

'Why? Had she perhaps heard about the diamonds, did she know something we don't? She bought that painting, and tried to sell it, only a few weeks later, so, again, why?'

'Are you suggesting that the diamonds are still somewhere?'

'What if ...' Sophie began, pondering again, then again looked into his eyes, noticing they were a lovely blue. 'What if Victoria and Jan Smettens, didn't work together? What if, this Smettens character, was the diamond thief? What if he was the one who had organised the fumigation to be done, and ...'

'What if this Victoria,' Martijn said, taking over the conversation, 'witnessed something, was suspicious, saw perhaps that the diamonds were being put into the frame ...'

'Hence putting her name on the back of that painting' Sophie again took on the conversation, 'but that doesn't make sense either ...'

'What if, having witnessed perhaps the process of placing stolen diamond into the frame, she had, later, when the opportunity arose, taken them out?' Martijn suggested.

'Or ...' Sophie said, 'placed them in another frame?'

They were both quiet for a few moments, thinking through their reminiscing, then it was Sophie, who said, barely louder than a whisper, 'So, Victoria Thompson, were you a naughty girl?'

THE PAST;

PERIOD 5

ROTTERDAM
DECEMBER 1969

'Why Victoria?' she asked. 'Who is she?'

She was lying on his lap in the couch of their small apartment in Hillegersberg, a suburb in the north east district of Rotterdam, looking up into his lovely blue eyes as he looked down on her.

She felt comfortable and content. She, Marijke de Vries, was totally in love with this Englishman.

They were set to be married in early January.

It was early evening on St. Nicholas day. She had explained all about this feast and celebration and he had been amazed at all the festive goodies and colourful shop windows in preparation for it.

James Samuel Price looked down into the sparkling blue eyes of the woman who lay on his lap. He was so in love; she was gorgeous and so attentive to him.

He was twenty-three and had only moved from London five months ago, after securing a position with the Shell company in Rotterdam.

There he had met Marijke on the very first day of work.

Now they were set to get married, in less than three weeks.

Whilst settling down after dinner, on the large couch and listening to the radio, they had been generally discussing their future plans.

Children came up in the conversation.

James said he would like to name their son Samuel, after his grandfather, who, at the age of 99, died the previous month, and after his father, Samuel Junior.

As Samuel senior lived in Vancouver, it was too far and too expensive to travel to his funeral. He told her that he had been an ambassador, even in the Netherlands at one point, in The Hague. He had sadly, never met him, or his grandmother, Elizabeth, who had passed away several years ago.

'And, what if we have a girl?' Marijke asked.

'Victoria,' he replied.

'Why Victoria, who is she?'

'She is my sister. She left to travel to Greece, back in 1965, didn't hear much from her at all, but she sent a Christmas card in 1967, then, nothing.

Mum and dad weren't happy at her going, but as you can imagine, quite sad at losing contact with her. So that's why I thought of Victoria,' James explained.

They both fell silent for a bit. Shocking Blue's 'Venus' came on the radio.

'So, is Victoria a family name then, going back further generations?'

'Ah, now this is quite an interesting story' James said, stroking the lovely long blond hair of the woman on his lap.

'Do tell,' she asked. Her English was mildly accented, though she had been teaching James Dutch. It surely wasn't an easy language to learn, usually in the evening though, she preferred to speak in English and just loved to hear his nice accent.

'Well, my grandfather, the ambassador, when he was appointed in Cape Town, had an assistant come to work with him, she had been sent from London, her name was Victoria … Victoria Thompson,' James said, having to think a little about the surname.

'She was his assistant for about eight years, went with him to Paris in 1904, I seem to recall from the stories my dad told me, then also went with him to The Hague,' James paused for a moment, bent down and softly kissed her lips, before sitting up again, continuing the story.

'We are now getting close to World War 1, and in 1912 my grandfather is recalled to London. Victoria again travels with him. But then he is posted to Vancouver, in Canada, and, Victoria, had now fallen in love, so she stayed on in England.'

James shifted his position slightly, then continued the story, 'So, my grandfather goes to Vancouver, where, he falls in love and marries. Her name is Elizabeth, they have a baby son, Samuel Junior. That is, of course, my father. Now, this is where the story gets really interesting.'

Marijke reached an arm around James', neck, pulls herself towards him and they kiss.

'Mm, now that was also interesting', James said to her, smiling. 'Anyway, to get back to the story, Victoria, remember, she fell in love. Well she married this chap, he was sent off to fight in the war, was killed less than three days after arriving on the front. Very sad, but Victoria was pregnant, gave birth to a girl, Jane.

Now, many years later, just before the second world war, in 1939, Victoria became very ill. She had never remarried, lived in London but also kept in contact with my grandfather.

'So, he got to hear of her illness, but he himself was not well enough to travel at that time, so my dad, Samuel Junior, he travels from Canada to see this Victoria whom he had heard much about. Arrives in London, sees Victoria, and …wait for it, he meets Victoria's daughter, Jane ...the rest, as they say, is history.

'They fall in love, but because of the war, they didn't get married until after, in 1945, and then, a great thing happened ... I was born!' he said smiling down at her.

'You know, when I was talking with Dad the other week, he and Mum were about to fly out to Canada, for Granddad's funeral. Anyway, I was telling him all about this feast, this 'Sinterklaas' time, that all the window displays were great and the assortment of various things, like speculaas and pepernoten and such, when he told me about a painting that grandad had.

'He apparently has a few good works hanging on the wall, but he has a painting called "Feast of St. Nicholas", by some Dutch artist.'

'Mmm, I have heard of it,' Marijke said, 'I have a book of Dutch masters, let me see,'

with that she pulled herself up, left the couch and came back only moments later with a book in hand.

James sat up straight on the couch, watching her turn the pages of this book, thinking how lucky he felt, and how glad he was that he had moved in with her. Not long now before their marriage.

'Here it is,' she exclaimed and beckoned him to look.

James looked at the picture in the book.

There it was indeed, a painting by Jan Steen, 'Feast of St. Nicholas'.

THE PRESENT;

ROTTERDAM

TUESDAY 21ST MAY

'Martijn,' Sophie said, looking up from the journal and catching his eye, 'come and take a look, let me show you something.'

Martijn moved to sit beside her and she explained.

'Here,' she said' is a photo of the Gauguin, "Woman on the shore", the one of which a copy was made at some point, the one, the real one, which I tracked down which had the name of Victoria Thompson written on the back.'

'Aha,' Martijn replied

'And here,' Sophie said, briefly giving him a sideways glance, and flipping the journal open to a different page, 'is a painting by Jan Steen, called "Feast of St. Nicholas", which the ambassador purchased in London, back in 1897, before he was posted to Copenhagen. Now, what strikes you about the two paintings?'

Martijn looked at the second one, then placing his hand upon hers where the first picture was in the journal, he opened it and looked, then back again at the second painting.

He then looked at her, 'The frame is, almost identical.'

Sophie smiled at him. In flash she quickly leaned towards him, kissed him on the lips, then said, 'you'll make a fine detective someday,' smiling at him.

'It's exactly what I saw, the frames are very similar indeed. Now, I know that the original frame, as shown in the photo of the Gauguin, was no more. Both the copy and the genuine painting now have a much smaller thinner frame. Even a darker shade as well, so, what, mister fine detective, do you deduce from that?'

Martijn looked into her brown eyes, her face was quite lit up, her eyes sparkled and she was smiling broadly at him.

The kiss had been quick and unexpected, though rather pleasant and had certainly set his heart racing a little faster.

He put on a mock frown, looking seriously at her, then broke into a smile and said, 'I think I know what you are thinking, so, first, let me ask this, were both paintings in the rooms which were fumigated, whilst hanging on the wall in Cape Town?'

Sophie smiled back, 'Yes, and, wait for it,' turning to another section in the journal, she opened a page which showed the large reception room at the Ambassador's residence in Cape Town.

Martijn looked, then back into her eyes.' Side by side'

'Side by side, indeed, and see how similar the frames look, seeing them next to each other.'

'Are you thinking the diamonds were placed in the wrong frame?'

'No, I think that, once this man Smettens had placed the diamonds in the Gauguin, which I'm sure he did, because that is the painting he bought four years later, no, I think this little Miss Victoria, swapped the frames at a later time.'

'After this Smettens guy had left the residence?' Martijn surmised.

'Yes,' Sophie answered, 'then she put her name, written neatly on a label, on the back of the Gauguin. I'm thinking she might have done that as a teaser so that once Smettens and his cronies, after buying the Gauguin in 1908, discovered that the frame was empty, they might figure out what happened.'

'Mmm, could well be. Quite the madam this Victoria. She was, how old?'

'A mere girl really, about twenty I think. We'll have to find out, also, we need to find out if the Ambassador ever sold the "Feast of St. Nicholas".'

Martijn leaned forward, kissed her briefly, then, looking into her eyes said, 'That will have to wait a bit,' then pulled her towards him. They kissed.

Sophie's phone lying on the coffee table, dinged, announcing a text.

Checking it moments later, she read the message from Chrissie and said' I have to go back to Paris first thing tomorrow' then settled back into his arms.

PARIS

Wheels touched down. Engines into reverse thrust.

Exhilarating.

Once again she was in Paris. The first time she had arrived here, fifteen years ago, had been an adventure, an eye opener as she was on the quest her grandmother had sent her on.

She had returned only a year later and had studied in a fine culinary school for nearly eight months, had then spent another two months working in a two Michelin star restaurant in the heart of the city before returning to New York where she had then purchased the restaurant where once she had been a waitress.

Now she was on a different quest. To help find Sam.

Though she'd only known Chrissie for just over a month, they had bonded, had become good friends. They shared a story.

Though she almost relentlessly teased Chrissie about Sam, she did appreciate how much she cared for him, Sam was important for Chrissie, therefore important to her.

Tammy had received an e-mail back from Sophie, who stated she had some new leads that might prove helpful, saying she would meet her at the airport. Tammy passed through customs and wheeled her case into the arrivals area.

Holding a sign that read, 'Miss Tammy', Sophie stood among several others holding signs and noticed a petite blonde woman heading her way.

She smiled and they greeted in French.

'Okay, well, I think it's about diamonds,' Sophie said, having let herself and Tammy into her apartment.

Their meeting and following taxi ride had been a matter of casual chit chat, Tammy telling of her experience in the city, Sophie of her upbringing and work. Both avoiding speaking of the reason they were meeting, until Sophie unlocked her door and they had entered.

Sophie took off her coat, and showed Tammy to the guest room. She continued speaking, 'Martijn, he's a Dutch detective, he knows Sam, helped me; likes me too, and I like him. Well, he is going to research the theft of the diamonds, which happened in 1903, in Cape Town, South Africa.'

Sophie interrupted herself to ask if Tammy would like a drink, and after an affirmative reply that suggested a coffee would be great, she continued to explain, 'He, Martijn and myself, went to Sam's apartment in Rotterdam yesterday. I still had a key as I had been there before, maybe Chrissie told you?'

Tammy smiled, 'Yes, she and Sam were on the trail of Chrissie's grandfather. She mentioned you had a run in with this woman who tried to sell a fake painting?'

'Oui,' Sophie answered, heading into the small kitchen area, 'thank goodness she is now in prison. Anyway, I asked Martijn to be there too, in case the woman who broke into our offices, most likely looking for Sam's Address, had also gone to Rotterdam.'

Sophie sorted herself out in the kitchen, preparing the drinks, all the while continuing to speak, 'So, he entered first, but no sign of any disturbance.

I knew that Sam had some journals, belonging to his great-grandfather, the ambassador. These journals had been of help before, so, looking through these we stumbled upon the diamond robbery, also came across a name I recognised that of a Mr Jan Smettens.'

Tammy leaned on the kitchen bench, watching the French woman getting the coffee ready, listening to her story and filing away a little bit of information with regard to Sam's possible romantic interest with this woman.

Sophie was attractive, but she had revealed a liking for this detective fellow, Chrissie would be happy with that news.

'So,' Sophie said, having made the drinks, 'we feel that this Smettens guy, was in fact the robber. He stole the diamonds, then he hid them in the frame of a painting, hoping to obtain this at a later time and retrieve the diamonds.'

'A good plan,' Tammy interjected. 'He had the opportunity to place the diamonds in the frame of a painting?'

'Oh sure, a plan and an opportunity. We also know which painting, because he purchased it at auction in 1908, when the ambassador sold it.'

'Wow, a long wait.'

'True, but also wise. The diamonds would no longer be a priority for the police, also the diamonds were now in France, not South Africa.'

'I see, but if that's the case, how can Sam's disappearance have any connection?'

'Well, this is where Martijn and myself struggled with any solid answers. You see, I discovered that the painting, the one where we believe Smettens hid the diamonds in the frame of, was copied, had a different frame put on and was put up for auction.

'The fake one, ended up in our auction room and it was Sam who saw it and queried it. I was adamant it was right, but it was proved a fake, however, I discovered where the real one was, and here we, that is Martijn and I, tried to think through possible scenarios. Anyway, let me show you something; it will be easier to understand.'

Sophie left the kitchen, headed for the lounge. Tammy, drink in hand, followed.

'This is one of Sam's great-grandfather's journals,' Sophie said, placing it upon a low coffee table and opening it up. 'I brought them with me to further investigate, Martijn said that would be okay. Now, look,' Sophie invited Tammy to sit next to her on the two-seater sofa.

'This photo shows one of the main reception rooms at the ambassador's residence in Cape Town. Now, look at those two paintings you see, what do you observe?'

Tammy studied the photo, then replied 'They are the same size and the frames are almost identical, but they are not by the same artist.'

'Very Good, indeed. The one on the left is by Gauguin. This is the one used by Smettens. It's where he hid the diamonds, we are pretty sure about that. The one on the right is by Jan Steen, it's called the "Feast of St. Nicholas". Now, I discovered that on the back of the Gauguin was a name that of Victoria Thompson. She was the assistant to Ambassador Price, in Cape Town and Paris, and also The Hague.

Now, having discussed the possibilities of several scenarios, we both agree that the most likely case is this.

Through these journals, we found out that the ambassador was away. Now, we think that Victoria saw Smettens put the diamonds into the frame of the Gauguin, but later ...'

'Took them out?' Tammy guessed, 'and put them into the other painting's frame?'

'Exactly' Sophie said, smiling, 'or, just simply changed the frames, as they were quite similar.'

They both sipped from the cups and sat back in the sofa.

'So' Tammy asked, looking across at Sophie, 'any idea who this woman is? The one that broke into your offices, the one who Sam captured on his camera and who is now, most likely with Sam, and, has, some leverage over him?'

'No, no idea,' Sophie replied. 'Martijn hopefully might find some connection. I think that if we find out more about this Victoria Thompson, then we might find a connection.'

'So, how can I help?' Tammy asked.

'Well, could you do a search and see if you can find out as much as possible about this Victoria Thompson? There is more in the journals about her, I'm sure.

Martijn found some relevant info, which I have highlighted with pieces of paper inserted in the pages of the journals, then I will do a further trace into the other painting, the one by Jan Steen, the "Feast of St. Nicholas".'

THE PAST;

PERIOD 6

THE YEAR 1972

Jane Shield lay comfortably in her bed. She was alone and deep in thought. The last few days had been mentally challenging. Glancing across over to the tallboy dresser, she saw the photograph.

Her wedding photograph, taken in London, 1945.

She closed her eyes briefly as she remembered the first time she saw him.

He had come from Canada to visit her mother who was very ill. She had written to her mother's former employer, the ambassador, whom her mother had been close to for many years, informing him of her mother's illness.

As he himself was not healthy enough to travel, his son had come instead.

Their greeting had been such a special moment, she reflected, as they both knew instantly that a spark had ignited.

James Junior.

He stayed, joined the war effort later that year, was wounded and ended up in the very hospital where she was a nurse.

They married after the war.

Jane reopened her eyes. Tore her eyes away from that photograph and looked on her bed where two diaries lay.

Her mother had passed only days after meeting James, happy in the knowledge of her obvious liking for this man. Her mother had that day, only hours before, handed her two diaries, one from the year 1903 and the other 1908. She didn't say why, didn't explain, but just gave her a look and handed them over.

Jane shifted slightly to a more comfortable position and again closed her eyes briefly.

She wasn't in pain, but knew she was dying.

She had the same illness as her mother and had found out that it only passed down the female line, though sometimes skipping a generation.

Opening her eyes again Jane knew what she had to do; post the letter she had already written, to her daughter in Greece.

They had received no news from her since 1967, a Christmas card.

It was approaching that time of the year again.

The second decision she needed to make was about the diaries.

With one thing and another, the outbreak of the second world war, the romance that was blossoming, the busyness at the hospital, she had put those diaries away.

It hadn't been until two days ago, when she had been given the results from her tests at the hospital, that she recalled them, dug them out and began reading.

Her mother had kept a secret.

It was a secret she could not share with her husband.

But was it one to pass on to her daughter?

She had written the letter, this most definitely had to be sent. She had to be made aware of an illness that she possibly carried in her body. One that could affect her, or most certainly her daughter if she ever had one.

But what about the diaries?

She had also written a letter to their son, James Samuel, who lived in Rotterdam with his wife Marijke and their baby Samuel, who had only been born a few months ago, in August.

A tear appeared on her cheek. She brushed it away. Then with a determined effort flung back the bedclothes and got up.

She slowly got dressed, took some medicine and a little breakfast, then got ready to go out to the post office.

She had made up her mind.

Together with the letter, she would send the diaries also to her daughter in Greece, hoping that the address she had, was still current and that the parcel would reach her.

Coming out of the post office an hour later, Jane could not possibly have even considered that the very diaries she had just posted to her daughter would one day be instrumental in the disappearance of her grandson Samuel.

THE PRESENT;

BOSTON

TUESDAY 21ST MAY

Chrissie sat, laptop on her lap, on the couch in her front room. It was just after seven in the evening.

A glass of red wine was on the low table in front of her.

They had not long ago had dinner. Currently Ally was clearing up in the kitchen after Chrissie had made the meal.

They had landed in Boston just after three in the afternoon. Had not long after that received an update from DS Saunders.

Sam and the mysterious lady had travelled by train from Halifax to Boston on the Friday evening.

The lady now had a name.

She is Alcina Patronas, from Greece.

From the airport they had gone straight to Chrissie's house.

Here Ally had set to work, using Sam's laptop that they had taken with them, to find out what she could about this Greek woman.

Chrissie had first of all sent an e-mail to Sophie in Paris informing her, and Tammy too, of the name of this woman and would they pass that on to the Interpol guy.

She had then phoned the auction house, insisted she spoke with one of the directors, told her it was to do with Sam Price, and was put through.

She didn't know whether it was Walton or Stanhope she spoke to, but knew about them as Sam had spoken of them.

She informed him of Sam's disappearance and asked if he had made any contact with them since Friday.

He had not, but if they could be of any help, just ask was the genuine offer.

She thanked him and promised to keep them updated.

Quite at a loss as to what to do next, Chrissie set about fixing dinner for herself and her 'rival' Ally.

She smiled at the thought of her calling Ally her rival. Yes, she was, but even after such a short time, with a common focus, they had bonded.

Ally, appearing in the kitchen in search of a drink after scrolling through social media for some time, noticed Chrissie and sensed her feelings.

'We'll find him, truly, we will, he will be alright,' she said.

Chrissie turned and gave a brief smile.

'Thanks, I know we will,' she replied.

Chrissie reached for her glass of wine, took a sip and continued to look at the screen of her laptop.

She nearly dropped her glass as a ping announced an incoming e-mail.

'Ally!' she called out, reading the message, which was from Sophie, briefly thinking it must be around midnight in Paris.

Ally came into the front room, drying her hands on a tea towel.

'Alcina Patronas is the daughter of Victoria Patronas, formerly Victoria Price, Sam's aunt, Alcina is his cousin.'

THE PAST

PERIOD 7

THE YEAR 1988

Joshua Parker stood still.

His body had only moments ago been trembling and shaking. He had been sobbing. Joshua was devastated, forlorn, lost. But the sobbing had subsided.

Taking a few deep breaths had taken control of his breathing and he now stood quite still overlooking the Pacific Ocean.

Not far behind him, sitting on a bench only metres from the graveside, were his father and mother-in-law, Zoltina and Millie, and in between sat his daughter, twenty-one-year-old Millie.

Emily had died.

She had been working in an excavation site in New Mexico. Her master's in geology secured her a leading position in the team that was investigating the discovery of some ruins believed to be Mayan. Also a large pit containing a huge variety of stones was uncovered.

Shortly after arrival she had spoken excitedly on the phone to Joshua. He had visualised her face as she spoke. The broad smile, the sparkling eyes.

He was trying hard to bring her face to mind as he stood looking at the ocean.

His thoughts turned to the time when he met her, some twenty-six years ago, in Trujillo, Peru, where he had stood in a cemetery with her ...

It had been the morning after their dinner together. After an initial somewhat quiet start, they had quickly discovered what they had in common.

And that was a man from the past, Henry Hopkins.

The cemetery was well kept. Having obtained the plot number from the man in the old stone building by the front gate, speaking in broken Spanish and English, Emily had communicated who it was she was looking for and a number along with a rough sketch of the various paths had been handed over to her.

They followed the route and easily found the correct tombstone.

Emily knelt down and read the inscription.

Joshua noted that it was one of the better quality headstones and that the grave looked well kept.

Although most Peruvians would have two names, the man, who's grave they stood by had just one.

Cisco Huanca.

This was her ancestor on her mother's side as far back as she would ever be able to go, she figured, reading the inscription.

The name of a woman, the wife, a name of a girl, the daughter, and there, carved in stone, the name Zoltina, after who her uncle was named.

Then in English, the words 'Truly a free man now,' below which were the words 'Sleep well my friend,' and the name Henry Hopkins.

'Well, well, Henry Hopkins' Joshua said, his voice soft as he stood beside her, his hand on the shoulder of the woman who, though he had not even known her for a day, meant the world to him.

Emily stood up, briefly looked at him, then took her camera and began taking pictures.

She took one of Joshua standing by the grave and he one of her.

'I know very little of Henry, other than his involvement in the mine in Harris.'

Joshua said, as they walked away.

Emily looked across to the man who had captured her heart. There had been something about this stranger when she had first seen him, stepping off the bus the previous day. She smiled at him as they walked on, thinking of her decision to get him to take her to dinner, leaving him speechless.

'I know his whole life,' she answered.' The journals are well written. You must read them. He was here, he was there, at the mine, when bandits attacked.

Though he writes humbly, I have no doubt that despite Cisco having been killed, he saved the life of Zoltina.'

'He was obviously close to them, seeing that headstone.'

He arranged the funeral, and yes, he was close. They worked here together in the mine, for a number of years.'

The couple exited the cemetery and headed back to the hotel.

'That inscription, 'Truly a free man now,' Joshua asked, 'not sure I get that exactly.'

'The answer is in the journals,' Emily replied, 'The name Cisco, means, free man'

The following day they had hired a driver to take them to the north of the city, to where the mine was located, some eight miles inland from Puerto Chicama.

It was Joshua who had the most information about the location. Though he knew little of Henry's work outside of the mine in Harris. He had done some research on the sculpture that stood outside the office building of CP Holdings.

He had told Emily about it, over dinner, a great evening which had gone on to the point of a friendly request to vacate the restaurant.

They realised then it was close to midnight.

He showed her a sketch he had made, which he'd brought with him in order to stimulate some sort of conversation as he had been worried as to what to say to this most beautiful woman.

He need not have worried as they bonded easily and were soon sharing stories.

He had explained to her that though no-one had seemed to know, he figured out that the shape of the rock sculpture, shaped from a large boulder they had mined, was chiselled out to form the map of Peru.

Then, doing some measuring and maths, and studying a large map he had purchased of the country, he discovered that where Henry had drilled a hole in the sculpture and inserted a green gemstone, corresponded with the location of Trujillo.

He had blushed when she had complimented him on his clever discovery.

He'd then swiftly continued with the conversation. He had searched through what he could find out about Henry, and come up with information about a mine, just north of Trujillo. This he had read in a file which had been compiled by Charlie Parker the third, with whom Henry had made a business deal.

It was that piece of information that had prompted him to head for Peru and find out more about the man who had been such an important figure in the town.

The following morning, when they met for breakfast Emily had produced an old map. It had been tucked in one of the journals, and, according to Henry, he had acquired it when mining in Ecuador as it had the details and location of a silver mine in northern Peru.

Joshua had been fascinated by this old map. Furthermore it had clear details mentioned that would make it, hopefully easy, to locate.

They gave instructions to the driver and found the mine. At least found an old building which had been part of it.

Emily explained that prior to leaving, they had blown the mine up, to prevent bandits from claiming it.

They walked around for a bit, then headed back to the port.

Here they got out of the car, and looked at the buildings that made up the port of Chicama.

'Zoltina left here, where he boarded a ship to Acapulco. There he set up a business, this was way back in 1821.'

They both stood for a while hand in hand. A natural progression in their journey together as they looked at the vast Pacific Ocean ...

Joshua took another deep breath, a wonderful memory from so long ago.

He turned, noticed the three of them still sitting on the bench.

It seemed like he had been away in his thoughts for simply ages, yet, it must have been only minutes.

He made his way towards them.

Millie slipped from in between her grandparents and walked towards her father.

Recalling what she had seen on the television.

The devastation of the tornado that had swept through the small settlement.

The commentator mentioning that it had swerved unexpectedly at one point, catching a couple of twister observers out, and taking hold of their vehicles and brushing them aside like toy cars.

However, for Millie the traumatic part of the news report was seeing the devastation of the excavation site where her mother had been at work.

Trees uprooted, tents and equipment flung in all directions. Seventeen people were injured, four died.

She reached her father. They hugged.

Zoltina and Millie came off the bench, and made their way to them.

Then the four of them walked slowly towards the entrance of the cemetery.

The sky was blue. The wind a mere whisper and the sound of the ocean seemed to be a soothing roar. Each with his and her own thoughts.

Zoltina, now seventy-eight, recalls fondly the day of the maiden voyage of his cruise boat, and six-year-old Emily standing excitedly at the rail, waving to the many folk on the pier. Her sixth birthday.

At the age of seventy, with no-one to take over the reins, Zoltina sold the Huanca Bay Transport company with its three vessels.

Millie thought of the many hours she and Emily had spent in the study, reading, chatting. Thought of the journals she had found and passed on for Emily to read. Journals that brought her into contact with Joshua.

Walking beside him now, her arm around his waist, she was thankful that Emily had found a caring and loving husband.

Young Millie was still in a daze. Ten days ago. Only ten days ago, she had embraced her mum as her mum had set of for New Mexico.

It was comforting to feel her father's hand on her shoulder. It would be a difficult time ahead for a while.

She was off to Milan, Italy, spending some time there in pursuit of her fashion career.

Her father would be heading to Canada, to the town of Harris, as he was about to take over the running of CP Holdings there.

Joshua was thinking about the very move that was on Millie's mind.

He would go, but never thought that he would be going alone.

The foursome reached the gates and left the cemetery.

THE PRESENT;

BOSTON

THURSDAY 23RD MAY

The phone buzzed. Chrissie stirred, saw her alarm clock showing just after two am. 'Hello?' she answered, her voice still sounding dazed and sleepy.

'Chrissie, it's me ...'

'Sam!' Chrissie sat bolt upright, instantly fully awake, 'Where are you? Are you okay?'

'I'm fine. Listen, I'll explain in a moment why I'm calling, though by the sound of it, you are aware to some degree, but first, I need to know ...'

'If Sophie is okay?' Chrissie interjected. 'Yes, she is fine, Tammy is with her, and so is detective Martijn ...'

'Really?' Sam said, surprised, 'you know more than I realised? How?' spoken softly and with a sense of relief.

'I flew out to your place, Contacted detective Karen. She took me to your apartment. We suspected something was up as you hadn't returned my calls or e-mails, she called Ally ...'

'Ally knows too?' Sam interrupted.

'We figured your disappearance might have something to do with her. We found the message on the mirror though, hence we made sure we got hold of Sophie. Sam, what is going on? Who is this woman that came to your place?'

'You know about her too? You found the memory card! Well done you!'

'And your laptop. Fancy hiding the mouse in the butter!' Chrissie said, laughing, yet almost crying as it was such a relief to hear his voice.

Sam could hear the break in her voice, 'Sorry Chrissie, couldn't call, couldn't do much really, until I found a way to get hold of you. Now that I know Sophie is safe, I can explain it all.'

'Where are you?'

'Right here in Boston, listen. I can leave from where I am safely now, so, I'll get to your house in, oh, about twenty minutes, but don't tell the police; wait till I get there, okay?'

'Okay, see you soon,' Chrissie answered, realising she was crying now.

The phone connection was broken.

She got out of bed, quickly showered and dressed, before entering the guest room to wake Ally.

'Hey, Ally, wake up. Sam is alright!'

'He is?' she asked, sitting up. 'Where is he?'

'Get dressed. I'll get the coffee going, he should be here in about fifteen minutes!'

'You spoke with him?' Ally asked, flinging the bedsheets aside.

'He rang; we spoke briefly. He doesn't know your here. We are not to talk to the police. See you downstairs.'

MEANWHILE, LESS THAN TWO MILES AWAY

Sam Price reached the petrol station and phoned for a cab.

It was a clear and mild night. The gas station was a 24-hour service station and Sam waited outside.

He would have liked a coffee right now, but was sure Chrissie would supply him with one very soon.

He had no money.

She had his credit cards. She did have his laptop, or actually the laptop he had purchased for Ally. She did also have his camera and passport, but he had those back now.

Now knowing that Sophie was not in danger, he knew the tables were turned.

The cab arrived.

The driver opened the trunk and Sam placed his small suitcase inside, then opened the back door and sat down. He was tired, but relieved.

Giving the driver the address, Sam looked out the window of the cab and thought back ...

Friday afternoon.

Habitually looking out the large living room windows overlooking the industrial estate he noticed the van.

Noticed that two men got out and stood waiting by the side of it.

Something churned inside of him.

He had a sense, a premonition perhaps. All was not well.

When one of the men looked up and directly at his apartment, Sam knew that trouble was coming.

His mind raced as he thought as to what to do. Who were these guys?

Friends of the Rozzinis perhaps?

Sam quickly grabbed his camera, he took a couple of shots, then another vehicle appeared and a woman got out.

Sam took two more photos, then, realising he would soon be in danger, set about to protect himself.

Taking the memory card from the camera, he took it to his bedroom, placed it under an unopened bar of soap in the en suite, then put a new memory card into the camera.

Next he placed the laptop, the one he had given to Ally to use, on his desk, took his own away and, moving towards the kitchen, noticed the two men and the woman were talking.

Wrapping the laptop in foil he placed it under a grilling rack in the bottom of the oven. Going back into the living room and back to his desk, he took the power cable and the mouse and mousepad away.

The mouse he hid in an almost empty butter container in the fridge. The power cable and pad he placed in the bottom of his wardrobe, underneath several jumpers.

Once again back in the living room he noticed the men were still standing by the van, but the woman was nowhere to be seen.

Next Sam checked his credit card folder, took out the one he used most and left the others there.

This card he then quickly put in an envelope and placed it among other envelopes in his desk.

Heart racing and still trying to figure out who these people were, and what they were after, Sam's next move was to get ready to phone Detective Sergeant Saunders.

Then there was a knock on the door ...

The cab pulled up at the address given.

Sam broke off his thoughts, checked on the fare, then told the driver he would get the money from the person inside the house.

Already the front door was open.

As Sam exited the cab, Chrissie came down the path, and, following behind was Ally.

Chrissie flung herself at Sam, saying nothing.

'Eh, hi guys, could you pay the cabbie, please?' Sam asked as he untangled himself from her only to be re-entangled by Ally.

The trunk popped open and Chrissie told the driver she'd nip inside and get the money.

Sam retrieved his case and closed the trunk.

Chrissie came back and paid the driver. Neither Chrissie nor Ally had said a word to Sam as yet.

He was surprised to see both of them together.

Both women making a fuss of him, they led him into the front room. Then the questions came, where have you been, who was that woman, what is it all about, where does Sophie come into it?

Sam turned and looked at them both, still in somewhat of a confused state as to how they knew so much, and moreover, how it was that they were together.

'It is really all to do with my father's sister,' Sam said, then walking towards them placed himself in the middle and hugged them both.

THE PAST;

PERIOD 8

THE YEAR 1999

Fifty-two-year-old Victoria Patronas walked along the waterfront promenade. The city of Thessalonica to her right, the Thermaic Gulf, part of the Aegean Sea on her left.

She was in thought. Deep in thought.

Stopping and facing the sea, she took in the fresh air. Sensed her eyes welling up.

She was lonely. She felt lonely.

Walking on a little further, passing the statue of Alexander the Great, she perched herself on a low white wall, and, again looking out to sea, let the tears that had been welling up, flow over her cheeks.

It was early on a Sunday morning.

A couple of church bells were chiming somewhere in the upper area of the city.

She had fallen in love, over thirty-four years ago in London.

She had been planning for a trip to Paris with a couple of friends, she changed it, going back to Greece with him.

The Adonis in her life. He was tall, deeply tanned, dark hair, brown eyes and his English accent was delightful.

Her parents were less impressed and suggested they write to each other, see how that developed, before making such a commitment.

She had argued.

She had left.

She recalls sending a Christmas card one year, the last time she wrote. Was it back in 1966 or 67? She had, she remembered, put her address on the envelope, hoping they might write to her.

But there had been nothing, from them, or from her older brother, though he had always been a good older brother to her.

Then, late in the year 1972, she had received the parcel, and the letter. It was in November, her first born, Alcina, only two months old.

A letter that revealed her mother's illness. A hereditary disease. She remembers crying that day, reading how this illness might affect her, or, holding her baby daughter in her arms, her child.

Then there were the diaries, just two of them, belonging to her grandmother, after whom she was named. Why just two, why those particular years?

Though she had wondered, it wasn't until recently that she had found them again, and had finally read them.

At the time she had been angry, angry with her mother, with her father, with herself too. But stubborn as she was, she put the diaries away for later and continued her life in Thessalonica, with her handsome Adonis.

Her life was good. He came from a wealthy family and she had all she wanted. A nice house in a great district of the city, a circle of friends that enjoyed the good times, a nanny and a housekeeper. Life was good.

She had travelled to many of the Greek Islands, had an all over tan, the best clothes and jewellery.

But the dream was shattered. The bubble of happiness burst.

Her Adonis found a new Aphrodite.

Her daughter was just three.

But she had been strong, been fierce, had a great command of the language, had made some good contacts and had survived. Not only survived, but had been able to set herself and her daughter up in a smaller but nice residence close to the waterfront. Had found work, had kept her head down and, stubborn and headstrong, had continued life in the city.

Though years passed, and seemingly quickly, Victoria began to feel isolated. Began to feel so very alone.

She was financially secure. But as she had lost interest in her work, spent much of the day lounging around her house.

Then came, what she had forgotten about, what she had deliberately put into the back recesses of her memory. She became ill.

She knew. She went to the doctor armed with a letter; the one her mother had written all those years ago; the one describing, in medical terms, the illness she was sure she now also had inside her.

The doctor, after the results of various tests, confirmed the diagnosis.

Only two months earlier, her now 27-year-old daughter had met an Australian and had moved with him to Perth in western Australia.

She remembers, as she still sat on the low wall and gazing out to sea that she almost was going to go into a speech about the dangers of such a move, but then thought back of how she had done the very same to her parents, all those years ago.

Who was she to even argue this arrangement.

Victoria got up, continued her walk, glanced up and over to where she could see her house, then once more turned to look out to sea.

Earlier, she had written a letter. A long letter, to her brother. A letter she would post in the morning.

Then, later today, she would call her daughter.

Explain the illness.

Then she would tell her about the diaries, and that there was a secret within, to be read only, after she had passed away, which, according to the doctors, was only a few weeks away.

Walking along the waterfront, a few more church bells ringing throughout the city, with the tears having dried up, Victoria wondered about what she had learned in those diaries, written by her grandmother all those years ago.

About diamonds and paintings.

THE PRESENT;

PARIS

THURSDAY 23RD MAY

Tammy wanted to ring.

Not long ago she had rung Chrissie when it was only six in the morning, with the news about the letter she had found. Percivald Quinton writing to his daughter about Bastiaan Bouten.

Now she had even more exciting news, but it was the middle of the night still in Boston.

When her phone rang, and she saw that it was Chrissie calling, she animatedly answered the call.

'Chrissie! Great that you rang. I have news, well, we have news ...'

'You're not the only one Tammy,' Chrissie interrupted, 'I have news too ...'

'This is too exciting,' Tammy spoke, interrupting Chrissie's interruption, speaking rapidly, 'Sophie and this Dutch detective, his name is Martijn, well, they figured something out, well, in between kissing and canoodling ...ow!'

'Tammy?'

'It's alright that was Sophie, she hit me ...'

'I can relate to that, but listen ...'

'No, hang on, this is really good, clever detective work really, but this whole thing, is about a painting ...'

'The feast of St. Nicholas,' Chrissie said interrupting.

'Yes, the feast …wait, what? How … Sophie and this Martijn just figured this out, how could you know about …'

'Sam told me,' Chrissie answered, letting that sink in for a moment.

'Oh. Well …hey! Sam's okay? Where is he? What happened? Is he alright?'

Chrissie smiled at the barrage of questions from her friend, then answered, 'Sam's okay, he is right here with us, with Ally and me, in Boston, but please say well done to Sophie. That was very clever, working it all out. Do you know why the painting is so important?'

'Diamonds!' Tammy answered.

'Again, yes, well done. Listen, may I speak with Sophie for a minute?'

Tammy passed her phone to Sophie, who stood right by her side, then rubbed her shoulder where she had playfully been punched by the French woman. She gave her a mock scowl as she handed the phone over. Sophie smiled, took the phone and quickly gave Tammy a peck on the cheek to show no hard feelings, then spoke, 'Sam is okay?'

She listened for several moment, saying 'oui' a couple of times before handing the phone back to Tammy.

'So, now what? Do you want me to come home? And you and Sam, and Ally? You need me to referee?'

Chrissie laughed, then answered, 'No, well not yet anyway. Can you stay with Sophie for a bit; help her with what I have asked her for? Can you do that?'

'Of course, but you have to tell me everything you know, I mean, everything, come on girl, talk to me ...'

BOSTON

When Chrissie finally ended the call the time on the kitchen clock said it was just after four o'clock in the morning.

Finishing her cup of tea, she smiled.

Sam was safe.

After she and Ally had made a fuss over him, they had listened as he told them what had happened since last Friday afternoon.

THE PAST;

PERIOD 9

THE YEAR 2014

Roberto Solari settled himself in the first-class carriage. He had spent a few days in Monaco with his ailing sister and was glad to be on his way home again.

Eighty-five years of age, he had arthritis in his fingers and knees. No longer could he easily hold a brush.

Added to that he had the onset of Parkinson's.

He regularly wondered why it seemed to affect only his right hand.

His painting hand.

A woman came bundling into the carriage with a mustard-coloured suitcase and a large handbag which she plonked on the seat opposite as she sat down.

Roberto noticed her hair was wet. Caught in the recent shower which his knee had earlier predicted would be imminent.

Rubbing his knee he studied her briefly as she was settling herself in.

Her somewhat bedraggled hair was shortish and blond. He noticed her clothes were of good quality, as was the handbag and suitcase.

She wore a nice watch but there was no sign of jewellery on her fingers.

She turned and noticed him looking at her. He smiled and nodded a greeting.

She smiled back.

A whistle sounded and almost immediately the train rolled away, leaving Monaco and heading for Paris.

The woman turned her case around, opened it and was fumbling around for a bit.

Roberto spotted something.

He saw a small painting.

Twenty by thirty centimetres. Oil on canvas, slim frame. He knew this painting, knew the artist.

'That's a nice painting,' he said to her, speaking French.

Two rows further along in the carriage, Alcina Patronas was observing the scene.

She too had observed the blond woman come bundling into the carriage with her luggage and her hair all wet from the recent shower.

Thankfully she had arrived early and had already been seated when the downpour had come down with force, aided by a gust of wind that blew the rain almost horizontally across the platforms.

When the old man mentioned about the fine painting she apparently had inside her suitcase, her ears pricked up. He said he knew the artist.

This was interesting. Was he someone connected with the art world. That might prove useful she thought.

The train picked up speed quickly, then rode smoothly along the tracks. With only a few people in the carriage, Alcina was able to continue to pick up bits of conversation between the woman and the old man.

She had earlier, upon arrival at the terminal building, noticed the woman as she appeared to be a little flustered, checking out the departure board, rummaging through her handbag. She wasn't sure what it was that drew her attention to her.

Now, as the train travelled at high-speed heading north, Alcina tried to piece together, from what snippets of conversation she heard, what it was about this woman that somewhat troubled her.

A conductress came through and she showed her ticket.

Paris.

She wondered if it would be up to her expectations.

Forty-two-year-old Alcina Patronas gave up after a while of listening in and relaxed in her seat, the landscape rolling by.

She thought back to why it was she was here, thought back to the circumstances that changed her life, thought back to the event that had started it ...

The letter. A letter from her mother.

It had been a Saturday morning and she had been sitting on the patio, having breakfast. The sun was already well up and the temperature climbing rapidly towards the twenty-five degrees.

Her boyfriend came through the sliding doors and placing the letter on the table.

He said nothing. Their relationship was deteriorating.

The contents of the letter was the straw that broke the camel's back.

Alcina read about the illness, one that had ended her grandmother's life, one that was now affecting her mother and one that, most likely, she would also have.

Taking the letter into the kitchen, she had explained its contents, but instead of sympathy and concern, he came out with a sentence that cut deep into her heart.

'Well that's that then. I'm not having children with you.' He turned and left the kitchen.

Standing there, totally devastated, she, some moments later, heard the front door slam.

She would not see him again.

That had been nearly fifteen years ago.

The high-speed train reached Lyon and stopped for seven minutes before it slowly pulled out of the station to continue towards Paris.

Several people had entered the carriage, but it was by no means full.

Alcina briefly studied the couple who had taken seats across the aisle from her, then again looked out the window and continued her reflections ...

Her mother had left home at the age of eighteen, leaving London behind to head for Greece.

Alcina had been twenty when she had met an Australian tennis player, had fallen in love and had moved to Perth.

That had been in 1992.

She booked her travel home three weeks after receiving the letter, left her job, relinquished the lease on her flat, put her finances in order and left Australia behind.

She flew from Perth to Dubai, then a connection to Thessalonica.

Eight years after leaving, she arrived home, only to discover and hear of another devastating bit of news.

Her mother had passed away the day before.

The years passed.

Alcina was financially secure.

The house, overlooking the waterfront, a prime property, was hers. Also there had been a substantial amount in the bank.

Three months after her mother's death, Alcina took herself to a hospital to do tests to see if she had the genetic illness that passed down the female line.

The results were inconclusive. Not enough information was available to establish a firm diagnosis, but the likelihood that she would contract it in later years was high.

She found work, lived day by day, was often angry, regularly bored and dissatisfied and kept looking for something to focus on.

More years passed.

Then one day, less than a year ago, she had a mind to empty a large wardrobe. Time for a change. Throwing everything on the bed Alcina then came upon a shoe box that she hadn't seen before.

Inside was a large brown envelope and two diaries, one for 1903 and one for 1908, both having belonged to and been written by her great-grandmother Victoria.

A plan began to form.

As she had wanted to go to Monte Carlo and wander around the casino, all dressed up and feeling like a Bond girl, she made plans to go.

Two days there and then the train journey to Paris.

Picking up on the conversation she overheard, she briefly wondered about speaking to the old man as he seemed to be knowledgeable about art. But as they arrived in Paris, she saw that the blond woman was all over him and in animated discussion.

Taking a taxi to the hotel she had booked, Alcine later that day called into the Paris Fine Arts Auction House.

THE PRESENT;

BOSTON

THURSDAY 23RD MAY

Chrissie stood in the doorway of the second guest room.

Leaning against the door jamb, she let tears roll down her face as she watched him, watched Sam as he lay fast asleep on the bed.

Ally came up to her, peeked through the doorway and looked at the woman who had become her friend, noticed the tears and realised how much Chrissie was in love with the man she too was in love with.

'Come on,' Ally said, as she reached through the door and began to close it, 'we need to follow up on what Sam asked us to do.'

Chrissie looked at Ally, nodded and turned allowing the door to be closed.

Going down the stairs, she looked at her watch, four-thirty in the morning, then replayed in her mind all that Sam had told them a little earlier ...

'Right, start at the beginning, last Friday ...' Chrissie had said.

'And don't leave anything out, come on ...' Ally had added.

Sam sat in the comfy armchair in the front room. The very chair he had occupied when he first came here, and first met Chrissie.

The two women were sitting on the couch, Chrissie nearest, Ally on the edge of the seat. Both looking at him intently. Both had obviously been concerned. Somehow they had got together in a search for him. They had said little, too little, about that. They wanted him to tell the story first.

Sam smiled briefly, looked at them both in turn, then sat back a little and began to speak. As he spoke, he not only took himself back to that Friday afternoon, but the two women on the couch, both giving their full attention, were taken along …

What he was working on that afternoon, was an affair of the heart.

Though having tearfully said goodbye to Ally, his feelings towards Chrissie were very strong. He was just recalling the time they had spent in Genoa.

Not mentioning his thoughts at that time, Sam began with when he noticed the van.

'I was walking through the lounge, when I noticed a van parked in the street opposite my apartment and saw two men get out.

They were talking to each other. One of them glanced at his watch a couple of times. Were they waiting for someone?'

And so Sam explained how he went into action as he had a sense of something that was not quite right. He told them how he hid the mouse and laptop, told them of the pictures he took and the hiding of the memory card.

Then came the knock on the door …

'Hello cousin Sam,' the woman said, smiling broadly, 'I'm cousin Alcina, Victoria's daughter, from Greece.'

'Well hello cousin,' Sam answered, warily, instantly suspicious of the dark-haired woman that stood before him.

'Come on in,' he said, standing aside.

There was no sign of the two men.

He led her to the living room.

'Would you like a coffee?' he asked, gesturing for her to sit as he made his way past her heading for the kitchen, 'or a cold drink?'

'No, thank you. I want you to sit down, and listen very carefully to what I will say.'

Sam turned, looked at her. The tone of her voice was unmissable. It was lightly threatening, and as he looked into her brown eyes, he could see that she was very serious.

'Very well. You had to have done some research as to where I was. Moreover, there must be something I can help you with, so, cousin or no cousin, do tell, what is it you want of me?' Sam replied.

He remained standing in the archway in between the living room and kitchen area.

'Very well,' the woman answered, frowning slightly as she had not expected that response. 'Your ... associate, Miss Sophie Pontiac, in Paris. One of my men is, well keeping an eye on her. Also, if you care to look out your window, there are two men right outside, if you're thinking of doing anything foolish. I need your assistance in locating something. Help me, and all will be well. I need to contact my man in Paris every three hours. If I don't, well, cousin, her life is in your hands'

Sam looked at her. He could tell she meant business. He felt for sure that she was sure of herself, moreover sure that she was in control of the situation.

'I don't know about you, but I need a coffee. Do you want one? Yes or no. Then, do tell how I may be of help.'

Sam kept his eyes locked on hers. He hoped his voice had sounded confident.

He also hoped she would take him up on the drink. It would give him a few moments in which to think on the situation he was in.

'Sure, black, no sugar.'

Sam turned and headed into the kitchen.

'I'm sorry for your loss,' he called out. 'I had picked up that your mum had died, some years ago now, early 2000 was it?'

'I am surprised you know, my mother left the family a long time ago, never went back home ...'

'Your mother wrote to her brother, my father,' Sam explained, having put the kettle on and fetching a couple of mugs.

He said no more; let her figure out how much he knew about the situation.

It was quiet for a few moments in the lounge.

Alcina had not appreciated that her mother had been in contact with Sam's father.

She had found nothing to suggest her mother had any contact with the family when going through her things.

How much did he know, she wondered.

'I lived in Australia for some years. Went back to Greece when she told me she was ill. I guess she must have written to your father as well at that time,' Alcina said, recovering from the initial surprise and determined to re-establish control.

'Guess so, 'Sam answered, pouring the drinks and carrying them into the lounge.

Placing them on the low table, Sam then sat down and said, 'As my cousin, I would normally help you anyway, if I could. Threatening a friend of mine, well, I guess what you need me for isn't, perhaps, legal?'

Sam again looked directly at her, again held her gaze.

She was still confident, though a slight touch of redness on her cheekbones, suggested she wasn't as sure as earlier.

Fishing a packet from her handbag, she took out a cheroot, then fumbling for her lighter, lit it, blew the smoke in Sam's direction and looking at her watch Alcina said, 'Two hours before the call. So, listen, you will accompany me to Boston. We will take the evening train. I will take your laptop, your camera and your phone.

Take a small suitcase and don't forget your passport. When we are on the train, I will explain what you need to do.'

'Sounds very intriguing,' Sam answered, trying to remain as calm as possible.

He reached for his coffee, still piping hot, blowing on it and taking a careful sip.

'I will need to have your phone straight away,' Alcina demanded, 'and don't try anything stupid. My threats are true threats. I mean business. There is a lot at stake, do you understand?'

Sam looked at his watch, calculating the time. He stood up, 'If we are to catch the evening train from Halifax, we have to go soon.' Then reaching into his trouser pocket, he took out his phone which he placed on the table.

'My laptop and my camera are there on my desk,' Sam said, indicating. 'I'll go and grab some clothes, pack a case, and my passport. I will not be stupid.'

Sam left the room, going through the kitchen to his bedroom.

Alcina got up, retrieved the laptop and the camera, then sat down and sipped her coffee.

She felt more confident again, more in control.

She put his phone in her handbag, got her own phone out and pressed some numbers.

She felt sure that her cousin wasn't going to risk the life of his friend.

Once Sam was in his bedroom, he quickly got his passport, took a suitcase from the wardrobe, then ran into the en suite bathroom where he put the hot tap on by the basin.

He let this run for a bit, whilst gathering his toothbrush, shaver and deodorant.

The mirror steamed up. With his finger Sam wrote, in the top left-hand corner of the steam, the words 'Find Sophie'.

He then turned the tap off, picked up his toothpaste and aftershave and continued to pack the case. As she hadn't asked for them, he left his credit cards behind, stuffing them quickly into a pair of socks in the drawer.

He hadn't timed himself, but was sure it was only moments ago that he left the lounge.

Shutting the door to the en suite, then shutting his bedroom door, he took his case back through the kitchen and entered the lounge.

Alcina was no longer alone, but had let in one of the men. Both of them were now smoking.

He noticed the coffee mugs were gone. No doubt his cousin had washed them and eliminating traces of her being there.

'Good, let's go,' she said. 'After you,' she gestured for Sam to leave first.

In Chrissie's front room both her and Ally were totally focused, hanging onto every word.

'I could smell the smoke,' Chrissie said. 'It's when I really became suspicious.'

Sam queried how come it was that they were both together and Chrissie had briefly explained that she had tried to call him and had instantly been suspicious that he hadn't answered.

When Sam had prompted for more, he was met with a united front of the two women demanding he speak first and tell all.

'Well, then, 'Sam continued. 'I left the message, left my laptop hidden and the memory card with the photos I took. I was not really sure who it might be that would come looking for me. Not just one, but two beautiful women makes me feel rather special.' He smiled at the women, but their looks suggested he better get on with telling the story.

'Cousin Alcina didn't say much on the drive to Halifax. I was in her car, the two men behind us in the van. We didn't stop until we got to the train station. She got out and made a call. She spoke in Greek, well I assumed it was Greek, couldn't pick up what it was she said, but if she was indeed speaking to someone in Paris, I wondered who it might be as by now it would be well after midnight over there.

'Anyway, she had a suitcase in the trunk, in which she had placed my laptop and camera, along with my suitcase. We entered the station and she threw the car keys to one of the men.

I assumed that they were to return the rental vehicles. Did you find out if they were?' Sam asked.

It was Ally who answered, 'Detective Sergeant Karen followed the trail, thanks to your photos. They were indeed rental vehicles, both the van and the car.'

Sam nodded, then proceeded with the story.

It was three thirty in the morning.

Sam was tiring. He had been speaking for some time, explaining the last few days, what his cousin had said on the train journey to Boston, and what the object of her forceful pursuit was.

Alcina had told him, 'My great-grandmother was Victoria Thompson and she worked as an assistant to your great-grandfather, the ambassador, Samuel Price.

She worked with him for nearly nine years.

Now, when the ambassador was posted to Canada, she stayed in London, about to get married. She was told, and I read this in a diary, that, upon the death of your great-grandfather, she would be bequeathed a painting. One she had taken a liking to when she first worked with the ambassador in South Africa.

She never got it.'

'Really?' Sam had asked, 'and what painting was this then, he owned a few.'

'The feast of St. Nicholas, by Jan Steen,' Alcina answered.

'My grandmother received the diaries, but did nothing about it. My mother received the diaries, also, did nothing about it. I now have the diaries, as I also have the hereditary illness passed down the generations, I want to do something about a promise not kept. I want that painting.'

'And you sought me out. Why? I don't have the painting. My parents don't have it either. The ambassador stayed in Canada, married there. It's very likely then that the painting would have gone to his wife or her family,' Sam suggested.

'This, my cousin, is where you come in. I found out a number of things, in researching the whereabouts of the painting. You, working for the auction house, you, with contacts and experience, you will find it for me. Furthermore, you'll ensure that I get it.'

Sam took it all in, and ran the story through his mind, as the train sped towards Boston through the evening landscape.

Though certainly a plausible story, to Sam it seemed too much of an overkill in order to obtain a painting that, though it may be reasonably valuable, surely wasn't worth all this effort and threatening behaviour.

Looking through the window, he could clearly see the reflection of his cousin.

He knew from a conversation he had with his father sometime back that his aunty, dad's sister, had this genetic illness, affecting the female line.

He'd not known a lot about it, other than that she had left home at eighteen, had gone to Greece and had never returned home.

Now the woman he observed in the reflection on the train window, a woman who had suffered the loss of her mother, and who now had the illness herself, was angry.

He could hear the tension in her voice, sensed the determination in her body language, and, he could see her face. Purposeful and focused.

But was it all the truth.

Sam had his doubts.

After some time of silence, Sam asked, 'So, what information have you got that will help in locating the painting's whereabouts?'

Alcina looked at her cousin.

Inwardly she was somewhat relieved. So far everything had gone to plan. He seemed to accept her story and looked to be willing to assist.

'I went to Paris, about five years ago, following up on information from the diary. I went to the Paris Fine Arts Auction House as they are a reputable firm that has been around a while. However, they didn't exist in 1908 and however much I tried, I came away without finding what I was looking for. Went back home.

Then, a couple of years later, I read an article in a Greek magazine, all about a painting by Gauguin that was discovered in a hotel room and went to auction in Amsterdam. This got me thinking. So, I then contacted this auction house, asked if they knew of a painting called "the feast of St. Nicholas", which had once belonged to ambassador Samuel Price. Low and behold, they said I should get in touch with you, Samuel Price, great-grandson of the ambassador, who is an art assessor and will likely know the whereabouts of that work of art.'

Alcina paused for a moment as she reflected on the day she made that discovery.

The train rolled smoothly through the countryside.

'I was ill for a while, had to be at home to recover, but in that time I discovered who you worked for. I had no idea of the whereabouts of your parents, my aunt and uncle, nor of you, but figured as you worked for this auction house that you would live in Paris.'

Alcina looked across at her cousin, noting that he was listening intently and, feeling no animosity from him, she continued to explain.

'So, I went to Paris again. This time I broke into the office there, found your file and found out you went to Canada, hence my journey here, and also my plan to ensure your assistance with some leverage. Just to be clear, my threat is serious. I really need to have this painting.

As far as the painting goes, I tracked it to having gone with the ambassador to British Columbia, to Vancouver, but nothing since, so that's around 1912. Hence I need your help.'

'So, why are we heading for Boston?' Sam asked.

'The auction house in Boston, Franck Huysen & Son, who you now, temporarily, work for, is one of the oldest established auction houses this side of the Atlantic.

'I figured that they may well have information in their archives of works of art that passed through there. You see, the ambassador, when he left London to travel to British Columbia, came via Boston.'

'Really?' Sam asked. 'Did he then go overland?'

'Yes,' Alcina confirmed.

'Why did you want my laptop and camera?' Sam asked, after another period of silence as the train approached Boston.

'Your job, as an assessor, must be a lot of research, very likely research that might help in finding this painting. I figure you to have all of that on your laptop.

As for the camera, certainly you would have one, if there was someone, who might wonder where you are and come looking, then they would assume you are away on a job.

My research suggests you live alone, but just in case, I told you, I mean business.'

'You're right, I do live alone, however, if someone should come looking for me, wouldn't they wonder why my car was still there?'

'Wishful thinking cousin. I know you live alone. I know you work alone, you have not been in Canada very long. You could well have travelled somewhere by train.

Your van being there wouldn't raise too many eyebrows.'

Sam wondered how long she had been in town, knowing he had a van, but dismissed the distraction. He needed to focus on what lay ahead.

'I have rented a place in Boston. There you will do your work, where I can keep an eye on you and keep in control.'

Sam was tiring. The coffee helped his focus, but he was longing for some sleep.

With two pairs of lovely eyes totally focused on him, he took a deep breath and began to tell all that had occurred since his arrival in Boston ...

'So, who were those two henchmen you hired?' Sam asked, after Alcina opened the door to the apartment and insisted he entered first.

'It's late, your room is at the end of the hall there. Bathroom is the door before. Get some sleep. The two guys, in answer to your question, are waiters at a Greek restaurant in Halifax, I persuaded them with a little story and some cash to help me out. Now, I sense you're curious and will do what I ask you to do, but what I said, I meant, so, get some sleep and don't try anything stupid.'

Sam gave her a look, then headed for his appointed bedroom.

She was right though. He was indeed curious. It would be an interesting challenge to start the investigation, whilst all the while also looking as to how he might turn the tables.

He was in Boston, certainly not a disadvantage. He knew how to access various record systems, also not a disadvantage. He wondered if anyone might possibly discover he was missing as he got into bed.

The following morning he rose early, as usual, showered and dressed and was in the kitchen fixing himself some breakfast when Alcina appeared.

'Good morning, cousin. Would you like a tea or coffee?' he asked, looking directly at her.

'No, not yet. Carry on,' she said and returned to her room.

Good, Sam thought. She'd started to relax more; started to believe that she had the situation in control. Exactly what he wanted.

He waited, sat at a small dining table, mug of tea to hand and eating a piece of toast.

'I'm ready, get the laptop, and I assume we have access to the internet?'

Sam was on the laptop practically the whole of Saturday. Alcina had given him several sheets of information that she had accumulated and he perused those, made notes and thought about where to begin his search for the painting that once had belonged to his great-grandfather, Jan Steen's 'Feast of St. Nicholas'.

Sam first concentrated on confirming the fact that the ambassador, en route to Vancouver, had indeed come via Boston.

In just over two hours, he had found a document of interest.

He called Alcina over.

'Okay, here is the manifest, the complete manifest. The ambassador must have been adamant that there were complete records of what had arrived in Boston, and what was to be loaded onto the train,' he said, pointing to a specific entry.

Alcina came over and looked to where he was pointing.

The painting was listed there.

'A good start,' Sam said, standing up and heading towards the kitchen.

'What next?' Alcina asked, still looking at the document her cousin had found.

'Follow the goods,' Sam answered, preparing a drink.

After some more digging and searching, Sam established that the ambassador went by rail from Boston to Cleveland, from there by ship to Thunder Bay in Canada, then back on a train to Winnipeg and onto Vancouver.

Quite the journey. As he was getting into it, and enjoying the search, Sam still had a nagging doubt that it wasn't just about the painting.

Lunchtime.

'Why can't you just look if the painting has sold in any auction?' Alcina asked.

Sam, in the kitchen making himself something to eat, looked up at her. 'Didn't you already try that?' he asked, to which she had no reply.

Getting back behind the laptop, he said, 'I have now established that the painting did indeed get to Vancouver. It's important that I have a complete trail, or else we will be fishing in the dark,' Sam explained. Though not exactly necessary, he wanted to take as much time as he could in order to formulate an escape plan.

He did also want to find the location of the painting, as this obviously meant much to her.

Alcina, in the beginning hovering around and watching that Sam didn't attempt to send any messages to anyone whilst logged onto the internet, began to relax more and more, and seeing that Sam was totally focused, decided to make dinner for them.

'My cousin did make regular calls, probably every three hours, when she spoke in Greek, but quite briefly, and I began to wonder if there was anyone on the line at all.

Anyway, it's tiring focusing on the screen all day long, and so, after dinner on the Saturday, I told her I'd do one more hour, than pack it in for the day.

'She didn't disagree, so that was good.

However, she had my phone and took the laptop into her room.

'Sunday I had no results at all and she did become a little frustrated, suggesting I might be stalling, but when I got up and offered for her to go ahead and look, she declined.

'I did try and start a couple of conversations, but she was still too wary to totally let her guard down.

Late Monday morning I had better results and clearer directions.

I discovered that the ambassador had retired, in 1922. He had married a Canadian woman in 1914. Her name was Elizabeth Claussen and they had a son, in 1919, Samuel Junior, my grandfather.

Had I the ambassador's journals, I would have easily found this out, but I didn't have those to hand of course.

Cousin Alcina was pleased with the progress; even more pleased when I discovered that the couple, with their three-year-old son, moved to Kamloops.

This is a town also in British Columbia. This also gave me a new reference point and I found out that he had sold two paintings in a local auction.

Alas, not the "Feast of St. Nicholas."

'By Tuesday I was pretty sure that the ambassador had not sold the painting we were looking for. Also, I noticed Alcina had not, at least as far as I was aware, made any regular calls.

I also, by that time, knew that she must sleep very soundly. Every morning I was up well before her.

So a plan finally took shape in my mind.

'Wednesday I began to put that plan into its beginnings.

I found the ambassador's death notice; he passed away in Kamloops at the age of ninety-nine. His wife had passed away a few years earlier. As they had only one son, I figured the belongings would likely go to him.

'However, my grandfather lived in London.

As a child I went to visit him a couple of times. I do not recall seeing that painting.

So it seemed likely that whatever the ambassador left behind, stayed in Canada.

I convinced Alcina that the next stop would have to be Kamloops in British Columbia. I told her that it would be quite reasonable that in his later years, especially after his wife died, that he would have donated or sold some paintings to the art gallery there.

'I also made the suggestion that the best way to travel there would be by train, as flights could be too difficult, especially if by now someone was looking for me.

She agreed and taking the laptop away, said she would make the arrangements.

'I kept my enthusiasm up during dinner and into the evening, but saying I had a headache, I went to bed early.

'Then I waited.

What I hadn't told her, of course, is that I actually found no trace of the painting at all and my own assumption is that although I don't recall seeing it when visiting my grandparents in London, I feel that surely granddad must have inherited, being the only son and heir.

'I heard Alcina go to bed at just before eleven thirty.

I was ready, packed and ready.

I did need the laptop, and wanted my passport and my phone.

My trusty little torch came in very handy.

'I had my stuff ready to leave the apartment, via a fire door escape.

Entering her room I could hear she was very sound asleep.

I located the laptop, my phone and my passport, but I also found something else.

An old newspaper article. She must have been reading it prior to going to sleep.

'I decided not to take it, but knew now, why it was she was so keen to find this painting. I put two and two together. It was all about diamonds.'

Sam stopped talking.

It was nearly four am.

Chrissie and Ally sat motionless for a while.

Sam broke into their thoughts.

'I would really like to get to sleep now.'

'Yes, yes of course,' Chrissie said, 'but what about your cousin?'

Sam got up from the chair, 'Do nothing. It will worry her, and, she still may follow the false lead. In the meantime, we will go in the right direction. Perhaps we can ask Sophie to help with that.'

'Come on, let's get you to bed,' Chrissie said.

'It's all in here,' Sam said, handing the laptop to Ally. Then looking at each of them in turn, 'When I wake up tomorrow, you will tell me your side of the story.'

PARIS

Tammy was relieved. She was pleased for her friend Chrissie. Sam was safe.

Rubbing her shoulder where Sophie had playfully punched her, she went into the lounge where the French woman had her laptop open and was scrolling away.

'You must work out or something. You hit hard!' Tammy said, sitting herself next to Sophie on the couch.

'Sorry Tammy,' Sophie said, 'you just touched a nerve. Yes, I do care for Martijn.'

Sophie flung an arm around Tammy and gave her a hug.

'So, what has Chrissie asked you to do?' Tammy asked

'You first,' Sophie replied, sitting back and looking at her new American friend. 'Tell me what happened, details, mon ami'

THE PAST;

PERIOD 10

FRIDAY JANUARY 30TH 2015

The service was over.

The family and friends had gone.

He was alone.

After the handshakes, the smiles, the hugs and kisses, Sam had wandered off, just walking around the grounds of the crematorium. Finding himself on a path on the east side, he sat on a bench. A couple of times he saw a plane take off into the sky from the nearby Zestienhoven Airport.

The many friends were mostly Sonja's, from work, and school friends of old.

The family were all hers.

His parents had three years earlier moved to live in Sint Maarten, where his mother could better look after his father who had developed dementia.

When he had rung his mother they had both cried and not spoken much, yet the connection was tangible. The sense he had of her presence was comforting.

Walking back to where he had parked his car, passing groups of people on the way to say goodbye to their loved one, he thought about his family.

The most interesting character would surely be his great-grandfather, the ambassador. He promised himself he'd look into the life of this man who had travelled far and wide and, according to his father, was a collector of fine art.

Sam remembers visiting his grandfather, Samuel Junior, in an area called Bromley in London, on a number of occasions. He and grandma Jane passed many years ago now.

His father, James Samuel, had worked for the Shell company since 1969 and retired at the age of sixty. He and his mother, Marijke, then purchased a house in Sint Maarten and spent most of their time there. When Dad showed oncoming signs of dementia, they moved there permanently. Not having been terribly close with his father, Sam and Sonja had never visited them there.

Sam reached his car. He had decided he didn't want to follow the hearse, but drive himself to the crematorium and await its arrival.

Opening the door he sat for a while before switching on the engine.

The service had been fine. One of Sonja's uncles, a minister, had conducted the service, with a smattering of humour, a time of reflection, a time of thankfulness.

Hymns sung and prayers prayed.

Sonja had prepared it all herself.

He was thankful. He was grateful for her having been in his life.

Sam switched on the engine, shifting into gear and drove off.

The last words she spoke, so softly, so comfortingly, so encouraging, came to mind as headed home.

'Go and find someone to love.'

'That's just not going to happen,' Sam said aloud to himself. 'There will never be another you sweetheart'

Little could he have imagined, driving with tears in his eyes, that at some point in the future, he would have feelings for three women.

THE PRESENT;

PARIS

THURSDAY 23RD MAY

Having relayed the whole story that Chrissie had told her to Sophie, Tammy then asked, 'So, what is it we are to do? What did Chrissie ask?'

'Two tasks,' Sophie answered, grabbing a sheet of paper upon which she had written some details. 'First, and this is the priority search, to look for the whereabouts of the painting, the "Feast of St. Nicholas".' She looked at Tammy then said, 'the other task, is to follow up on the clue that you found, in that letter to your grandmother. Chrissie told me to search for the trail of this Bastiaan Bouten.'

BOSTON

Chrissie went downstairs and into the kitchen. She stood there, by the sink, for a moment, when she sensed someone behind her.

Turning, there was Ally.

They stood, facing each other, some six feet apart. Each fixing her eyes on the other.

Like two gunslingers in the old wild west.

How can she look so beautiful at six in the morning, Chrissie was thinking.

Sam was safe, he was asleep. The search was over.

Was she now looking once more at her rival?

It was Ally who broke the silence.

'You are very much in love with him,' she said, walking towards Chrissie.

Reaching her, Ally placed her hands gently on Chrissie's shoulders.

Chrissie could find nothing to say. She looked up into Ally's eyes.

Yes, she said to herself, yes, I do love Sam.

Ally broke her gentle hold, turned away and spoke, 'I love him too.' She then turned and again faced the other woman, 'The man saved my life. He risked his and, goodness knows how, but he pulled me to safety. If it wasn't for him, I would be dead Chrissie, so, yes, I love Sam.'

Then walking towards her again, taking hold of Chrissie again, she said, 'But my love is different from yours.' Then again releasing the hold, she stepped back, still holding her gaze on Chrissie, 'Do I want to be with him? Sure, yes I do, but I can't. I can't be with him knowing how much you love him, and, you know, Sam, I believe, would choose you, should choose you.'

Chrissie could still find no words to say.

Her eyes were tearing up.

Ally stepped forward again, this time she embraced Chrissie.

They hugged each other for a moment.

Then it was Ally again who spoke, 'Sam needs you Chrissie. He won't hurt either of us. He won't make a decision. He is still so vulnerable. I need to be with my daughter. I'm going to be with her, and you, my rival,' Ally said, smiling and reaching forward to wipe a tear from Chrissie's face, 'you need to be with Sam.'

'So, come on, will you help me sort out a flight back to San Francisco. I'll pack and I'll be gone before Sam wakes.'

Chrissie finally moved, she took a step towards Ally and again they hugged.

'You're the best rival a girl could have,' she whispered.

'We both love Sam. That's why I have to leave and you have to go and get him. It's the best for him, leaving him with the only option.'

IN ANOTHER PART OF THE CITY,
NOT FAR AWAY

Alcina stirred.

She could hear birds chirping and the light that was coming through the curtains suggested a bright day.

Stretching she was pleased with herself. Pleased with the progress. Pleased that she had her cousin under control, had him hooked on the search. She could see it in his eyes. His excitement yesterday upon finding the most likely whereabouts of the painting was good to see.

It was rather early to get up, seeing the time on the bedside clock read six-twenty.

But they had to get ready to travel.

To make their way to Kamloops.

Throwing the sheet from her, Alcina sat up, stretched some more and then became aware that something was wrong.

The laptop was missing.

Suddenly she felt her stomach muscles tighten. She leapt from the bed, quickly checked the second drawer down of the chest of drawers upon which she had placed the laptop.

Gone!

His camera, his passport, his phone! Gone!

Alcina left her room, marched through to the other bedroom, her heart racing.

He was gone!

Cursing herself silently, she strode throughout the apartment.

When had he gone? How had he not disturbed her? Where had he gone?

Forcing herself to calm down, she stood for a moment to think.

There were no police knocking at the door.

He had surely created a false sense of acceptance, had surely been sincere in the search he did.

Perhaps he was wanting the painting for himself?

If so, he had a head start.

She needed to move, and move quickly.

One thing she was happy about, he had no idea of the real reason why she wanted that painting so bad.

Cancelling the train tickets she had already purchased, she phoned for a cab.

THE PAST;

ANTWERP, BELGIUM

THE YEAR 2018

It was a frosty and cold day early in December, but the weekly Sunday market was being set up as usual.

The many stalls with bric-a-brac, stalls with vintage clothing, others with a variety of records and posters, still others with foods like cheese, fish, meat, eggs and vegetables.

Adriaan Bouten walked up to the front door of a building on the corner of the square, looked at the bunch of keys in his hand, selected one, and inserted it into the lock.

The door opened.

A dusty smell hit his nostrils and it was cold.

In view of the change of circumstances in his life, this inheritance came as a welcome relief.

Closing the door behind him, the thirty-eight-year-old architect looked around the two-bedroom cottage. It had once belonged to his grandfather, and he had been here on a few occasions. It seemed to look a lot smaller than he remembered.

He had set out from Breda in the Netherlands early this morning. The first opportunity he'd had, since receiving a letter with regard to his inheritance.

The marriage of his parents had faltered and broken. His mother was now remarried and living in Hilversum, his father had moved away and was now residing in northern Italy.

Adamant that his own marriage would be a solid one, it had not been the case.

Six years.

One day she had just left.

He had been at a conference in Dubai, looking at all the new architectural innovations there, and had returned to a letter on the kitchen bench.

Not only had she left him, but left him with very little, their bank account reduced to almost zero.

But then, amongst the mail that had been posted earlier and was on the doormat, was a letter from a solicitor in Antwerp.

Two days later, having changed the locks on the house, opened a new bank account and instructed his own lawyer to prepare divorce documents, he had travelled to the Belgium city and had received his inheritance.

The house and all that is in it.

Adriaan looked out of the dormer window in the second bedroom. The market was getting busier. The view brought him back to many years ago when he had stayed here as a child.

He shivered. Get some heating going that was his first task.

Nearly a month. She had been gone nearly a month.

Where had she gone, who had she gone with? Where did he go wrong?

A little over five months later, someone would knock at his door.

THE PRESENT;

PARIS

THURSDAY 23RD MAY NOON

Tammy was preparing lunch for them both.

Sophie was on the phone to Martijn. It was her second call to him as she had already called to pass on the latest information that Sam was safe.

Finishing the call she entered her kitchen and saw what Tammy had prepared.

'Wow, that looks and smells great. I feel privileged, having a great chef cook my lunch.'

Tammy turned, smiled, then protecting her shoulder, smilingly asked, 'How's Martijn?'

Sophie smiled in return, 'He's fine.'

Since the call from Chrissie, both young ladies had got busy in starting the research asked of them.

Sophie concentrated, through her own auction house, her previous connections with the world of art and a few other sources, on the location of the painting by Jan Steen.

Tammy, starting with the new information she herself had found with regard to Bastiaan Bouten, set about to trace his movements and subsequent family line.

Just before noon, they were both successful.

It was then that Tammy got up to fix the lunch, pleased with her progress, looking forward to relating what she had found to Chrissie and Sam.

It was then that Sophie made her second call to Martijn.

Ally couldn't believe her luck.

She had earlier quickly packed whilst Chrissie sorted out the travel arrangements, and though with time in hand before her flight, had left the house.

In the cab on the way to the airport, she had allowed herself a few tears.

When would she see Sam again, she wondered. Or Chrissie.

She had become fond of the woman she had once thought of as her rival. A feeling of rivalry that had not lasted once she had met her.

Drying her tears, she was glad she was on her way to her new home. San Francisco.

On her way as to be able to see her daughter this coming weekend.

Still so much to catch up; still so much they could learn from and about each other.

When she had noticed Chrissie standing in the doorway to the bedroom in which Sam lay sleeping, she had felt the woman's love for him.

A love that was deeper than how she felt.

As the taxi drove through the city, she was happy with herself for the decision she made. Whilst they both loved Sam, she knew that Chrissie was the one he most likely would choose. Leaving made that so much easier, for them both; the only option left, she had said to Chrissie.

After checking in and having gone through security, Ally was again thankful for Chrissie, not only to have found a flight so quickly, but first-class travel.

Then, as she was walking through the various perfume counters, she spotted her.

There was no doubt.

She had seen her photo, the one Sam had taken, the one on the memory card she had found.

It was her. Cousin Alcina.

At an opportune moment, and knowing how she was going to approach the situation, Ally walked up beside her.

'Hello Alcina,' said Ally, to the woman, who startled and froze, 'We need to talk, unless you want me to call attention to you?'

Receiving no protest, Ally went on, 'Over there, let's sit shall we?'

In a row of four vacant seats, Alcina sat down. She was stunned, her feet barely able to move and she was desperately trying to think. She turned to look at the woman.

'Listen to me, and listen carefully,' Ally began, her eyes fixed upon the other woman's with a stare that demanded attention.

'First of all, Sam is the most kindest, caring and loving man I know, he means the world to me.' Ally began, letting that sink in for a moment.

'Now, I'm guessing, looking at that flight departure board over there that you are most likely heading for Vancouver. From there no doubt going to Kamloops,' Ally continued, seeing the shock in Sam's cousin's face, her tanned features now rather pale as she sat, almost slumped, in the chair.

'You think that the painting you are looking for might have been donated to the local art gallery there, something that Sam suggested might be very probable.' Ally again paused briefly, saw that she had all her attention, and went on, 'Seeing as the ambassador died in 1969 and the art gallery didn't come into existence until 1978 that seems very unlikely.'

Again Ally let that sink in. Alcina's eyes briefly lowered and she gazed at the floor for a moment, before again giving all her attention to what was being said.

'Sam's friend, Sophie, in Paris, she's fine, they found out about the break-in and have you captured on film. Furthermore, Sophie, very clever girl, spent some time and investigated, finding out the real reason why you want this painting so bad.'

At this point, Alcina's jaw opened slightly. She was aghast as to how that could have been found out.

'Your great-grandmother,' Ally continued, 'found out about the robbery, found out what was going on. I think she really liked the ambassador. I'm sure, like Sam, he was a kind and caring man. Anyway, she found out, and switched the frames of the paintings. Now, we don't know her intentions, but when she got to London, she fell in love. In the end she let the diamonds be. We figure that she may well have written down what she had done, a diary perhaps?'

Alcina couldn't help but nod in affirmation.

Ally briefly smiled, 'Thought so. Well, to go on, your grand-mother also didn't act upon that information, nor your moth-er. I know of your illness, Miss Alcina, I'm sorry. But you need to go home, you need to be with friends and other family that you may have, you do not need diamonds.'

Ally stood up, looking down at the other woman, said, 'Go home'.

Then Ally walked away toward the gate where her plane to San Francisco would soon be boarding.

Alcina sat in silence.

EPILOGUE;

SUNDAY 26TH MAY

Samantha Price walked through the market stalls on her way to the house with the dormers on the corner of the square.

As she past the wooden bench, she thought that it had only been just over a month since she had sat there, with Sam. Just over a month ago that he had presented her with a banker's cheque for a quarter of a million American dollars.

When he had e-mailed her two days ago and asked whether she was in Acapulco or Antwerp, she had replied that she was in the Belgium city for another week before going back to Mexico.

When he asked her if she could do him a favour, she had instantly replied that of course she would.

Passing several more stalls she was closing in on the house.

An American woman would be awaiting her, her name was Tammy and she was the granddaughter of Rosemary Quinton.

The woman, a petite blond, was already there, saw her approach and smiled.

'Hi, I'm Tammy,' she said, extending her hand, 'thank you for coming.'

'My pleasure,' Samantha answered. 'So, you're Rosemary's granddaughter, and I'm guessing that this is about the miniature? Sam didn't reveal anything.'

'My grandmother fell in love. Chap's name was Bastiaan Bouten. He travelled with her to New York. However, he was never mentioned

688

in Grandma's letter. Sam discovered who he was and confirmed that he and her shared a cabin on the ship.

Just the other day, I found a letter, from my grandmother's father, his name was Percivald. Now it was a short letter, and in it, he stated that he had this Bastiaan character investigated, found out that he was actually married, and sent him packing back to Belgium.'

Tammy let Samantha take all that information in for a moment.

'Well,' Samantha then spoke, 'that means ...'

'Exactly,' Tammy interjected, 'that's what we thought.'

It was Samantha who again spoke, 'Sam and I, we went into the tunnel that pedestrian and cycle tunnel, just over there,' indicating with her head, 'So, with this chap coming back here ...'

'Very possibly retrieved it,' Tammy finished. 'He lived here, this house now belongs to his grandson, whose name is Adriaan. I spoke with him the day before yesterday. He would like to meet me. Sam suggested, and I agree, that you should come along. I'm glad you are here, thank you.'

'It's most considerate. What are you hoping to find?' Samantha asked.

Tammy knocked on the door, then turned and said, 'The answer.'

The door opened and Adriaan Bouten greeted the women and invited them in.

MEANWHILE IN THE HAGUE

Sophie and Martijn stood side by side in a large room in the basement of the Mauritshuis Museum.

Also present was the chief of the Rotterdam police, a personal friend of Sam's who had assisted Martijn with the search and arrest of Elsa Wagenaar, then there was the museum's curator and two women who were on the preservation team.

On a table lay a painting.

The 'Feast of St. Nicholas', by the artist Jan Steen.

Radiology equipment had just moments ago picked up an anomaly in the left-hand side upright of the ornate frame.

The two ladies were carefully disconnecting this section.

All of them watched and waited.

Sophie decided to grab Martijn's hand, he firmly clasped hers. She smiled.

Moments later there were gasps all around, as diamonds came tumbling out, one by one by one, a whole stream of them.

Sophie, in her delight, reached up and kissed Martijn on his cheek.

The detective coloured slightly, to the amusement of the chief who had noticed.

The South African diamond robbery of 1903, had been solved. Later it would be found that the total number found in the frame, was almost exactly the same as had been reported stolen. There was one diamond missing.

BACK IN ANTWERP

After the initial greeting, Adriaan asked the ladies to follow him upstairs where he took them to the second bedroom.

Stopping at the foot of the double bed, he turned to Tammy and Samantha and said, 'After your call, Miss Tammy,' looking at each of them in turn, 'I hunted in the attic; found this trunk.'

They all looked at the old trunk that was on the bed.

'Look' Tammy said, who stood next to Adriaan, leaning over and pointing, 'I see a label. That's a shipping label, it reads, "Madison". I recall that name. Sam discovered that this was the ship they sailed on to New York, back in 1946.'

'He went to America?' Adriaan asked, 'when you said that we are probably related and that Bastiaan, my grandfather, was likely your grandfather too, I thought ...'

Tammy looked at the man beside her. He was a good-looking man, a shade under six foot, a mop of brown hair and brown eyes set in a pleasant, clean-shaven face.

'You thought, perhaps a romance?' Tammy said, then, looking back at the trunk, 'No, he went with her to New York, but then it was found that he was ...' Then looking at Adriaan again, said, ' ...he was already married.'

Adriaan thought about this, then nodded, working things out in his head, then he leaned over and opened the trunk.

'I looked into it last night; haven't looked at it all, noticed the tools,' he said, indicating.

Both women looked.

There were a number of tools.

'Bricklayer's tools,' Samantha said.

Tammy looked at Samantha, then said, 'Yes, of course, Grandma wrote he was a bricklayer.'

'Yes, he was,' Adriaan said. 'Also he was a street paver, but something doesn't make sense.' Looking directly at Tammy. 'He sailed, in 1946, to New York, with your grandmother, yes, and, if you think we are related, then, I guess your grandmother was pregnant?'

Tammy nodded an affirmative.

'But I know from records I have just been reading, you see, I only recently inherited this house, from him, from my grandfather, and he didn't get married until 1948. He wasn't married when he met your grandmother.'

Tammy thought this through, then looked at the man beside her.

'I'm so sorry,' she said, I know that my grandmother's father, my great-grandfather, was ...wait, here, let me show you ...'

Tammy opened her handbag, drew out the letter she had found, and showed it to Adriaan.

'Looks like he was not happy with her choice ...' he said. Then looking at Tammy, 'He is cold, no?'

'He is cold, yes!' Tammy agreed, then looked in the trunk.

Spotting something, she exclaimed, 'Oh my, look that scarf. It looks familiar. It's certainly a woman's scarf ...'

Adriaan leaned over and went to get hold of it, then said as he took hold of it to lift it out, 'It has something inside it.'

He freed the scarf, then, in front of them, unrolled it.

Three pairs of eyes saw a black leather pouch appear.

Samantha gasped.

'Oh my,' said Tammy.

Adriaan took the pouch, loosened the leather cords that bound it, then taking Tammy's hand, slipped the contents onto her palm.

'Oh wow, it's beautiful!' Samantha exclaimed.

'He did retrieve it,' Tammy whispered, 'but kept it, wrapped in one of grandma's scarves. Gosh,' then looking up at Adriaan,

'I'm so sorry, I believed the note, it seems your grandfather was a good man, I think he must have been heartbroken.'

'This belongs to you,' Adriaan said, handing her the pouch and scarf.

'Wait,' Samantha said, taking her phone out. 'Let me get a picture of the two of you and the miniature, I'll send it to Sam.'

Tammy smiled, then, turning to Adriaan, putting the item back into the pouch, said, 'Thank you so much. Actually, the scarf I'll keep, but the miniature belongs to someone else. She will decide what to do with it. It's quite a story, would you like to hear it?'
    'I would very much like to hear it. I shall make some coffee?'

'Of course,' Tammy said, smiling, 'I guess, half cousin of mine?'

Leaving the bedroom and heading down the stairs, he said 'Actually, no, I was adopted.'

'Really?' Tammy said, suddenly feeling her heart beat a little faster.
    Samantha, right behind Tammy, noticed the American blush a little and once downstairs, quickly whispered into her ear, 'He's a nice man isn't he?'

Tammy turned and smiled. For once someone was teasing her.

'Please send that photo to Sam.'

BOSTON

The morning light was beginning to show through the curtains.
    Sam had been awake for a little while, and was sitting up in bed and reflecting on the past few days.

He had called DS Saunders and thanked her for everything, explaining briefly the turn of events and that no further action was required.

Ally had called and with the speaker phone on had related her encounter with Alcina at the airport to him and Chrissie.

Sophie had e-mailed him with an update of the painting.

She had, in rather quick time Sam thought, and had conveyed as much in his reply to Sophie, traced the 'Feast of St. Nicholas'.

Turns out his great-grandfather, having spent several years in the Hague as ambassador, had promised the work by Jan Steen to the museum there after his passing, and there it had gone in the year 1970.

In her e-mail Sophie said that she, together with Martijn and his friend the chief of police, were going to the museum on Sunday, to check out the painting.

Then Tammy had called Chrissie about the relative of Bastiaan Bouten that she had found and where he lived. When Sam discovered that this was indeed the house where Rosemary Quinton had stayed after meeting and falling in love with this Bastiaan, he had then contacted Samantha, so that, if she was in the city, she could accompany Tammy.

She was and she would be more than happy to do so.

Sitting up in bed he felt content and happy.

His phone, on the bedside table, pinged.

He wondered if it was from Sophie.

It was from Samantha.

He opened it and beside him, Chrissie, having heard the ping, stirred.

'Wow,' Sam whispered.

Chrissie, sitting up, moved across to look.

'Wow.'

'There it is,' Sam said, putting his arm around Chrissie, kissing her forehead. 'It's no longer a missing item. It belongs to you girl.'

Chrissie looked at Sam, quickly kissed him, then said 'I will donate it to a museum. You can help me decide which one, perhaps one that had other pieces of art by Breughel.'

'Great idea, and, I know just the one.' Sam answered. 'It's the only option really, it's where a painting he did, of the same scene, hangs.'

Another ping sounded, this one from Sophie, also accompanied by a photo.
'Wow!' Sam said.
'Wow indeed, 'Chrissie agreed, 'that's a lot of diamonds.'

'After all that excitement, it's really too early to get up yet, don't you think?'

'Oh, much too early' Chrissie agreed.

THE END

EIN HERZ FÜR AUTOREN A HEART FOR AUTHORS À L'ÉCOUTE DES AUTEURS ΜΙΑ ΚΑΡΔΙΑ ΓΙΑ ΣΥΓ
ΓΙΑ FÖR FÖRFATTARE UN CORAZÓN POR LOS AUTORES YAZARLARIMIZA GÖNÜL VERELIM S
HJERTE PER AUTORI ET HJERTE FOR FORFATTERE EEN HART VOOR SCHRIJVERS TEMOS OS AU
ÖINKÉRT SERCE DLA AUTORÓW EIN HERZ FÜR AUTOREN A HEART FOR AUTHORS À L'ÉCC
ΛΟ ВСЕЙ ДУШОЙ К АВТОРАМ ETT HJÄRTA FÖR FÖRFATTARE À LA ESCUCHA DE LOS AUT
MΙΑ ΚΑΡΔΙΑ ΓΙΑ ΣΥΓΓΡΑΦΕΙΣ UN CUORE PER AUTORI ET HJERTE FOR FORFATTERE EE
ÖINKÉRT SERCE DLA AUTORÓW EIN HERZ F
ÇÃO ВСЕЙ ДУШОЙ К АВТОРАМ ETT HJÄRTA F

The author

Hendrik Hoitinga was born Leeuwarden in Fries-
land, the Netherlands, and emigrated to New
Zealand at 10. After travelling extensively during
his teens and twenties, he married his wife in
Auckland, before relocating to the UK. They have
two children. Hendrik worked in retail for 26
years. He and his wife were then commissioned
and ordained as officers of the Salvation Army in
1995. They have since served in England, Belgium,
Wales and Scotland. Hendrik has been able to
focus on his writing since he retired in 2017. Now a
grandfather, living in Wick in Scotland, he still loves
travelling, music from the sixties and seventies and
he collects Dutch comic books.

The publisher

He who stops getting better stops being good.

This is the motto of novum publishing, and our focus is on finding new manuscripts, publishing them and offering long-term support to the authors.
Our publishing house was founded in 1997, and since then it has become THE expert for new authors and has won numerous awards.

Our editorial team will peruse each manuscript within a few weeks free of charge and without obligation.

You will find more information about novum publishing and our books on the internet:

w w w . n o v u m - p u b l i s h i n g . c o . u k

Printed in Great Britain
by Amazon